Andrew G. Lockhart

THE GAMMADION

Magda Green Books

The Gammadion

*A **mission** for the princes of Europe precipitates Venetian nobleman Giovanni di Montercervino into romance and danger at the court of Arghun, Mongol ruler of Persia.*

***Arghun,** the great-great-grandson of Temuchin, is dying. But there are those who would hasten his death for political reasons, while others would sacrifice his wife Nadia for personal ones. Beautiful and talented, but victim of a barbaric Mongol marriage law which passes her from ruler to ruler, Nadia desires only to protect her son until he reaches manhood. Torn between her duty as a wife and her love for the Christian envoy, she must discover the identity of her secret enemy before it is too late.*

***And must** Giovanni compromise his faith to save the Muslim woman her loves?*

Publishing History
First published as a paperback in 2002
under the title *The Il-khan's Wife*
ISBN : 0-9543923-0-2

The Gammadion
Published in 2021 and 2022 in a new complete edition
by **Magda Green Books**
ISBN: 9798363493348

Original cover photo by Vladimir, courtesy of *www.pexels.com*

O ye who believe!
Ye are forbidden to inherit
Women against their will
(Qur'an S.IV.19)
**

Force is always beside the point when subtlety will serve.
(Herodotus, quoting King Darius of Persia)
**

In the year 1256CE - 653AH of the Muslim calendar - the Great Khan Mangke, grandson of Genghis Khan, sent his younger brother, Prince Hulegu, to consolidate and strengthen Mongol rule in Persia.

A large part of the country was already part of the Mongols' Empire. It had Mongol-appointed governors and paid Mongol taxes, but there were pockets of independence and of resistance to foreign rule. The hot and, in Mongol eyes, inhospitable south had been left largely alone; Persian Iraq, specifically Baghdad, had been relatively untouched by the earlier invaders. The Abbasid Caliph, al Musta'sim, whose father had refused help the Persian resistance in 1227 - though he later chalked up some minor successes against the Mongol generals - was still lording it there in all his glory.

Hulegu's first major campaign, in the winter of 1256, was against the Islamic sect known as the Assassins, under their leader Rukn ad-Din Khurshah, who were entrenched in fortresses high in the Alburz Mountains, to the south of the Caspian Sea and not far from present day Teheran. These Assassins, more properly called Nizaris, were Muslims of the Isma'ili faith, a branch of Shi'a Islam. They were unpopular with, even hated by, the orthodox Sunni, who did not mourn their humiliation . . .

THE FAMILY OF TEMUCHIN

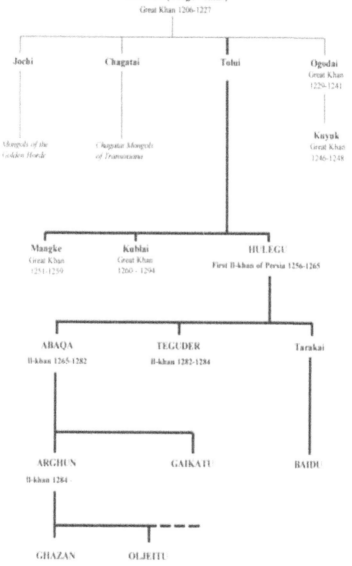

Temuchin (Genghis Khan)
Great Khan 1206-1227

Jochi

Chagatai

Tolui

Ogodai
Great Khan
1229-1241

*Mongols of the
Golden Horde*

*Chagatai Mongols
of Transoxiana*

Kuyuk
Great Khan
1246-1248

Mangke
Great Khan
1251-1259

Kublai
Great Khan
1260 - 1294

HULEGU

First Il-khan of Persia 1256-1265

ABAQA

Il-khan 1265-1282

TEGUDER

Il-khan 1282-1284

Tarakai

ARGHUN

Il-khan 1284 -

GAIKATU

BAIDU

GHAZAN

OLJEITU

Prologue
Alburz Mountains, Persia, 1256 CE

The envoy shivered. It was only a month till the solstice and, though no snow had fallen, the sharp mountain wind chilled his bones. It was true he had known colder winters, but the circumstances of this journey were exceptional. Fear played a part in his discomfort as much as the temperature.

He wondered what his reception would be like - a polite audience, immediate death by the sword, or a slow, bloodless execution in what he had been told was the traditional Mongol manner, suffocation beneath a pile of carpets. Khan Hulegu's reputation for savagery equalled that of his grandfather Genghis, but the new ruler of Persia did not seemingly have the Great Khan's patience.

The envoy drew his camel-hair shawl more tightly around his shoulders and urged his pony into the gully. A few stones dislodged by its hooves clattered onto the rocks below. At least he was away from the grim mountain-top fortress and breathing the free air again. Whatever awaited him below, it could scarcely be worse than the stifling of his intellect as a Nizari slave. Perhaps a quick death would be preferable to the slow destruction of his soul.

He glanced at his three-rider escort. They were well wrapped against the cold but, unexpectedly, no armour was visible. Instead, they wore felt coats with fur-trimmed sleeves and collars. There was also fur on their boots, and on the ear flaps of the helmets worn by two of their number. The third man wore a Persian hat and a thick scarf to protect his ears and lower face from the wind. The envoy could see none of the faces clearly but he could picture the pale skin, prominent cheekbones and narrow eyes that marked the Mongols as a race apart.

None of the three had spoken, simply indicating by signs the direction in which they wanted him to go. Perhaps they did not understand his language, or had been instructed to bring him to the Mongol camp, no more. The questioning would begin later, he told himself, when he had delivered the Grand Master's message. Then he would learn his fate, and whether Hulegu was truly the monster the emirs depicted, striking down indiscriminately all who opposed him and the innocents who served them. A mirror image of themselves, he reflected bitterly, only the Nizaris killed by stealth, with poison and daggers in the night.

How would his family fare then, he wondered: prostitution for his wife and daughter; at best, conscription to the Mongol army for his sons? And he could do nothing to protect them. He shivered again. The Khan's patience must surely have run out. His campaign had begun early in Ramadan and his siege battalions had been camped in the mountains for a month.

They had climbed to the other side of the gully and had almost reached the outlying tents. The path was less treacherous now and the envoy began to take note of his surroundings. The Mongol camp was spread out over the southern hillside, makeshift grey awnings surrounding the round, whitewashed *gers* of the princes. Identification pennons hung limply in the winter air. Skin-clad human figures stamped their feet and swung their arms against the cold; others exercised their ponies in the spaces between the tents and round the war engines. Behind, the dark crags of the Alburz, their peaks hidden in cloud, cast an ominous shadow over the whole scene.

The envoy noticed the third rider was studying him with interest. In the dim light, he could make out a pair of dark eyes peering at him from between the rim of the Persian hat and the folds of the muffler. The two helmeted Mongols were already some distance ahead and seemed bent only on reaching their destination. Suddenly, to his surprise, the man addressed him in the Persian language.

'What is your name, Master Ismaili?' It was a young voice, well modulated, with the accent of the southern provinces.

'I am called Nasr ad-Din Tusi,' the envoy replied. 'However, you are wrong in your assumption. I'm not of the Ismaili faith!' The angry sharpness of his denial surprised him, but the cold had made him irritable.

'So you have no love for the Grand Master?' The eyes above the muffler flashed. 'Yet you serve him, and come to Hulegu as his spokesman.'

'A man may serve another unwillingly, and without loving him,' said Nasr.

'He might also serve willingly without loving his master. Allah sometimes leads men into strange situations.'

Nasr stared at the speaker. 'So you follow the teachings of Mahommet? That is unusual in a Mongol.'

The escort laughed. 'I am no Mongol, Nasr ad-Din,' he said. 'Just as you are no Ismaili. And no soldier either, if my information is correct. By all accounts you are a physician and translator of great works from the Greek. An astronomer too. A man who sees the future in the stars.'

'You are mocking me!' Nasr detected irony. What could this youth know of the magic of herbs, the beauty of Homer, or the mystic paths of the planets?

'That was not my intention,' said the escort more humbly. 'Like you and much of Hulegu's army, I'm a Persian and a follower of Islam. I was a scholar too before my conscription and your name is known to me. Hulegu has great regard for men like us, and great use too. He is a Buddhist but treats all faiths equally. And his awe of scholars is exceeded only by his awe of priests.'

'And so you serve willingly?'

'Why not?' The escort's voice rose in pitch and he spoke with youthful impatience. 'If nothing else, we Persians are survivors. Our country has been ruled by men who forget kings are kings by the will of God and seek to further their own glory. To build private wealth. It was so at the time of the last Sasanian monarchs and is no different now. We owe the Caliph no favours. And Shah Mohammed Ali, for whom many people weep bitter tears, was a foreign usurper. A Mongol ruler can be no worse.'

'I shall weep no tears for the Caliph of Baghdad, or for the Shah of Kwarazm,' said Nasr. They had reached the camp and he saw the escort had spoken the truth. Many of the outpost guards had the dark features and neat beards of his own countrymen. 'I have heard though that Mohammed Ali's son Jalal was a man of whom Persia could be proud.'

The escort slowed his pace and urged his pony closer to Nasr's mount. 'Be careful!' he warned. 'Even Mongols have ears for the Persian language when it comes to certain names. And Jalal is a name Hulegu fears.'

'I shall be careful,' said Nasr in an undertone. 'As you say, I'm a scholar, not a soldier. One with a family to consider. I do not count bravery among my virtues, nor foolhardiness among my faults.' He glanced at a passing group of fur-draped Mongols but they took no interest in him or his companion. 'But though I have lived more than twenty years in a cage, I'm not entirely ignorant of recent history. Surely Jalal al-Din is dead, his sons murdered by Genghis's troops, their bodies thrown in the Indus, his daughters given as brides to the Mongol princes?'

'If you speak openly of what I'm about to tell you, it could mean your death,' the escort said. 'Hulegu is superstitious. It's not an old enemy he fears, but the legends surrounding that enemy. From a priest of the old religion he heard that one of Jalal's sons survived, and lives with a sister in Kerman. The Khan is haunted by the prospect that the story is true.'

'Supposing it is?'

'I'm not yet in Hulegu's confidence, but I'll tell you what I think. He will reduce the castles of Maimun-Diz and Alamut to ashes. The Grand Master has defied him too long. Then, if the omens are favourable, he'll turn on Baghdad, depose the Caliph and adopt formally the title *Il-khan*. Then he'll subdue the south. Its climate is not to the Mongols' liking, but they'll take hostages to ensure obedience. They'll execute any men who resist and abduct the women of prominent families as wives for their nobles. Thus Hulegu will take care of the heir to Jalal if one exists, dilute the blood of the Shahs if there's a daughter, and guard against insurrection in a single measure.'

'It may be as you suggest,' Nasr said wearily. 'I do not have your obvious grasp of politics. I care little what happens to Maimun-Diz, the Grand Master, or even the Caliph, but there's a fine library at Alamut, and instruments I use in my work. It'll be a great pity if . . .'

'Rest easy, Nasr ad-Din.' The escort laid a hand on his arm. 'Hulegu will not destroy anything that can be used in his service. Pledge him your loyalty and you will be free to carry on your work in the sciences. We will find a worthy task for you to undertake in the new empire.'

Nasr had often met ambition in the young, but rarely such self-assurance. There was arrogance in this youth too, he thought, a quality that might be the undoing of a weak man. Yet he liked him, and found comfort and hope in their conversation. His terror had abated and, despite the cold and the tiredness that was creeping over him, he managed a smile. Hulegu might not be the ogre depicted in the Nizari tales. Perhaps life in Mongol service could indeed offer him what he craved, to once again think his own thoughts and explore new ideas, free of the invisible fetters that bound him to the Grand Master.

'And what does Fate have in store for *you* in this new empire, I wonder?' he asked warmly.

'My ancestors once held the hand of kings and shaped the policies of kingdoms,' said the young man proudly. 'I ask no more of Fate than she allows me to emulate them.'

'Pray Allah grants your wish,' said Nasr. 'What is your name, and how will I know you again?'

The escort pushed back his hat and unwound his scarf so that his brow and chin were visible. He had a handsome face which wore the gravity of expression that usually comes with middle age. His nose was aquiline. His beard was jet black and trimmed to a point.

'My name is Ahmed Kartir.'

'Kartir,' echoed Nasr with a wan smile. He had not slept well since the Mongol siege began. 'That is a noble Persian name and not one to be forgotten in a hurry. He who first bore it was among the greatest of our sons.

'But you should be careful too, Ahmed Kartir,' he added as an afterthought. 'If you'll take the advice of an old man, do not let your ambition become a prison for your soul!'

*

PART ONE
The Il-khan's Wife

I
Kerman, 1290 CE

The fire temple had existed since the time of King Ardashir. Half a morning's ride from the walls of the city he had founded, it was, like the city itself, almost entirely surrounded by mountains. It lay on the road to Isfahan, a monument to old days and old beliefs. In summer, it basked in sunshine. In late autumn and early spring, cool breezes blew over it from the barren, rocky wastelands above, whipping up the sand into frequent storms that swept its deserted terrace and battered its crumbling pillars.

The city had grown and prospered in the thousand years since Ardashir's day and had long been known by the name of the province in which it stood - Kerman - proud, independent and largely untouched by the politics of the Khanate. Those who clung stubbornly to the Mazdaite faith had long found more convenient and judicious meeting-places for the practice of their rituals, and the temple had fallen into disuse except as a tryst for illicit lovers or men of business.

Though spring was not yet over, the signs of summer were everywhere. The winds had abated and only an occasional flutter of breeze disturbed the sand which settled on the ruins. The sun had not yet unleashed its full power, but the plain shimmered in a heat haze. The ring of mountains was blue and distant.

Ahmed Kartir, civilian governor of the province, halted his mount by a broken, half-buried column. He raised himself out of the saddle while the animal relieved itself in the sand.

'So what are you up to, Nizam?' he asked his companion, breaking their long silence.

'May not a man ride with an old friend without incurring suspicion?' the other man retorted.

Time had been unkind to him, Kartir thought. He was below average height, which accentuated his stoutness. His jacket and breeches were plain, his boots well worn. A sweat-stained yellow turban was wound round his brow. It seemed too large for him and dipped untidily over his right eyebrow.

Kartir hoped he had aged more gracefully. His once jet black hair and beard were streaked with grey and his aquiline features were deeply lined, but he held his tall frame erect. And he had always taken pride in his clothing. It was never ostentatious. He chose and wore it carefully, as befitted his position as a man of means.

'We were never truly friends, Nizam,' he said sharply. 'I haven't seen you for ten years, and we exchanged no more than ten civil words in the ten before that. Tell me what you want, and why you have dragged me out to the desert in this weather.'

'The place is symbolic, Kartir. The gods of our ancestors are all around us.'

Kartir rested his eyes on the cracked altar stone. 'It's rather late for an apology to them, don't you think?' He could not disguise his sarcasm. 'We both know the old faith was doomed from the moment temporal power broke with spiritual. Religion is now a political matter, and I for one am a pragmatist.'

'Keep your beliefs to yourself,' said Nizam irritably. 'I did not propose this meeting to argue about religion. Events may be going well for us at last.'

'Still dreaming of the glory of Persia, Nizam?' laughed Kartir. 'Why don't you just admit the scheme failed? We are both twenty years older than we were then, and the world is a different place.'

Nizam scowled. 'I'm sorry you see fit to mock my dream. It was once yours too. But, despite your derision, I repeat: events may be going well for us at last. Perhaps our hopes are half realised, without our lifting a finger.'

Kartir's amusement died. 'I've no time to play power games,' he said. 'I'm nearly sixty, as you must be, and would like to enjoy my old age in peace. Tell me what you're doing in Kerman. Explain your reasons for requesting an interview, and do not take all day.'

'Have you forgotten our first meeting here more than twenty years ago?'

Kartir had not forgotten. He sighed. 'At least twenty-five. A long time.'

'In those days you were in service to Hulegu,' resumed Nizam. 'You believed he would unite Persia in peace and justice. But our first Khan was superstitious. He was haunted by the spectre of his grandfather's enemy, Jalal. He had heard a story that two of Jalal's children survived the massacre on the River Indus, a boy and a girl living with the priests of Zoroaster in Kerman. Then Nasr Tusi with his fortune-telling persuaded him he had nothing to fear from ghosts. If he attacked Baghdad he could not fail. You should be grateful to Nasr. He diverted Hulegu's attention.'

'As I intended. Give me credit for recognising Tusi's fine intellect.'

Nizam ignored the interruption. '. . . So Hulegu forgot. You, on the other hand, wondered if the story was true and asked my help. We met at this very spot. You had returned from Baghdad to take up your appointment as viceroy. Jalal's son had not survived, but his daughter was alive, and *her* daughter Roxanne. I found them for you.'

'And you were paid well enough! Please get to the point.'

Nizam's face had not lost its scowl. 'You remember our next meeting?' he enquired smoothly.

'How could I forget!'

'In the intervening years you had become disillusioned. The Mongols were the same as other conquerors. Though still governor here, you no longer enjoyed the same trust. Hulegu was dead and his son Abaqa of a different disposition.'

'I should have listened to my own predictions,' said Kartir. The conversation was stirring painful memories. Abaqa had wanted to be Khan, not just in name but in reality. He could not overlook the south and had ensured its obedience the only way he could.

'But I offered a solution,' pursued Nizam. 'The seed of Jalal. An alliance by marriage between Roxanne's son and your daughter, though they were children at the time.'

'The boy had a father too, Nizam!'

'He was unimportant. The priests wanted only to preserve the line. Anyhow, you approved my suggestion. You betrothed your daughter to the lad. A new dynasty would arise, one that would recapture the empire of Darius and drive the Mongols back to the steppes. The old Magian prophecy would be fulfilled!'

Kartir shook his head sadly. It was a sign of the times that men revelled in the glories of the past. They looked to the skies for portents that would herald the new age - the birth of a Persian Alexander, foretold by the Magians of Istakhr a thousand years ago. The old gods would awake; the sacred fires would be rekindled.

'Prophecies and dreams! I should have known better.'

'If you had acted sooner . . .'

'Always if!' snapped Kartir. 'Abaqa needed more power. He went on conscripting our youths to his ranks and kidnapping our maidens to be wives to the Mongol aristocracy. The young man on whom I pinned my hopes was sacrificed in a senseless war. My daughter Nadia is trapped in marriage to Arghun, the new Il-khan.'

'A marriage that has never been consummated, if reports from Tabriz are to be credited.'

'That's small comfort to me, Nizam, when she's a prisoner,' said Kartir bitterly. 'Anyway, the fact they have no issue proves nothing. How can you say events are going well; that your plan is even one tenth realised?'

Nizam swung round in the saddle and faced him with a knowing smile. 'There is the boy. Your grandson.'

'How dare you involve Hassan in your schemes!' Kartir felt his stomach tighten and his chest burn as the acid rose into his mouth. 'He is only ten years old, and can be of no use to you.'

'You're a politician, Kartir, but you show little understanding of the politics that matter. The child is a Persian.'

'One who was weaned and raised at the court of the Mongol,' objected Kartir. 'I'm not as naive as you think, Nizam. I love the boy for Nadia's sake, but he is tainted. He is learning their customs and is being trained to bear their arms. He'll grow up with Mongol thoughts and habits.'

'Perhaps you underestimate your daughter's strength and influence,' said Nizam. 'I hear she supervises her son's education. She provides him with the best teachers, and he is being instructed in the

Islamic faith by the imams. For all that, it seems Nadia does not scorn the old religion as you do. She obtains favours for its adherents.'

'I do not scorn the old religion,' said Kartir. 'Mazdaism is irrelevant, that is all.'

'Maybe so. But what I hear too is that Arghun is enamoured of Nadia, and that Hassan has become his favourite.'

'You hear a great deal for a humble administrator in a provincial government,' said Kartir. The man's demeanour irked him, but he was still curious to learn the reason for his sudden appearance in Kerman after a decade, and what scheme he was hatching. 'But supposing your reports are correct, where does it lead us? You can't expect Arghun to make the boy his heir. He has sons.'

'He has. But your grandson is Persian. On your side he has the blood of the Magians, on Roxanne's the seed of Jalal al-Din. In a few more years he'll be a man. The people will support a Muslim claimant. Perhaps even the Mazdaites will subordinate their faith to the good of our country.'

'You're living in the world of fairy tales, Nizam.' Kartir laughed again. 'May I remind you the people supported Teguder when he declared himself a follower of the Prophet and took the name Ahmed.'

'Teguder had his eye on the main chance and was a Mongol,' spat Nizam. 'The popular support withered when the princes showed their disapproval.'

'And they would do so again, only more so. My loyalty to Arghun is hollow but it was purchased at a great price. I'll not be party to anything that could bring Mongol wrath down upon Nadia and her boy. If the Il-khan were to hear of Hassan's blood line - and the prophecy - and link the two . . .'

'From whom would he hear it?' scoffed Nizam. 'All who knew the true facts of Roxanne's birth are long dead. Roxanne herself died before her son reached puberty. Only two old priests of Zoroaster knew our secret. Khalafi converted to Islam and departed this life twelve years ago, though he was senile long before that. Gobras was killed during Abaqa's assault on Kerman. We two alone know that Hassan is the great-great-grandson of Jalal al-Din and heir to the empire of the Kwarazm Shahs.'

'Even so, Arghun's eldest son, Ghazan, will not forgive a plot to disinherit him.'

Nizam wrinkled his brow earnestly and looked around as if they were in the middle of a crowded market-place. He laid his hand on Kartir's saddle-horn.

'Listen to me, Kartir. You said yourself the world is a different place. Our country has changed for the worse since Hulegu's reign. The Mongol empire is no longer secure or at one with itself. Arghun pays only lip service to the authority of Kublai Khan. The troops of the Golden Horde perform manoeuvres on the shores of the Caspian. The Chagatai Mongols mass on the border of Khorasan, and Ghazan is hard pressed to keep them in check.'

'So?'

'To the west, the Mamluks are always a threat to Arghun's hold on power. And there lies the seed of our success. Sultan Ashraf's dearest wish is to see Baghdad the capital of Islam again.'

'An Egyptian rather than a Mongol ruler? Small consolation.'

'Not a conquest, Kartir - an alliance,' said Nizam triumphantly.

'And what would your master, Baidu, Prince of Baghdad, have to say about your proposed alliance?' asked Kartir. They were on dangerous ground.

'Baidu is young and dissolute. He will be easily swept aside when the time is right. Only a few princes retain their loyalty to the ambitions of Genghis, and they too are weak drunkards. The junior officers have intermarried, and their offspring are half Persian. The ranks are swelled by men of Persian birth. Once an enslaved minority, they are now the backbone of the army. You have influence, Kartir, and a loyal following. If you were to mobilise, the people of Fars and Yazd would follow. And with the forces of the Mamluk Sultan supporting our cause in the west, the princes would be overwhelmed. Think. You might be regent!'

Though the candle of Kartir's youthful ambition had long since been snuffed, Nizam's persuasive tone stirred the still-glowing embers of his pride. But his instincts warned him to tread warily. He was too old to take risks.

'Ghazan will not take a rebellion lying down, and he'll not be swept aside so easily.'

'Perhaps Ghazan will not survive his father.'

'The Lord Ahriman has entered your heart, Nizam,' cried Kartir in horror. His companion's sinister meaning was only too clear. 'I have no love for the sons of Arghun, but I'll not be a party to assassination. I've seen too much of it in my lifetime.'

'So you remember the names of the old gods!' Nizam snorted. 'Anyway, such drastic steps may not be necessary. Ghazan has discontent among his own generals, as well as the Chagatai, to worry about. As for Arghun's other son, Oljeitu, it's rumoured he's being raised as a Christian by his mother. He'll never be accepted as ruler.'

'Don't forget I'm viceroy here and could have you arrested for just thinking those thoughts,' said Kartir. 'Are you so sure I'll not betray them to Arghun?'

'As you say, they are thoughts only. By betraying them, you would compromise yourself. Anyway, I know your heart too well. Like me you're a patriot.'

A patriot, but not a fool, thought Ahmed Kartir. He was struck by the enormity of what he had been for a second contemplating. Nizam's arguments were too glib, his motives and true loyalties unclear.

'You're wasting your time, Nizam,' he said. 'Your scheme is madness.'

'Still the same arrogant Kartir!' rejoined Nizam angrily. 'I hope you don't live to regret your decision.'

Kartir's temper too was rising, but he controlled it. 'Coming here was a stupid mistake,' he said. 'Go back to Baghdad and your accounts, Nizam. Learn to accept Fate as I have done. Allah will return our country to us in His own good time.'

'And if I cannot accept?'

'Ignore my advice if you like,' warned Kartir. 'It's *your* head and severed limbs that Arghun will display on the gates of Tabriz.'

'That's your final word?'

'One more! If you decide to turn your thoughts to action, take care that no harm befalls my daughter, or her son. In either case, Prince Baidu will not protect you, and your unseeing eyes will look down from a spike on the gates of Kerman.'

Kartir watched Nizam ride off ill-humouredly towards the city. When the dust trail had vanished, he dismounted and sat pensively on the crumbling temple steps. The meeting had reminded him of events he would rather have forgotten. He breathed slowly and evenly, trying to ease away his tension. Gradually his indigestion subsided.

It was not Nizam's fault the plan had failed. The hand of Allah, All-wise and All-powerful, had intervened. Yet Kartir had known in his heart they could not succeed. That one man, not out of his teens, could change the course of history as Alexander of Macedon had done seventeen centuries earlier was no more than a mad dream. Though the deeds of Jalal had already passed into legend and Jalal himself, dead more than forty years, would soon become a cult figure in Persian mythology, that an unknown and probably spurious descendant could rally the shattered forces of Islam was a pious hope.

But he had been desperate.

At Alamut it had been different. His belief in Hulegu's unifying mission had been genuine, his ambition fired by the prospect of emulating his ancestral namesake. What the first Kartir, High Priest of Zoroaster, Grand Wazir to the Persian kings, had done a thousand years ago was to give pride and unity to the nation in the name of Ahura Mazda, god of the Magians. He, Ahmed Kartir, would restore that pride and unity in the name of Allah, and in another thousand years men would remember *him*, and honour *his* name.

Disillusionment with the Mongol cause came gradually. He accepted even the bloodletting in the early days. Empires were not built without blood being spilt, even innocent blood. The fate of the Caliph left him unmoved. Later came the doubts.

The turning point came in Khorasan. Once the land had been rich, its fertility assured by the network of underground irrigation channels, maintained by generations of peasant farmers. Now, much of that province was sparsely populated and the network had fallen into disrepair. He had witnessed none of the supposed atrocities himself: the rotting corpses in the streets; the stench of burning flesh; the piles of bleached skulls left as a warning against defiance. But he had seen too much death, too many elegant buildings fired, too many hostages taken. And he could not close his ears to the stories.

Kartir remembered the words of Nasr ad-Din as if they had been spoken yesterday. *A man may serve unwillingly and without love.* He had never imagined they would one day apply so aptly to his own situation. Love had never been part of his relationship with Hulegu but he had respected, even admired him.

I have lived more than twenty years in a cage.

His career had flourished in the early years, but he was losing the idealism of youth. By the time of his posting to Kerman he knew the bars of the cage were closing round him. His ambitions had been achieved at the expense of his conscience. They had become his prison and he could not escape. The Il-khans did not tolerate desertion.

He had first heard the story from Juvaini, the Il-khan's secretary. A group of priests of the Zoroastrian brotherhood, returning to Kerman from a pilgrimage to India had found a young girl wandering near the River Indus, at Peshawar, with an infant boy in her arms. In terror of her life, she had told them she was Roxanne, daughter of Jalal al-Din, Shah of Kwarazm, Khorasan and Transoxiana.

'Highly improbable,' Juvaini had joked. 'The Gabars can't forget the days when they held the hand of kings and would like to do so again.'

Kartir knew some Gabar myths but this was one tale he had not heard. He was intrigued.

Of course, history told a different story. The battle of the Indus had taken place two generations earlier. At first, Jalal's troops routed the Mongols, but his army was torn apart by rivalries. Genghis's forces had regrouped and driven him back to the river. The Shah had escaped by leaping fully armed into the current. The Mongols had butchered his sons and married off his harem and female issue.

Supposing it were not myth. How then would he have heard it? The followers of Zoroaster, the Gabars, did not openly declare their faith. For more than two hundred years, the law had persecuted them and forced their conversion or exile. They practised their religion behind locked doors. Their secrets were theirs alone.

He had been given no opportunity to investigate. He was posted to

Maragha to work with Nasr on building an observatory, and had remained there for three summers. He had cemented their friendship by marrying Nasr's daughter. After Maragha had been Baghdad, his reward a finance ministry under Juvaini. Four years later, he had been with Hulegu when he annexed Fars and Kerman to the empire. Nadia had just been born. For his loyalty, he was appointed Wazir.

Even then, it would have been unwise to ask openly about Jalal's children, but by an accident of Fate he made the acquaintance of Nizam, a steward formerly in the employ of the deposed Emir. Nizam had offered his services as agent, and for five hundred silver dinars, Kartir had bought the information he wanted. He was too late. The Shah's son had not survived and his daughter Roxanne, now an elderly matron, was dying in the care of the Mazdaite priests. However, there was a granddaughter, also named Roxanne, and *her* son, Mahmoud Hassan. Khalafi, the Gabar patriarch, had sworn to the story's truth.

Within a year, the first Il-khan was dead. His son and successor, Abaqa, was less trusting and, while confirming Kartir in his appointment, had taken measures of his own to ensure allegiance. The generals came. There were more hostages. The conquerors' grip of Kerman became a stranglehold.

Kartir had borne it philosophically. Though his loyalty had begun to waver, he had a wife and child. He never doubted that, without his co-operation, not only would their lives have been at risk, but the treatment meted out to the province would have been much harsher.

In Nizam's proposition he had seen hope. He instinctively distrusted the man and there were risks involved, but beneath his growing doubts and cynicism still burned some of the idealism of Alamut. The Mongols had failed him, but perhaps he could indeed become the father of a new dynasty. His ancestors were noble - Magians, the priestly tribe, rulers of Persia in all but name. Nadia and young Mahmoud were already playmates and he had little to lose by agreeing to a betrothal. Whatever the outcome, that was an investment in the future of his race.

Abaqa stayed away, but the threat of further oppression was always there. The military commanders came and went, each demanding commission from the poll tax in return for their protection. Though the cage imprisoning his conscience was growing ever smaller, Kartir endured it. His life was comfortable, the people of Kerman uncomplaining. And he had his family.

His private pain had come later. The death of his wife, just as Nadia was growing into womanhood, drove him to the depths of despair. He had no understanding of a maiden's needs and had pressed ahead with the marriage contract too hastily. But Fate had intervened once more. Without warning, the Il-khan's forces again attacked the south. The new bridegroom was conscripted to fight against the Golden Horde and never returned to Kerman. Kartir had to bear the agony of his pregnant daughter's abduction as security for his continuing allegiance.

For a decade, he had governed without interference. Once he had been summoned to Tabriz, and that had been six years ago, by Teguder. He had not seen his daughter or her child since: Nadia, prisoner of a barbarous marriage, victim of an ancient Mongol custom that demanded she be passed as a chattel from one ruler to the next; Hassan, the grandson he would not see grow up.

A curse on the brood of Genghis, thought Kartir. And on Nizam for dredging up these memories. But though his new proposal was insane, it had just enough logic to tempt a desperate man.

Nizam did not look back until he saw the minarets of Kerman loom up through the haze. He slowed his pace, spat out a mouthful of sand and wiped some foam from his horse's neck. The animal was snorting and trembling from exertion.

The ring of mountains seemed closer. Over the peak of Segoch, away to the south east, hung a solitary white cloud in an azure sky. Nizam scanned the horizon from left to right. Satisfied that the road behind was deserted, he stopped, unhooked a water-bottle from the saddle-horn and took a long drink.

Nizam had no reason to believe he was being pursued, but his native caution was honed by ten years as a double agent. In his world of suspicion and deceit, of lies and secrets, survival depended on being able to outthink and outrun the enemy, on having quick wits, sharp eyes and a glib tongue.

He was satisfied with his morning's work. Kartir would put spies to work and discover that al-Ashraf did indeed aspire to conquer Baghdad - that a Mamluk force was already encamped west of the Tigris river, not far from ar-Ramaddi. Perhaps he would learn that Ashraf and Baidu had already exchanged dispatches. But he would not interfere. Though he might risk a visit to his precious daughter, he would not go to Arghun with his intelligence.

That was the one certainty. The scheme might have failed but Nizam had covered his tracks well a decade ago and the viceroy still believed the lie that had been spun round him. To confess to the Il-khan would be to confess his own treason.

Nizam mopped his brow with the loose sash of his turban and swallowed another mouthful of water. Yes, he had done well and hoped Baidu would be reassured. The prince might be dissolute, but he was no fool. He had his own spies and would act decisively and fatally at any sign of a double-cross.

A pang of fear rose in Nizam's belly. For a moment he doubted his own resolve and whether even his profound hate for Kartir outweighed his terror of the Mongol.

Umid Malikshah pushed aside his empty plate and gave a satisfied belch. His eyes settled on a fruit-laden basket placed just out of his reach. Kartir slid it towards him and watched his supper guest's hand hover over it briefly before falling back on the table.

'Your hospitality is overwhelming, Excellency, as ever!'

'Then, if we have finished eating, let us talk,' said Kartir. 'What intelligence do you have of Tabriz? How has the city changed in the last six years?'

'Truly, it has changed little. Trade is good, and I always return to Kerman a happier man than when I left.'

'I'm pleased to hear it.' Kartir smiled. Fine food and good company always cheered him and he was in a much better mood than on the previous morning. 'Is that all you have to say? No rumours or gossip among these mighty men of business of whom you are so fond?'

'You know I do not move in such exalted circles as yourself,

Excellency,' said Umid with friendly indignation, 'but do not mock my humble profession. As gatherers of information, we merchants are unequalled. The spies of the Khan himself are blind and deaf compared to the sellers of carpets, silks and fine spices.'

Kartir knew this was no exaggeration. Since before Mongol times, the weavers of Kerman had been unequalled for the elegance of their designs and quality of their handwork. Their products were known from Damascus to Samarkand. The industry had suffered greatly during the Conquest, but due to men like Umid it had recovered and was flourishing again. He and his company of merchants pursued their business fearlessly from India to Genoa, from Herat to the deserts of Arabia.

But hand in hand with their trade in carpets and blankets went a trade in information and Kartir was only too aware that, while the whole province benefited from the former, no one relied upon the latter more than himself. Though almost twenty years his junior, Umid was his most valued friend and confidant.

'What is Arghun like as a ruler?' he asked.

'Shrewd, my friend. Like his predecessors, he's a Buddhist, but tolerant in religious matters. You knew he had appointed a Jew as Grand Wazir?'

'I'd heard something of the sort. This tolerance could be his downfall.'

'Indeed, Excellency,' agreed Umid, 'though the Jew seems a capable enough man. A more interesting piece of news is that Arghun has recently received an envoy of the Christians, from their patriarch in Rome.'

'Jews and Christians together? Perhaps I should not judge so hastily, but that usually bodes ill. What do the Christians want?'

'I haven't been able to find out,' said Umid, 'but when I do, you'll be the first to know. I plan to be in Tabriz shortly, and I'll return there again in autumn.'

'Actually, I have a another commission for you, Umid, or rather for your army of intelligence gatherers. I may go to Tabriz myself while the weather is still bearable, and there's someone whose activities need careful watching.'

The idea had been growing in Kartir's mind since his meeting with

Nizam the day before. He would visit his properties at Qazvin and Maragha, neglected for six years. From Maragha he would travel on to Tabriz, request an interview with the Il-khan. If he achieved nothing else, he might at least see Nadia again, and her son.

He related the substance of the interview at the fire temple, omitting mention of Jalal's children. Some secrets were better buried.

Umid raised his eyebrows quizzically. 'Nizam, eh? I heard something in Baghdad. A slippery fellow by all accounts. His ear always to the ground.'

'And it's not friendship that prompts him to renew my acquaintance after ten years,' Kartir added. 'Once he was useful to me, that is all.'

Umid scratched his beard. 'It's true that Ghazan is hard pressed in Rayy. If Sultan Ashraf is contemplating invasion, with or without Persian help, there could be no better time.'

Kartir only nodded. Umid's counsel was always helpful and reassuring.

'Still, if you'll pardon me,' went on the merchant immediately, 'a visit to Tabriz by Your Excellency might be untimely. Perhaps the princes think of Kerman as a backwater, merely a hot, dry desert of no importance. But again, perhaps not. Suppose the Mamluks have already formed an alliance with the Islamic underground. If Arghun's agents have wind of it, he may see the most innocent journey as a threat.'

Kartir considered this advice. He did not want to act hastily and a month or two would make no difference. 'You're right!' he agreed. 'I shall remain in Kerman, at least for the present. But I'll be satisfied only when I know Nizam's intentions.'

'You may rely on me. Whatever his intentions are, I'll keep an eye on him. But be careful, Excellency. This Nizam is a dark horse. Drunkard or not, Baidu pays his wages. And he might resent your standing in the province. If, as you say, he once served the old royal house, he would lose status when Hulegu replaced the Emir. And if you also passed him over when forming your administration . . .'

'What of that? Nizam tried hard to ingratiate himself with me, but he did not merit a post. I doubt he ever had influence with the Emir.'

'A man may reach fifty and still harbour envy and secret ambitions,' said Umid. 'And because he is fifty, there's less time for him to achieve them.'

*

II
Tabriz, Autumn

'He rides like a Mongol!'

Arghun, Il-khan of Persia threw back his head, took a long draught from a decorated metal cup and fetched the Italian ambassador an energetic blow on the back.

Giovanni di Montecervino stood his ground. He absorbed the blow and acknowledged his host's enthusiastic observation with a polite smile. After nearly four months in Tabriz, he had become used to Arghun's moods, his bouts of drinking and his spontaneous outbursts.

The Khan was a large man, about forty years of age, with muscular shoulders and arms. He might once have been handsome, thought the Italian. Now his hair was sparse, excepting that which grew from his upper lip in a thick moustache. The flesh of his neck was puffed, the pale yellow skin of his face blotched. His features were those which to outsiders distinguished the Mongol race, a flattened nose and curiously elongated eyes, the latter presently glazed from the effects of alcohol.

The two men stood on a platform overlooking a stretch of bare, dusty ground, on which had been raised, to left and right, a line of poles.

Each pole supported an overripe gourd.

'And he handles the bow like a Mongol!'

This second vociferation was uttered as the object of their attention wheeled his pony at the end of the line and, crouching low in the saddle, spurred the animal forward. Simultaneously he raised a diminutive bow and drawing six arrows in rapid succession loosed them at the gourds on his left side. Each found its target. The rider halted, wheeled the pony again, and prepared to make another pass. From his lips came a bloodcurdling battle-cry.

The second flight of arrows was no less successful. Six found their targets and four of the gourds were toppled to the dusty earth. Arghun raised his cup in salute, took another swig of liquor and again clapped Giovanni between the shoulder-blades.

The rider reined in his pony at the foot of the platform and looked up at them. He was a boy of ten or eleven years of age, slim and dark-complexioned, with curly black hair. His nose was prominent, but not large enough to detract from his pleasing, handsome looks. His dark oval eyes under long black lashes sparkled with excitement, his lips were parted, and his breathing was fast from exertion.

'How was that, My Lord?'

'Well done indeed, Hassan!' Arghun drained his cup and refilled it from a flagon at his feet. 'Now we'll have to test you in the hunt.'

Giovanni regarded the lad with a mixture of surprise, approbation and curiosity. 'He is only a child, Your Majesty,' he gasped. 'I had not imagined he would be so young.'

'We don't pamper our children as you do, Ambassador,' laughed Arghun. 'It's true he's only a boy, and his bow is half the normal size, but we Mongols are warriors, and this training is no game. Hassan must learn to hunt, fight, and drink like any true descendant of Genghis Khan.'

'Shall I make two more passes, My Lord?' asked the boy eagerly.

'No, Hassan. That'll do for today. Go to your mother. I fear she'll cast a spell on me with those wide eyes of hers if I detain you too long.'

Hassan dismounted, retrieved his arrows and led his pony through a gate into the courtyard at their rear.

Giovanni hesitated, then turned to Arghun. 'The boy will be a credit to your noble ancestor, Sire, of that I am sure,' he said. His inquisitiveness was beginning to overcome his diplomatic reticence. 'However, if you will forgive my boldness, he does not look like a Mongol.'

'Nor was he born one,' said Arghun casually. 'But he's the son of the third wife of the Il-khan of Persia, and'll learn Mongol skills, just as if I seeded him myself.'

'You have other children, your majesty?'

'Two sons and two daughters by my current wives. That I acknowledge! The eldest governs for me in the eastern provinces. Who knows how many others I may have spawned? But tell the Prince of Venice that the Il-khan treats all his wives' children equally.'

'Your Majesty's wisdom and impartiality are well known,' the Italian acknowledged tactfully. The alcohol had loosened Arghun's tongue and seemed to have heightened his feeling of conviviality, but flattery was always a diplomat's most powerful weapon. 'I'm certain *all* your children will be a credit to you.'

'Let me tell you frankly, Sir Giovanni,' said the Il-khan, 'I've a great fondness for this Hassan. He's a clever lad, and no less skilled than my own son Oljeitu, who's about the same age. His mother is not as other women. I married her as was the custom when my father's brother, unfortunately . . .' He winked knowingly. '. . . met with an accident. I once suspected the child was my uncle's, but now I doubt it. Nadia had a husband or lover in my father's time. In truth, I'm rather afraid of the woman and don't like to ask about the boy's parentage. Breathe a word of my weakness and I'll cut off your tongue, then your balls!'

He laughed coarsely but good-humouredly.

Giovanni felt a dryness in his mouth. He took a sip of his own drink. The taste revolted him, but he tried not show it. He laid the cup at his feet. 'Your wife, Hassan's mother, is a native Persian then?'

'Her home was in Kerman. In the south. She was brought here to Tabriz as a hostage during my father's reign. Her people were Gabars.'

'Gabars, Sire?'

'Of the old beliefs. They worship a god called Ahura Mazda. Their prophet is Zoroaster. My grandfather encouraged them. Their priests dress in white robes and ridiculous hats, not unlike the shamans of the old Mongol religion. They light fires all over the countryside, sacrifice dogs, and pour wine on their altars. What a waste! But my ancestors had a great awe of priests, whatever their faith. My mother was a Christian. You didn't know that, I suppose?'

'No, Your Majesty.' Giovanni knew, but sometimes it was tactful not to admit one's knowledge; in any case, the Nestorians were no true Christians. He stood back while Arghun descended unsteadily from the platform clutching both his cup and the half-empty flagon, then he climbed down.

The Il-khan's eyes were more glazed than ever, but they seemed to miss nothing. He had noticed Giovanni no longer carried his goblet and ordered a soldier to fetch it. 'What was I saying?' he asked, slurring his words noticeably.

'About the Gabars, Sire . . .'

'They're of no importance,' said Arghun. 'I treat all faiths equally.

You can tell your prince *that*. But I must tell you about my wife, Nadia. She must be a witch, I think. She has the blackest of eyes, and a way with medicines. She wears an amulet . . .' He traced a shape in the dust with the heel of his boot, a cross with its arms bent at right angles.

'A gammadion, Sire,' Giovanni identified. 'That is the Greek word for it. It is a good luck charm.'

Arghun took another gulp of liquor from the flagon and broke wind. 'The woman never removes it from her neck,' he said. 'There it lies between her tits, mocking me, daring me take my pleasure of her.'

Giovanni allowed his goblet to be filled and, under his host's watchful gaze, took a draught from it. The drink, a fermentation of mares' milk, was potent and sickly. He would have given five years of his life for a cup of the best wine from the vineyards of the Po valley. His senses reeled, and he felt the nausea rise in his throat. Thrice he had managed to empty the cup in the sand. The ground below had been damp from the excess spilled by the Il-khan and his discourtesy was unlikely to have been noticed. Here on the threshold of the royal residence it was a different matter.

'Where was I?' drawled Arghun. He staggered, and Giovanni felt his arm gripped tightly. 'Oh yes, a witch. But I love her. I love all my wives. Tell the Prince of Venice that too. Yes, I love the witch. And I'm very fond of Hassan.'

He righted himself again and, with his hand on Giovanni's shoulder, adopted a steady walk towards the castle gate. They passed along several corridors, traversed a courtyard and entered a building constructed in decorative brickwork inset at intervals with coloured tiles. At the end of yet another corridor was a doorway guarded by two burly fellows with swords.

'This family talk has made me quite thirsty,' said Arghun. He put the flagon to his lips once more, threw back his head, and drank. Only a few drops remained. There was a pause during which he swayed again, then patted the Venetian's shoulder in a brotherly fashion. 'Now there are other matters we must discuss . . . now that we're better acquainted. We must settle the question of Damascus, and how we might join forces to destroy our common enemy.'

'Indeed,' acknowledged Giovanni gravely. 'Your Majesty knows I only await his pleasure in that matter.'

Arghun did not reply. He staggered across the sumptuous apartment they had just entered, flopped drunkenly onto a cushion, and promptly and unexpectedly fell asleep.

Giovanni bent over him cautiously, uncertain what the rules of diplomacy demanded. The most powerful man in Persia, descendant of Temuchin, Conqueror of the World, was snoring like a hog. His nostrils flared, his upper lip twitched and, as he exhaled, the Venetian caught the rancid odour of his breath. The feared ruler, whose long arm stretched from the Caucasus to the Arabian Sea, who, it was rumoured, controlled a hundred thousand horsemen and an army of twice as many conscripts, could not control his own senses.

During his stay, Giovanni had many times wondered at the Mongol capacity for alcohol. Italians caroused, but their revels were a joyful diversion from the stresses of toil, trade and war. To the Mongols, intemperance seemed a duty, a way of life. He had wondered too that the abstemious followers of Islam had suffered for seventy years under the Mongol yoke. He had observed the princes' excesses and asked himself whether, despite his natural distrust of Muslims, the alliance he pursued was with the wrong people.

Yet he found the Il-khan less intemperate than many. Beneath his coarseness, Arghun had an ordered mind, a sharp intellect. Between his bouts of drinking, he often showed a friendliness and good humour that seemed absent in others of his race. But he was deeply melancholic too and these moods alternated in him unpredictably.

Giovanni studied the features of the sleeping monarch, watching the eyes for signs that he might be stirring. The Il-khan's brow was set with furrows and his head moved restlessly from side to side as if he wrestled with an insoluble problem. His sonorous breathing was punctuated with moments of utter silence in which it seemed he might have ceased breathing altogether. His mouth would open wide, his shoulders relax and his chin sink onto his chest. Then the nostrils would flare again and the snoring resume.

The slumber was profound. Satisfied there was no danger of him being judged impertinent, Giovanni breathed a sigh of relief and made his way past the stern, unseeing guards to his own quarters.

It had taken him a month to obtain his first audience and he suspected the Il-khan's chief minister of delaying him for private motives. There was no political advantage in doing so. Arghun, in his eagerness to smash the Mamluks, had twice written to Rome seeking a Christian alliance. Giovanni used the month profitably, studying the customs, history and language of Persia and of the people who had conquered it. That Hulegu, grandson of Genghis Khan, had succeeded in destroying Baghdad and the power of the Caliphs, enemies of Christendom, was fortuitous. That he had married a Christian, albeit one from an aberrant eastern sect, was auspicious. It was a beginning.

His first meeting with Arghun was in late spring. The Il-khan examined his credentials and politely received letters from his uncle, the Duke of Venice, from the German Emperor, and from Pope Nicholas himself. His second meeting was no less formal. At the third, Arghun was drunk and talked of nothing but his wives and hunting. Giovanni listened. While in this loquacious mood, the Il-khan might impart information that would be of value to the Christian cause, would justify the risks of a lengthy mission and would, from the religious imbroglio of the Il-khanate, bring relief to the princes of the City States.

At his fourth audience, in mid summer, he managed to steer the conversation round to the proposed alliance. Arghun, true to his reputation for unpredictability, showed no interest, preferring to test Giovanni's knowledge of alchemy and to demonstrate his own. There were other meetings too, with the Il-khan alone or jointly with the Wazir, but they too were unproductive. It was at the last of these that Arghun spoke of Hassan, and invited Giovanni to be a witness to his son's skill with the Mongol bow.

Summer was almost over when Giovanni first saw the woman. She was no longer youthful but had a timeless beauty that stirred his soul and caused a tingle in his loins. Her hair was the colour of finest ebony, tinted with strands of rich gold. It was braided and tied at the shoulder. She made no attempt to cover it or to hide her face behind the veil that was common among Persian women. Her skin was dusky and her eyes deep brown. It was the eyes that held Giovanni's attention, not because she looked at him, but rather because she did not.

The window of his apartment opened onto a corridor tiled in blue and green mosaic, with an archway at its western end through which the setting sun threw its pale light on her graceful figure. Giovanni had stood behind the central mullion as she passed, watching those eyes, wide and enticing, but touched with sadness and an understanding of the world. He was reminded of a portrait of the Madonna that he carried in his baggage.

He tried to dismiss the thought. The woman was a heathen. Christians in Tabriz were few and far between. Yet he could not rid himself of her image, nor of the feelings she awakened in him. How many years was it since he had truly loved, how long even since he had lain in a woman's arms?

When he saw her again she had a child with her and, again, he caught in her animated countenance that sublime quality of the Blessed Virgin as she cradled the Christ in her arms. He dared to follow them until they turned a corner and disappeared through a curtained doorway guarded by two Mongol soldiers.

On the third occasion they passed one another in the archway. Giovanni bowed. She acknowledged his politeness with a smile. Their eyes met, and it seemed to him she looked into his heart and saw the desire that was burning away all his resistance to her charms.

He had not known who she was. Now Arghun, in his eagerness to show off his stepson's prowess with the bow, had made everything clear. The object of his desire was Nadia, third wife of the Il-khan of Persia, as unapproachable and inviolable as the Madonna in the portrait.

Having stabled his pony, Hassan hurried to his mother's quarters. Her apartment was functional rather than luxurious. The divan was plain and comfortable, the carpets rich in colour but sparsely laid, and the single cedar wood table decked with an assortment of bottles and jars containing perfumes and spices. Closets off the main room were hung with curtains to hide their contents from the general view, and to afford privacy when needed.

Nadia sat on a cushion at a narrow window, overlooking a garden. Her hair was unfastened and hung loosely about her neck, shoulders and upper arms. She was pounding some substances with a pestle. The window seat was her favourite place in the room, where she could work in all seasons without need of a lamp, and from where she could see without being seen anyone who passed on the pathways below. She ceased her occupation and kissed her son warmly on the cheek.

Hassan could scarcely control his excitement. 'Four passes only, Mother, and only one arrow missed its target. Twenty-three gourds out of twenty-four, and ten were toppled. Arghun came late and didn't see my error.'

'How is your stepfather today?'

'He praised me and promised I could join the hunt when winter comes. But I don't think he is well, Mother.'

'You noticed the unhealthy tone of his skin, the paleness, and the swelling, as I asked you to do?'

'I saw all that, Mother,' replied Hassan gravely, 'and I'll swear he had drunk more than usual.'

'The liquor dulls his pain.' Nadia knew there was no going back. 'And he will require more of it soon.'

'I don't want Arghun to die,' said Hassan. 'He has always treated me fairly, and I know he honours you above other women, even though you are not first in rank. Can you not prevent his death?'

Nadia smiled tolerantly. 'I can delay it perhaps. I can bring him respite from his pain, but I cannot cure the sickness that eats away his inside.'

'Then he'll die, and Ghazan will rule in his place. That won't be so bad, though I'll mourn him.'

Nadia embraced him but she avoided his eyes. 'Have you any other news for me?' she asked at length.

'The ambassador from Italy watched me today,' went on Hassan, brightening up. 'He was with my father on the platform, and applauded. He's very stern, and doesn't drink the fermented whey. Once I saw him pour his cup into the dirt when Arghun wasn't looking. He is wary, but they seem fond enough of one another's company.'

'Has anyone else observed their familiarity?'

'Yesterday they were both with the chief minister of the treasury and, three days ago, when Prince Gaikatu arrived and had an audience, the Italian was there too.'

Nadia frowned. She patted Hassan's head while he fingered the arms of the hooked gold cross that hung at her breast. 'Well done, my little spy,' she teased. 'Now, Hassan, have you no lessons with the imam today?'

'None, Mother. Remember, in two days time I'm to go to Maragha. This afternoon I'll challenge Oljeitu to a game of chess, or to a fight with the wooden swords.'

'Let him win today, Hassan.'

'Why should I do that, Mother?'

'You'll understand one day,' said Nadia, 'but for now, obey me in this, I beg you.'

Arghun awoke at dusk. His first thought was of the dull ache that spread across his body, squeezing his organs in its unrelenting grip. The feeling of well-being brought about by intoxication was gone and he was left with only the after-effects, a throbbing in his head and a sour taste in his mouth. He despised himself for his own weakness, but knew that before long more liquor would be needed to render him insensible to the pain he had suffered so many weeks.

His second thought was that he was not in the place where he had fallen asleep. He was lying in his own bed. Through half-closed eyelids he was aware of the pale glow of lamplight. His ears caught the rustle of silk, the clink of glass against metal, and the sound of gentle breathing. He opened his eyes and raised his pounding head to see Nadia kneeling by the side of the divan. She was busying herself with some objects on a silver tray. There was a goblet, full to the brim with clear liquid, an open box containing a white powder, and several phials. As he watched silently, she picked up one of these containers, covered the opening with her forefinger, and shook it. Having done so, she raised a second phial and poured its contents into the first.

A movement of his arm distracted her and she looked up.

'My Lord Arghun. You are awake.'

'How did I get here, Nadia?' His throat was dry and the words came forth as a hoarse rasping sound.

'I could not move you from the cushion alone, but once the guards had lifted you to your feet I was able, with Hassan's help, to support you on the short walk to your bedchamber.'

'I walked?' croaked Arghun.

'You were half awake, My Lord, and talking to yourself,' said Nadia, reaching for the goblet and the box of powder. 'Now drink this, I beg you. It will wet your throat, counteract the sourness in your mouth, and purge your bowels of the alcohol.'

She emptied the contents of the box into the liquid, stirred the mixture with her finger and held the cup out to him. The mixture hissed and bubbles rose to the surface.

'What is it?' demanded Arghun in a hoarse whisper.

'Only water, My Lord,' said Nadia. 'Do you doubt me? It is water - water to which I have added a salt purchased from the apothecary at great expense. Now, drink it before the effervescence stops.'

Arghun laughed half-heartedly, took the cup obediently and drank. The bubbles tickled his palate, but the medicine refreshed him. 'And now this, My Lord.' She gave him the phial in which she had combined the two substances.

Arghun frowned.

'Put it on your tongue and swallow it quickly,' she instructed.

The Il-khan did so without demurring and lay back on the bed. For a while he studied her shapely figure and alluring profile then, struck by a sudden disturbing thought, he raised himself on his elbows. 'Was it you who found me in this condition, Nadia?' he enquired. His voice had almost recovered its usual resonance.

'It was Hassan. He had told me you looked unwell this afternoon, and I asked him to bring news of you when he returned from his play with Oljeitu. He saw you lying on the cushion and alerted me.'

'Unwell, yes,' grunted the Il-khan. 'The guards did not enter this apartment?'

'I have said so, My Lord. They lifted you to your feet, no more. The soldiers would not dare cross the threshold of the Il-khan's bedchamber.'

'Yet you dare, Nadia.'

'I am your wife.'

'I have other wives, Nadia,' said Arghun, ' and they wouldn't enter unless I commanded them.'

Nadia did not reply. To his surprise, Arghun realised his headache was ebbing. The pain in his chest and side remained, but it was no worse.

He reached out and took her hand.

'Sit beside me on the bed, Nadia. I want to talk to you.'

'Talk, My Lord?'

'You know we never do anything else,' said Arghun. 'There are things I don't want to leave unsaid. I know I'm sick. And it has become worse over the last few weeks. I drink more and more wine and other rotgut to rid myself of the pain. You've noticed these things, I know.

'My wives - Tolaghan and the others - they come only when I command them for my pleasure. This lump of flesh in my groin erects and I have a few brief moments of passion, but I gain no lasting satisfaction from it. With you I'm quite impotent. Yet in my dreams it's your face I see. It's your skin I caress, and it's between your thighs that I find lasting ecstasy.'

He became agitated. 'Can you explain it to me, Nadia? Can you explain why it is, though I find pleasure in an hour of your company, though I delight in the sound of your voice and gain satisfaction from watching you prepare your medicines, that I'm unable to share your body as a man should. You're more beautiful than the others. Now that this sickness has taken hold of me, it's you who comes unasked to offer me comfort. Yet you remain as much out of my reach as ever.'

He searched her dusky complexion for some warmth of response, but could see nothing there. Her eyelids only flickered.

'Is it that you hate me so much? Is this visit to my bedside a mockery? Have you come to watch me die, to hasten my end with these medicines?' He sighed. 'None of that is true, I know, yet it was my people who dragged you from your homeland, who forced you into marriage, first with my uncle Teguder, then with me. Did you bewitch us both, that neither was able to touch you?'

'With you, it was not always so,' breathed Nadia. 'And I do not hate you, My Lord. It's true I did not marry Teguder from choice, and would not have married you on his death had it not been the Mongol custom. But I have offered myself to you many times, as was my duty as a wife.'

'Duty!' echoed the Il-khan. 'I know it, Nadia.' He sighed again. 'Would that I could make amends for the grief brought to your family by my kin. And would that you could offer me a medicine to cure this unnatural impotence.'

*

III

Giovanni suspected his patience was being tested. He was no closer to his objective than when he left Italy. He looked forward apprehensively to each meeting with Arghun, never certain whether the Il-khan would be drunk or sober, unable to anticipate which subject his host's capricious mind would introduce next into their conversation. Moreover, the tedium of waiting had dulled the enthusiasm and high expectation with which he had begun his adventure.

Three times Arghun had absented himself from Tabriz for a week or more and Giovanni was left to negotiate with the Wazir, who continued to prove stubborn and unhelpful. Although admitting that an alliance would be in the Il-khan's interest, he made plain his distaste of his master's potential ally. Giovanni had known in advance he would be dealing with a Jew, but he had not expected to encounter one so influential in foreign policy and so much in control of the purse-strings. Sa'd ad-Daulah's appointment a year previously was a second setback to the Christian hopes only months after they were enlivened by the visit to Rome of a Mongol envoy.

Five years earlier, the cause had seemed hopeless. Hulegu was succeeded as Il-khan by his son Abaqa, also tolerant in matters of religion. Arghun, son and presumed heir of Abaqa, inherited this tolerance but not the kingdom. On Abaqa's death, the Muslims conspired to raise Hulegu's second son, Teguder, to the throne. That news was received badly by the Holy Father. There were rumours that Teguder had poisoned his brother, but no proof.

The third Il-khan, despite a Christian upbringing, converted to Islam in order to consolidate his power base and broaden his popularity. However, he succeeded only in angering the Mongol aristocracy who commanded the army. With the generals' help, Arghun seized power. Teguder was executed, smothered and beaten to death beneath a pile of carpets. Mongol law forbade the shedding of a prince's blood.

Two days had passed since Arghun ended their last interview in such a dramatic manner and Giovanni received no further summons. His quarters were comfortable enough and he was free to walk unhindered in the greater part of the castle and its grounds, along its maze of corridors and round its courtyards and gardens. Those areas forbidden to him, the women's quarters, the treasury and, surprisingly, the kitchens, were well protected, and he had only to stray a few steps from the permitted walkways to find his passage barred by two or more sentries.

On the morning of the third day, while strolling aimlessly in a hitherto unexplored section of corridor, he was awakened from a reflective mood by the sound of chilling Mongol battle-cries. The shrill whoops and screeches were accompanied by the noise of shuffling young feet, the occasional grunt, and the dull thud of one object striking another. He took a few steps in the direction of the sounds, turned yet another corner, and came upon a closed arena in which two small boys were engaged in what appeared to be mortal combat.

They wore full battle dress in miniature. Each carried a round shield made from animal hide, reinforced with strips of metal in the shape of a star. The short wooden swords they swung to and fro were cleverly carved replicas of the weapons worn by Arghun's guards, but having their edges and points blunted and thickened. Their helmets were pulled well down over their brows and, though the padded leather flaps hid their ears and part of their faces, Giovanni recognised one of the combatants as Hassan and the other as the Il-khan's youngest son, Oljeitu.

Fascinated, he watched, uncertain whether to intervene. The contest was so earnest, the blows struck so savage, that he believed at first the outcome would be serious injury to one or both participants. He then noticed the fight was supervised. A young man wearing a leather corslet and armed with a wooden sword stood unobtrusively by a pillar at the rear, noting every move and calling out as one boy penetrated the other's defences and scored a hit on his well-protected person.

'Five to four!'

The boys circled one another warily, each looking for an opening in his opponent's guard. They were well matched in size and agility, but Giovanni noticed differences in the styles and manner of their attack and counter attack. He found himself wondering if their approach to the contest reflected fundamental dissimilarity of race and character.

Oljeitu applied himself energetically in a renewed assault on Hassan's shield. He cut and slashed from right and left, using the full strength of his arm and the weight of his body to beat the Persian boy back.

Hassan's shield absorbed the blows and he used his feet to good effect, turning sideways so as to present the narrowest possible target. Having taken momentum out of the attack by the deftness of his retreat, he reversed the position of his feet and, holding the shield close to his body, went on the offensive. However, his sword thrusts had less menace than those of Oljeitu, and the Mongol boy met them with sword and shield together.

For a few moments they grappled. Oljeitu gritted his teeth and stoutly held his ground, using the edge of his shield to try and force Hassan's sword from his grasp, and cleaving the air as his opponent stepped nimbly aside to avoid a fierce stroke aimed at the shoulder.

Oljeitu began yet another savage attack, and once again Hassan allowed himself to be driven back. Nimble as he was, however, Hassan was careless and shifted the shield fractionally to the left, exposing a small but significant section of breastplate. Seeing his opportunity, Oljeitu lunged and scored a hit just below Hassan's right collar- bone. Hassan gasped and fell on one knee.

'Kolokol!' cried the young Mongol, stepping back and sportingly permitting his antagonist to recover. 'The fight is mine.'

'Five hits apiece,' announced the supervisor. 'The next touch of the sword will win the game.'

Hostilities recommenced. With excited shouts of bravado, the boys fell upon one another. Again Giovanni was aware of the contrasting styles. Oljeitu, aggressive and brash, relied on his strength to beat his opponent into submission. Hassan, quick on his feet and deliberate in his other movements, sought to use the Mongol prince's weight against him, and to strike when his rival was off balance.

In this fashion it ended. Hassan, pushed hard towards the wall of the arena and apparently vulnerable to the wildly-swinging sword, pivoted on his legs and with a movement of his wrist deflected the wooden blade from his shield. Oljeitu stumbled, dropped his guard, and

Hassan's weapon swept down on his opponent's unprotected left arm.

Hassan gave a whoop of joy and threw his shield in the air. 'Six to five. The game is mine!' he yelled, prancing up and down in delight.

'Six to five. Hassan is the winner,' confirmed the score-keeper, coming forward and applauding both combatants.

Oljeitu looked disconsolate in defeat. He briefly raised his sword in salute before stalking off, helmet pulled even further down over eyes wet with tears.

'I won't play chess with him today,' Giovanni heard him mutter as he passed.

Hassan exchanged a few words with the fight supervisor, removed his helmet and crossed the arena. The ambassador, though full of admiration for the boys' skills, was still recovering from his uneasiness at the violence inherent in their play.

'Did you see the whole game?' enquired the victor. His curls were flattened by the helmet and damp with perspiration. His dark eyes held a glint of triumph.

'I regret that I watched only a small part of the contest,' replied Giovanni with diplomatic politeness. He was not used to children. 'However, may I be allowed to congratulate your highness on your win.'

'Haven't I been taught well?' pursued the boy. He indicated the score-keeper. 'Ibrahim says I've improved of late. Oljeitu always used to win, but I've beaten him six times since my birthday. And he never wins at chess.'

'How old are you, if you'll forgive me asking?'

'Ten,' answered Hassan. 'Oljeitu is half a year older, but we're the same height.' He pulled his shoulders back and stuck out his chest.

The Venetian could not help smiling. He was reminded that this grim, battle-weary warrior was a mere child. 'I fear you'll play no chess with Prince Oljeitu today,' he said solemnly. 'As he passed me I heard him remark to himself that he did not have the inclination.'

'Then you will be my partner, sir!'

Giovanni was taken by surprise. 'I, your highness?'

'It would please me greatly, sir,' pleaded Hassan, 'that is, if I don't detain you from affairs of state.'

'I await only the pleasure of your stepfather, the Il-khan,' said Giovanni. There were no simple friendships in his narrow world of men and politics and his fear of commitment was especially strong in this alien country and among its heathen people. Yet he was warming to the boy's charm. He forced another smile. 'I am at your disposal.'

Hassan beamed and held out his hand. Giovanni felt his fingers gripped tightly and found unexpected pleasure in the contact with the child's small, sticky palm. He was led along several corridors and through a gateway or two, until they reached a door guarded in the usual manner by two fierce Mongols. Without realising it, he had returned to the quadrangle in which his own quarters were located, and was in the corner diagonally opposite his own door, though separated from it by the gardens and terraces.

Hassan halted in front of the guards, drew himself up to his full height and in a shrill, imperious voice demanded to be admitted. Giovanni saw a flicker of tolerant amusement cross the face of one of the sentries, but both obediently stepped aside and made no effort to hinder him from following the boy into the room beyond.

The apartment was like none he had seen since his arrival in Persia and reminded him of a monk's cell. There were no cushions or rugs. In one corner, beneath the window, was a table covered by a parchment on which was drawn innumerable geometric figures. On one wall hung Hassan's small bow and a quiver of arrows. Some toys and games, mostly having a military theme, were scattered on the floor.

The chess pieces had pride of place on a second table, inlaid on its surface with alternate squares of light and dark wood, highly polished, and clearly of recent manufacture. The pieces themselves were beautifully carved to match the colours of the board. The faces and figures of the kings and queens were formed with an intricacy of detail unmatched in any pieces to be found in Italy. The front ranks of footsoldiers carried tiny swords, the knights on their prancing horses were frozen in the act of loosing arrows from their diminutive bows and the priests, instead of bishops' vestments and mitres, wore long, flowing robes and conical hats. The castles occupying the corner squares were in the form of miniature pagan temples.

'It's a very fine set,' remarked Giovanni in admiration.

'My grandfather had it carved for me,' the boy said proudly. 'He represents the Il-khan in the province of Kerman, where my mother grew up.'

He squatted on the floor beside the playing table. Giovanni, seeing no stool to sit on, followed suit.

'What may I call you, sir?' asked Hassan.

'My name is Giovanni. You may call me that.'

'And you must call me Hassan. I'm tired of being a highness. As you agreed to play with me, we should be friends - and friends call one another by their proper names.'

'I shall be happy to be your friend, Hassan,' Giovanni said sincerely.

They played. Giovanni, who had studied with an Italian master, won the first game. In the second, Hassan forced him into an error whereby he lost his queen. The boy then pressed home his advantage and needed only six more moves to achieve check-mate. Though he had recognised his opponent's talent from the outset, Giovanni had not considered the possibility of defeat by one so young and he damned his own complacency. In his current profession he could afford to underestimate no one, not even a ten-year-old boy.

'So, Hassan,' he said humbly, 'you are adept in contests of the mind, just as you are in trials of arms. You have been well taught in both.'

'If I have any skill in chess, it's due to my mother,' said Hassan. 'She is my teacher in most things. I played quite well, Giovanni, and will be satisfied at beating you, if you'll deny that you allowed me to win.'

'I deny it most vehemently,' laughed Giovanni. 'You are an accomplished player and did not need my condescension in order to win. Why do you accuse me?'

'I didn't mean to offend, only my mother says I ought to allow Oljeitu to beat me sometimes, at chess as well as in swordplay. But I always try hard to win, and don't understand why I should do otherwise.'

'Your mother speaks wisely, Hassan.'

'Then you would have allowed me to win after two or three games?'

Giovanni looked across at the deep brown eyes but saw no guile in them. He had to remind himself that this young philosopher was only ten years old. 'I cannot say, Hassan,' he said. 'Sometimes it is wise to enter into another's feelings. Perhaps your brother's pride will be hurt, as mine was a moment ago, if you win constantly. In time he may resent it.'

'Should I fear his resentment, Giovanni?'

'I do not know Oljeitu. All I can say is, listen to your mother.'

Hassan made a face. 'My stepfather is always saying that.' He reset the chess pieces in their proper places in readiness for another game. 'But I don't always pay attention, then I'm scolded . . .'

'Hassan!'

The ambassador turned to see Nadia on the threshold. In full daylight and at this proximity she seemed younger than he had at first thought her, and even more beautiful. He felt a thrill of pleasure. She had a full, shapely figure, in no way disguised by the looseness of her gown. The silk fabric covered her shoulders, but the bodice was cut away at the collar to reveal the upper curve of ample breasts. The glint of her unusual necklace drew his eyes from her dusky throat to the dark, inviting hollow beneath. The material of the skirt seemed to be attracted to the contours of her hips and thighs like iron to a lodestone.

Giovanni fought against his feelings. Apart from the boy he was alone with her and that knowledge filled him with apprehension. He had been warned of the barbaric customs of eastern princes, who treated their women like cattle yet would emasculate or put out the eyes of any man daring to address them. Even if the travellers' tales were myth, he had no desire to put them to the test.

'Have you forgotten, Hassan?' Nadia rebuked her son. 'The escort awaits to take you to Maragha, and you cannot go dressed in that fashion. Armour is for fighting. Wear something more befitting a scholar!'

Hassan leapt to his feet. He stammered an apology and ran off. Giovanni bowed and would have withdrawn too if Nadia had not addressed him directly.

'Are all children so wayward?' She watched the boy go with a gesture of despair.

'I fear so, madam, - though I am no expert in the matter.'

'And you were encouraging him, sir,' she chided. Her large brown eyes were fixed on Giovanni's face, and he fancied he saw a touch of mischief in them.

'I swear I had no knowledge of a prior appointment, madam,' he said defensively. 'His Highness asked me to play chess with him, and I obliged.'

'You beat him, I trust.' She smiled. 'Hassan gets too big for his little boots sometimes.'

'It was one game all when you arrived, My Lady,' said Giovanni, relaxing his guard a little. 'Your son is a fine player for someone his age. I confess I should have seen his ploy but did not.'

'He is good but erratic,' said she. 'His mind flits like a butterfly from one flower to the next, tasting the nectar only briefly before passing on to more colourful petals. But I admit to being well satisfied with his progress in most things. He studies mathematics and the sciences with one of Persia's greatest minds, my uncle Shirazi of Maragha, and shows some skill at improving the master's theorems, or so I'm told. I teach him what I can of physic and healing - a little knowledge I had from my mother, and he learns the teachings of the Qur'an from a venerable mullah.'

She touched Giovanni lightly on the arm and he felt a tingling at the spot. 'But that is enough talk of my son. Walk with me in the garden and tell me of your country and its people.'

'It is permitted, madam?'

She laughed at his discomfort. 'Do Venetians shut up their women and forbid them intercourse with strangers?'

'Not at all,' said Giovanni, 'but would His Majesty not disapprove of us being alone together?'

'Tabriz Castle is no *harem*. The Il-khan would wish only that I show hospitality to a guest. Besides, we shall not be alone. I do not think you would harm me, but were you to try, the guards have well-whetted swords. She indicated the two Mongols patrolling the corridor then beckoned Giovanni to follow her. He did so, fearful of causing offence by refusing.

She led the way to a small arboretum where he was surprised to note that, despite the lateness of the season, the trees still bore all their leaves and the wood had retained its fragrance. Some mellowed fruit hung on the upper branches. A narrow footway zigzagged between the trunks, joining two points of the perimeter path.

Giovanni glanced at her frequently as they walked. In places, the way was overgrown with low-hanging foliage and they could scarcely pass through without their bodies touching. Twice he experienced a thrill of delight as the silk fabric of her gown brushed his knee.

Nadia did not draw back from this fleeting contact, nor did she exhibit any sign that she was aware of it. She showed unexpected interest in his description of the basilica in Rome and gasped as he endeavoured to convey the splendour of the Holy Father and his cardinals in their ceremonial robes. She seemed enthralled as he talked of Venice, of its palaces and churches, its waterways, and the great lagoon with its many islands. The sadness he had seen once in her eyes was no longer evident. Her face was animated like that of a child listening to a well-loved story.

'So it's really true that your people live upon the water,' she asked when he had finished, 'and that they travel everywhere by boat rather than by carriage? I heard this from a countryman of yours when I was a child but did not believe it. He was a boy called Marco Polo,' she went on reminiscently. 'I'll always remember that. He wrote his name in a book for me. The letters were strange and he taught me how to sound them. He came to Kerman with his father and uncle. They meant to travel to China, but could not find a ship at Hormuz, so they came back and took the overland route.'

'The Polo family is known to me, madam,' said Giovanni. 'Marco remained in China and now serves the Great Khan.'

'Kublai has honoured him then,' Nadia said. 'There can be few of your race who have found favour at the Mongol court, though many travel the Silk Road.'

'Indeed, madam. The kingdoms of Italy value greatly their trade with the Orient, and it is no secret that my purpose in Tabriz is to secure an alliance that will aid that enterprise. Sadly, I make little progress. I have still to persuade His Majesty of the benefits an alliance will bring.'

In voicing his disappointment at the failure of his diplomacy, Giovanni intended to do no more than make conversation. It was she who, from the chance meeting, had initiated their dialogue, and once assured that it would be innocently regarded by the Il-khan, he saw no reason not to prolong it. Motivated partly by his growing attraction and partly by the curiosity that Arghun's words had aroused, he wished to take full advantage of the opportunity to learn more about this woman who evoked feelings of such intensity in his soul. He also entertained the hope that, whatever Nadia's personal faith, neither she nor Hassan was beyond redemption and might yet be brought to the Cross of Christ, the Saviour.

But now he wondered if he had gone too far. His frustration at the months of wasted effort must have shown in his tone. Nadia threw him a penetrating glance and, for the second time since he had seen her, Giovanni imagined the beautiful wide eyes were able to look past his countenance and read his very mind. However, when she spoke, there was no displeasure in her voice.

'Be patient with my husband,' she counselled. 'He is persuaded, but dare not act with haste. Already there are some who accuse him of showing undue favour towards Christians and Jews. That is unjust. Arghun wishes only to rid the bureaucracy of corruption. But to rule effectively he needs the good will of the people as well as the support of the Mongol princes.

'Most of our people follow Islam, and have done so for six hundred years. They have not forgotten the destruction and slaughter that followed the march of Genghis's armies. They distrust the Il-khan's good intentions and do not realise their present misfortunes are a result of the ambition and greed of a few influential families who rose to power under Hulegu and Abaqa. Because these families also profess the Muslim faith, they are listened to.'

Giovanni wondered at her political astuteness, but her words depressed him. For all his doubts about the wisdom of his mission, if the Muslims gained the ascendancy it would surely fail.

'This distrust you speak of - can it be overcome?'

'In time,' said Nadia. 'Given freedom, ad-Daulah will reform the treasury and introduce a liberal tax regime. Persia's wealth will find its way into the public coffers to be used for the benefit of the people as a whole, rather than lining the pockets of a few bureaucrats who are traitors to the religion they profess.'

She became quite animated and fingered her gold talisman. The ornament was much too large to escape notice but until now Giovanni's attention had not been unduly drawn to it. It was like no gammadion he had ever seen. Both the cross and its chain were gold. Where the arms met, the metal was thickened and bore the engraving of a radiant sun.

Now he was scarcely able to take his eyes off it, yet knew he had to, because of where it lay, pulling his gaze towards the cleft between her breasts. He felt heat mount in his cheeks and was sure Nadia must hear his pounding heart. Thankfully, she had paused to examine a single flower that remained on one of the shrubs and seemed not to notice his discomfort. Instead, she plucked the flower and held it to her nose.

'On the other hand,' she continued after a moment, 'it is the Mongol princes who hold military power. Arghun is dependent upon their loyalty, and they in turn rely on the treasury to provide funds. Without pay, the ranks will not stay contented long. Moreover, the princes do not like Christians any more than they like Muslims. So, you see, Arghun must not be precipitated into an alliance which could antagonise those on whom he depends, until he is ready.'

'I understand His Majesty's caution,' said Giovanni. 'However, I fear that Sa'd ad-Daulah is hostile.'

'Perhaps so,' agreed Nadia, 'but as the Il-khan's servant he too will hold back for the reasons I explained. I also suspect Jews and Christians have no cause to love one another.' Her dark eyes looked directly into his, unblinking, questioning, and again he thought he noticed a trace of humour. 'You would convert Daulah if you could!'

'I confess it, madam. It is the mission of every Christian to spread the teachings of Jesus wherever he can.'

'I know,' said she. 'You are just like the followers of Mahommet in that respect.'

They had reached the outer path. The sentries passed on the veranda above but gave them hardly a look. Her manner had been so relaxed throughout their discussion, that Giovanni had lost his inhibitions against a free exchange of views.

'We would spread the gospel peacefully, madam. The Muslims would spread their religion by conquest!'

The humour in her expression vanished. 'I will forgive such an indiscretion only because you are a stranger in our land,' she said sharply. 'The message of Islam is also peaceful. It is men who oppose the will of God by making war on each other. And it is we women who suffer. Can you deny that Muslims and Christians are equally guilty?'

Giovanni stammered an apology, but he was puzzled. Her defence of Muslim philosophy was at odds with what the Il-khan had told him of her. 'I admit to having little understanding of Persia and its people,' he said humbly, 'but I wish to learn. Tell me, does your own faith also have a peaceful mission?'

'I do not understand your question.'

'Forgive me, madam. His Majesty informed me that you held different beliefs from the majority. He called you a Gabar.'

'The Il-khan has misled you,' said Nadia. 'No single faith holds all the secrets of life and death. But I was brought up to follow the Islamic creed, like my father. Hassan studies the Qur'an as I told you. Gabar is the name given to the followers of Zoroaster. Yet perhaps I can suggest how the misunderstanding has arisen. My father's name is Kartir.'

'How is that of significance?'

'Your knowledge of Persia is truly imperfect,' smiled Nadia. 'I do not blame you. There are many of our own people who do not remember. The name Kartir is famous in the annals of the Iranians. He was a Magian, high priest and chief minister to the first Sasanian kings, next only to the king himself in power, and in certain respects even more powerful. In those days, the temporal and spiritual ruled together, and the Persian empire prospered. Later kings became more concerned with their own personal glory, and the influence of the priests gradually declined. Some blame the fall of Persia to the Arabian armies on that fact.'

They had turned into yet another footway and she stopped by a vine-covered pergola to pluck some over-ripe and shrivelling grapes which she held out to him. There was a warm sensuality in all her movements and Giovanni's pulse began to race once more. With an unsteady hand he took a grape. It was sugary but still palatable.

'The old religion was tolerated at first,' Nadia went on. 'But as the Persian and Arab cultures merged, new dynasties arose that were less sympathetic to the Zoroastrian beliefs and customs, and they persecuted those who adhered to them. Many fled the country. Others converted to Islam to obtain tax advantages, or to protect their families.

'Some defied the prejudice and continued to worship their gods openly. Even today there are those who do so and in Kerman, where I spent my childhood, there is a Zoroastrian tradition. My father's ancestors were descended from the Magian priestly caste. Though the family converted generations ago, the name Kartir is still associated with the past. But I think he is a popular governor.'

Again she paused. Giovanni realised they had made two complete circuits of the garden. There was more he wanted to ask, but his instincts urged him to proceed slowly. Taking advantage of the short silence, he bowed and made his excuses.

'Thank you for clarifying so much for me,' he said. 'I shall try to be patient in my dealings with His Majesty, as you recommend. But I fear I am detaining you. You must have many responsibilities to attend to.'

' 'Tis I who have detained *you*, sir,' replied Nadia. 'I hope we can talk again on another occasion. Meantime, I am grateful for the friendship you have shown my son. In return, I presume to give you one piece of advice. Hassan tells me you have made the acquaintance of my husband's brother, Prince Gaikatu, the governor of Rum Province. Do not trust him even when he smiles.'

Giovanni bowed again and turned to go, but she halted him.

'Your way lies over there,' she said with a smile, pointing in a direction opposite to the one in which he was heading. 'These courtyards and gardens are confusing to anyone unfamiliar with them.

'And remember,' she added. The smile was no longer evident. 'The other princes show their hate, but Gaikatu disguises it well.'

*

IV

The old town of Maragha lay in a valley to the south of Tabriz and separated from it by the forbidding heights of Mount Sahand. To east and west, as far as the eye could see, stretched fertile rolling grassland. Leafy orchards, carefully planted and diligently farmed for their prolific crops of fruit, dotted the mountain's lower slopes and lined the approaches to the town.

Maragha boasted many fine buildings of neat, decorated brickwork, and of the mottled white stone that generations of local masons had quarried and cut, dedicating the products of their rough labour to the glory of their gods. The stone was much admired for its colour and texture, and for the delicate veins of red and green that gave it its essence.

Dominating the skyline were three towers dating from the Turkish occupation and the magnificent dome of the Maragha observatory. The former occupied a central position in the town, and though few in Maragha cared which of their many Seljuk rulers were entombed there, none could pass about his daily business without encountering a stark reminder of his own mortality. Written clearly on the wall of one of these monuments to forgotten conquerors were the words *All Men Must Savour Death*.

The observatory stood at the town's western end, easily accessible from the Tabriz road. Built by Nasr ad-Din Tusi under the patronage of Khan Hulegu, it was testimony to the life of the great scholar and home to the finest scientific instruments in the whole of Persia. Its library was stocked with the best literature of the age, giving pride of place to several works by the master himself, as well as historical treatises and mathematical texts rescued from the sack of Alamut.

One of the guardians of this treasure-house was a man of unscholarly appearance. The right side of his face was pleasing enough and he might have been considered handsome had it not been for the overwhelming impression of ugliness given by the left. Where the eyebrow should have been was a white scar, long healed. The eye socket was empty, and a mass of shrivelled scar tissue stretched across the cavity in his face from temple to jaw. He might have been a soldier whose luck on the battlefield had run out, and who had been forced to live out his retirement in constant pain and misery, an object of pity or ridicule.

In fact, Jafar al-Salah had always been a scholar. Although the memory of his pain remained, the pain itself had long vanished. Pressed into Ismaili service as a child, he had once been a scribe in the great library of Alamut. Fleeing from the onslaught of Hulegu's army, he was trapped in a burning section of the castle, where a falling timber struck him a glancing blow on the head, tearing and singeing the flesh around his left eye and crushing the cheekbone below. Resigned to an agonising death in the poisonous fumes from the fires, Jafar was pulled from the crumbling building by one of the Il-khan's retainers, a man little more than his age, and a Persian like himself.

Terrible though his wounds were, Jafar recovered. Through the skill and patience of Nasr they healed and, despite the disfigurement, he regained his zest for life and work. For the past thirty years, that life had been devoted to Maragha. For ten, he had assisted Nasr in observing the heavens and in compiling a table of planetary motions. For another six, until the Master's death, he had studied the mathematics of the circle, endeavouring to improve upon the theorems of Ptolemy. He had become fascinated by the theory of numbers and preoccupied with the search for a new meaning to life in the triangles of Omar Khayam. In time he had come to terms with the loss of his mentor and friend and now, in his fifty-sixth year, he had become a teacher of the young and a translator from Greek and Arabic.

It was in this capacity that Jafar was to make the acquaintance of Prince Hassan. It was no part of his normal duties to give tuition to members of the Il-khan's household. That task fell to the Master of Maragha alone, Qutb ad-Din Shirazi, Nasr's adopted son and successor to the post. However, Hassan's position was unique.

Shirazi had praised the boy's intellect. 'The child has a superior mind,' he said. 'His curiosity about the natural world, about the heavens, and in all matters relating to the sciences is insatiable. He already has a grasp of the Greek language, as well as Arabic and Persian, and I have been told he converses freely in the Mongol tongue.'

'I've heard that the Il-khan's eldest son, Ghazan, has an aptitude for languages,' remarked Jafar with no great enthusiasm. 'I wouldn't, however, think of him as a scholar.'

'Ghazan is an artisan by inclination,' replied Shirazi. 'Our task was to teach him the skills that a king might need. Hassan will never be a king, but he may yet be a scholar. He must be nurtured carefully and taught to curb his wilder passions.'

'This child has been adopted by the Il-khan who wants to turn him into a Mongol prince,' said Jafar grimly. 'Arghun will not thank you for interfering, Master.'

'I do not see the conflict, Jafar,' rejoined Shirazi calmly. 'Throughout the long history of our people there have been many conquerors but, on the whole, it is they who have changed and our ways that have survived. Even if that were not so, I would have to take the risk of offending Arghun. I owe it to the boy's mother.'

Jafar tried to smile. It was an effort he knew made his disfigurement even more grotesque. 'The beautiful Nadia? You are on dangerous ground, Master Shirazi. Not content with making a philosopher of his stepson, you would make the Il-khan cuckold.'

'Believe me, she is a woman worth dying for, my friend,' said the Master of Maragha with a sigh. 'As we are both men with raw desires, I confess that, though we are blood relations, I have lain often with her in my dreams. But my waking motives are honourable. My duty is to the memory of my father, and hers.'

'How so?'

'They were friends. If Nadia had had a brother, his education would have been placed in Nasr's hands and it would have been undertaken gladly. Since she never had one, the contract is unfulfilled. Thus I undertake the education of *her* son in my father's name.' The Master paused and licked his lips. 'The fact that my duty takes me into her company is neither here nor there.'

'And the blood relationship you spoke of . . .?'

'Nadia is my niece. She is the daughter of my sister.'

'I never knew that.'

'There was no reason for you to know, Jafar. My sister left Maragha more than twenty years ago, and I never saw her again.'

Jafar muttered words of sympathy. 'I envy you sometimes, Master,' he said bitterly, after a silence. 'Over the years, I have observed that, though you already have a wife, other women eagerly seek your company. Would that even one could gaze at me with love, rather than pity and loathing. It is true I have had two wives, but neither permitted intimacy unless my face was covered with a leather mask.'

'The life of a scholar can be lonely if there are no diversions,' conceded Shirazi with a solemn nod. 'You have my sympathy and understanding. I respect and admire your many excellent qualities. You envy me, you say. Sometimes I have envied you your courage, your superior knowledge and your experience of life. Throughout our long association I have never pitied you. Only the pitiable are to be pitied.'

Jafar was conscious of a pleasant, warm glow radiating from his solitary cheek. Such a testimony more than balanced days of anguish and self-effacement. He loved Shirazi as he had never loved any woman, though his love was intellectual and spiritual, and both his inclination and his religion forbade him seeking any sexual gratification from it.

'So Hassan progresses well in our care?' he asked to hide his embarrassment.

'He does indeed,' replied Shirazi, 'so much so that I am ready to ask for your help in the nurturing of which I spoke.'

'My help, Master?'

'You are familiar with the library, and your knowledge of Greek is greater than mine. Hassan should broaden his understanding of that language and be given a grounding in history. You are ideally qualified for both tasks.'

'That may be true, but . . .'

'Hassan is a lively boy. Mischievous too sometimes. You'll like him. Come, Jafar, what do you say? What I have in mind will also give you an opportunity to meet his mother. Nadia wishes to lessen her son's travelling and proposes a tutor for a month or two in the royal residence. She assured me Arghun will not object. Hassan will pay a visit in a day or two. You shall take him in hand, then return to Tabriz with him.'

Jafar was uncertain, but not because he doubted his own ability. In the observatory and its library he felt secure.

'I think you should accept the commission,' continued the Master kindly but firmly. 'Your duty to Hassan and his mother may even be greater than mine.'

'He is a Mongol prince,' frowned Jafar. 'I am not prejudiced on that score, but why should I have any duty in regard to his education?'

'I know nothing of his origins, Jafar,' said Shirazi. 'However, I suspect he was not sired by a descendant of Genghis Khan. His mother is not only beautiful and my niece. Her father, and my brother by marriage, is Ahmed Kartir, viceroy of Kerman.'

For the second time that day, Jafar felt the flush of blood in the veins of his right cheek, and a surge of excitement fired his whole being. His expression as he stared at Shirazi was one of astonishment mixed with reverence.

'Kartir!' he cried. 'Then you know I cannot refuse the commission.'

'May I study the histories on this shelf, Jafar?' asked Hassan, pointing to a row just out of his reach.

Jafar looked up from his reading and scrutinised the eager young face. After only a few days acquaintance with the boy's talents, he had come to understand Shirazi's enthusiasm, though he found Hassan's company wearing and his behaviour sometimes fickle.

'Have you finished the text I set you?' he enquired suspiciously.

'It's done, Jafar. You may correct it if you wish.'

Jafar doubted that the boy could have completed translation of the Greek passage in the time available, however he nodded in acquiescence. Without waiting for permission, Hassan had already mounted a stool and was balancing on his tiptoes. Now, at his tutor's signal, he reached upwards and toward the topmost shelf. The stool wobbled on its uneven legs and he leapt clear as it toppled.

'Let me take them down, Your Highness,' said Jafar tolerantly.

He picked two volumes at random, laid them on the table, and took up the paper on which the boy had written. To his amazement, the translation was not only complete, but Hassan's interpretation was almost flawless. Not for the first time Jafar wondered why Shirazi had chosen him for this task. He looked round to see Hassan already engrossed in one of the histories and, satisfied he might have at least a few moments peace, began to search the shelves for a Persian work that might be used to more thoroughly test his pupil's ability. Hassan had translated with ease from Greek into his own language. Let him attempt the exercise in reverse.

While he was debating this plan with himself, Jafar's one true eye noticed a volume that had fallen on its side. The parchment was discoloured and the script faded, but the binding was secure. It was a history of the Sasanian kings, one he had often browsed for its sympathetic treatment of the old religion. This work would provide the boy with the very challenge he needed.

Jafar set the book on his lectern and carefully turned the pages until he found a well-remembered passage.

When Tansar had departed to the Tower of Silence, Ardashir, King of Kings, invested Kartir with the symbols of his office. And Kartir forgot neither his vow nor the prophecies, and he prayed to the god to strengthen his hand and to strike down Persia's enemies. So it was by the power of Ahura Mazda_that Kartir held sway over men and the elements like the Magi in ancient times . . .

A sudden breath of air ruffled Jafar's hair and made him turn round. Hassan had risen from his table and was endeavouring to read over his shoulder.

'What is it you have there, Jafar?' asked the boy, apparently unconcerned at his rudeness. 'I noticed the leather is very worn and the parchment yellow.'

'Did you indeed, Hassan?' said Jafar severely. 'Are your eyes always so sharp that you can keep the right on your studies and the left on other people's business? Spare a thought for me who have only one eye, and when that is absorbed in study I see naught else.'

Hassan seemed taken aback by the rebuke but he recovered quickly. 'Is it a Greek history like the other?' he persisted.

'Not Greek, Hassan,' said Jafar. 'The language is archaic Persian. Your next task will be to translate it into the Hellenic, and it may be you will find the text especially interesting. It relates the history of Kartir, high priest and chief minister to the first Sasanian kings, and possibly an ancestor of yours. He held the kingdom together during six reigns, and our country owes much to him.'

'My grandfather is also named Kartir,' exclaimed Hassan. He righted the fallen stool and seated himself on it, an elbow on one knee and his chin resting on his fist like a Greek philosopher. 'I haven't met him that I can recollect, but my mother says he's a great man, just like the Kartir in your book. May I begin the translation straightway?'

Jafar nodded pensively. He studied Hassan's face with its high cheekbones, prominent nose and serious eyes, and a memory, painful still after the space of almost thirty-five years, stirred and rose to the surface of his consciousness. He was again at Alamut. He felt the heat of the flames and the slow, engulfing suffocation of the smoke. Through the haze of pain, he saw bending over him the tall figure of his rescuer, grasping him by the armpits, pulling him from the burning timbers. It was only later that he had learned through Nasr the name of the young man who saved his life - Ahmed Kartir ad-Din Kermani, once a scholar himself but now in the confidence of the new ruler of Persia.

This knowledge had created for Jafar a dilemma of conscience. Though Mongol rule had brought a tolerance not seen in Persia for six hundred years, his dislike of the conqueror was almost as great as his hatred of the Ismailis, with their self-righteousness and relentless persecution of all who held different beliefs from themselves. His rescuer, bearing the name of the great disciple of Zoroaster but for all that a devout Muslim, had willingly enlisted in the service of the invaders. Such things were beyond Jafar's understanding. Yet he owed the Il-khan's viceroy a debt, and after thirty-five years it was still unpaid.

Now, through a twist of fate, he had made the acquaintance of the boy, so like his grandfather in his eagle-like features and gravity of expression. Had Shirazi foreseen that a bond would grow between them, and had he consciously chosen him as Hassan's tutor for that reason? How strange it would be if the child became the means whereby his debt was settled.

Jafar lifted the heavy manuscript and placed it on the table. 'Indeed you may begin now, Hassan,' he agreed solemnly. 'This book must not leave the library, but I shall copy some more of the writing and give it to you when we return to Tabriz. Then I shall test your knowledge of Sasanian history as well as your understanding of the language.'

Jafar was gratified to find himself so well lodged. The floor of his schoolroom was carpeted, and there were already a small table, chair and lectern. Beneath the single window was an alcove, large enough to provide shelving for the small selection of histories in Greek, Arabian and Persian that Shirazi had permitted to be removed from Maragha. At the rear of the apartment was an anteroom containing a bed and some scattered cushions.

He had parted from Hassan and his escort at the castle gate and had not seen the boy since. Two servants had carried his chest containing books, parchments and personal belongings to the room that was to be his home until winter, and there they had left him alone.

The sights and sounds of Tabriz both excited and terrified him. He had been to the city only once before, during Abaqa's reign. Then, the multifarious travellers, colourful bazaars and crowded streets with their babble of different tongues had all sparked his interest. What tales might these merchants tell in the caravanserai: the Westerners with their blond hair and pink, sun-scorched faces; the sallow Orientals; wild desert Arabs who rode or led camels instead of horses; mysterious black men with flat noses and crinkly hair from the lands beyond Egypt? Tales of places they had visited, mountains they had climbed, rivers they had forded; of beautiful women and forbidden pleasures? Tales worthy of Firdausi, or of Shahrazade herself? They had seen life whereas he, Jafar, could only dream.

But the dream had ended abruptly. He had been jostled by a crowd of youths who mocked his disfigurement and his scholarly garb. It had been one of the most bitter experiences of his life, one that had not left him so that, when he saw again the turrets and minarets of Tabriz rear up out of the plain, he felt his insides churn with anxiety. As he rode from the city gates to the castle, he imagined the eyes of the population were on him and he began to regret his decision to leave the solitude of the observatory.

There were moments when he saw, or thought he saw, Nizari faces in the crowd. These were memories from the more distant past of a different, more subtle torment, one in which the tormentors hid their fanaticism behind a benevolent mask. Jafar told himself this could not be, that his Ismaili gaolers had been scattered to the four winds, and when he looked again he saw only the features of strangers.

Though these encounters disturbed him deeply, the journey was without incident and, as the day wore on, Jafar's fears subsided. His tension eased. During the afternoon, one of the servants had returned bearing a tray with food and refreshment. Though not talkative, the man had told him the apartment adjoined Hassan's own and that through the corridor to the left of his door access was gained to the quarters belonging to the boy's mother.

The building in which he was housed occupied a corner position in a quadrangle. The door of the room opened onto a covered veranda which connected together other apartments. The corridor on the left was closed by a curtain and to the right was a terrace with steps leading down to a garden. Jafar was surprised to find himself in a part of the royal residence so close to a wife of the Il-khan. He had often listened to tales of the old Caliphate, how the ruler of Baghdad and the sultans of the Muslim empire had numerous wives; how they were housed in a separate building, the *harem*. This appeared not to be the rule here. Apparently each of Arghun's wives inhabited different sections of the castle.

Only the continuous presence of the Mongol warriors who guarded the curtain and patrolled the corridor made Jafar feel uneasy. Soldiers of both the Mongol and Persian races were not uncommon at Maragha, but their visits were usually of short duration. They loitered inside the gates of the observatory, sometimes taking advantage of the high wall of the courtyard to shield themselves from the midsummer sun. However, they did not venture near the library, nor those other areas most frequented by the scholars.

By the time darkness fell Jafar had distinguished two separate watches. The arrival of a third disturbed his evening prayers. Their coarse conversation and laughter as they changed places carried plainly through the door. Jafar lay down on the bed. Hours passed but he could not sleep. The new sentries' boots sounded noisily in the corridor and the continual shifting of the position of their lamps threw alternate light and shadow across the walls of the room.

Suddenly the noise stopped and the lights were still. Jafar heard a dull thud, a faint cry, and the sound of someone moving past his door towards Hassan's apartment.

*

V

Giovanni woke with a start. The moon was almost in the first quarter and there was just enough light entering his narrow upper window to impart a silver eeriness to the room and its sparse furnishings. The quietness was broken by the buzzing and chirping of night insects. However, he had become accustomed to these sounds during the summer months and knew that something else must have disturbed his rest.

Of late he had slept well, and in the moments before oblivion his thoughts were invariably of Nadia. Before their walk in the garden, he had become resigned to the possibility of returning to Rome with his mission unfulfilled. Now his hopes of securing the treaty were revived and, with them, the kindling of hopeless sensual longing. He was unable to put her from his mind in waking hours. When he dreamed, it was she who filled his fantasies.

A week had passed and he had seen her only once. In that time, he had twice been summoned by Arghun who had been not only friendly but quite sober. However, at both meetings the Il-khan had skirted round the subject of the alliance. Instead, they had talked of architecture and trade until Giovanni suspected again that his sincerity and endurance were being tested. He had also participated twice in the communal feasting that provided a diversion for the royal party, but these were occasions for overindulgence rather than reasoned conversation, and he had escaped from them as soon as he could without insulting his host.

He lay motionless and listened, but could hear nothing unusual. Several minutes passed. The moon completed its transit across the tiny aperture and disappeared from view. Now he could scarcely see the door of his room or the shuttered lower window. Suddenly he knew what was wrong. The guards posted from dusk to dawn in his corridor always carried lamps, so that even on moonless nights a continuous pale glow through the slats on the lower window enabled him to discern the outlines of his table and chair. The muffled noise of the soldiers' feet as they patrolled, though it did not disturb his sleep, must have impinged sufficiently upon his subconscious, so that when it ceased he was immediately aware of it.

Giovanni swung his legs to the floor and sat on the edge of the divan rubbing the sleep from his eyes. He grasped the short sword that lay unsheathed within reach of his right hand as he slept and felt comfort in the cold metal of the hilt. Then he fumbled with his feet, found his sandals and slipped them on.

He rose in the darkness, unbarred the door, stepped into the corridor and crossed quickly into the shadow of the pillars bordering the veranda on the other side. Moonlight bathed part of the courtyard and gardens below, but the junction of his corridor and the one leading to the Hassan's apartment was in total darkness. Things were not as they should be. There was no lamplight, and no sign of the patrol.

Giovanni edged his way along from pillar to pillar until he reached the corner. He wondered if he should raise the alarm. It was none of his affair if the Il-khan chose to leave parts of the palace unguarded or if the soldiers, bored with their long vigil, slipped away for an hour with their paramours. However, Giovanni's instincts told him simple explanations would not do. Not once in his four-month sojourn had the corridor been left unguarded. And Hassan had returned to the castle only that afternoon. Mischief could be afoot and be directed at the boy he had befriended.

He had just reached the corner pillar when he saw a light blink at the far end of the adjacent veranda. Giovanni lengthened his stride and in an instant reached the spot where he had recently passed through the curtained opening. In the gloom, his bare left toe collided with a solid object lying across his path. At the same time his right foot slipped on a wet patch on the tiles and a warm, sticky fluid permeated the gap between the foot and the sole of his sandal. He knelt and explored with his hand.

No lamp was needed to tell him what had happened to one of the guards. He felt the leather corslet with its metal reinforcement. The man's arm was fully outstretched and his callused hand still gripped his sword. He must have been struck from behind with considerable force and with an extremely sharp weapon for, as nearly as Giovanni could tell, the head had been partly severed from the neck.

Feeling fear and nausea, Giovanni rose. The curtain had been pulled aside and the first two doors beyond were slightly ajar. The broad corridor was lit by a single lamp, hung about halfway along and head-high. Taking the sword of the dead guard as well as his own, he entered cautiously, flattening his body against the wall lest an intruder emerging from one of the apartments ahead should catch his shadow and be alerted to his presence. He had gone only a few steps when he heard the unmistakable sounds of a struggle coming from the nearest room.

Two men, neither of whose features he could distinguish, were engaged in a deadly wrestling match, the outcome of which seemed certain, given the relative build of the participants. A third man had Hassan in a powerful grip, one hand clasped round the boy's waist and holding him so that his feet were clear of the floor, the other held over his mouth to prevent him crying out.

Giovanni hesitated no longer. He sprang into the light and launched himself across the threshold at Hassan's captor. Seeing the threat, the latter released his hold of the boy's waist and went for his weapon, but the Italian struck him in the neck with his short sword. The man groaned and slumped to the ground, mortally wounded. Giovanni was allowed no time to assess the situation, and he had no clear sense of what followed.

In the dimness of the room, he had underestimated the number of intruders. A pair of strong hands gripped him by the throat and threw him to the floor, where a heavy knee pinned him, crushing his chest and forcing the breath from his body. He dropped the short sword in the fall and, though his left hand still grasped the weapon of the dead guard, he could not summon the strength either to use it or to wriggle free.

He heard a childish yell and something whizzed past him in the half light like a buzzing mosquito. Then there were sounds of hurrying footsteps and adult voices. He was aware that the pressure on his chest had relaxed, and that a small figure was bent anxiously over him, shaking him by the shoulder and repeating his name over and over again between sobs. In the doorway stood Nadia, carrying a lamp. She was accompanied by a fierce Mongol who held a sabre in front of her protectively.

'Giovanni. Giovanni!'

Nadia came forward and pulled the boy away. 'Be easy, Hassan. He is alive and not much hurt, unless appearances be deceiving. But he's in great danger of injury if you do not release his robe. Look to Jafar. He is bleeding. Find some rags and hold them tightly to that sword cut in his arm.'

Comforted by her assertion, Giovanni tried to rise but found himself held by the weight of his late assailant's legs. With effort, he threw the body aside, sat up and looked around him. There was now enough light to clarify the result of the recent struggle, if not its primary cause. Apart from Nadia, her protector, Hassan and himself, there were four people in the room. Two were dead. The man whom he had struck in the throat sprawled across the boy's divan, a trickle of blood from the corner of his mouth and the staining of the cushions confirming what the attitude of the body made only too obvious. His second antagonist stared sightlessly from his crumpled position on the floor. A tiny arrow had penetrated his temple and buried itself to half its length in his brain.

The third man, whom Nadia had referred to as Jafar, sat weakly against the door frame. Clearly, he had been a defender rather than an attacker. Giovanni noticed the hideous disfigurement of his face and realised he must be the tutor he had heard about. His arm was bleeding freely. Despite his smaller stature, he had managed somehow to wedge a stiletto between his opponent's ribs, and the latter, although still alive, lay on the floor twitching uncontrollably.

As Giovanni watched in horror, Nadia's guard swung his sabre and the head of the dying man was parted at a stroke from his body. Having dispatched him in this way, the Mongol dragged both torso and head into the corridor and stood to attention, awaiting further instruction.

Nadia, who was endeavouring to staunch Jafar's bleeding with a cushion, paled at this apparently savage action but recovered herself well.

'Remove the other two bodies from my sight, Sartak,' she ordered. 'And sound the gong. I'll be quite safe now.'

The Mongol did as she bade him, then departed.

Hassan, his tears dried, had watched the decapitation with curiosity. He collected some bandages and, with his mother's help bound the wounded man's upper arm tightly. His miniature bow, which he used with such accuracy for sport and which had been the means of saving Giovanni from throttling at the hands of one of the intruders, was strung across one shoulder as he worked.

'Did you see, Mother,' he cried excitedly, 'did I not use the bow to good effect?'

'You showed courage,' said Nadia. 'The deed is done, but do not glory in the death of an enemy. Now, run and fetch me my box of medicines.'

Giovanni, on his feet again, felt obliged to offer her his assistance.

'Be so kind as to support Jafar,' she begged. 'He is weak from loss of blood. This room smells of death, and he should be lodged elsewhere for the time being. My son too!'

Giovanni hoisted Jafar with ease and, carrying him like a child, followed her to another apartment. There he laid the tutor on a couch. Hassan returned bearing a shallow box filled with bottles, jars and phials of various shapes and sizes. Nadia selected a small beaker, and Giovanni watched in fascination as she mixed some substances in it, added liquid and, having raised the tutor's head from the cushions, made him drink the mixture. Jafar sank back on the divan with a sigh and remained still.

'What have you given him, madam?' Giovanni asked. 'Are you a physician as well as a stateswoman and mother?'

'Merely a strong sleeping draught.' Nadia laid the beaker aside and inspected Hassan's bandage. 'We have stopped the bleeding, God be thanked. Jafar will live. Now, pray tell me what you know of this affair. It seems I am indebted to you a second time, Ambassador. On the first occasion, I had cause to thank you for entertaining my son. On this, I have to be grateful for his life.'

'I did little, madam,' said Giovanni. 'You owe much more to that brave scholar who lies there. He faced an enemy twice his size and conquered him.'

'Nevertheless, you risked your own life for his sake.'

She raised her eyes and Giovanni felt again a surge of pleasure. His instincts alone had drawn him into this night-time adventure, yet he could not deny the satisfaction her words gave him or calm the rapid beating of his heart that arose from his proximity to her. He related his suspicions on waking and how he had interrupted the intruders but had underestimated their numbers.

'In the darkness I saw only two - the one who fought with Jafar, and the other who held your son.'

'And in another moment, my throat would have been cut,' interposed Hassan, seemingly none the worse for his experience.

'Pardon me, madam,' said Giovanni. 'It is none of my affair, but I do not think that was the intention. These were desperate men, prepared to kill a sentry and any other who stood in their way. If their plan was assassination, Hassan would have been dead before I was halfway along the corridor. This was an attempt at abduction, nothing more.'

'I take your meaning, sir,' Nadia said thoughtfully, 'but I can think of no reason why anyone would wish to carry off my son.'

'Perhaps for a ransom,' suggested Giovanni. 'Such kidnappings are common in my country. Or perhaps to gain political advantage. Are any of the intruders known to you?'

'The one whom Sartak despatched was the second sentry, to judge by his clothing.' Nadia shuddered as she spoke. 'I did not look closely at any of the faces, but I do not think I know the others.'

Giovanni noticed the quivering of her limbs. Despite her apparent coolness in the presence of violence and death, she was reacting like any mother whose child had just been victim of a cowardly attack. He was aware that under the cape covering her shoulders she wore only flimsy night apparel. The outline of her breasts and the darkness of her nipples were visible through the material. Giovanni averted his eyes. His heart was beating faster than ever and he almost gave way to a mad impulse to put his arm around her and comfort her.

The arrival of Arghun accompanied by a troop of militia drove all sensual thoughts from his mind. 'What's the meaning of these midnight goings-on?' The Il-khan was only half dressed. A mail tunic covered his torso and genitals, but his legs and arms were bare. 'The corridors are littered with bodies and wet with blood. If Sartak had not told me something of the affair, I would take it extremely ill to find one of my wives and a foreign ambassador together in their nightwear.'

Nadia lowered her eyes. 'If Sartak has told you anything, My Lord,' she said, 'you will know that Signor di Montecervino has assisted in foiling a plot against my son.'

The Il-khan's gaze fell on the sleeping Jafar. 'And who is this, pray? Yet another man in his nightwear that I find in my wife's company, and the ugliest I have ever seen.'

'This is the tutor brought from Maragha,' said Nadia. 'You will remember agreeing he should be engaged for Hassan. I am thankful we lodged him in the next apartment. He too came to Hassan's defence and received a grievous wound in the process.'

'Then I'm grateful for their intervention,' growled the Il-khan, 'but I want a more precise account of events.'

Giovanni repeated his story and his suspicion that abduction had been the intention.

Arghun's brows darkened. 'Assassins can be purchased for a gold coin or two,' he said. 'They do their work and vanish without trace. You're right, Ambassador. A deep plot has been hatched and, by Genghis's bones, I'll find the truth of it if I've to wake the whole city. What can the tutor tell us?'

'He is hurt, My Lord,' said Nadia. 'I have given him a draught to ease his pain and allow him to sleep. He will awake by morning, and you can question him then.'

'Hassan?'

'Only that I was roused by a hand over my mouth and another round my waist. I tried to bite the fellow but he held me tighter. Jafar must have heard the cry of the guard or the commotion in my room. There was a third man and it would have gone ill for us if Giovanni had not arrived.'

'It's unfortunate one of these fellows couldn't be taken alive,' growled Arghun, 'but it can't be helped. I suggest, madam, you take your son to your own apartment and Sartak will keep watch until morning . We owe a debt to you, Ambassador, but you too should retire for what remains of the night. This autumn air is rather chill.'

*

VI

Arghun was feeling better. For the week prior to the attempted kidnapping, he had eaten only in his chamber, taking what Nadia brought him and washing it down with a mixture of wine and water. The gnawing ache in his side had not gone away, but under the influence of her potent draught, swallowed daily, the discomfort had eased. He had asked to be allowed two doses a day so that the pain would be eliminated entirely but Nadia refused, saying that an increase in the dosage would be fatal. However, she promised that if he followed her prescription he would notice a improvement in his condition.

The Il-khan relied upon this assurance and, as the medicine brought him some respite, he bore his discomfort stoically and continued to follow his wife's advice. There were moments when he feared the improvement might be temporary. He formed in his mind a picture of his father on his deathbed and wondered if it might be only a few years, or even months, before he reached the same agonising end. But Arghun enjoyed life. Hope prevailed and he dismissed these terrifying thoughts.

He was mortal, and there were a hundred other ways in which a man could die. And there were certain things to be attended to without delay in case his life was to be cut short. He must settle the succession in favour of Ghazan, recall him from the northern frontier to receive the formal approval of the princes. Nadia's future too had to be secured, and for that reason he must make peace with her father, Kartir.

And he would conclude a treaty with the Christians. He had waited long enough. The Venetian had proved his sincerity. But he had not always been a diplomat. He had a strong right wrist and the muscles of his right forearm were more developed than those on his left. His daring in going to the boy's aid only confirmed it. The ambassador had once been a swordsman, even if too young to have taken part in the Egyptian Crusade.

Arghun's first task in the morning following the assault on Hassan was to increase castle security, his second to pay a visit to the tutor. However, Jafar was still dazed and in pain, and could not improve upon the Italian's account of events. Disappointed, but resolved to find a clue to the mystery, Arghun next summoned his brother Gaikatu to an audience.

The prince was a young man of about twenty years of age. His features bore a resemblance of sorts to those of the Il-khan, but his skin was smoother, his hair healthier, and there was none of the puffiness about his eyes and neck that marked his brother's condition. The two men were of a similar height, though Gaikatu appeared the taller on account of his slighter build.

'Well, Brother,' demanded Arghun. He was never able to hide his dislike and distrust of the prince. 'What do you know of this affair?'

Gaikatu stared hard. He smiled with his teeth, but there was little warmth in the smile. 'And what affair is that, Your Majesty?' he countered insolently. He had not taken kindly to the summons, nor the manner in which it had been delivered. 'You know I am a man of many . . .'

' . . . that are conducted for the most part in the bedroom,' Arghun finished angrily for him. 'You know very well I'm referring to an attack on my stepson, and I'm waiting for your answer.'

'What do you mean?' Gaikatu ceased smiling and frowned nervously.

'I mean, Brother, that there has been a vile attempt to abduct Hassan from his bed. The perpetrators are all dead, thanks to a puny scholar and the Venetian ambassador. I want to know if you had a hand in it.'

'What have I to gain by harming Hassan?' rejoined Gaikatu, his toothy smile returning and becoming broader than before. 'He's a fine lad, though he does not have our blood. And his mother is a fine lady!'

This prevarication angered Arghun even more. 'Don't play the fool or the innocent with me!' he roared. 'I can still put paid to your many affairs by having you hung up by the foreskin. Do you deny any involvement in the kidnapping?'

'I deny it absolutely!' screamed Gaikatu in his turn. 'What's your evidence for this unwarranted accusation? They told me you were indisposed, Brother, but I did not imagine it was an illness of the mind that you suffered from.'

'I haven't accused you of anything,' said Arghun, controlling his temper, 'but you're the author of so many devious schemes that I can't help looking in your direction when mischief is afoot.'

Gaikatu uttered a low laugh. His teeth continued to smile but his eyes were wary. 'So your enquiries have proved futile and you want to know what I've heard,' he said coolly. 'The answer is *nothing*, Your Majesty. I had no involvement in an attempt to carry the boy off, and know of no one who did. Believe me, Brother, had I any reason to resent Hassan and the favour he enjoys, there would be ample opportunity to effect his disappearance without resorting to night-time adventures. And since you know me so well, you must also know that, had I been the instigator of this crime, it would not have been bungled so disastrously. No agent of mine would have been caught off guard by a meddling Venetian.'

'You should thank the gods for his meddling, Gaikatu. If anything had happened to the boy, I would have used bare steel first and asked questions afterwards. It's just possible your ever-smiling mouth would have been shut for ever. Old customs mean little to me. Why should I care whether my enemies die by the carpet or by the sabre?'

The prince bowed with clearly feigned respect. 'My apologies, Your Majesty, but may I suggest you look in another direction for the perpetrators of this offence. Though I don't pretend to be your bosom friend, I have never sought to be your enemy. Might there be those among your supposed friends who harbour secret grudges, or whose hatred burns unquenched beneath a smiling exterior?'

The Il-khan looked at his brother through narrowed eyes. He understood the game he played only too well. 'What nonsense is this, Gaikatu?'

'There are many in Persia who still hate our race, Arghun,' went on the prince, again showing his teeth. 'We both know it. Others are driven by the religions they profess to make war, openly or covertly, on those who hold different beliefs. One such holds the nation's purse-strings. Daulah grants favours to his family and other Jews he has imported to the civil service. The Wazir is lining his own pockets with gold from the treasury.'

'When was there a Grand Wazir who didn't help himself?' snapped Arghun. 'The state coffers are full, and the economy in better condition than at any time since Hulegu's reign. The troops have full bellies; you and the other princes have your little luxuries. Daulah owes his position to me, and is loyal. If he pockets a few coins, it's his reward for good management.'

'I'm glad you have such confidence,' muttered Gaikatu slyly. 'Let's say then the Jews are innocent. Have you considered that Oljeitu's mother, Tolaghan, is a Christian, and might conspire to remove any threat to *her* child? He's your true son, yet you show him no preference over Nadia's bastard. Are your other wives above suspicion? And what of Ghazan? He is banished to the far reaches of Khorasan, but perhaps has eyes and ears in the capital. Would he not . . .?'

'To what end are you deliberately provoking me?' interrupted Arghun in sudden fury. He grasped the loose folds of Gaikatu's tunic and lifted him clear of the floor.

Gaikatu fumbled for the dagger at his waist but then seemed to think better of it. 'Calm yourself, Arghun,' he hissed. 'I speak only your own thoughts. Instead of cutting out my liver, consider what I've said. Can you trust anyone but yourself? Can you be sure this new tutor is no more than he seems? Or that this Italian who talks of alliances does not have deeper motives for cultivating your good will?'

Arghun lowered his brother to the floor but maintained the grip on his tunic. 'Pox on your twisted brain, Gaikatu!' he growled. 'Do you see conspiracies everywhere, or do you merely put up a smoke-screen for your own? This audience is finished. Get out while I'm still in a pleasant mood, lest today's the day I forget we had the same father.'

Gaikatu inclined his head and hastily withdrew. He did not allow his face to lose its smile until he had reached the door and turned. He hoped Arghun had not seen the relief in his expression.

Outside, he relaxed his jaw and began to breathe freely. Rumours of the previous night's disturbance had been round the castle by daybreak and it amused him how the morning gossip had diminished their credibility. Four assailants had become six and then ten, while the daring of both the tutor and the Christian ambassador had grown in the telling.

Least credible in Gaikatu's mind was the fact that whoever was responsible had waited until Hassan was in the relative safety of his bedroom before mounting the attack. The boy had just made the journey to and from Maragha watched over by only one swordsman. Why, the prince wondered, had the assassins not seized their opportunity then? That was the real mystery.

He did not really care who the boy's enemies were. His plans would not be affected on that score. However, despite his insolent bravado, Gaikatu had been chilled by his brother's last words. His support among the generals was considerable, but it was not yet time to engage in the final struggle for power. Arghun still commanded the majority, and the Il-khan did not make idle threats. And if he were to suspect the truth . . .

'By the tomb of Genghis Khan, I took great risks this morning,' he said to himself, 'but it was worth it if the seeds of suspicion have taken root. Now I'm nearly ready to move on.'

Though Arghun distrusted his brother, he was convinced by his argument. Of all the princes of royal blood, he knew Gaikatu best. He knew he would not have launched an attack in this fashion. In political terms the boy was an unimportant member of the household. And Gaikatu would not have left the relative safety of Rum if he planned mischief now. He would have found an excuse to ignore the summons to the capital.

The Il-khan reasoned that the day would come when his brother's treachery would threaten the stability of the kingdom, and then he would cut him down as he had done his other enemies, without mercy. But not yet. Gaikatu kept the others in check. His death would upset the delicate balance of power among the generals. Strike off one head and two others would appear in its place, like the monsters in Greek legends.

Who else would wish harm to the boy, and for what reason, Arghun did not know. He had been tired by the audience and could no longer think clearly. He rested for an hour and afterwards, partly refreshed, received despatches from Kerman and from China. He tried to revive his sagging spirits with thoughts of the hunting trips he planned on Mount Sahand. However, his body had begun to ache again, and as it was not yet the hour for his medicine, he ordered a servant to bring a flagon of liquor. Having consumed half on an empty stomach, he felt sick and lay back with his eyes closed to await Nadia's daily visit.

'At least I have one piece of information that'll please her,' he muttered as drowsiness overtook him. 'Kublai Khan's news I'll keep to myself for the present.'

Prince Gaikatu's appetite for liquor and carnal pleasures was matched by that of his small circle of friends. If they did not follow their inclinations or practise their vices openly, it had little to do with respect for the unwritten laws of the Yasa that had bound their ancestors on the steppes of Mongolia, or for the moral code of the population they had conquered. The conversation of the prince and his companions, when not rendered unintelligible by the over-consumption of alcohol, was such as could be engaged only in private.

By noon, Gaikatu had consumed his usual ration of fermented mares' milk without feeling any ill-effects whatever. An hour's relaxation in the arms of two of his mistresses, women of Greek and Egyptian origin who willingly sold their charms for a few gold coins, rid him of the unpleasant taste of his recent audience and he was in good humour, ready to make light of the whole episode. He was joined for the midday meal by two of his closest associates, who were impatient for him to recount the events of the morning. The two women hovered at his shoulder and Gaikatu stroked their buttocks almost absent-mindedly.

'What did Arghun want?' asked a handsome youth with fresh complexion and beardless chin. A flat-chested Persian girl clung to his arm.

Gaikatu showed his teeth. 'Is there more than one topic of conversation round the city today?' he remarked, turning to the third man, the most senior of the three though scarcely into his thirtieth year. 'What do you think, Timur?'

'You know I don't listen to rabble gossip, Prince. Has the Il-khan's night-shirt caught fire and singed his privates, or has he caught the pox at last and his nose fallen off?'

'Either way, there'll be parts of him missing!' cried the young man who had spoken first. He raised the pitch of his voice to a squeaky falsetto.

'*Lend me your sweet lips, My Queen. Let thy moist tongue quench the flames that consume my cock. Let thy sweet breath cool the burnt flesh !*'

'By all the gods, you make a fine eunuch,' exclaimed Gaikatu. He pushed the women away, thrust his hand between the youth's legs and patted his crotch. 'I could almost believe you have already lost your manhood, Cousin Baidu.'

The Persian girl giggled stupidly. The three men fell back on their cushions, laughing raucously.

Gaikatu himself was first to recover. He adopted a more serious air. 'Has none of you heard of the kidnapping?'

His friends regarded him innocently.

'Kidnapping?' enquired Timur.

'Attempted kidnapping, I should say,' corrected Gaikatu. 'An attempt was made in the night to carry off the boy Hassan. Arghun wanted to know if I had anything to do with it.'

'Did you, Cousin?' asked Baidu.

'What's Nadia's bastard to me?' grunted Gaikatu. 'If I had wanted the boy dead he would be. Instead, at least four more maidens in Tabriz are without husbands.'

'Then who was responsible?' enquired Timur.

'Who knows or cares?' Baidu shrugged impatiently. 'One of Ghazan's spies - a jealous wife? Perhaps even the Christians or Jews? I didn't come all the way from Baghdad to play guessing games. We've more important matters to discuss.'

'You're right, Cousin,' agreed Gaikatu, 'and I suggested to the Il-khan he explore these very avenues. The would-be kidnappers are dead and we should be grateful to them for diverting attention from our activities. With luck, Arghun will be occupied for a week.'

'Then we should act now,' frowned Timur. 'The common rabble begin to see hope in the policies of the Jew. If we delay, Arghun will achieve what Teguder, with all his fake Muslim piety could not, and become a popular ruler.'

'I agree with Timur,' said Baidu. 'You know you can count on my battalions if you claim the throne, but some of our potential allies are wavering. A full treasury means regular pay for the lower ranks, and the distribution of a few bonuses among the commanders could easily buy their loyalty. A charitable project or two; some new houses; a school; a mosque even, and the people will be licking Arghun's backside.'

Gaikatu applied himself meanwhile to the business of eating. His victualler had provided a plentiful supply of fish from Lake Urmia, and the prince tackled it with relish. A large part of his diet consisted of liquid nourishment, and a jug of liquor sat at his elbow. The Greek and Egyptian courtesans sat with him, fondling his ears and running their fingers through his hair. Occupied as he was, Gaikatu did not however miss any of his companions' words.

'Ad-Daulah must be dislodged quickly,' said Timur. He drained his goblet and refilled it.

'It's my game, and we play by my rules,' said Gaikatu, almost choking on a mouthful of food. 'I say it's too soon. The emirs are not ready.'

'Since Fate appears to be on our side, surely we should take advantage of it,' persisted Timur excitedly. The liquor was beginning to have an effect. 'A few managed riots against Jewish nepotism wouldn't be difficult to arrange. We need a dozen Muslim martyrs. Once the Jews are seen to be the enemy, it'll be easy to denounce the Wazir as a traitor. Arghun'll not stand in the way.'

'The matter is in hand.' Gaikatu looked up from his meal. His gaze flitted calmly to each of the other men in turn. 'But it must be managed with cunning. We mustn't act so hastily that the blame falls on us.'

'So much the better if Arghun were to perish in a mob attack.' Baidu's handsome face distorted in a vicious scowl. 'That could also be arranged.'

Gaikatu glared at him. 'Don't be a fool, Cousin. Our plan depends upon inciting the Muslims against the Jews. We can't risk making the Il-khan himself a martyr.'

'If he's dead, he can't make an alliance with the Christians,' Baidu muttered, rising from his cushion and pacing the room. The Persian girl tried to attached herself to him again but he threw her off. 'Our ambitions are threatened from that quarter too. With the Mamluks sandwiched between the armies of the German emperor and our own forces on the western front, Arghun has every chance of securing a truce. His popularity will grow once Persia is at peace. And have you forgotten

Ghazan? He has a powerful army of his own.'

'I haven't forgotten him,' growled Gaikatu. 'When the time comes, Ghazan will be fully occupied. My agents are working in Rayy and Khorasan. As for the Christian alliance, I'm undecided.'

'It can easily be thwarted,' growled Baidu under his breath.

Gaikatu turned on him in fury. 'You too may be prince of Genghis's line but by his balls do not defy me. Arghun will live unless *I* give the word.'

'That was not my meaning,' said Baidu fawningly, lowering his eyes. 'But you know the Christian alliance will destroy us. It can be prevented without the Il-khan's death. The Italian is the key. Trust me and I can do us both a great service.'

Gaikatu recovered his temper as quickly as he had lost it. 'Your meaning is clear, Baidu,' said he, 'but if you have a plan, keep it to yourself, and see to it I'm not blamed if some misfortune should befall the Venetian ambassador.'

Baidu made no reply. He only nodded, returned to his cushion and beckoned to the girl to join him. He filled his goblet with wine from the barrel that had been placed at his disposal. However, he refrained from drinking and watched the other two men as they gradually succumbed to the effects of the fermented milk.

'I'm not such a fool as Gaikatu thinks,' he mused. 'And he's not Il-khan yet. My cousin is too sentimental. He has a yen for this Nadia, and wants her to think pleasurably of him, so his judgement is clouded. What if the Venetian were to die and *Arghun* were to be blamed for his death? And what if the woman were to be implicated? She has a deal too much influence for my liking.' He drew open the Persian girl's robe and fondled her small breasts. She thrust her hips forward provocatively. 'As for the supposed kidnapping, it was a useful diversion, but I wonder if Gaikatu protests too much. Perhaps I should discover whether Hassan *does* have value as a hostage.'

*

VII

While the interview between the Il-khan and his brother was going on, Nadia wrapped herself in a cape to cover her silk dress and hide her gold cross, as well as to protect her from the cool of the morning. She saddled a pony, left the city by the south gate and, proceeding a short distance, reached the point where the path forked, one branch to join the Silk Highway to the east, the other to begin a tortuous climb of the lower slopes of the mountain which eventually brought travellers out on the road to Maragha.

She took the latter route and, after riding at a fast trot for half an hour, came to a grove of olive trees where the path forked for a second time. This plantation bordered a settlement of grey villas, once the property of industrious farmers, but allowed to fall into decay under stringent tax regimes that rewarded diligence by the imposition of punitive levies on property and profit, and encouraged at least the outward appearance of sloth. There had evidently been a recent resurgence of interest in the cultivation of the green oily fruit for, here and there, the undergrowth had been cleared, the harvest gathered, and the trees pruned.

The smallholdings were deserted and there were a few travellers on the road. Nadia did not attract undue attention. She left the path, traversed the plantation at its narrowest point and arrived in a dusty lane that skirted several tiny gardens and the houses behind. Stopping at one of these, she knocked twice on the plain door. It was opened by a woman about her own age.

'My Lady Nadia!' The tone was polite but by no means servile. 'You are expected.'

'How can that be, Djamila, when I decided on this visit scarcely an hour ago?'

'I do not understand these things, My Lady,' the woman replied. 'Most of us are denied glimpses of the future, but for one who spends half the time remaining to him in the world of spirits, who knows? I say only that the Patriarch expects you.'

She led the way across an unfurnished anteroom, past the main apartments, to a flight of stairs that descended towards the rear of the house. The walls bore signs of neglect and the floor tiles, once brightly coloured, were faded and cracked. In places they had come away altogether to expose the crumbling clay beneath. In contrast, the floor at the lower level was carpeted and the walls were hung with damask and dyed astrakhan, giving the impression of comfort rather than opulence.

Nadia followed her guide into a long room, at the end of which was a panel of burnished metal with inlaid decoration. Below the panel was an elevated brick hearth where a fire burned with a bright orange flame. To one side, on a pile of cushions, and alone save for a large spotted dog, sat a shrunken figure of a man. His ancient, wizened features were all but buried in a white beard that began at the corner of his eyes, where the bushy eyebrows left off, proceeded across the cheekbones to the upper lip, continued round the mouth and lower half of his face, and fell in three long strands over his neck and chest. He was dressed in a plain white toga and conical cap. With one yellow, bony hand he stroked the ears of the animal as it rested its head contentedly on his lap. He did not look up when Nadia entered.

'You are welcome, Nadia, daughter of Ahmed Kartir,' said he in a firm voice that belied his age, ' - all the more since your visits are fewer than they once were.' He indicated a second pile of cushions on the opposite side of the hearth. 'Seat yourself comfortably and we can talk.'

Nadia removed her cape and squatted elegantly. 'How are you, Patriarch?' she enquired, scrutinising the tired face and allowing her gaze to fall with more than passing interest on the dog. 'You have not forgotten how to eat?'

'I'm as well as can be for a man who has lost count of the years,' he replied with a chuckle. The beard parted to reveal a mouth of broken, yellowing teeth. Still he did not look up. 'I do not starve, but my needs are few, just a little bread, softened with wine. Have you noticed my companion? He is four-eyed, as you can see. They tell me the black spots on his forehead move when he wrinkles his ears. When death and the Tower of Silence call, they will not have to search far in order to perform the last ritual for me. Your family has forsaken the teachings of Zoroaster, but I think you know some of our ways. Such a dog has to be brought to the altar with the corpse. We preserve the old customs when we can.'

'I remember what you once told me of the funeral rites, Gobras,' Nadia began, and waited for Djamila to withdraw from the room. 'I always enjoy debating with you on religious matters, but today I'm here on a different errand.'

'I suspected as much,' declared the old man. 'Although my eyes have become useless, the visions in the fire have become more frequent. I used to see only the outline of events, or their shadows, but I now see faces in these daydreams of mine. Yours I remember from days gone by and I have seen it more than once, along with another I do not recognise. I do not know what troubles your heart, Nadia, but do not deny it is troubled.'

'My husband is ill, Gobras. If his death comes too soon, it will unleash disorder and bloodshed on this kingdom. I have laboured all these months to preserve his life and ensure my son has a protector until he reaches manhood. But it seems Hassan's life is already threatened by swords and daggers in the dark - by agents of a faceless enemy who would carry him off.'

Gobras listened, his face sunk in his beard, while she related the events of the previous night. He had ceased fondling the dog's ears and sat motionless on his cushions, his arms folded inside the toga. Only the brightness of his sightless eyes betrayed him as a living being, rather than a figure carved in stone. When Nadia had finished her narrative, he gave a long sigh, but otherwise remained silent, staring unseeing into the fire. Nadia waited, not daring to interrupt his trance, almost afraid that the sound of her voice would shatter the fragile statue he had assumed.

At length he stirred, withdrew his bony arms from the folds of his robe and turned his benign countenance in her direction. 'Is it as Nadia, daughter of Kartir, or Nadia, Arghun's queen, that you come to me?'

'Though my marriage to Arghun has the force of Mongol law, I am not his queen, merely his wife,' said Nadia. 'And it is neither as Arghun's wife, nor as Kartir's daughter that I have come, but as Nadia, the mother of a ten-year-old child. It is as a mother that I wish to learn who my son's enemy is, and what he hopes to gain. And it is as a mother that I ask whether it is possible this attempted abduction relates to the secret you and I share.'

The Patriarch again showed his yellow teeth. 'A mother need fear only another mother's jealousy,' he said. 'Yet a king has many enemies. A viceroy too perhaps. Enemies who may use a wife, or a child to gain an advantage.'

'I too have these thoughts,' said Nadia. 'In my head they intermingle with others I do not understand, and of which I am ashamed. I know that a priest of the Magian god does not betray a trust, but reassure me, Gobras. Reassure me I need not fear that others know the father of my son.'

Gobras raised a shrivelled hand to calm her. 'Do you really think me capable?' he asked. 'I have nursed memories of terrible times, when the horse soldiers of Genghis Khan swept across the plateau. That was more than a lifetime ago. I was a boy then. At Parwan I saw what remained of the bodies of three of Jalal's children after the Mongols had cast them from a cliff into the Indus river. I saw another, a daughter, snatched from the jaws of death, clutching her infant brother. We hid her, dressed as an acolyte, until we had crossed the invader's lines and reached Kerman. I escaped with my life. We all did, because Mongol superstition forbade them from harming priests.'

He ruffled the ears of the dog and it emitted a throaty gurgle. 'Fate allowed me to escape a second time when Abaqa's army overran Kerman. Herded with those destined for execution, it was again my priest's robe and white cap that saved me. All around me men, women and even children were dying, put to the sword and fire. I was brought here with the hostages and allowed to go free when the Il-khan saw I could do no harm. I had already survived more than seventy winters. I was ill, and did not attempt the journey home. It was no matter they thought me dead in Kerman. Most of my friends had long gone to the Tower of Silence, and I would not be mourned.'

He sighed reminiscently. 'There were few in this province who adhered to the old beliefs. They were persecuted, reviled and ridiculed. Their meagre incomes were taxed excessively, and even in poverty they were assaulted by the Muslim collectors and their womenfolk abused. However, I found a place among them and became their patriarch. I kept the sacred flame burning, and our beliefs live on.

'I remembered your father with affection, and you as a joyful child, and it was with a mixture of joy and sadness I learned one day that you had been brought to Tabriz, and married forcibly to a Mongol prince. But you had a son, and when I stared into the sacred fire I saw visions. I prayed, because that is all a man of nearly eighty years can do. I prayed and I believed.

'Yes, you had a son, Nadia, and I looked on him with hope. That is why I shared my memories, and my secrets with you.'

The flame in the hearth had sunk to a mere glow and the air had cooled. Gobras rang a bell at his side and Djamila reappeared. She added fuel to the fire and it flared up again brightly. Nadia, surprised as always that the priest's frail body could deliver a monologue with such strength and eloquence, had listened in silence. Now she felt the need to speak.

'The persecution of your people has eased,' she said gently when they were again alone. 'I use my influence when I can. Arghun is not perfect, but he is a tolerant ruler and would extirpate injustice.'

'We are grateful for your intervention,' said Gobras, 'but Arghun does not see everything, and some abuses continue. But we shall not speak of that now. You know I would not betray you, yet you seek reassurance. I shall give it as best I can.

'My ancestors came from Media at the time of Cyrus the Great. Our race bred priests and kings who shaped the history of lands beyond the frontiers of Persia. We followed the teachings of holy Zoroaster, resisted the temptations of evil Ahriman, and strove for perfection of thought, word and deed. Our philosophy was not always tolerant of others but it was never stagnant. New ideas were absorbed when they were seen to aid the search for truth.'

He held out his wrinkled hands to the warmth of the flame and the joints of his arms cracked audibly. 'I have seen evil in my life, Nadia, but that has not deflected me from the true path. I told you that your presence here gave me hope, and despite your confession I still cherish that hope because of the prophecies of a priest of my order in the days of Kartir the Great. Should I abandon the search for perfection at the end of my life and perhaps destroy yours which is scarcely half lived? I have not spoken my secrets, or yours, to any living soul. It would serve no purpose to speak now.'

Throughout this testimony, the Patriarch's voice rose and fell until, at the end, seemingly exhausted, it faded to a whisper. He sank his head in his beard as before and resumed his trance-like posture. In the silence, Nadia found herself contemplating the panel above the hearth. It was in the form of a triptych, each of its three sides depicting scenes from Mazdaian mythology in the inset tessellated tile. She had seen it a dozen times without paying attention or attaching any meaning to it. It now seemed to her that, in the intricate, skilfully-laid representations of gods, kings and demons, or in the firelight playing on their colourful figures, there might be a solution to the puzzle that perplexed her. For an instant the vision was there, then the fire was dark.

'Then the deed makes no sense at all,' she said almost to herself. 'It's true my husband treats Hassan as a son, but he has always made it clear that Ghazan should succeed him as Il-khan. Gaikatu, who would seize the throne now if he could, or dared, has nothing to fear from a ten-year-old boy and his mother.'

If Gobras heard, he gave no sign, but continued to sit motionless with his sightless eyes directed towards the sacred flame.

'Do you still wear that beautiful necklace?'

After several minutes silence, Nadia was startled by the sound of the Patriarch's voice and the unexpectedness of the question.

'You remember my father's fylfot?' During the early years of their acquaintance she had often seen him peer at the charm with his failing sight, but he had never remarked upon it. 'That was the name he called it by. I am never without it.'

'Do you know its history?'

'Only what my father told me. It had been in his family for generations, passed between father and daughter, mother and son. His forebears believed that ill-luck would follow if the cross were passed from male to male, or female to female. There was a legend that such a cross had been fashioned from gold of the gods by King Jemshid as a present for his mistress and that Kartir, priest of your religion, had worn the original and from it had derived his authority.

'My father had no time for superstition. There must be many good-luck charms in the world, and many fylfots with the sun's picture at the centre, though perhaps few like this one. Its arms unscrew at the elbow. They are hollowed out and I use them to carry my perfumes.'

She lifted the chain over her head, held the cross in one hand with one of its arms pointing upwards, and turned the bent section two full revolutions. It parted to reveal a tiny thread. She raised the charm to her nose, sniffed gently and replaced the seal. Then she took the priest's hands and pressed the cross between his palms.

'Here,' she said lightly, 'you may feel and smell it. You can still detect the aroma.'

Gobras stroked the ornament. 'And whence comes your knowledge of medicines, and your healing skill?'

Nadia saw no connection between this question and the first, nor could she imagine how either related to the subject of her visit. However, she had never known Gobras to engage in idle conversation.

'That was learned mostly from my mother - the daughter of Nasr Tusi. Surely I have told you that already. But how does that relate . . .?'

The Patriarch seemed able to read her mind and he anticipated the question. 'Be patient with me, Nadia,' he begged. 'I am an old man and forget sometimes. There is a reason for everything, and the reasons for this plot against your son may be deep and sinister. You remember the question I first asked when you came today?'

'Did I come as the wife of a king, or as the daughter of a viceroy? And I replied, I came as a mother.'

Gobras nodded. He returned the gammadion to Nadia and again began staring sightlessly at the flames. The spotted dog licked his hand and he stroked its muzzle. He spoke slowly and deliberately.

'Any wife who is jealous of another's beauty or resents her influence might poison the husband's mind against her rival. She might even slay her in a passion. I do not say it is impossible for a mother to strike down her rival's child, but a coolly planned kidnapping is not such a woman's weapon.

'Your son's life might be in danger if it was thought he threatened the succession, not only from the mother of the true heir, but from any of the princes who aspire to the throne. As it is, without knowing Hassan's father, any one of them might act out of fear, but assassination, not abduction would be the solution.

'I do not think it is the enemy of Nadia, Arghun's wife, nor the enemy of Nadia the mother, that you must expose, but the enemy of Nadia, daughter of Kartir; Nadia, who understands secrets and can heal sicknesses that defy physicians; who sees visions in the flames . . . '

Nadia gasped. 'How can you know what I have seen?'

'Tell me it is not true,' breathed Gobras. 'Tell me it is not true that, as a maiden, visions came to you in the flames on your hearth, or in your glass, or in the clouds. Visions of things yet to come - things you did not wish to see and therefore feared. I suspected your gift was there from the beginning, but it is only now I can guess its meaning.'

'It's true,' she said. 'However imperfectly, I saw things and was afraid. Even now, visions come upon me like gusts of wind: Arghun's death; the kingdom at war; lands I have never seen; dread plagues. Today, the fire is dark for me, but if you have seen the answer, tell me who my enemies are.'

'If only I could be certain, Nadia,' said Gobras. He fondled the dog's ears. 'You know how my people were betrayed, and by whom . . .'

'But that was long ago, Patriarch. Even if your betrayer is still alive, neither I nor my child poses any threat to him!'

'Still, it is possible. How better to attack an enemy than through his children? Such hatred does not die.' He had turned his face towards the sound of her voice, and it seemed to Nadia as if his sight was recovered, so bright did his eyes become. A bony finger was raised and wagged, unerring and ominous, at her gammadion. His voice became more urgent. 'Yet there is another possibility.

'You deny that ornament you wear has any significance beyond its beauty. Your enemies may believe otherwise - that it is a talisman beyond price. They may see in your child the fulfilment of a thousand year-old prophecy; they may try to destroy him, or to set him on the throne of Persia, not as a descendant of the Shahs, but as the son of Nadia, descendant of the Magians, and wearer of the Cross of Jemshid, the Gammadion of the Sun!'

'There are few in Persia who remember the old legends,' sighed the Patriarch. He had returned to his former posture, hunched over the fire, his head sunk in his beard. 'This is what the Magians told to their children in Istakhr and Ctesiphon.

'Jemshid, son of Tahmuras, ruled Persia wisely and justly for seven hundred years. No one was more skilled as a forger of weapons, a weaver of cloth, or a goldsmith. He discovered medicine, and knew how to treat all the sicknesses of mankind. His most valued possession was the seven-ringed cup, one ring for each of the planets, a gift of the gods, in which he could see the whole world, past, present and future.

'He had two beautiful daughters, Shahrinaz and Arnawaz, whom he loved more than the gods themselves, and on whom he showered gifts of jewels and articles of precious metal. Among these presents were two golden *su-asti*, crosses of well-being, on which each of the four arms was bent at right angles. Shahrinaz received the cross whose arms were bent to the right. In its centre was engraved the emblem of the sun god, Ormazd, for Shahrinaz had fair skin and golden hair. Arnawaz had complexion and hair as dark as a starless night, and to her was presented the left-handed cross, on which the engraving was of the crescent moon, symbol of Ahriman, god of darkness.

'The adjacent country was ruled by Prince Zohak, who had been corrupted by a *daeva*, and tricked into murdering his own father. But one throne was not enough. At the head of a huge army, Zohak crossed the borders of Persia, determined to seize that kingdom too. Because King Jemshid was arrogant, one seventh part of his magic cup was dark, and he did not see the danger until it was too late. And because Zohak was handsome, Arnawaz became enamoured of him and conspired with him to slay her father, so that she might become queen at his side.

'Whereas Jemshid had ruled justly, Zohak used magic to oppress the people. On his shoulder and that of his queen, where once they had been kissed by the evil *daeva*, grew two black snakes that consumed human brains, and each day they offered two of their subjects as sacrifice to these monsters. And because Arnawaz wore the emblem of the dark god round her neck, she held the real power in the kingdom, and through her Zohak ruled for a thousand years.

'Shahrinaz wished to avenge her father. She was patient, and prayed to Ahura Mazda to help her. The sun god answered.

' "Is light not always greater than darkness? When the sun rises, does not the moon flee? You already have the means to lift the shadow of your sister from the land. She is Ahriman's creature, and cannot bear the sunshine. Take the *su-asti*, the cross your father gave you. Go to the palace. Hold my image in front of your sister, so that daylight is reflected upon it, and the power of the one she wears will be broken. Then you will see Arnawaz as she really is."

'Shahrinaz hesitated. "But even if my sister is destroyed, Zohak is still king."

' "You cannot harm Zohak," answered Ahura Mazda, "for I have already decided his fate. He will be overcome by your son, Faridan, bound with celestial chains and imprisoned below the earth in a cave of fire, until the end of time. When Arnawaz is dead, give the *su-asti* to Faridan, so that he will be protected from evil, and can accomplish the task I have set for him."

'Shahrinaz did as the god proposed. When she held up the cross of the sun, Arnawaz screamed in terror, and her human form shrivelled up until all that remained was the black serpent.

'Then Shahrinaz said to her, "Because you were once my sister, I will spare your life, but from today you are banished from human company. Crawl away to the desert and the wild places of the earth where you belong."

'As the venomous creature slunk away, the cross of the moon fell from its body and was lost for ever in the shifting sand.

'When Faridan was twenty years old, Shahrinaz placed the gammadion of the sun around his neck.

' "Now you are ready to fulfil your destiny," she said. "Go, break for ever the power of Zohak, lift the shadow of fear from the people and restore justice to the land. The *su-asti* of the sun god will protect you as long as you do not allow evil into your heart for, were that to happen, it would be as if you wore the left-hand cross of Arnawaz. Goodness would be despised, and the creatures of the night would rule again in the world.

And, because the *su-asti* was a present to me from my father Jemshid, and because I have now given it to you, it should always be passed from father to daughter and from mother to son, down through the generations." '

When he had finished his narrative, Gobras sighed again and with his bony finger beckoned Nadia to approach the hearth. She did so with trepidation and stood with wildly beating heart before the tiled panels. A slight movement of his head directed her attention to a section of panel just above the altar floor. Set in the finely-cut tile was a representation of the myth. On the right was Shahrinaz, her beauteous face surrounded by a halo of golden fire. To her left knelt a second female figure. Where her head should have been grew the neck and jaws of a serpent that seemed to sway, contort and wither in the fire's light. Behind sat Faridan, wearing a crown and bearing in his hand the seven-ringed cup of the gods.

As Nadia watched his image, it seemed to her for a brief instant to dissolve and, instead of contemplating the intricate work of the artist, she was staring at the youthful features and dark curls of her child.

On her return to the city, Nadia found that a small crowd had gathered in the shadow of the walls. An elderly mullah, conspicuous in his white shawl, was attempting to cool an argument between a group of artisans and their employer. The atmosphere was tense. Several soldiers stood watchfully by, hands on weapons, ready to intervene if the dispute escalated into violence.

'What is amiss?' she asked a woman bystander.

'The workmen claim they've been cheated,' replied the other with a shrug. 'It's a common enough occurrence, and scarcely warrants the attention of the militia.'

Nadia continued on her way. Such altercations were indeed common in Tabriz, and there were more important matters to occupy her attention. Though relieved that the secrets she shared with the Patriarch were safe, she had taken small comfort from her visit.

She knew that if Arghun weakened the royal princes might at any time conspire to depose him, and to murder Ghazan, his rightful heir. But Hassan did not stand in their path to the throne. However uncertain her own future in a kingdom ruled by Gaikatu, Arghun's brother could gain nothing by harming her son.

That Hassan could be a target of conspiracy because of *her* birth and parentage had never occurred to her. The occasional glimpses of the future that plagued her existence had never hinted at that. She had known for almost six years what her father had planned in Kerman with the man Nizam, and how she had been forced to suffer as a result. She had wondered if Kartir had learned the truth, or even if the truth mattered any longer. It had been so long ago. Could it really be that past and present had converged - that her abduction and the Gabars' betrayal were related to the matter that now so tortured her mind?

And as for the fylfot, surely that was fantasy. Yet, as she ran her fingers over her necklace, Nadia was overwhelmed by dark forebodings that her fate, and that of Hassan, was somehow bound up in its pattern. What would she do now? Other than the Patriarch, there was no one in whom she could confide. She had no friend to whom she could confess the emptiness she sometimes felt or with whom she could share her secret longings.

She found herself thinking of the Italian ambassador. She had watched him as they conversed and knew he would be hers if she desired it. But could she trust him with her suspicions and fears without endangering her position as Arghun's wife?

Between her and Mahmoud Hassan, her first husband, a childhood bond had existed, but it had been a marriage without love. Politics had been behind Kartir's insistence that the union take place, and she had been a dutiful daughter.

Then her child bridegroom had gone to war. She had parted from him sorrowfully, but it was the girlish sorrow of saying goodbye to a friend, not the desolation of a woman losing an intimate part of herself. Knowing what she knew now, she felt only pity for him, sacrificed as he was because of a vengeful lie.

With Arghun, she had come closer to love than with any man. She had first seen him at Kerman, a young general in Abaqa's army, strikingly handsome in his red cloak and polished helmet with its luxurious plume, and astride a lively grey pony. Her father was away from home the day the Mongols came. Though he had always warned her against wandering alone in the city streets, she had been curious to see again these people whom he had at first served willingly, and now feared.

Mongols! Nadia had strange memories of them from her childhood days - eyes narrower, skin paler and hair silkier than the native people of Iran. But these youths who had come to Kerman were not what she remembered. Most were dark and indistinguishable from the young men of the south. They defied the teaching of the Prophet. They had been drunk with liquor and had wished only to humiliate her. Then Arghun came, tall and with a fine moustache, and had behaved differently towards her.

That too seemed so long ago. Nadia had known what her fate as a hostage would be - marriage to the Mongol prince as security for Kartir's continued loyalty. A widow at the age of sixteen, deprived of companionship, but with a passionate nature, she had thought the prospect not unattractive. However, Arghun had been denied his inheritance and instead of union with Abaqa's handsome son, she had been taken by his scheming uncle Teguder. It was then she had discovered the power she was able to exercise over men.

Again she thought of the handsome Venetian. That power was with her still, Nadia reminded herself, if she chose to use it. The question was, did she dare?

When she reached the palace, she went immediately to Arghun's quarters and found him impatient for a dose of the medicine that kept his pain at bay. She could see he had been drinking.

The Il-khan reclined on a couch. He was paler than he had been the night before and the greyish colour had returned to his skin. 'So you have not forsaken me, Nadia,' he sighed.

'How could you think that of me, My Lord?' she asked. 'I have only been searching for the truth behind the plot against my son.'

'And my enquiries have proved useless,' said Arghun bitterly. 'However guilty Gaikatu is of wishing my death, it seems he is innocent of designs on your child. Where have you been?'

Nadia saw no reason to lie. 'I visited the Gabar patriarch. He is wiser than the mullahs of Islam, and often sees visions.'

'I don't understand these things, Nadia,' said Arghun wearily. 'What did you discover?'

Nadia had begun mixing ingredients for his medicine and she continued to do so without looking up. 'Nothing,' she said, trying to keep her voice steady.

'You know there are revolts afoot,' Arghun went on. 'Gaikatu is planning something aided by that decadent cousin of ours. These are dark days. I must send for Ghazan and confirm my wishes for the succession.'

'You may have many more years ahead of you, My Lord,' said Nadia quietly, still absorbed in preparing her mixture.

Arghun sat up. He put a hand under her chin and tilted her face so that their eyes met. 'And I may not,' said he with a bitter laugh. 'You know it - though there is more grief in your expression than I had expected to see.'

Nadia drew her face away and resumed her task. She raised the two tiny phials with steady hands and poured the contents of one into the other.

'Some good may come of my death,' Arghun continued after a short pause, during which he watched her keenly. 'I've decided to end your bondage. You'll not become one of Ghazan's chattels against your wishes. My son is likely to have more wives than he can satisfy. There is Tolaghan, some others whose names I forget, and little Keremun of course.'

Nadia's hands shook. Quickly she returned the phials to her tray to avoid spilling the contents. Her voice quivered. 'You of all men know I did not come to Tabriz willingly, My Lord,' she said, 'but you know too, for I have told you often, that I have been content as your wife, and grateful to you for being a father to Hassan. I wonder what I am to do with the freedom you so generously grant me. Am I to be cast adrift in the world with no protector?'

'Your father grew rich in my grandfather's service and is a man of influence. You will be returned to his house.'

Nadia turned to face him again. She stood submissively while he reached out and fondled her breasts. 'My Lord?'

'You will go to your father, Nadia,' Arghun concluded. 'I have summoned him, and he is now only a week's journey from Tabriz.'

*

VIII

Prince Baidu lay back indolently on a divan piled high with cushions, a flagon of liquor at his elbow. His youthful face wore an expression of disdain as he surveyed the person of his visitor. The man wore the garments of an artisan. The air smelt of grime and sweat.

'Well,' demanded the prince. 'What did you find out?'

'Regrettably nothing new, Highness. Two Persians bribed one of the guards from the night shift. He slit the other's throat and was in turn slain by the tutor with a lucky blow. The boy would've been jackals' meat if the Italian ambassador hadn't intervened.'

'And the Persians?'

'One killed by the Italian, Highness. The boy shot the other with an arrow.'

'It becomes interesting!' cried Baidu. With a steady hand he raised the nearby flagon to his mouth, took a long draught of liquor and smacked his lips with relish. 'Were these Persians recognised? Is their motive known?'

'They were strangers, Highness.'

'So,' said Baidu, wiping his mouth with his sleeve, 'two strangers try to carry off the bastard son of some unknown conscript. It's just the kind of trick my cousin Gaikatu is capable of. He has a taste for young boys as well as wenches. His face broke into a grin. 'Still, I believe his denials. What's the tittle-tattle in the city saying?'

'The most favoured theory is that Tolaghan, mother of Oljeitu, arranged it,' said the artisan confidentially. 'It's no secret that His Majesty pampers the boy more than his own. Another I heard was that the boy's father still lives and tried to snatch him.'

'After all this time? Very plausible, no doubt,' said Baidu sardonically. 'Does this father have a name?'

'I've never heard one mentioned, Highness,' said the artisan. 'However, there's one other piece of news. The Il-khan has summoned the Viceroy of Kerman to Tabriz.'

'Nadia's father, Kartir, former intimate of Hulegu. Now that *is* interesting. Does the fact have some significance, d'you think?'

'I don't know, Highness.'

'Don't know, don't know,' mimicked Baidu. He took another gulp of liquor. 'Have you nothing else to say?'

The man hesitated. 'About the Lady Nadia, Highness . . .'

'Well?' snapped the prince.

'It may be nothing, My Lord, but this morning she left the city on horseback and took the Maragha road.'

'Alone? You followed her?'

'Yes, Highness. On the hill are some farms. Melons, pumpkins and olives. An apple orchard or two. The Il-khan's wife went to a house at the other side of the olive groves and was there two hours or more.'

'Who lives in this house?'

'I don't know, My Lord. I didn't want to draw suspicion and betray myself by enquiring. It's not unusual for the Lady Nadia to visit the homes of citizens, both inside and outside the walls. She has skill with potions and salves I'm told . . .'

'Yes, yes, yes,' cried Baidu impatiently. 'I know all about that. Make further enquiries about these farms and who lives there. You have my permission. If Gaikatu finds out, I'll make up a plausible story to explain our association. What of the other matter - my cousin's grand plan?'

'The counterfeit money has been distributed as ordered, Highness. Already there have been incidents. Workmen complain of being paid light coinage.'

Baidu tossed the man a bag of money. 'Here are some real coins. An added bonus for you trouble? Remember, say nothing to my cousin of our meetings. It would only lead to complications.'

The man muttered his thanks and withdrew, almost colliding at the door with two new arrivals.

'Why do your spies have to smell so bad, Baidu?' said Timur, pushing his way roughly past the artisan and entering the apartment.

'Good agents are hard to come by,' snorted Baidu. 'Is there any sign of Nizam?'

'He'll be here! Timur bent low over the divan. 'But are you wise to trust him, Prince? Given half a chance he'll go scuttling back to Ashraf.'

'I know, and I'd sooner trust an Egyptian viper,' said Baidu. 'Still, he has his talents, and I have a job for Master Nizam that'll test his loyalty.'

He grinned maliciously, signalled to Timur to approach even more closely and whispered in his ear. Both laughed. Baidu then beckoned impatiently to the second newcomer, who was waiting obsequiously by the door. He was a spindly, dark-skinned man wearing only a plain white jubbah that was much too large for him, and sandals. Both his face and head were clean-shaven and were scratched and raw from recent contact with a blade.

'You took your time,' said the prince acidly, 'but now that you *are* here, let's talk about religion. You can give me some information in exchange for the ten silver dinars you were paid in advance. Tell me, how zealous is Arghun in his observation of the Buddhist faith and, while you're at it, what significance has a gold cross with bent arms and an engraving of the sun at its centre?'

Ahmed Kartir shaded his eyes and scanned the road for signs of movement. It seemed to stretch out endlessly into the hazy distance and was deserted save for a few lizards. The sun was still far from its zenith, but the ridges of the Zagros had already taken on the rich golden colour of honey. The stone on which he sat was warm through his jubbah. He was perspiring heavily and envied the two younger men, for ten days his sole companions, who effortlessly reloaded the pack animals. They seemed to suffer none of the disagreeable effects of the long journey - the aching thighs, the stiffness in the back, the dust- and sand-scratched throat and the constant thirst.

Kartir did not care that it was Ramadan. He took a drink of water from his flask, removed his sandals and rubbed the soles of his feet to relieve the cramp and promote the circulation. He felt a surge of apprehension, but knew he could not turn back. The Mongol despatch riders they had encountered at the last town would have reached Tabriz by now, and Arghun's wrath would fall on Nadia if he failed to keep his appointment.

He had taken Umid's advice and remained in the residency throughout the hot summer. Rumours reached him of troop movements on the borders of Mesopotamia, but such activity was not unusual. Fate had decided the timing of his journey north. At the onset of autumn, he had received despatches from the Il-khan himself, and a summons to wait on His Majesty's pleasure in Tabriz.

Umid had returned to Kerman and they travelled together as far as Isfahan, gathering intelligence as they went. There they had parted, Kartir to continue his journey by way of Hamadan, Umid to make a detour via Baghdad and Mosul.

'We were right in all our suppositions, Excellency,' Umid had said as they shared their last meal together. 'Arghun is a strong ruler but too tolerant in matters of religion. There is much resentment among our brothers in the Faith. The new chief minister has dispensed favours to his fellow Jews who now hold the most influential appointments. Some think Arghun is unaware of this nepotism, though a few mullahs are claiming he encourages it.'

'I've seen no resentment thus far,' said Kartir. 'Neither in Yazd nor here in Isfahan. If anything, Arghun's rule seems to have brought security. It was the same in the smaller towns we passed through.'

'It simmers beneath the surface, Excellency. There has already been minor unrest in several towns, and even demonstrations against Jews. One day soon it may break through.'

'You mean a popular rebellion?' said Kartir. 'That will do more harm than good to the people's standard of life. The Mongols' grip on power has not weakened. They will crush a revolt and impose greater sanctions as a punishment. If indeed Arghun is blind to the goings-on, the best course of action will be to acquaint him of it and persuade him to adopt a more even-handed policy.'

'Or to adopt Islam itself,' suggested Umid. 'I hear that some of the generals already attend the mosque. But if that is your proposal, Excellency, may I suggest you ask your daughter to deliver the message. The wagging tongues are saying her influence exceeds even that of the Wazir.'

'I feel sure the wagging tongues exaggerate,' said Kartir. 'However, I'll soon learn if that is so. Have you ascertained what the Christian ambassador wants?'

'A treaty, no less. Rome hopes that Arghun will support it in a war against Sultan al-Ashraf to take back Jerusalem. That information cost me twenty dinars. The most serious news cost me forty. It seems Nizam did not lie to you. Baidu is treating secretly with Ashraf, and has promised him Baghdad for the Muslims. Nizam himself carried the letters!'

'Perhaps I shouldn't be surprised.' Kartir laughed grimly. 'So Baidu's in bed with the Egyptians, and Arghun with the Christians? Interesting, is it not?'

'Indeed, Excellency. And it was worth another ten dinars to find out that Baidu has twice been to Tabriz since spring. He and Gaikatu are there now. What better place to plot than under the Il-khan's nose?'

'What news of Nizam?'

'Sadly, his trail was lost. The man is not without native cunning. He may have suspected he was being watched and slipped out of Baghdad by night.'

'Has he hatched a double-cross with Ashraf, do you think?'

'Quite probably. He can have no real love for Baidu. The man's an enigma. I've been unable to discover much about his early history, though it may be he was Baghdad-born. There are few in Kerman who remember the Emir, let alone those who served him.'

'I have long regretted my association with Nizam, and regret even more letting him out of my sight,' said Kartir. 'But dredging up his past can serve no purpose. We should concentrate on picking up his trail. He could be anywhere by now.'

'I'll do my best to find him, Excellency,' said Umid. 'My own business takes me again to Baghdad and that is as good a place as any to begin. Let us rendezvous the first day after the ending of Ramadan in the square of the Great Mosque, in Tabriz.'

Kartir mopped his brow. He pulled up the hem of his jubbah and sat contemplating his knees and shins. A sudden soft breeze from the mountains above stirred up the dust and ruffled the hairs on his leg. A lizard scuttled over his left sandal and disappeared into a crevice.

He knew it was not the climate that made him sweat so freely. It was past the autumn equinox, usually a pleasant time to travel and, since Isfahan, both night and day had indeed become progressively cooler. But as he neared his destination, his initial uncertainties had become fears. Why had Arghun summoned him? Even Umid had been unable to suggest an explanation.

Much of Kartir's dislike of the Mongols and disillusionment with their cause had been built on a single fact - that his daughter had been taken from him. He had set out for Tabriz bitter, resentful, and determined to find in Arghun a man made in his father's image, arrogant, suspicious, a tyrant and a bully. In his mind, he painted the Il-khan as a lecherous, intemperate monster, and in his nightmare fantasies he often exacted terrible revenge for Nadia's degradation.

Yet, this picture was clearly incomplete. Such a man did not invite his enemy to sup before driving a dagger into his belly. Surely, if Arghun wished his death, or wanted to replace him as viceroy, there would have been no warning, just the unexpected and fatal touch of cold steel against the neck, or the final agonising breathlessness of an arrow between the shoulder blades.

Was the invitation a test, or did Arghun already suspect the South of a plot against his rule, and had he devised this subtle means to acquaint himself of the detail? If that were the case, was he to be tortured before suffering the fate with which he had threatened Nizam?

Kartir swallowed another mouthful of water and replaced his sandals. The horses were ready and it was time to move again. Though still weary, he could delay no longer. His companions had already mounted. Their animals snorted and tread the dust impatiently.

He glanced north along the deserted road. Only Maragha and Sahand now separated him from his destination and whatever awaited him there.

*

IX

After his nocturnal adventure, Giovanni tossed and turned on his divan for an hour or more, trying to make sense of the deadly events in which he had become involved.

His inquisitiveness could have cost him his life. He had helped to foil the attempted abduction, but if it had not been for Hassan his mission might have been over, his body and not those of the would-be abductors lying on cold stone or in an anonymous grave.

Why had he interfered? The domestic politics of the Tabriz court were none of his business. Yet to ignore any circumstance that might change the balance of power in the Mongol capital could lead to the failure of his mission. And he might despise Arghun's intemperance and fickle humour, but there was no one else with whom he could have meaningful negotiations. It would be foolish to dismiss lightly an attack on the Il-khan's extended family.

Thus Giovanni argued, but his heart told him it was not thoughts of his mission that prompted him to go to Hassan's assistance. He had acted impulsively according to his nature, throwing aside the guise he had assumed for a few moments of danger and excitement. And he had nearly paid the price of his carelessness.

However, that was not all. His mission itself was an adventure, but one in which the risks were calculated. Sacrificing his life for the sake of a Muslim child was not part of the plan. Though he liked Hassan, Giovanni knew it was not concern for the son that had spurred him along the dark, blood-soaked corridor, but his growing passion for the mother. He would have given half his fortune for an hour at Nadia's breast, for a taste of her lips, for a fleeting moment of joy in her embrace.

Yet he was baffled by his feelings. Only once had he ever truly loved a woman and she had died in his arms, her cheeks sunken, her lips pale and her once lovely face scarred by smallpox. He had been twenty-three years old, she eighteen. Afterwards, he had taken comfort in the sword, but neither skirmishes with the ambitious Genoese for dominance of the sea routes, nor the more intense Sicilian War, where he had joined the struggle against French tyranny, were able to heal the wounds in his soul.

On his return to Venice he had embarked upon a series of affairs, all of them frivolous and insincere. As sole heir of the Montecervinos he enjoyed wealth and position, and there was no scarcity of women competing for his favours. But Giovanni was tired of high-born fortune seekers. He longed for the anonymity of a tradesman or artist, to be able to court a maiden who would marry him for his own sake, and for hers, not because her father desired it.

Still restless, he had taken service with the Vatican and, as the years passed, he gradually forgot his pain. He was a young man with no desire to commit himself to the life of an ascetic, and he took Roman mistresses. Some were beautiful, he recalled, others clever and amusing, and all of them desirable in their way, but among the women of the Christian capital there had been none whose company and conversation he craved as much as that of her who was not only forbidden him by his Church, but tied to another by a heathen polygamous marriage. He had risked all to gain Nadia's gratitude, but it was for nothing. She could never be his.

Finally, his inner struggle unresolved but with his body and mind tired out from exertion, he fell into a dreamless slumber, to be wakened by the rays of the autumn sun striking his eyelids through the upper window.

He washed, said his prayers and breakfasted on some fruit brought to him the previous evening by the anonymous, veiled attendant who saw to his needs. Having dressed, he opened the shutters and was startled to see a face pressed against the window. A muffled voice called his name. Seeing it was Hassan, he unbolted the door and opened it.

The boy sprang down nimbly from the window ledge. 'Are you coming to play chess with me this morning, Giovanni?'

'Your mother will chastise me if I interfere with your study.'

'Jafar is not well enough to give me lessons, and my mother has business outside the castle,' said the boy. 'Besides, she likes you too much to scold you.'

Giovanni felt a flush of pleasure creeping over his cheeks. 'I'm flattered that your mother should think highly of me,' he said, trying to control the trembling in his voice. 'By all means let us play chess but first, if you have no objection, let us visit the tutor.'

'Let us do so then,' said Hassan. He adopted a stately pose which Giovanni noticed with amusement was intended to mimic his own, and together they set off across the courtyard.

Jafar was on his feet, but he was pale and drawn. The awful scarring of the left side of his face, conspicuous enough by lamplight, was now revealed in all its horror, and Giovanni instinctively shuddered at the thought of the agony the injury must have caused. Though neatly bound, the wounded arm had continued to leak blood and the cloth was stained dark red near his elbow. Jafar responded civilly to enquiries about his health, but Giovanni detected hostility in his manner.

'You are a long way from your homeland,' the tutor said, seating himself on the chair by the lectern.

'Indeed, sir, but I am by no means the first of my race to travel to Tabriz.'

'Many travel and pass on their way. Few seek the favour of our conquerors.'

Giovanni glanced at Hassan who had taken up a book and appeared to be paying no attention. 'I ask no favours,' he said with dignity. 'I only serve my country as best I can.'

Jafar sighed and closed his one good eye. He was evidently in pain. 'I thank Allah that you chose this particular time to do so,' he conceded quietly, 'but as to favours, you will receive none from the seed of Genghis.'

Giovanni could see that nothing was to be gained by prolonging the interview, so he wished Jafar a speedy recovery and withdrew. Hassan followed.

'Tell me something of your life here in Tabriz, Hassan,' he said when they were alone in the boy's small apartment. 'Is this the only home you have ever known?'

'I was born here, or so my mother says,' Hassan replied. He began arranging the chess pieces on the board. 'I have several times been to Maragha, and twice visited the sea coast. Last winter, my father took me to Baghcha where he has a palace, a few villas and some splendid tents.'

'Your father? You mean His Majesty the Il-khan?'

'I always think of him as my father,' said Hassan. 'I never knew another.'

'And what is your ambition? Do you intend to be a soldier, a scholar, or a merchant perhaps.'

'I will be a viceroy, Giovanni. That is my grandfather's title, but he is an old man. When Ghazan is Il-khan, I will have him send me to Kerman to collect his taxes.'

Giovanni smiled. 'And you will rule nobly, I'm sure. Do you have any other relatives - a grandmother? Cousins? Another grandfather? It's normal to have two.'

'Master Shirazi is a distant uncle, I believe, but there are no others that I've heard of, Giovanni,' answered Hassan frankly. He finished setting up the game and began it by moving a pawn forward. They continued to play.

Giovanni won the first game. Remembering their earliest encounter, he began the next with a more cautious gambit. Hassan saw his ploy. He played with skill and energy and twice forced Giovanni's king into check. On finding himself with four pieces against three, Hassan gave a great whoop of joy.

'Kolokol!' he cried. 'I've won!'

'Never underestimate your opponent, my young master,' said Giovani calmly. He moved his one remaining knight and neatly turned the tables.

Hassan's face fell with disappointment.

'In chess, just as in life, there are times for boldness and times for cunning,' Giovanni told him. 'When your enemy is in the open and crying victory is often the time to strike. To be truthful, I thought you had learned that in your swordplay.' He grew more serious. 'And when your enemy hides himself in dark corridors, that is a time for caution.'

'I didn't think I had any enemies, Giovanni,' said Hassan, who had obviously understood the allusion. 'In truth, I don't like Gaikatu and Baidu or some of the emirs much but I can't believe they would want to take my life. Jafar blames the prophecy for everything.'

'The prophecy?'

'Oh, it's a fairy tale only,' said Hassan, putting on a lighter face. 'From an old book. Jafar made me translate it into the Greek language.'

'Tell me about this prophecy,' said Giovanni, intrigued.

'Wait, I'll show you!'

Hassan leapt up from the chess table, rummaged in a corner and returned with a parchment on which was some close writing. He pushed it into Giovanni's hands.

Giovanni smoothed out the paper. He had just enough knowledge of Greek to decipher it:

There were men in Istakhr telling lies about the priests of Zoroaster. Kartir banished them from the city and from any other place where he found them. After that only a few liars remained and they stayed in hiding practising magic and doing evil deeds. And so good and evil waged war all over the land, but it was goodness that prevailed as it had at the beginning of time.

The false Mazdaites vowed to be revenged on Kartir and his sons and daughters. They called on Ahriman to help them destroy the empire of Darius.

Then the priests of Zoroaster foresaw the end of the empire after a thousand years and prophesied it might be saved only by a true son of Kartir bearing the cross of Jemshid.

'So what is the meaning of this fairy tale, Hassan, and who are Ahriman and the false Mazdaites?' Giovanni enquired when he had finished reading.

'Ahriman is Satan,' Hassan said. 'Jafar says his evil is all around us. On the way from Maragha he talked a lot about these Mazdaites, and people called Nizaris, but I didn't understand any of it.'

'And what is the cross of Jemshid?'

'It's the necklace my mother wears, Jafar says.'

'The gammadion?' Giovanni was curious. The Il-khan had attached mystical significance to the symbol, and here was the boy doing the same. 'And this Kartir? Your mother told me something of him. You are a descendant, it seems.'

'A true son, Jafar says. And my mother has the cross.'

'Surely this tale is only fantasy,' said Giovanni. 'What does your mother think?'

'I haven't told her yet.'

Giovanni studied the earnest young face. Was it possible that an ancient prophecy had some bearing on recent events, he wondered? He knew only a little of Persian history, but he believed Satan and his evil forces were at work in the world and might use even a child in their plot to win men's souls. Again he imagined the darkened corridor; the spilled blood of the sentry; the lamp; the boy in the grip of his would-be assassin or abductor; the raised swords. Although the day was warm, he suddenly felt cold.

'I recommend you do so, Hassan,' he said. 'And meantime, take great care.'

Three days passed. Giovanni noticed the militia had been augmented both in and around the castle. The number of night-time guards in the corridor outside his room was increased from two to four.

On the first morning, he had another meeting with Arghun, but made no further diplomatic progress. Encouraged by Nadia's opinions, he tried to see the Il-khan, not as a conqueror, but as a man with his country's interests at heart. They talked of the Crusaders and their last abortive attempt to take Cairo. Giovanni felt much more at ease. Whereas previously he had only listened and answered questions, he now took an active part in the conversation, correcting Arghun's misconceptions about the Christian faith and even challenging some of his opinions on military strategy.

To his surprise, he found himself warming to the man. Beneath the Il-khan's coarse exterior was a sharp mind with a profound knowledge of the world. Even if misguided in his religious beliefs he seemed sincere in them. He might deserve the reputation for Mongol ruthlessness against his enemies, but he was someone who valued friendship and rewarded loyalty.

Giovanni spent the second and third mornings roaming in the Tabriz bazaars. Since the early weeks of his stay he had known where the western merchants, Italian, German and English, congregated to negotiate terms and exchange gossip. He encountered a Venetian whose caravan was passing on the way to Bukhara and who was able to give him the latest news from the City State. His family was well.

His wanderings took him into hitherto unexplored lanes in the Christian quarter, where he found several churches. Thinking he might make his confession, he entered one, but found the walls plain, the furniture stark and the atmosphere alien. He did not see a priest and left the building wishing he had stayed outside.

By contrast, a Buddhist temple erected by Hulegu, which he passed on his way back to the castle, was nobly constructed and richly decorated, at least on the outside. For a while, he stood contemplating the ornate stone on the threshold and considering whether he should go in. The call to prayer of a muezzin from the tower of the nearest mosque brought him to his senses. What was this city doing to him, he wondered?

Never for a moment had Giovanni questioned the teachings of the Holy Church, or considered what it would be like to follow the tenets of another religion, but he was beginning to see Tabriz with a Persian perspective. Its cosmopolitan population mingled and jostled in the markets with no sign of hostility in their faces. The good-natured bartering between men of different faiths spoke a tolerance that would be difficult to imagine in a city of only one. Had he mistaken the tutor's distress and natural reserve for intolerance, and was Nadia right? Was the intolerance in him, and did men, whether Christian, Muslim or Jew indeed oppose the will of God by making war on one another?

Hassan had not resumed his formal lessons, and in the afternoons he invited Giovanni to his cell to play chess. The boy's tactics seemed to have vastly improved and Giovanni, to his great embarrassment, lost two games.

On the third afternoon after the attempted abduction, they were joined by Oljeitu who, having been too long deprived of his playmate's company, had come to seek him out with the object of engaging in swordplay. The atmosphere became less dignified, the chess was abandoned and the two boys wandered off leaving Giovanni in sole possession of the cell. He gathered up the splendid chessmen and carefully reset them on the board. Turning to leave, he saw Nadia standing expectantly in the corridor.

'Your son had already left, madam,' he said somewhat needlessly.

'Indeed,' said she.

'He was in need of company his own age,' said Giovanni. 'Perhaps he has been too much in mine of late.'

'If you're weary of him you have only yourself to blame,' said Nadia lightly, 'but, in truth, I'm glad I found you here. Will you walk with me in the garden? I have news that I hope will please you.'

Giovanni gladly consented. Since their last conversation, the arboretum had seen the first real signs of autumn. Leaves, blown across the pathways by a slight wind, rustled beneath their feet.

'It is almost time to leave Tabriz,' said Nadia, pulling the shawl she wore more tightly round her shoulders. 'Soon it will become very cold here. The Il-khan will invite you to spend the winter with him at the palace of Baghcha to discuss your alliance. It seems even the Wazir has now admitted its benefits.'

'That is good news indeed, madam, and I thank you for being the bearer of it. I had almost given up hope. Will you and Hassan also winter in Baghcha?'

'We will not go immediately. At the end of Ramadan, there is an important festival in the calendar of our faith. But I shall certainly join His Majesty by the middle of the month of Shawwal, if not sooner. Do you hunt, Sir Giovanni?'

'I have been known to do so, madam.'

'At Baghcha there is good hunting, and some other sport. There is a wide river and fine forests. Sometimes the rain comes down in sheets from the skies. Near the palace is a lake with fish as large as your arm. When it freezes over, as it does sometimes, the soldiers fit cloths to the ponies' hooves and use them to pull wheelless carts over the ice.'

'It sounds delightful, madam.'

'I trust you will find it so. But tell me more about *your* country, sir,' she went on light-heartedly. 'How do you spend the winters there? Is it very cold, and do your splendid canals freeze? How are your houses warmed, and what do you do for water? What are the women of Venice like, and how do they dress?'

Giovanni laughed at her high spirits and wondered whether the prospect of a change of scene alone could have led to the change. 'That is a great deal of knowledge, My Lady,' he said. 'Where do you wish me to start?'

'Let us start with the women. Are they beautiful?'

'Some of them, My Lady. However, I have to say that few can match in face or form what I have seen in your country, and none in the manner of dress. In Venice, the ladies wear heavy fabrics, cover their heads with jewels and walk stiffly with their garments trailing in the dust. They look splendid, but do not have the simple elegance of Persian women.? As he said this, he looked directly at her so that she could be in no doubt that the compliment was intended for herself, and he noticed from the brightness of her eye that she understood.

'Have you known many Persian women?' she asked. She had stopped walking and was defying his gaze.

'I judge by the example before me,' he replied.

Nadia lowered her eyes and turned away from him.

'Forgive me, madam,' he said hastily, afraid that he had been too daring in his compliment, and had incurred her displeasure. 'That was an impertinence.'

'You are forgiven,' said she. 'My mood today is frivolous, and I meant to tease you. There has been so much good news. My father is coming to Tabriz, and I have not seen him for six years.'

'And your mother?'

'She died when I was twelve years old.'

'I'm truly sorry, madam. Is your father really descended from the great Kartir who lived in Sasanian times?'

'Who knows?' Nadia shrugged. 'It's more than a thousand years since King Ardashir ruled. I know only that there were priests and kings among my father's ancestors.'

'Your son's tutor seems to assume a connection,' Giovanni observed casually. 'He has been filling Hassan's head with tales of evil men and magic crosses.'

'I have already admonished Jafar,' said Nadia. 'Hassan showed me the passage of translation and I'm obliged to you for persuading him to do so. He seems to pay more attention to you than he does to me.'

'There are many legends in my country, My Lady,' said Giovanni, feeling it to be tactful to ignore her observation. 'For example, it is held that Romulus and Remus, the founders of Rome, were suckled by a she-wolf. I have a great interest in the tales from other nations.'

'If it pleases you I will tell you what I know of the false Mazdaites, though I'm not a great believer in prophecies. Touching the cross of Jemshid I'm even more sceptical, having learnt the legend only a day or two ago.'

They continued their walk.

'In the days before Mahommet,' she said, 'the disciples of Zoroaster worshipped Ahura Mazda, the god of light. It is from his name that the word Mazdaite derives. But there was also a god of darkness. His name was Ahriman and he was akin to Satan in Christian and Muslim teaching. Now, while Kartir was Grand Wazir, there arose in Persia a new philosophy, spread by a priest called Mani who claimed divinity for himself. Like Jesus, this Mani had twelve disciples.'

'Then you know something about my beliefs, madam?'

'Islam acknowledges the prophethood of Jesus, though it denies his divinity,' Nadia replied. She smiled. 'Perhaps one day we can debate the merits of our two theologies.'

'Perhaps,' echoed Giovanni, '- but tell me about Mani.'

'Persia was very different in the days of Kartir,' she went on. 'Rather than deny the tenets of the Mazdaites, Mani added to them, bringing in ideas from other religions. His teaching enraged the priests of Zoroaster. They claimed he was in league with Ahriman and accused him of using magic in his rituals. He was charged by Kartir, found guilty of heresy and executed with a number of his followers.'

'But what connection does this have with recent history?' frowned Giovanni. 'And who are the Nizaris?'

'They too were heretics - heretics of the Islamic faith. Some called them Ismailis. They attributed magical meanings to the law of Mahommet, and claimed that only their adherents had the right, and power, to understand it. Like the followers of Mani, these Ismailis added the tenets of other faiths to their philosophy. Thus they adopted beliefs and practices of the ancient Mazdaites and the Hellenes. And they slew by the dagger or by poison those who opposed them. This my father taught me. He was at Alamut when Hulegu burnt their castles to the ground.

'Those who survived the purge, it was said, were scattered to the four winds. But Jafar, like my maternal grandfather, was their prisoner and suffered for many years at their hands. He sees their spectre everywhere, even in an ornament about my neck.'

She laughed and fingered the gammadion, but Giovanni saw that some of the gaiety had gone from her eyes.

'The tale of the fylfot is even more fanciful,' she concluded, 'and will keep till another day. Though it is beautiful, it is neither magic nor worth a king's ransom. Still, until my son's enemy is discovered, there will be a small corner of my heart that fears its secret power.'

Giovanni received the promised invitation three days later. Arghun was alone and planning a hunting expedition. He was in good spirits.

'You'll join the party of course, Ambassador,' he said jovially, clapping Giovanni between the shoulder blades. 'Master Hassan is most insistent that you should. It'll be his first hunt, along with my son Oljeitu. They are to be blooded.'

'Blooded, Your Majesty?'

'You will see!' laughed Arghun. 'It's customary.'

He sent for some wine and, while they drank, began reminiscing of his own childhood and describing in gory detail the excitement of his own first hunt.

Giovanni listened with only one ear. He was thinking of Nadia, and of the look in her eye when he complimented her.

He might indeed complete his mission at Baghcha. However, it was no longer the mission that drove him on, but the momentary sparkle of longing he had glimpsed in the second before she turned away. He could barely stifle his apprehension that, in weeks of closer proximity with Arghun's household, he would be unable to disguise his growing feelings of love for her.

*

X

The morning of the first hunt was the coldest Giovanni had experienced since his arrival in Persia. It was scarcely daylight when they set out. There was already snow on the mountain peaks. Giovanni could feel the chill of the wind on his teeth and gums, and the air he drew into his lungs was icy. The broad back and rounded belly of the pony he had been allocated did not suit his stature. The stirrups were too short and his knees stuck out uncomfortably.

He rode on the Il-khan's left. With him was Nadia's father, Kartir, newly arrived in Tabriz. It was Giovanni's first opportunity to observe the viceroy at close quarters and he now saw in the high cheekbones and aquiline nose the origin of Hassan's gravity of expression.

All around them were gathered the princes and emirs of Mongol blood, among them Gaikatu smiling toothily. A leather liquor flagon hung beside his weapons on the saddle. His face was flushed, and not merely from the exertion of the ride. To his rear came Prince Baidu. He too had been drinking but, instead of fostering high spirits, the liquor seemed to make him morose. Giovanni, for no reason he could identify, was slightly uneasy at his presence. More than once he had the feeling that the prince's glare was fixed on his back, though when he casually turned, the sullen eyes were always directed elsewhere.

The women too had joined the expedition. Some drove wagons, others were mounted on animals no more sedate than those of the male hunters. Nadia was not amongst them.

In mid morning, they came to a plateau dotted with low-lying shrubs and stunted trees. Denser woodland surrounded it on three sides. The hunters now formed two wings that drew away from the royal party and into a wide arc. There were eighty or more riders, Giovanni estimated, armed with swords and clubs as well as bows. He watched their manoeuvres with interest.

'It was different in the old days, Ambassador,' Arghun said wistfully. Though the wine and liquor was flowing freely, he seemed to have abstained. 'The whole army hunted for weeks at a time. Now we make do with a platoon or two!'

He urged his piebald pony into a trot and Giovanni followed his lead. The whole line moved forward. Hassan and Oljeitu, restrained until now, leapt into the van with whoops of delight. Their tiny bows were strung over their saddle-horns.

'They will gradually move into a circle, driving the game before them,' Arghun explained. 'Then the circle tightens so that no animal can escape. Don't you hunt in this manner, Ambassador?'

'Customs are rather different in Italy, Your Majesty,' said Giovanni. 'Our parties are small and we work with dogs or hawks.'

'At Baghcha we'll see what can be done,' said the Il-khan. 'Perhaps we can find a bird or two for you.'

Gaikatu and a group of his followers had drawn level. The prince was none too steady in the saddle. Arghun followed him with his eyes as he pulled ahead. He seemed to lose interest in the conversation he had begun.

'You'll have observed my kingdom has its problems, Ambassador,' he growled. 'You know I'd dearly love to support your venture against the Egyptian Sultan, but I don't want my grandfather's empire to fall into the hands of perverts.'

'Perverts, Your Majesty?'

'By Genghis's balls, Giovanni, can't you see that ever-grinning ape that is an apology for a brother. Gaikatu and his cohorts would destroy the Il-khanate. He spends his days with whores and small boys. Neither he nor my cousin Baidu with whom he's so close has any interest in statesmanship. I don't pay tribute to Kublai Khan, but at least I show him respect. My would-be successors have respect for nothing. I can't leave the centre of my realm undefended while I engage in a war against the Mamluks!'

'Of course, Your Majesty,' began Giovanni, surprised by this sudden confidence and by the vehemence of the speech. 'But if Sultan Ashraf were to turn on Baghdad . . .'

'No buts, Giovanni,' cried Arghun. 'Three more months. Time for my son Ghazan to return from Khorasan. He has battalions to keep the wolves at bay. He suddenly slapped his thigh, gave one of his heartiest laughs and increased the pace. 'Three months for you to sample the pleasures of Baghcha. We'll talk some more, then I'll give your treaty my approval. I'll write you a letter to take to the Christian Patriarch!'

At the unexpectedness of this offer, Giovanni lost a stirrup and almost unseated himself. His pony went into the canter. 'Your Majesty is most gracious . . .' he panted.

'Pox on your soft diplomacy, Master Venetian,' Arghun shouted back at him. 'At Baghcha, we'll discuss our campaign in detail. Now, let us enjoy a man's sport!'

They reached the woodland. Arghun and the nucleus of his party had forged well ahead and some hunters had already disappeared among the trees.

Though the sun was nearly at its zenith, they were higher on the mountain and Giovanni was still cold. Now, his ears were assailed by the sound of animal shrieks. He did not risk the pace of the Mongol riders. His satisfaction at having made progress in his mission had not overcome his discomfort. He was chafed from contact with the unfamiliar saddle and his joints were stiff from maintaining the unnatural position in the stirrups. He found himself separated from the rest of the party, and only the cries of the hunters and the shouts of encouragement from the women assured him he had not been left alone in the wilderness.

The separation was only temporary. Giovanni's pony had the scent of its fellows. It snorted and jerked at the reins. Giovanni gave it its head and it bounded forward eagerly until they had crossed the threshold of the trees. Here it was sheltered. Some natural warmth returned to his limbs and he breathed more evenly.

Beyond a dense thicket which hindered his progress, the trees thinned out again. Giovanni found himself in a another clearing, surrounded by scrub. Arghun's party was just ahead. Hassan and Oljeitu were with them.

The Mongol hunters had formed themselves into a huge circle and were driving the animals into its centre. There were wild hogs, rabbits, a few deer and one or two wolves and foxes. The circle tightened until there was no gap through which the smallest creature could escape.

Arghun drew his bow, took aim at a hog and brought it down with an arrow in the forehead. One by one, the princes took their pick of the game. Finally, the other hunters raised their weapons and loosed a torrent of arrows into the milling and screeching pack that remained. The cries of the terrified creatures as the missiles found their mark mixed with the whoops of the youths, the ecstatic screams of the girls and the yells of triumph from the experienced archers.

Giovanni felt ill at ease and sickened in the presence of such mass slaughter. He had often hunted, and had found pleasure in it, but this hunt was ritual killing, akin to genocide. The arrows flew thickly without respite from all sides of the copse, and the hunted fell, wounded and dying. The hunters dismounted and moved in with sword and club, despatching any beasts that had survived the onslaught. A deathly quietness reigned over the plateau. Even the ponies were silent.

The Il-khan rode into the centre accompanied by two wagons bearing the princes' women. He dismounted and strode into the midst of the slaughter where his son and stepson waited, flushed and triumphant, by the beasts they had killed. Oljeitu had brought down a mountain cat, Hassan a deer. Arghun drew his sabre and cut both animals' throats. He dipped his hand in the creatures' blood, smeared it on the boys' brows, then clapped a large hand on their respective shoulders.

'Now you are both full Mongol warriors,' he said.

All round the copse, groups of hunters had been silently awaiting the completion of this ritual. Now the Il-khan's words were the signal for general cheers and the gathering up of the spoils. The two boys joined in. The dead beasts were loaded onto the wagons. Arrows were loosed into the sky.

Giovanni found Kartir at his elbow.

'Is it not good sport, if a trifle bloodthirsty?'

Giovanni nodded his agreement. He had noted that, like himself, the viceroy took no part in the killing.

'And another week of it is to follow,' Kartir added. 'Take my advice and learn to like it, as I had to do once. Our royal host takes his hunting very seriously and expects others to do the same.'

On the homeward journey the spirit of the party became wilder and its conversation more and more raucous. Arghun drank sparingly but, even so, became quite merry. He rode among his followers, clapping them enthusiastically on the back and congratulating them on their success. Giovanni could pretend no enthusiasm and prayed he would be spared any attention.

His prayers were answered. He reached Tabriz without incident, crept unnoticed to his apartment and, weary and nauseated, threw himself onto his bed.

The process was repeated the following day. Giovanni learned that, instead of being merely a spectator, he was expected to participate in the kill. He had never used a Mongol bow, so the armoury provided him instead with a weapon of Persian construction, not unlike the bows he had known in his own country.

The game was just as numerous and again Arghun had the first choice of victim. Having brought down a large wolf, he wheeled his pony and signalled to Giovanni to approach.

Giovanni hesitated but, as he was vainly searching for a reason to decline, he found Kartir again by his side.

'It's a great honour to be allowed to follow after the Il-khan,' said the viceroy in a loud whisper. 'You cannot refuse!'

Giovanni ached in every limb from the previous day's ride. The nausea rose in his chest. He fought it down, fitted an arrow to his bow and took careful aim at a buck gazelle on the edge of the melee. The arrow pierced its neck just above the shoulder and it fell stone dead.

Arghun raised his arm in salute and the slaughter began as before. The spoil was loaded, the wine drunk and, amid general high spirits, arrows were loosed into the air.

As they began the descent from the mountain slopes, Giovanni found that the Il-khan himself had joined him.

'We'll make a hunter of you yet, Ambassador.' Though he had been drinking, the Il-khan sat erect in the saddle and was quite sober. 'That was a fine beast you brought down. What do you say we honour you by cooking it for supper?'

Giovanni accepted the invitation with misgivings, inwardly cringing at the thought of a whole evening spent in Bacchanalian celebrations. In the event, the party was small, the wine was of better quality than any he had sampled previously, and he quite enjoyed himself.

He awoke with a mild headache, which had gone by noon.

There was no hunting that day. Arghun departed in mid morning with his wife Tolaghan, his daughters Oljei and Doquz, and Prince Oljeitu.

'He has gone to Maragha to see my Uncle Shirazi,' explained Hassan while they played chess. 'From there he'll ride to Van, and then on to Baghcha. We are to meet him there, he said. You are to look after me, Giovanni.'

'I look after you, my young master?' laughed the Venetian.

'It is the festival of 'id al-Fitr, - the ending of Ramadan. When that's over, we'll travel to Baghcha together, with my mother. My grandfather will come too. He thinks it's too cold here and wants to go back to Kerman, but Arghun has persuaded him. General Taghachar will give us an escort.'

'I see that Prince Baidu has also left the castle,' said Giovanni. 'Has he gone to Maragha too?'

'No, to Baghdad,' said Hassan with unusual vehemence. 'I'm glad. I don't like him. He insulted my mother.'

Giovanni chose not to respond. He moved a piece on the board. It would be unwise, he thought, to express an opinion as to the prince's character, even to his new friend. Hassan, however, was determined to vent his feelings.

'Baidu is nearly always drunk,' he continued with a grimace of disgust, 'and last year, at the celebration of the Il-khan's birthday, he vomited in front of everyone.'

'What did His Majesty have to say at that?'

'Arghun swore dreadfully and ordered Baidu to be beaten and thrown into a dungeon for three nights. Baidu's face was very red, and he just laughed. Then Arghun said it should be six nights, and that he would cut off Baidu's privates if he ever saw him again. Baidu was so drunk he went on laughing as the soldiers dragged him away. I think Arghun forgave him later, Giovanni, but I never shall.'

'Because he insulted your mother?'

'He called her a Persian whore,' said Hassan. He had become quite animated and seemed to have lost interest in the game. 'That was when

Baidu came to Tabriz in the summer. I overheard him talking to his friends. There was Prince Timur and some others I recognised. And a stranger - a little fat man wearing a turban. I didn't catch all the conversation, nor did I know what a Persian whore was, but I asked the imam and he said it was an awful insult.'

'Insults by themselves cannot cause harm,' Giovanni said simply. He gestured at the chess table. 'It's your move, Hassan. Shall we continue with the game?'

Hassan fingered a piece then released it as if undecided on the move. 'I didn't tell my mother what I overheard, just as I didn't tell her about the prophecy until you asked me to,' he said. 'Should I do so now?'

'I recommend you say nothing to your mother,' advised Giovanni. 'It will only distress her.'

Hassan hesitated. 'It's just that thinking of Baidu brought it to mind. I've seen him again.'

'Seen whom?'

'The little fat man in the turban. Baidu's friend. The day before the hunting began I went with Jafar to the mosque and saw him talking to a mullah. Only, I couldn't remember where I'd seen him before. But I do now. He has side whiskers and a stubbly grey beard, and the turban falls over his eyes. I remember too what name Baidu called him. It was Nizam.'

The hunting was resumed the following morning, and was led by Gaikatu. Giovanni's heart wasn't in it and decided to plead a bad stomach. However, remembering Kartir's advice, he prepared to join the outing with as brave a face as possible if the prince showed any sign of displeasure. Gaikatu shrugged off the excuse. He had his own circle of friends and appeared to be wrapped up in his own thoughts.

The governor seemed to be genuinely unwell and had taken to his bed.

'It's the weather,' Hassan explained. 'The cold is bad for my grandfather's health and he caught a chill. My mother has prepared some medicine and we will both stay behind today and keep him company '

'I am truly sorry to hear your news. Be sure to give your grandfather my good wishes for a quick recovery.'

On the fifth morning, Gaikatu departed with his retinue for Rum Province. There was heated argument as to who should take his place, and the task of leading the hunt was finally given to General Taghachar, the city commander. Again, Giovanni considered excusing himself, but Hassan was as enthusiastic as ever and, since he no longer had Oljeitu for company, begged him to join the expedition. For the second time, Kartir appeared unwell and remained behind in the castle.

They ventured further into the hills than before. As usual, a group of women followed behind in wagons and for the second day in succession Nadia was in their company. Hassan seemed to take her presence as an incentive for excessive high spirits and from time to time would gallop up and down the line with some older youths, whooping all the while.

A suitable ground was chosen and the line of riders began to manoeuvre into a circle, driving the game from its cover into a clearing. The final ring was much tighter than previously and the game therefore less plentiful. Giovanni was glad. He had already seen too much slaughter.

The discipline of previous outings was missing. The hunters took up their bows without regard for rank. They let loose at the yelling, squirming pack and moved in to finish off the survivors. The carts were brought. The riders emptied their flagons and with drunken whoops and obscenities began shooting their arrows in the air.

Giovanni had no ear for the sounds of merriment. He heard a sudden swish of the air and felt a stab of pain. Then he was staring in horror and disbelief at the red stain spreading over his tunic and breeches, where a deadly shaft had buried itself in the flesh of his right thigh. His senses swam and he fell helplessly from the saddle.

*

XI

Nadia drove her wagon through the ragged circle of hunters. She had seen Giovanni fall. Hassan left his prize and pony and ran towards her, his eyes wide with alarm. Timur, still in the saddle, glance down at the Venetian's body and turned away incuriously. He began loading his game.

'It seems our cousin's Christian ally has no head for liquor, Taghachar,' he scoffed. A few nearby hunters laughed drunkenly.

'How easily you forget, Timur,' grunted Taghachar, dismounting and beckoning to an attendant to hold his pony. 'It's scarcely a year since you had to be carried to your bed in a drunken stupor. Help me raise the Christian to his feet.'

He bent down to grasp Giovanni by the armpits and Nadia saw him grow pale with anger. 'By the pox, this is no joke,' he thundered. 'The fellow's been stuck with an arrow. His clothes are soaked in blood. What fool was shooting low?'

Nadia's heart leapt into her mouth. She jumped down from her cart and ran towards the general. Hassan followed. The laughter had stopped. In the other wagons there was a burst of excited chatter and startled faces were turned in their direction. Timur had ceased his occupation and was staring unemotionally at the spreading red stain on the Venetian's thigh.

'Is he badly hurt?' cried Nadia. She knelt beside Taghachar as he broke off the protruding part of the arrow.

'He's breathing and the wound doesn't look serious, My Lady, but there's too much blood for my liking,' he exclaimed. 'By the Great Khan's beard, if he dies, Arghun's vengeance will be terrible!'

'He'll not die,' said Nadia, 'but his leg must be compressed and bound to slow the bleeding. Allow me attend to it.'

'Yes, yes, My Lady,' agreed Taghachar hastily. 'Someone help me put him in the cart. He's in no condition to ride even when he wakes up.'

They lifted Giovanni and laid him in the wagon. Nadia peered at the bloody clothing.

'I do not think this can wait,' she said anxiously. 'The arrowhead must be removed and the opening cleaned. There is plenty water in our provisions, but no herbs or ointments to staunch the bleeding. We should return to the city without delay.'

'Your son can travel with you,' said Taghachar. 'We'll bring the ponies. Do what you can for him!'

The party split. Two riders were assigned by Taghachar to accompany the wagon. Nadia climbed into it and directed Hassan to drive. At her signal, he whipped the horse forward. She tore the leg from Giovanni's breeches. She used a piece of animal skin as a tourniquet, incised the wound, cut out the barb of the arrow, cleaned the flesh with water and bound the thigh with strips of saddle-cloth. Giovanni did not fully regain consciousness, but groaned pitiably throughout the operation.

They travelled for an hour and almost reached the cultivated slopes on the outskirts of Tabriz. Every jolt of the cart seemed to increase the Venetian's distress, because he groaned more loudly and began to rave in his own language. Nadia felt his pulse and touched his brow. It was hot and damp with sweat. She ordered Hassan to halt and called out to the escort, which was some distance ahead.

The riders turned in the saddle and, seeing the stationary wagon, drew rein.

'I shall take Signor di Montecervino to the villa of an acquaintance,' said Nadia when they had come abreast. 'His fever is worsening and the castle is too far. He is delirious, and the motion of the cart aggravates his condition.'

'Don't you wish us to accompany you, My Lady?'

'It's unnecessary. There's nothing more you can do, and I shall be well enough chaperoned.'

'Are you sure, My Lady?' said one of the escort doubtfully. 'The Commander was most explicit that we should not desert you.'

'I will see to it Taghachar is informed the decision is mine,' replied Nadia. 'You will not be blamed. Please return to the hunt, and thank you for your assistance.'

She waved her hand and the two riders, relieved of their responsibility, galloped off back the road they had come.

'Eager enough to be gone,' muttered Nadia when they were out of sight. She took Hassan in her arms and tousled his dark hair.

'The world may believe this to be an accident,' she whispered, kissing him on the forehead, 'and, an hour ago, I would have sworn to it. The injury is simple and should not have brought on this fever. There can be no doubt Giovanni has been poisoned, which means the act was deliberate and planned.'

'Who is it you suspect, Mother?' Hassan hissed in her ear.

'I wish I knew, Hassan,' she replied softly. 'More than one enemy has been at work lately. We shall have to take extra care as long as we remain in Tabriz. But help me take Giovanni to the Patriarch's villa. Then unhitch the horse and ride like the wind for the castle. Bring my box of medicines. Speak to no one! We'll decide later what else needs to be done.'

*

XII

Darkness had fallen when Nadia finished attending to Giovanni's wound, and it was dawn before she and Hassan returned to Tabriz.

The bitter cold heralded the approach of winter and, though well protected by furs, she shivered in the weak sunlight that crept over the roofs and turrets of the city, bathing the tops of the minarets in a red glow. The call to prayer, high-toned and tremulant in the thin, chill air, lingered in her head long after the sound had gone and added to the eeriness of the morning. Many of the Faithful were already abroad in the streets, their breath white and spectral as they hurried along in answer to the muezzin's summons.

Nadia had chosen this early hour as she had no desire to face the inevitable questioning her arrival would cause. News of the ambassador's misfortune would have spread quickly, generating much speculation and perhaps even sympathy. However, if she was right in her suspicions that the wounding was no accident, a would-be murderer was at large, masquerading as one of Arghun's friends and until Giovanni's enemy was identified it was better his whereabouts remained her secret alone.

Hassan seemed unaffected by the cold or by her anxious mood. He had passed the night in innocent slumber while she had tossed and turned restlessly on a makeshift bed by the Venetian's side. When she closed her eyes she saw the broken arrow, the spreading red stain and a ring of indistinct faces. She had tried to tell herself that she had acted for the purest motives, that her concern for Giovanni's well-being was no more than she would have felt for Arghun's most miserable subject, but she knew this to be untrue. Her rapid pulse as she washed the blood from his thigh, the warm prickling of her flesh as she gazed unobserved at his broad chest and muscular limbs, told a different tale. For a few hours, despite the invisible chains that bound her to her current life and duty, she had been free. Whatever cruel Fate might have in store for them, together or apart, she could not - would not - allow the Venetian to die.

Few of the castle's residents had stirred. Hassan whipped the shaft-horse through the open, unguarded gate and the wagon trundled unchallenged across the main courtyard towards the stables. Leaving him to attend to the animal, Nadia proceeded on foot to her quarters. The sentries on duty in the corridor saluted sleepily in recognition and moved aside to let her pass. She had been apprehensive of her reception and breathed a sigh of relief as the curtain fell back into position behind her.

For several moments Nadia sat on her divan, calming her racing heart, allowing a plan to take shape in her mind. She knew what had to be done, but needed to summon the strength to carry it through. Though her servants might be trusted to perform simple commissions, they could not be relied upon to remain tight-lipped under interrogation. But could she confide in her father and ask his help without disclosing, at least in part, what she had always resolved to keep to herself: the betrayal of Gobras and his people in Kerman; the secret of Mahmoud Hassan's true identity? And if he did not already suspect, how he might react she could only guess. Righteous anger? Hurt pride? Since his arrival in Tabriz, they had been alone only once but, though the years had changed him, she could tell he was still a proud man. And if he refused her, what would she do then?

 Nadia threw off her furs, rose and drew back the curtain of one of the closets. A long mirror rested against the wall at the rear and she studied her figure in it critically. Her hair was disarranged by the ride and her face bore the dirt of the mountain road. The hem of her dress was torn where she had brushed against a nail in the wagon, and both bodice and skirt were smeared with dried blood.

Two pitchers of water lay untouched from the previous evening. Grateful that her absence had not disturbed her servants' routines, Nadia removed her soiled clothing, bathed, combed and refastened her hair, and oiled and perfumed her body. She selected a gown of green silk from her wardrobe, dressed in it and stepped back to admire the result.

For an instant, the reflection in the glass was not of herself but took the form and face of the Christian ambassador. He stood on a hillside, among vines laden with grapes. Round him danced five or six happy, laughing children. A feeling of excitement, unlike anything she had ever experienced, swept over her, and she realised she was trembling. In a twinkling of the eye the vision was gone, and she cursed the daeva who ad sent it to her. If that was her secret desire, it could never be fulfilled.

With a sigh, she refastened her gammadion about her neck and, still trembling, but firm in her resolve, went in search of her father.

Nadia knew that Kartir had long neglected many of the prescriptions and traditions of the Muslim faith. Though admitting the benefits of prayer, he denied the value of the thrice daily ritual, arguing that those who were the most scrupulous in its observance were often the least honest and sincere in their daily lives. However, he had always been an early riser by habit, and had indeed been dressed for an hour or more when she knocked at the door of his apartment. News of what occurred during the hunt had reached him, and he had become anxious when she did not return the previous evening.

He listened silently and impassively while she gave him a true account and confessed her suspicion that the incident had been planned.

'Can you be sure this was not a second attempt on Hassan's life?' he frowned.

'I am sure, Father. Hassan was some distance away when the ambassador fell. This attack was no domestic affair. It's a matter of politics. Signor di Montecervino is a threat to whomever plans to destroy this kingdom. His proposed alliance against the Egyptians will bring Arghun prestige and will strengthen his rule.'

'What do you know of such things, Nadia?' exclaimed Kartir. 'I have no desire to be ruled by the Mamluk sultan, but he is at least of our faith, and might be preferable to an Italian or a Frenchman.'

'The Christians do not threaten our country, Father,' she answered sharply. There had been reproof and condescension in his manner and it irritated her. She was no longer the naïve child he had once known. 'But there are others who wish for Arghun's death, both outside and within Persia.'

Kartir seemed taken aback and gazed at her in surprise. 'And you care, Nadia?' he said insensibly. 'His death will bring you freedom.'

Panic took hold of her. The years had not softened his dislike of the Mongols, and he would not help her. She felt tears well up in her eyes and turned away so that he would not see them.

'There will be no freedom for me or for Hassan if Gaikatu or Baidu rules,' she cried vehemently, ' - if my husband is torn from me before his time. I'll not allow Persia's enemies to destroy my son's only protector!'

Kartir followed her across the room and touched her on the shoulder. 'Surely you do not love him?' he said more kindly.

Nadia did not look round. 'What else should a wife do?'

'He is a Mongol.'

'He is a man!'

'But *love*, Nadia ... You were a hostage ...'

'Love!' Nadia echoed, facing him at last. 'Yes, I was a hostage. And for many years I asked myself *why* I was a hostage, what it was you had done to bring the Il-khan's anger down on Kerman. I doubted you, Father, and I doubted myself, until I learned the truth of what happened there.'

'The truth? The truth is, Abaqa was a savage.'

'Abaqa was sick and dying. He truly believed Kerman was a hotbed of treason.'

She saw his face grow pale. He did not know; he did not even suspect. This was not how she had meant it to be, to accuse him, to blurt out like a child the secrets the Patriarch had confided to her, but her pent-up emotions were now released, and they rose up, flooding her reason.

'Yes, Father,' she went on. 'Gobras told me what you planned. About Jalal's children!'

Kartir's face drained of colour. 'Gobras ... the priest of Zoroaster ... he is alive?'

'Yes, Father, though he is frail and blind. He too was a hostage, deceived and betrayed, just as you were.'

'Deceived and betrayed?' repeated Kartir hoarsely. 'How was I betrayed?'

'It was all a lie, Father. The man Nizam deceived you. Mahmoud Hassan was not Jalal's heir.'

Kartir's body stiffened and he swayed dizzily. Nadia put out her arms to assist him and he righted himself again.

'The priest cannot have told you that.'

'It is true, Father. Roxanne was an impostor.'

'But Khalafi swore .....'

'Khalafi's wits were addled,' said Nadia. 'He was easily persuaded to support a lie. Nizam hated you bitterly, Father, and planned his revenge. And when he had you where he wanted you, believing in the lie, humiliated and compromised, he betrayed you to the generals.'

'But why? We had spoken of Jalal's children when I first arrived in Kerman. It was only later that I rejected him as an administrator. What had I done to deserve his hatred?'

'How could you know? Even Gobras was deceived. But you had done everything, Father. You allied yourself with the invaders - with Hulegu - against the old order - against the Caliphate!'

'What is this nonsense, Nadia?'

'Nizam was a fugitive. He came to our province with a dozen others, men and women of the Caliph's blood, the spring after the fall of Baghdad. They were being hunted by the Mongols. The Mazdaite priests are good people, Father. They would not refuse help to refugees, even Muslims.'

'Yes, I was at Baghdad, Nadia,' said Kartir. 'I never pretended otherwise. But I had no hand in the Caliph's death, nor in the hounding of his family.'

'I know that, Father. However, Nizam was a bitter man. In his eyes, you as a Muslim were even more guilty than Hulegu himself.'

'Even so ....'

'Nizam was also a cunning man,' she went on hurriedly. 'Not only did he remain in Kerman but he took service with the old Emir. That was an honour unheard of for an outsider; even Gobras did not know how it was managed. And in the Emir's employ he had status, an income and perquisites. You took that from him. After only five years, he again had nothing.'

'So he had every reason to hate,' Kartir mused. 'Twice exiled because of me.'

'Save your pity, Father. He had none for you, and none for the Gabars, when he betrayed you all for gold. She remembered how the Patriarch had looked when he told her the story, his face pale and rigid like a piece of marble, his bony hands clenched tightly over the white knuckles. When he had confessed his own shame, the near-sightless eyes had been moist, the voice unsteady. Yet part of the tale had been true, in the beginning. There *were* two children, brought by the priests from Parwan. The girl alone had survived to womanhood and had indeed given birth to a daughter. But *she* died in childbirth, along with the son she conceived.

Kartir was staring at her, his eyes pained and disbelieving. 'And Roxanne - our Roxanne ...?'

' ... was Nizam's mistress and part of his plot to bring you down.'

'And Mahmoud ...?'

'Mahmoud was a legitimate child of Roxanne's marriage. But the husband had just died, and she was poor.'

The viceroy slumped with a groan onto his divan. Nadia sat beside him, put an arm round his bent shoulders and laid her head against his pale cheek as she had done as a twelve-year-old maiden.

'You knew this, Nadia? You knew all this, yet you did not tell me.'

'How could I tell you?' she asked. 'I have not seen you for six years, Father, and I did not know it then. At first, the result of the deception seemed harmless enough. Gobras learned of it and did nothing. He saw how fond we were of Mahmoud and his mother. Only when in one lucid moment Khalafi revealed to him what Nizam was - what he planned - did Gobras threaten to tell you. It was not merely a flogging that Nizam feared. How would the laws of Islam, or the Yasa of Genghis Khan, have punished his adultery? Roxanne's husband was alive when Nizam first took her to bed.'

She raised her head and looked at him questioningly. He was still pale but the pained look in his eyes was being replaced by a fierce rage. Though he was a merciful man, she knew very well how he would have reacted to such intelligence.

'And when you rejected his services, Nizam found others more willing to use them. For years he had been selling information to the military commander of Kerman. Now Gobras was accused of harbouring the Il-khan's enemies. Even before my nuptials were celebrated, ten men, women and children of the Zoroastrian faith were dragged from their homes. Gobras's robes saved him, but the others were not so fortunate. The men were executed, the women and children forced into prostitution.'

'I did not know, Nadia. Believe me. They told me Gobras had died in a skirmish when the Mongol troops rode through the city.'

'That might easily have happened. Abaqa believed Nizam's testimony and sent a regiment to Kerman. Many innocent Muslims and Gabars were killed in the purge that followed. You were too valuable to be killed, so I was taken instead ......'

Nadia had again averted her damp eyes from his and she spoke this half-lie easily, after ten years almost believing it, but wondering if she had said too much. Her doubts had not destroyed her love for him, her duty to him as a daughter, and she knew he would have died if she had not convinced Arghun of his loyalty, if she had not offered herself in return for his life. But that was one secret she would not give up unless he forced it from her.

She had not released him and for a while they both sat silently. Her tears began to flow again, but she no longer care that he saw them. Kartir pressed her hand and from time to time gave a disbelieving shake of the head. She could feel his anger cooling.

'And I did nothing to prevent your suffering,' he said at length, ' - though my foolishness was the cause of it. Do you forgive me?'

'There is nothing to forgive. The past is gone, Father, and I do not blame you. Let us forget Nizam. It's the present that matters, and the future. Persia's and my son's!'

'So be it,' said the viceroy. 'I have long harboured revenge in my heart, but it was revenge against Abaqa for what he did to you. Arghun is not a man I can hate. What do you want me to do?'

Nadia embraced him gratefully. 'Take a letter to Ghazan. I will write it for you. He must come to Baghcha. But, first, I need your help to load Giovanni's boxes. I cannot go to his quarters, nor do I wish to remain in Tabriz longer than I have to. Hassan and I will stay with him at Gobras's house until, God willing, he is well enough to travel. Then we shall hurry after Arghun.'

'But these attacks. On the Christian. On Hassan. The viceroy broke away abruptly from her embrace.

'What is it?' Nadia breathed.

'Can it be he is still pursuing his hatred and revenge?' said Kartir, almost to himself. 'Nizam ...!'

There was fear in his face and Nadia herself became fearful as a result. 'Father? If you know something of this plot, tell me, I beg you.'

'Nothing of poisoned arrows, I promise,' said Kartir, 'though what you have told me explains much else. Ask me no more. Leave the city now. Attend to the Venetian, but in late afternoon send Hassan to guide me to the house of this priest of yours. Allah grant that by then I shall have some answers for you.'

Giovanni's dreams were disturbed by thoughts and visions of death. His whole body was on fire. He was being carried aloft on a wooden stretcher by four faceless demons. At his side, an anonymous priest intoned the last rites. Ahead of him, the doors of Purgatory lay wide open and the flames of purification spilled from the entrance like the tongues of a thousand vipers.

As his body was about to pass through, his legs were seized and, just in time, he felt himself being pulled firmly away from the dreadful gates. The heat gradually abated. The demons dissolved into thin air. In his dream, he opened his eyes and saw Nadia's face looking down at him from the foot of the bier. Beside her stood a priest, dressed all in white and wearing a grotesque, pointed hat on his hoary locks. The flickering light from the slowly closing doors struck the object he held aloft as he pronounced the benediction, and Giovanni recognised Nadia's gammadion necklace. Its brilliance dazzled him and he turned away.

When he looked again, the images had vanished and he was alone at the top of an open tower. All around him were human skeletons, picked clean by the flock of birds that now hovered overhead. As he watched, the bones turned to dust and two more priests in white robes swept the residue over the edge into nothingness.

He became conscious of the violent throbbing in his right thigh and a brightness beyond his closed eyelids. He awoke. He was lying on a divan in a low room with two small windows at almost ground level. There was a chimney and a hearth in which a small fire burned.

His body was covered by a woven blanket. The rising or sinking sun had reached a point in the sky that aligned with one window opening, and its subdued winter rays illuminated the plain mosaic wall opposite.

Giovanni had lost his sense of time. As the horror of his dream faded, memory of earlier events began to return, though imperfectly. He remembered the first hunt, the smell of animal blood and the initiation of Arghun's sons as Mongol warriors. He recalled his own discomfort in the strange saddle, his weariness on the first night and the festivities of the second.

Then came the memory of the last day, the sudden stab of pain and the spreading red stain on his breeches. Surprised and angry faces were outlined against the trees and sky. After that, nothing.

Giovanni tried to shut out the pain while he took stock of his surroundings. The ceiling of the room was in shadow, but he discerned that it was vaulted and painted with figures of creatures from oriental mythology. Ignoring the stiffness in his neck, he turned his head to the left and saw that a set of three steps led from his bed, past the hearth, to a stone platform set between two columns supporting the roof. The area behind the columns was in total darkness.

The room had no visible door, and he was considering whether the platform led anywhere when he heard the sound of breathing coming from somewhere to his right and behind his head. He turned again, this time apprehensively. At first, he thought he must still be dreaming for, to his infinite surprise, he beheld in the shadowy corner, sitting calmly on its haunches, a large white dog with black ears, and twin black spots on its forehead just above the eyes. Its teeth were bared in a silent growl. He was searching in vain for a means of defending himself against this nightmare monster when it squealed, rose to its feet, ambled round the divan and up the steps, and disappeared behind one of the pillars. For minutes there was silence. Then came a rasping sound followed by wheezing, the rustling of garments and the pad of aged footsteps. From the exact spot where the dog had disappeared came an ancient man, a living copy of the priest in his dream. His shrunken head was swallowed up in the absurd conical cap and his wizened face was almost completely hidden by his beard.

'So the sun has done its work and you are awake, Master Christian?'

From one so frail and emaciated, the voice was surprisingly powerful.

'What is this place?' demanded Giovanni weakly.

'That is of no importance,' said the ancient warily, 'but you are safe for the present.'

'Safe?'

'You have enemies in our country, it seems,' said the priest. 'I can say no more than that.'

'At least honour me by telling me who you are, and how I came to be here.'

'My name is Gobras. And you were brought here by Arghun's wife, the Lady Nadia, and her son.'

'Nadia is *here*?'

'She has been and gone, but will return.'

'And Arghun?'

'Three days ago he left for Maragha and then his winter villa. That is all I know.'

'Three days ago? How long have I been here, Gobras?'

'You do not remember? Perhaps that was to be expected. The poison was strong and will have affected your mind just as it paralysed your body.'

'Poison?'

'The arrow's barb was poisoned, but the would-be assassin's aim was faulty, or else you moved unexpectedly,' said Gobras. 'Had the point struck a little higher and deeper, you would not have survived one hour, far less the full day you have been in my care. As it was, it took all of Nadia's skill to treat the wound and counter the poison's effects.'

Giovanni raised himself on an elbow and lifted the blanket. He saw that he was wearing beneath it a toga like the priest's and that his legs were bare. His right thigh was bandaged from the groin to the knee. 'Surely it was an accident,' he muttered, lying back. His head began to ache. 'I have no enemies in Persia.'

'Everyone has enemies,' replied Gobras with a chuckle, '- though I do not know whether the target was you, the boy Hassan, or even one of the emirs. I am a priest and have no knowledge of politics.'

Giovanni groaned. His slightest movement made the hot throbbing in his leg and the pounding in his head all the worse. 'An eastern

Christian?' he asked.

Gobras chuckled again, showing his yellow teeth. 'Not so, Master Italian. My faith is much older than that. My ancestors worshipped the true God centuries before the birth of Jesus, and a millennium before that of Mahommet.'

'A priest of Zoroaster then - of the old religion?'

Gobras inclined his head. 'We can talk of that later. Meantime, you should rest. The poison may still be in your system. Here, I have brought you a draught prepared by the lady, to be given to you when you wakened.'

Giovanni did not protest. Gritting his teeth against the pain, he sat up. He took the beaker of bubbling liquid that the priest held out to him, swallowed it in one gulp, and allowed his body to sink slowly back on the divan. His last thought as he drifted into disturbed sleep was to wonder by what means and for what reason Nadia had brought him to this dim cellar.

Nadia found Hassan in Jafar's room, though neither showed any enthusiasm for study. The tutor had not recovered from the trauma of his wound and his arm had begun to pain him again. He expressed the hope that he would be allowed to return to Maragha where, by resting until spring, he might regain his strength. Nadia agreed readily to his request and bade him make his preparations for departure. She instructed Hassan to assist and, once Jafar's arrangements were completed, to fulfil a few more simple commissions before showing his grandfather the way to Gobras's villa.

As the Il-khan and that part of his entourage who had left for Baghcha were not expected to return before the onset of spring, the militia had been withdrawn from several sectors of the castle. Only the occupied apartments were guarded, but Nadia took no comfort from the sentries' presence, fearing that any one of them might betray her to whomever had employed the bowman assassin. Her sense of foreboding did not leave her until, her preparations complete, she quit the castle again.

When she returned to the villa, Giovanni was asleep from the effects of the medicine she had prepared, but he was still restless. She bathed his face and neck then, with Gobras's help, raised his head and forced him to drink some water. He stirred and his eyelids fluttered, but he did not awake.

'Seeds of the poppy make a powerful remedy,' said the Patriarch with a chuckle.

'And a dangerous one too, in the wrong hands,' said Nadia. 'So you identified my preparation. How?'

'I was curious, and sampled the liquid,' the priest replied. 'My taste is sharp as well as my hearing.'

'And it gives you great delight to baffle me with your skill,' said Nadia. She seated herself on the edge of the divan beside the sleeping Venetian. 'You are right. Now I must hope I have not overestimated my own, and that his fever will continue to cool.'

'It has almost died away, if I am not mistaken,' said Gobras confidently. He touched Giovanni on the temple. 'Listen how his breathing slows and feel how the blood pounds less violently in his veins.'

'You would have made a great physician, Patriarch. Are you so sure he will recover?'

'We both know it, Nadia. It is not his fate to die unloved in this secret cellar.'

Nadia drew in her breath sharply. 'Why do you say that?'

'The human soul may glow as fiercely as the hearth, and reveal its secrets just as plainly. Stay with the Christian and look into *your* soul, Nadia, while I return to my fire.'

When Gobras had left her, Nadia studied the unconscious figure on the divan. The Italian's head was turned slightly towards her and, though his eyes were closed, she imagined them fixed on her with the same intensity she observed each time they conversed. The sensual desires it was in her nature to feel, but which she had long denied, stirred in her heart.

Giovanni moved. In his sleep, his left arm, which had rested on his blanket, rose and fell again on her lap. His good leg shifted towards her and Nadia felt his muscles tense against her side. Her flesh tingled and an aching emptiness opened in her inside. On impulse, she leant over him, laid her body on his impassive breast and pressed a kiss on his unresisting lips.

'If only my soul were free,' she murmured longingly, 'but it is not.'

*

XIII

Giovanni was dreaming again. Nadia knelt over him, her naked thighs resting on his belly and her breasts almost touching his chest. He could not see her face because it was hidden in the tresses that tumbled from her forehead and brushed his cheek and neck. He knew her only from the gammadion that hung by its gold chain from her delicate throat.

With mounting desire, he unfastened it and threw it aside, then he reached up and pulled her down, pressing her body against his and burying his face in her long hair. Now he could see her face clearly and he spoke her name over and over, at each pronouncement kissing her eyes and lips.

Just at the moment of ecstasy he awoke to find the dream partly realised and the object of his desire bending over him. She was wearing a green silk gown that emphasised to full effect the beauty of her face and figure. Her hair was fastened but loose strands fell from the clasp and touched his forehead. To his mortification, Giovanni realised he was in fact gripping her gold necklace fiercely. There was no sign of the priest.

'Nadia!'

She did not seem to mind the familiar form of address. 'So you are on the road to recovery, Sir Giovanni, and for that I am thankful,' she breathed. She raised her hand to her throat and rested her fingers gently on his. 'But you will surely strangle me if you do not release my fylfot straightway.'

Giovanni mumbled an apology and relaxed his grip on the cross. 'Have I been raving in my sleep, madam?'

'No more than anyone in your state might have done.'

Giovanni withdrew his fingers from the necklace and raised himself from the divan. His leg ached abominably again and his headache had returned. He was now over-conscious of his strange apparel, and that it may have been Nadia herself who divested him of his own and dressed his wound. Perhaps too she had also been present throughout his latest dream.

She seemed to read his thoughts. 'Your wives should be content that you dream so amorously of them when so far from home,' she remarked with a coquettish smile.

'I have no wife,' replied Giovanni in embarrassment, '- and Christians are allowed but one. It is only that lately, in my profession, I have not found time for courting.'

' 'Tis a great pity,' said Nadia, avoiding his eyes. She sat on the divan at his side and he felt the warmth of her body next to his. 'Yet it seems that, despite your denial, you have found a mistress here in Persia, since you whisper her name so fondly in your sleep.'

Giovanni's heart beat wildly and his mouth was dry. 'And what name did I whisper?' he stammered.

'I did not properly catch it, though the sound was not unlike mine,' she laughed. 'Think nothing more of it. The ramblings of delirium are easily forgotten.'

Giovanni struggled to free his mind of the wild, sensuous thoughts that were taking control of it. She knew of his desire and was playing with it. In spite of that, and of his pain, he wanted her as he had never wanted any woman before. He would have taken another in his arms, and he would have taken her too if he had dared.

'It seems that your debt to me is paid, madam,' he said. The throbbing in his leg was easing again. 'Not many days ago you thanked me for preserving your son's life. Now it seems you have saved mine, though I cannot believe I was the intended victim. Perhaps by chance I placed himself in the line of the arrow.'

Nadia shook her head. 'I fear not,' she said, 'though I may wish otherwise.'

'The priest spoke of poison, and of secret enemies, but would say no more....'

'Gobras is discreet,' she smiled, 'but there are good reasons for his silence. His people are often persecuted for their beliefs, and he is wise not to trust strangers, even when they appear as friends. I will tell you my suspicions, but we should converse in more comfortable surroundings. We shall be given adequate warning if anyone approaches the villa.'

'Are we in Tabriz?'

'Perhaps an hour's ride from there.'

'But why have you brought me here rather than to my quarters in the castle?'

'Your fever was high. It is a fair distance to the castle and you may not have reached it alive. I was afraid too that, whoever your enemy is, he might be lurking there and make a second attempt. In any case, though the royal apartments are quiet, I could not have treated you there. You are a man and a foreigner. It would be unseemly for me to go to your room.'

'Then I am grateful for your decision,' said Giovanni.

' 'Twas no more than a duty.' She rose abruptly. 'But come. Show me whether you can walk.'

Giovanni threw off the blanket and eased his legs to the floor. It was bare stone, and cold in spite of the warmth of the fire. The movement caused the violent throbbing to return to his leg as the blood began to flow normally, and again the pain was scarcely bearable. He could feel Nadia's eyes watching him.

'I see that the leg still troubles you,' she said. 'Come, can you manage a few steps if I lend you my shoulder? When we reach the next apartment I'll see what is to be done.'

Giovanni allowed her to place his arm round her neck and to take some of his weight on her shoulders. His pride was hurt but he was grateful for her support. They climbed the steps. Behind the pillars was a passageway, just wide enough to accommodate two persons in close proximity. Only the diminishing grey light from behind and a chink from an opening ahead broke the pitch darkness. Despite her warmth at his side, he felt the fetid dampness of an underground tunnel.

'It's only a short distance more,' Nadia whispered when they reached a point where the floor began to slope upwards. 'Stretch your hand out in front of you and after six paces you will feel the touch of metal.'

Giovanni did as she bid him. He counted to six and felt his probing fingers encounter a smooth surface. Nadia touched a spring and the panel slid back with a metallic creak to reveal a long, partly-carpeted room. At the near end was a raised brick hearth in which another fire burned. Close to the fire, Gobras sat motionless on a pile of cushions, his bony fingers clutching the mane of his white hound.

Released at noon from his obligation to the tutor, Hassan lost no time in obeying his mother's instructions. The corridors were quiet and he passed from his own room to Giovanni's without encountering anyone other than the familiar guards, who saluted him in friendly fashion. His tiny bow hung across his chest and he carried a bag in which he had stowed a few valued possessions, including his splendid chess pieces.

The Venetian's larger boxes had already been packed and removed, but some pieces of clothing lay on the divan. Symbols of the Christian faith still decorated the walls and furniture. Hassan had not previously entered Giovanni's quarters and he dallied there for longer than he intended, fascinated by the portraits and icons. In particular, he was drawn to the carved wooden cross with the naked Christ figure stretched helplessly across its arms. He had no understanding of Christian beliefs and rituals, but found it strange that the followers of its teaching had nailed their god to a tree, and incomprehensible that the god himself had permitted this barbaric humiliation. Yet he had grown to admire Giovanni and did not believe him capable of a cruel act in the name of religion. He decided the crucifixion must have an esoteric explanation.

Prominent among the other artefacts was an icon depicting a man in splendid apparel, sitting on a golden throne and holding in his right hand a golden sceptre. Hassan had seen nothing quite like it before and stared at the portrait in admiration. At length, remembering his mission, he packed it in his own bag along with the clothing and other items. He slung the bag over his free right shoulder, glanced quickly round the room, and was about to quit it when he spotted an object that had fallen on the floor. It was another icon depicting a mother and child. The bag was already fastened but sensing the portrait might have some special meaning for Giovanni and wishing to please him, he picked it up and pushed it inside his leather corslet.

He made his way to his grandfather's apartment, but Kartir was nowhere to be seen. Unable to fulfil his mother's wishes in precise detail, he decided no harm would be done if he went back later. He visited the armoury, where he refilled his quiver with diminutive arrows and armed himself with two swords. The shorter, a scimitar, he tucked unsheathed into his belt, the other, a man-sized rapier, he hung in its scabbard over his left shoulder, beside his bow.

Thus armed, he returned to Kartir's quarters but they were still deserted. As it was by his reckoning late afternoon, and despite his mother's charge that he should be the guide, Hassan reasoned that the viceroy must have already set out on the mountain path. If this were so, he would receive a reprimand if he did not overtake him before he reached the Patriarch's villa. After all, Kartir was an important man and had been to Tabriz before. It was inconceivable that he did not know the way.

Assured that he had made the correct decision, Hassan went to the stables and saddled three fresh horses. Two grooms glanced up from a game of dice but did not interfere. They grunted a greeting and resumed their pastime. Having fastened the larger sword to the pommel of one saddle and tied his bag to a second, Hassan mounted the smallest animal and, leading the others, left the castle.

He made his way through the Jewish quarter to the nearest city gate, but had scarcely traversed two streets when he found his way barred by an angry crowd, armed with swords, stones or heavy sticks. Hostilities had broken out between two or more factions. In the middle of the road, one fellow was struggling in the arms of two captors and putting up spirited resistance. He had almost succeeded in freeing himself when he was struck on the knees with a cudgel and crumpled to the ground. Other rioters moved in, savagely kicking his head and beating his body with their sticks.

Close by lay yet another man, his head and body twisted in an unnatural position. Hassan thought of going to his assistance but was deterred by a group of ruffians that had crossed the street in front of him, hauling their captives by the feet or the hair and pausing occasionally to strike them with whatever weapons were to hand. About twenty rioters had possession of a garden on one side of the street and were hurling stones at the houses opposite.

Hassan's young heart beat in terror. He had never before seen a crowd out of control. The violence made no sense to him. The rival gangs were indistinguishable. He urged his pony sideways into the shadow of a building, looking around desperately for an alternative route to the walls.

Just then, a detachment of soldiers wearing Arghun's colours passed him, moved in on the fighting and began driving the mob back along the roadway. No one seemed interested in him or his three horses and, with a thankful glance at heaven, Hassan turned them into a side road.

The way to the west and north gates was blocked. The shortest route now lay in the direction of the commercial quarter and from there to the south wall. His alternative was to return to the castle, make his way from there to the east gate, join the Silk Road and double back westwards. Guessing he might attract unwelcome attention among the shops and bazaars, he decided to adopt the latter option.

With the curses of the rioters resounding in his ears, he spurred the pony back along the road he had come and soon arrived at the field where he often practised his archery. He pulled up with a start. Four men had just emerged from the castle gate. Two rode in the open while the others were on foot and in the shadow of the overhanging wall. With relief, Hassan recognised both riders as servants of his stepfather, and was about to call out a greeting when their companions emerged into the daylight.

As he gazed at the four, Hassan's pulse began to race, and sweat broke out on his forehead. It was not the third man who caused the growing apprehension in his breast. He was Prince Timur. However, the fourth was short and fat with a stubbly grey beard, and he wore a turban that fell untidily over his eyebrows. He was Baidu's friend, whom Hassan knew only as Nizam.

Nadia touched a raised section of the panel and it slid back into place, concealing the tunnel.

'How is our guest?' asked Gobras. He raised his head in the direction of the newcomers.

Giovanni realised that the old priest was blind. His eyes seemed to stare straight ahead at the fire, and there was a grey film over them which the Venetian had often noticed in persons of great age who had become partly or wholly sightless.

'Signor di Montecervino's leg is very painful,' said Nadia, 'and, if you'll permit me to abuse your hospitality for an hour or two longer, I shall attempt a cure.'

'You are welcome to my humble apartment for as long as you need,' said the priest graciously. He waved his hand in the direction of a divan that lay against the wall below a window. 'May Ahura Mazda guide your hand.'

Nadia supported Giovanni as far as the divan and bade him be seated. 'Do you trust me as a friend, Giovanni ....' she asked.

'Madam, I ...,' Giovanni began, stammering a little. Her nearness still made him uneasy.

' ... trust me enough to put your life in my hands?'

'It is already in your hands, I'll swear.'

'Then will you also swear on your honour as a Christian never to breathe a word to my husband of what you are about to witness?'

'I will swear it by Christ's blood and the Cross on which He died.'

'Good,' said Nadia. Her voice was more gentle than he had previously heard. 'Will you lie back on the bed and give me your whole attention.'

Giovanni obeyed. His eyes sought hers and held them. He knew now that, not only did he trust her, but he loved her with a passion that exceeded his love of prince and country. Yet it was a passion he could never satisfy. He was in Venice no longer. Even if, according to Christian teaching, Nadia's marriage was no true one in the eyes of God, she was the wife of another man, a ruler at whose hands he could expect no mercy were even his smallest indiscretion to be discovered.

Nadia sat on the edge of the divan. When she spoke, her voice was little more than a whisper. 'Fix your eyes on my necklace and on the sun's image you see at the centre.'

Giovanni did so. The hooked cross lay snugly between the gentle swellings in her gown. He could see the engraving at its centre quite clearly, and, as he watched spellbound, it appeared to grow to twice its normal size - a living sun with rays so bright that they engulfed the whole room.

'Watch how it glistens in the firelight,' she went on in the same bewitching intonation. 'It has the power to heal.'

He began to think it might be true, what Arghun had said in his state of semi- intoxication, that she was a witch. He no longer cared. The gammadion held him in a spell from which he could not escape, a pleasant drowsiness through which he could hear her voice coming from a great distance.

'Your eyes are filled with sleep. As they close, your pain is melting away. Do not resist. Think not of the pain, but only of the warmth of the sun's healing rays.'

Giovanni was unsure whether she spoke the words in reality or whether they were the voice of his own desire to sleep and forget the hot throbbing in his thigh and the pounding of blood in his head. As this thought occurred, so the pain and throbbing seemed to lessen. He closed his eyes and opened them again what seemed only a second later.

He sat up with a start. His headache was gone. His leg still hurt but it was no more than an inconvenience. Nadia stood at the foot of the bed. The fire was now low in the hearth and Gobras sat motionless on his cushions, keeping sightless watch over it.

'How long have I been asleep?'

'An hour - no more,' she smiled.

Giovanni regarded her tenderly and with a certain amount of awe. 'What is this magic you are able to work,' he asked. 'A few moments ago I was ill and in pain. Now ....'

'If there was any magic, it was in you,' she interrupted. 'The human body has a great capacity for healing itself. I had but to divert your mind from the pain with this pretty necklace. Your limbs relaxed, you slept, - and sleep is a panacea. Now you must have something to eat. For a whole day you have taken no nourishment, other than the plain water I forced into your throat and a draught made from poppy seeds.'

Gobras rang a bell and a woman appeared bearing a tray of food. There were assorted meats and fish, a few loaves, some fruit and a flagon of wine. Nadia poured a cup of wine and broke some bread into it. She gave this mixture to Gobras who supped it slowly.

Giovanni needed no further invitation to satisfy his hunger. 'Was I so ill?' he asked between mouthfuls.

'Near death.'

'This house with its secret cellar ...?'

'It is the home of the Patriarch of the Gabars, and is both villa and temple. In olden times, the followers of Zoroaster built fire temples where they made oblations to Ahura Mazda and other gods. For centuries their practices have been forbidden or, at the very least, discouraged. The temples have been demolished or have fallen into decay. As I told you already, these people continue to practice their religion out of public view, and it's in places like this that they offer their prayers and perform their rituals. They also come to Gobras for spiritual advice. Some came yesterday. It was best they did not see you, so we brought you to the room behind the panel. It has another secret door to the outside.'

'But you told me you were a Muslim - that you did not follow the old religion,' Giovanni protested.

'That is true,' said Nadia. 'However, I do not hold with persecution. These are my people, whatever their beliefs. They mean no harm and they cause none. In any event, I am persuaded there is only one God. I can deny neither Gabars nor Christians freedom to worship Him in their own way.'

Giovanni offered no challenge to this avowal. He helped himself to more food and there was silence while he ingested it. He poured some wine and drank it thirstily.

'Do you feel better?' Nadia enquired when he had drained the cup. 'Well enough to ride?'

'To ride, madam?'

'I am determined to follow my husband without delay,' she said. 'There is a plot against him, of that I am sure. And someone wishes to prevent his alliance with your country - wishes it strongly enough to make this attempt on your life.'

'But suppose I were not the intended target - if the arrow was meant for Hassan?'

Nadia shook her head. 'My instincts tell me otherwise. Arghun has long suspected Gaikatu, Baidu, or one of the other princes of conspiring against him.'

'You warned me against Gaikatu before. But why would either he or Baidu wish to prevent the alliance, or to kill me? If their ambition is to rule, only Arghun stands in the way. I do not.'

'Perhaps they see the alliance as a threat,' Nadia ventured. 'Were your proposed campaign against the Egyptian to be successful, it would give my husband prestige. He would then be more difficult to dislodge.'

'Or else the princes are in league with the Egyptians,' suggested Giovanni. 'The Mamluk sultan might be very grateful to an ally who drove a wedge between Persia and Christendom.'

'It may be as you say,' agreed Nadia. 'It might explain what puzzles me.'

'Madam?'

'Mongol warriors do not tip their arrows with poison,' she said. 'There is no need. You have seen how skilful Hassan is with a bow and he is ten years old. I have seen a man bring down another at two hundred paces. If a Mongol bowman wished to take your life, he would not have missed. Nor would he have relied on the drunken aftermath of the hunt to disguise the deed. There is a subtle mind behind this. It was meant as accidental death, not murder, but they did not count on my intervention.'

'Perhaps,' said Giovanni. Her argument was convincing, though he was perplexed by her apparent support for his cause. Success of his mission would benefit Arghun but the benefits to the Muslim people were more nebulous.

He watched her closely. She half turned towards the priest as if meaning to seek his opinion but then seemed to change her mind. Giovanni followed the direction of her gaze to the metal panel behind the hearth. He saw her eyelashes flicker and a single tear fall on her dusky cheek. Instinctively he reached out his hand and touched the sleeve of her gown.

Nadia did not withdraw the sleeve. With her free hand she wiped the tear away and turned towards him with lowered eyes. 'Giovanni, I am afraid, and greatly in need of a friend!'

'Madam?'

'My father always believed the Mongol conquest of Persia to be not only the will of God but in the common good. In the days before Hulegu's invasion, Persia was under the control of men who, though professing the Muslim faith, were corrupt and godless. Hulegu destroyed them. My father became prosperous under his patronage. He enjoyed Hulegu's confidence and because of his loyalty was posted to be viceroy of Kerman.'

'Much of this you have told me already, madam.'

Still Nadia did not withdraw her sleeve. 'When I was a girl,' she went on, 'my father pledged me in marriage to a boy called Mahmoud Hassan who had been my childhood companion. I did not love him as a woman loves a sweetheart, but I loved my father and was eager to obey him. Shortly after we were wed, my husband was conscripted to the Mongol army. I never saw him after that.'

'I am truly sorry, Nadia.'

'By then, Hulegu was dead and Abaqa was Il-khan. Abaqa feared an uprising in the south and invaded. My father could not prevent my becoming a hostage. I was forcibly married to Abaqa's brother, Teguder, and when he died, under Mongol law I became Arghun's bride. In the meantime, I had given birth to Hassan.

'For six years, since Arghun's accession, Persia has been largely at peace. It begins to enjoy prosperity again. There is tolerance. And as long as my husband lives and is able to keep our enemies at bay, the prosperity will grow. The tolerance will remain.

'Arghun has promised me freedom on his death. I do not love him, but I fulfil my duty to him as best I can because he is a good man and fond of my son. Persia matters to me, but Hassan matters more.'

Giovanni's heart beat more strongly in his chest at this confession. He was filled with hope that one day he might be free to pursue her. But there was despair in his heart too. Arghun was no more than forty years old and, barring accident or assassination, might expect to reign for many years still.

'My life in Tabriz is not unbearable,' continued Nadia, tearful again, 'but I'm sick of intrigue, of being continually on my guard against those who would betray and destroy the kingdom. The Patriarch understands my inner thoughts, but he is an old man and unable to bring me the comfort a woman needs. Arghun protects me. He bends to my occasional wish, and I do believe he loves me in his way. As his wife I have influence. His brother and cousins dare not attack me openly. I have servants who obey me; I have spies who bring me information for a few silver coins; but there is no one I can truly call a friend.'

She looked so appealing that Giovanni again forgot himself. The hand that had held her sleeve now slipped down and grasped her hand.

The Patriarch sat as a statue, blind and unaware of his indiscretion.

'I will be your friend, Nadia,' he breathed, 'and much more if you desire it. If your son is in need of a father, I will be he.'

Slowly she pulled her arm away. 'I am grateful for your friendship,' she said, ' but for the time being I can neither give nor take more.'

*

XIV

Hassan pulled his charges into the shadows. He had not been seen. His heart was racing again. He instinctively disliked the little man, Nizam, and was sure his presence could mean only treachery.

'Your news is most welcome, Qutlugh,' said Timur. He took a bag from his belt and threw it to one of the riders.

The Mongol officer caught the bag and Hassan heard the chink of money.

'The unrest has begun, General,' he said. 'Blame for the light coinage is already falling on the Jews. The Muslims are exacting compensation in the Jewish quarter. A skirmish here, a beating or two there. No one will suspect it was planned.'

'Since one cousin is already in Baghdad!' laughed Nizam sardonically. 'And with the other halfway to Rum by now, both are as innocent as a eunuch's stump.'

'But take care events don't proceed too hastily,' said Timur, ignoring him. 'The evidence against ad-Daulah and his favourites must be stronger still. The Wazir has powerful friends. Unless the emirs are convinced of his treason, they'll not act.'

'It won't be long,' answered Qutlugh. 'Our agents are already at work planting false accounts. Taghachar may keep order for the present, but when his platoons discover their pay has been misappropriated, they'll quickly change sides.'

'I wish I understood Taghachar better,' mused Timur. 'He appears to carry out his duties with greater loyalty than ever. Continue to use the dinars wisely, Qutlugh, and if you can expose the city commander's weaknesses, so much the better. You understand my meaning.'

Qutlugh pushed the moneybag into his boot and saluted.

Nizam turned to the second rider and addressed him. 'I would've been happier to see the Christian's body,' he growled, 'but it seems the attempt failed.'

'You may yet see him a corpse,' the man replied. 'The woman couldn't have saved him.'

'By the pox, nothing is certain, Orda,' cried Qutlugh. 'This wife of the Il-khan dabbles in magic.'

'He's dead!' sneered Orda. 'When she returned to the city this morning, she was alone, except for the child.'

'She arrived alone!' screeched Nizam, his face becoming livid. 'Why didn't you tell me this before? And if the Christian is dead, what has she done with his body?'

'How should I know?' shrugged Orda. 'I was given no orders concerning the woman.'

'Calm yourself, Nizam,' said Timur, 'or your veins'll explode.'

Nizam scowled but calmed down.

'So, Orda,' enquired Timur, 'can you say where Nadia and her boy are now?'

'Still in the city, I think,' said Orda. 'As I've said, I wasn't detailed to spy on them. The woman went to her father, and the boy to his tutor. That's all I know. The Christian is either dead or dying. Even if he's not, the plan can't be tied to us. Who will believe the wound anything but an accident?'

'You're right, Orda,' said Timur. Another bag of coins changed hands. 'Still, you had better disappear for a while. The air is fresher east of Qazvin, or so I hear.'

'How does all this affect the plan?' enquired Nizam.

'Not at all, as far as I'm concerned,' Timur replied. 'If the Christian is dead, he can't make a treaty. If not, there'll be another opportunity. And we should certainly watch the woman. What's the matter, Nizam? Cold feet?'

'Nadia is not to be harmed,' said Nizam nervously. 'Not here in Tabriz.'

'Keep your turban on,' said Timur coarsely. 'I said watch, not lay her, much as I'd like to!' He lowered his voice, but not so much as to prevent Hassan overhearing. 'Arghun has already left for Baghcha. Isn't it time you ....'

He broke off suddenly as one of Hassan's horses, tired of remaining still on a short tether, whinnied and shook its tackle noisily. Timur whipped round with a sword in his hand.

Hassan gave a cry of terror, kicked his pony violently and urged it into a canter.

'After him!' yelled Timur, ignoring Nizam's protests and waving his sword at his two mounted henchman. 'It's Nadia's bastard - behind the pillar! He has overheard us. Don't let him reach the city gate! Delay, but don't harm him!'

Bent low and hugging the pony's neck tightly with his one free hand, Hassan crossed the open ground at a fast gallop and turned into a street of colourful villas. He could feel resistance in the tethers of the other two animals and could hear the angry shouts of the Mongol riders as they gave chase. He did not look back. The east gate could only be minutes away, but, even if he reached it, where would he go? Hampered by the two larger horses, it would only be a matter of time before Qutlugh and Orda caught up with him.

He released the tether and kicked his pony hard on the flank. Ahead of him, the east gate was wide open and beckoning. Now he could make his escape. Alone he could easily outpace the heavier riders. But his elation was short-lived. Freed so suddenly, the two horses collided and tangled in the loose reins. The pony reared. Hassan, caught unawares, would have been thrown but for his hold of his mount's neck. Qutlugh, who was heading the pursuit, overtook him and seized the pony's mane and bridle.

At that moment, four Persian merchants emerged from a side road. They were middle-aged, dressed in plain jubbahs and turbans, and walked beside their heavily-loaded beasts. Their leader was a man of average height with a neat grey beard and piercing black eyes.

'Hold there,' said he with authority. 'Leave the boy alone!'

'Mind your own business, old man!' cried Qutlugh. He raised one arm to protect his face from Hassan's flailing fists, but kept firm hold of the pony's bridle.

'It *is* my business when I see two grown men molest a mere child,' said the newcomer angrily. 'What has the boy done?'

'We caught him stealing horses,' said Orda glibly, catching up and regarding the travellers with contempt.

'That's a lie,' fired Hassan, now struggling in Qutlugh's grip. The Mongol had managed to partly unseat him and was trying to pull him free of the single stirrup that held him to the saddle.

'If he has stolen, there are laws in Tabriz to punish him,' said the Persian.

'I've stolen nothing,' gasped Hassan. 'These men are assassins. They've tried to poison the Venetian ambassador and are now planning to hurt my mother.'

Qutlugh hit him in the face and drew blood. The merchant took a step back and pulled a short sword from beneath his jubbah. Behind him, his companions did likewise.

'Release the boy,' cried the Persian grimly.

Qutlugh bared his teeth in a savage grin. He dropped Hassan to the ground and reached for his own scimitar. Orda let go of his mount's reins. He too drew his weapon and aimed a savage cut at the merchant's head. With surprising agility, Hassan's would-be protector dodged the blow, took another step back and stood in line with his friends, his guard raised.

Orda spat an expletive and both Mongols launched themselves into the attack. It was two against four. The odds seemed unfair, but the Mongols were taller and stronger, and none of the Persians was young. The fight swung from side to side. Qutlugh and Orda lunged and swept. Their antagonists dodged and parried.

Hassan sat up dizzily, wiping blood from his nose. Where there were six men, he saw twelve. In his humiliation, his one thought was to escape and find his mother. Tears welled up in his eyes and he rubbed them away with dirty and bloody fists. This cleared his vision and he saw that Qutlugh and one of the Persians was wounded. However, the merchants were tiring and unless the battle was ended soon, the Mongols' youthfulness and superior strength would win the day.

Through his tears, Hassan saw that his pony had strayed some distance. Its saddle had been torn from its back and lay only a few paces away with the miniature bow still attached to it. Most of his supply of arrows had fallen out in the struggle, but two remained, partially embedded in the leather of his quiver.

He scrambled onto his knees and crawled towards the fallen saddle. He unhooked the bow, tugged one of his last arrows free and with trembling fingers fitted it to the string.

Orda's sweeping scimitar felled one of the Persians and he turned to fend off a blow from one of the others just as Hassan shot. The Mongol's grim jaw fell and his eyes widened in horror as the tiny arrow pierced his neck just below the ear. He dropped his sword and was dead before his hands reached the shaft to pull it free.

Now totally outnumbered, Qutlugh swung wildly at his three remaining antagonists and retreated towards his horse. Blood dripped from a slash in his forearm. Two of the Persians would have pursued him but their leader called them back.

'Let him go, and look after Khalid,' he said, replacing the short sword underneath his jubbah. 'He badly needs a physician!' He extended his right hand and helped Hassan to his feet. 'And what is your name, young warrior?' he added gravely, with a glance at the miniature bow.

Hassan's tears had dried, but his nose still hurt where Qutlugh had struck him. He touched it gingerly, tracing his finger over the blood clot that was forming on his upper lip. His left knee stung painfully where he had scratched it in the fall. He wanted only to feel his mother's soothing hand as she applied one of her magical embrocations.

'Hassan,' he replied. 'I am Mahmoud Hassan, son of his majesty Arghun, Il-khan of Persia. Who are you?'

'I am Umid Malikshah, son of no one in particular, a trader in fine carpets,' said the Persian. His tone was friendly, his smile reassuring. 'And, by the beard of the Prophet, Fate has a strange way of bringing people together. I do believe you are the grandson of His Excellency Ahmed Kartir, Governor of Kerman. My friends and I are newly arrived in Tabriz and are anxious to speak with him.'

'Hassan is taking his time,' said Nadia. She seemed affected by a new mood and began pacing the room. At every slight sound from the floor above she glanced expectantly towards the door.

'He will be here soon enough,' said Giovanni reassuringly. 'There has scarcely been time for him to fulfil the commission you gave him.'

'You are right,' Nadia said, 'only a mother always worries.'

'He will be here soon,' Giovanni repeated, but he was uneasy. The day was wearing on. The fire had almost gone out and the Patriarch had not called for it to be rekindled. The old man seemed to be asleep.

To pass the time, Giovanni had asked to hear the legend of the gammadion and Nadia had consented to tell it. Having finished her narrative, she had taken off the necklace and given it to him. He still held it in his hand now and he turned it over slowly, running his fingers over the hooked arms, admiring again the beauty and ingenuity of their design.

Nadia had stopped pacing and was watching him. He returned the gammadion to her with an apology.

'It's nothing but a pretty ornament,' he remarked, but as he spoke he felt a chill of foreboding. 'As I look at it now, the hooks bend to the right. Turn it round and they will bend to the left. I acknowledge the miracle of your voice, but there is no magic in the gold.'

Nadia weighed the necklace in her palm. 'Perhaps, Giovanni,' she said thoughtfully. 'But, for all that, I'm sometimes tormented with thoughts that the symbol holds meaning for my life - for good or for ill.'

Kartir had gone to the mosque. Despite his avowed pragmatism, there were times when he felt the need for spiritual uplift and guidance. It was also the third day of Shawwal and Umid had promised to meet him in the great square on the first. He had made the acquaintance of the merchant's proxy in Tabriz and had waited with him in vain the previous two afternoons. A two day delay in a business man's schedule was hardly cause for concern, but Kartir was by now eager for his friend's intelligence. He badly needed his advice.

His reception in Tabriz had astounded him and shattered his every illusion. Arghun had welcomed him as a friend and entertained him with lavish hospitality. His daughter was comfortably quartered and treated with respect, even honour. The child he had last seen as an infant had become a handsome youth and dutiful son.

On the subject of Nadia's abduction, the Il-khan was apologetic, judging Abaqa wrong to doubt Kartir's loyalty, and condemning the deed which had negated all of Hulegu's trust.

Kartir's astonishment was all the greater when the Il-khan promised that Nadia would be released from the obligation to enter into further marriages and would be, on his death, free to return to her family.

He realised the Il-khan was a man of scarcely forty years of age, and that it could be many years before Nadia was returned to Kerman, but that did not diminish his joy at the news. Even if he were dead, Muslim sons cared for their mothers, and by then Hassan would be fully grown.

He had politely declined the invitation to spend a whole winter at Baghcha. The northern climate was much colder than he was used to, and he was afraid his health would not tolerate long exposure to the dampness of the coastal plains.

'A month only then?' Arghun had said persuasively. 'Remain with your daughter here and come with her when she leaves to join me.'

Kartir had accepted the compromise. There would be time for him to get to know his grandson while he awaited the arrival of Umid in Tabriz.

Nadia's revelations had turned his whole body cold, leaving him empty and sick in the belly. How could he have been so completely fooled? The Mazdaites were a close community, fearful of Muslim authority, and he had penetrated it too easily. His eagerness to believe had fogged his judgement, and he had been compromised.

Now the mysterious attack on Hassan took on new meaning. Kartir had dismissed the idea of Nizam's involvement as laughable, but now it seemed less so. Were the kidnapping and the Venetian's death necessary elements in a plot to deprive Arghun of the throne, and did Nizam have a role in both? And, if he had escaped the watchful eye of the merchant network to come to Tabriz, what would he do next?

Kartir left the mosque. He had to find the boy. Whatever new intelligence Umid might have gathered, he had to tell Nadia of his suspicions. Her safety and that of her son were paramount. It was best that they should leave the city. He retrieved his sandals and, distracted now by new doubts and old memories, strolled barefoot across the great square.

How many years was it since he had given hospitality to the Italian jewel merchant and his excitable nephew? They too had been Venetians. How old had Nadia been - seven or eight? She had adopted the youth as her own, had pledged him undying love and had followed him everywhere in the residency, listening wide-eyed and innocent to his dreams of visiting China. Then when the Polos' caravan had left, she had climbed on his knee and whispered how one day she would go and live in the Christian city of lakes and lagoons.

He wondered if she remembered. Had he only imagined a hint of warmth in her expression and a softness in her eye when she spoke of the wounded ambassador? Fate was indeed capricious, but would she be cruel enough to tear his child from him a second time, moreover to give her to a man who denied the message of the Qur'an?

As he tortured himself with this sudden unpleasant thought, the viceroy became aware of a group of travellers coming out from the shadow of the tower, and that one of them was gesticulating furiously in his direction. Almost at the same moment as he recognised Umid, a small boy, who had been riding at the dishevelled merchant's rear, dismounted from his pony and began running across the square towards him.

*

XV

Though Arghun had no inkling of Timur's treachery when he took the road to Maragha, he was already aware of his cousin's liaison with the Egyptian sultan. He would give Baidu just enough rope to hang himself. Unknown to any of the princes, he had mobilised two regiments in preparation for an assault on the Syrian capital. They lay within a day's ride of Persia's western border and their commander awaited orders at Van.

Arghun had waited patiently for a reply to his letter to the King of France but when, after half a year, it remained unanswered, his patience had turned to frustration. An incursion by the Golden Horde into Armenia in the spring had demanded a response, and this engagement had diverted his attention from his chief objectives, to gain revenge for his grandfather's defeat at the hands of the Mamluks and to extend his borders to the shores of the Mediterranean.

With the Armenian threat gone, he was ready to resume his war against the Mamluks. If only he could trust the Christians.

The arrival of Giovanni di Montecervino in Tabriz, alone, and apparently with the long awaited answer to his own diplomatic overtures, was just the omen he had needed. Arghun had studied the despatches carefully and taken every opportunity to test the sincerity of the bearer. His agents had confirmed that the Christian knights in the Syrian fortresses were under pressure but were not ready to quit Asia Minor without a fight. Satisfied that Western support would be forthcoming, he had repaired what he saw as fragile relations with his governor in the south and was ready to commit his armies in the great struggle.

It was almost noon. The chill of the early morning had gone and Arghun could sense the warmth of the late autumn sun through his thick corslet and tunic. He began to feel uncommonly alive. From Urmia he would send sealed orders to Van for a spring advance as originally planned, and once at Baghcha would conclude the Christian treaty and mobilise additional troops. Ghazan would drive the Chagatai back, would patch up his supposed quarrel with his deputy governor, and would throw his six regiments into the war. If Gaikatu chose to oppose them in

Rum, he would be crushed, as would Baidu.

Once his kingdom was secure, he would turn his attention to matters of religion. He would erect temples to his own faith and a mosque or two to show his gratitude to the Muslims. He would not forget the Christians and Jews either. Their temples were dismal places when set against the splendour of the Buddhist shrines in the cities of Khorasan. He would enlist the finest sculptors and metalworkers in Persia to build statues and mould artefacts honouring their prophets.

Men should honour the gods of other faiths as well as their own. Why should they not do it together? Nadia was right. Arghun could not remember her exact words, but she had told him the gods were the same whatever men called them. Perhaps he could found a new religion embracing all the others. The idea that he would be remembered in history for that added to Arghun's feeling of well-being, and he almost forgot the pain of recent months. Such was his faith in Nadia's ability that he began to believe again he would enjoy a long life.

That faith was born of more than ten years acquaintance with his wife's unusual talents. Arghun had inherited his forebears superstitious nature and did not doubt for a moment that these talents had a mystical and supernatural origin. At first, he had been attracted to Nadia by carnal desire. Gradually, desire was replaced by admiration, and admiration by awe. She continued to visit his dreams as a mistress, but in his reality she inhabited a plane far above weakness of the flesh. To Arghun, she was physician, adviser, priestess and goddess in one perfect human form. Sober, he worshipped her; drunk, he feared the reproach of her dark eyes. In his experience, hostages suffered their bondage in silent resentment. Nadia tolerated his fickle tempers with good grace and an understanding smile.

Arghun knew the Maragha road well. He had visited the observatory several times, most recently the previous autumn when he had listened with interest to Shirazi expounding on the alchemist's creed. The Master had introduced him to an Indian sage who claimed to have found the secret of life. It was the stark reminder of his mortality - the motto cut in the stone of the Turkish tower - which prompted him to enquire if death could really be conquered.

'The artisan who cut words in that tower was wise, Your Majesty,' Shirazi had said. 'It is only when a man is reminded how short life is that he truly lives it.'

'You are forever philosophising about the nature of life, Master Shirazi,' the Il-khan replied. 'I wonder you don't spend more time experiencing it rather than shutting yourself up here and looking at the stars.'

'I travel, Your Majesty,' said Shirazi. 'A month ago I was in Khorasan at the request of your son, Prince Ghazan. And you will recall we met at Lake Urmia only last year. I have been to Hormuz, to Arabia, and to India. Yet it is in this observatory, as much as in those faraway places, that life in all its many facets is to be found. Those who work here, young and old, come from all corners of the nation and the world.'

Arghun sighed. 'But all are mortal, Master Philosopher. Not one has found the secret of eternal youth.'

Shirazi tugged at his beard. 'The alchemists who search for the Philosopher's Stone would have us believe the secret lies therein,' he said. 'They say its power is infinite - even the power to cure sickness and prolong youthfulness. Allah in his wisdom may one day grant that we find the means of transmuting base metal, but I fear that men are forever doomed to grow old and die. And whether we remain healthy or not depends on the skill of our physicians. That was my father's philosophy!'

'So you deny the existence of an elixir?'

'I will not go that far, Your Majesty, but I am a sceptic.' Shirazi eyed the Il-khan meaningfully. 'Were it to be given to great men like yourself to live forever, I should nevertheless be content to grow old with my friends. Else the world would become an overly crowded place.'

'By the pox, I agree with you.' The Il-khan laughed. He clapped Shirazi jovially on the back. ' An eternity of fornication! There's a prospect that my deviate brother would find to his liking, I'll swear. However, to take up your implication - if kings alone were to be immortal, mankind would greatly benefit. Would you not say so?'

'I shall not argue to the contrary,' said Shirazi. The muscles of his face twitched slightly, but he did not lose his serious expression. 'But if Your Majesty is intent upon pursuing the matter further, I can recommend to you an Indian mystic presently at Maragha. He claims to have retained his youth and strength through meditation and the regular swallowing of a potion he has discovered.'

The Indian was a man of indeterminate age. He was short and round of figure. His skin was nearly black, but that could be judged only from his bare, podgy arms, which lay crossed on his breast when he was silent, and fat hands, which gesticulated expressively when he spoke. Almost nothing could be seen of his face, which was concealed behind the blackest of beards. Only a nose and a pair of the brightest eyes were in evidence.

'Is it true you have discovered a formula that can prolong life?' Arghun enquired.

'I can recommend it to you, O Most Great and Noble Majesty.' The Indian spread his arms wide and, despite his girth, bowed so low that his beard touched the ground.

'You have it with you?'

The Indian produced a tiny casket from the folds of his robe. Arghun noted it was decorated with a symbol resembling the one Nadia wore around her neck.

'Is it your desire to taste my humble preparation, O Great One?' asked the sage, removing the lid and holding out the box. It contained a grey paste.

Arghun dipped his forefinger in the mixture, raised it to his nose and sniffed suspiciously. 'The odour is passable,' he remarked.

'Your Majesty may safely taste it,' said the Indian. He scooped up a small sample of the paste and licked it from his finger.

Arghun waited a few moment and, seeing no harm befall the Indian, he sniffed the paste before depositing some on his tongue. 'There is a sweetness about it,' he said. 'What does it contain?'

'It is a blend of sulphur, quicksilver and honey in secret proportions, O Greatest of Kings,' said the sage, closing the box. 'To be effective, it must be taken in small doses over many months, in addition to a normal diet. If it is Your Majesty's desire, I shall manufacture a supply for you.'

Arghun had returned to Tabriz with sufficient of the mixture to last until the winter solstice for by then, the sage assured him, he would have obtained optimum benefit. Now, as he approached the observatory a year after his supplies had run out, foremost in his mind was to enquire the whereabouts of the Indian and whether an additional amount of the elixir might be blended for him.

Since his last attack of severe pain, he had eaten and drunk sparingly and resisted his craving for fermented mares' milk. Every three days, he had taken Nadia's draught and with each dose his condition had improved. However, he argued that, before Nadia could join him at Baghcha, his sickness might recur and worsen unless an alternative to her treatment was to hand. The Il-khan was not a man to rely on one medicine when he could avail himself of two.

Shirazi received him with customary politeness and advised him with regret that the Indian had returned to his own country.

'That's a pity,' the Il-khan grunted. 'I was determined to speak with him again.'

'It seems the sage anticipated your wish, Sire,' said Shirazi. 'He has sent you a gift. Another of his countrymen brought it here not a week ago. If you will wait a moment I shall fetch it for you.'

The gift proved to be a small casket of the same design as that which had earlier held the elixir. It was made of wood, and the lid bore the symbol of the gammadion, carved in relief.

'It's a good omen,' said Arghun, running his fingers slowly over the decoration. He opened the box and saw it was filled with the greyish paste he had first tasted a year ago.

'Your Majesty must have found the Indian's preparation of great benefit,' said Shirazi cautiously. 'A medicine whose essence bestows eternal youth . . .'

'Pox on you, Master Shirazi,' retorted Arghun with good humour. 'What kind of fool do you take me for? Not even kings live for ever. The sage claimed no more for his elixir than the property of promoting health and vigour into old age. You will know, as a student of history, that my ancestor Genghis was active well into his seventh decade, whereas my father Abaqa died young. My ambition is to emulate the founder of our dynasty.'

'Your Majesty, I did not mean to imply . . .'

Arghun did not allow him to finish his apology. 'No, you meant to flatter me as you always do,' he boomed. 'Come, Shirazi, tell me the truth. What is your opinion of this Indian's claims? It isn't my intention to deprive you of your tenure because you speak your mind.'

Shirazi relaxed. He had always found conversation with Arghun difficult in the past, and flattery had proved the only sure way of remaining in his monarch's good graces. However, the Arghun of today seemed different.

'I am a Muslim, Sire,' replied the Master of Maragha. 'Allah grants men a natural life span of seventy years, which may be cut short in many ways: by illness, by poisoning, or by death in battle, for example. Good health may be maintained by prayer and proper fasting, and by the judicious taking of herbal extracts. But one cannot cheat destiny.'

'And what is my destiny, Master Philosopher?'

'Only Allah can answer *that*, Sire, but I'm sure - indeed I hope Your Majesty will continue to rule wisely for many more years.'

'You cannot hope it more ardently than I do myself,' said the Il-khan. 'Now, if you don't mind, there's some business I wish to talk with you. Fetch me, if you will, the map of the lands occupied by the Egyptian.'

*

XVI

Nizam sensed he was trapped, and that made him nervous. He had not expected to be taken into Baidu's confidence completely, but all the months spent worming his way into the prince's favour, tolerating his debauchery, answering his every whim, should have brought some reward. Instead of skulking in Tabriz, he should have been marching into Baghdad with Ashraf's armies.

The Sultan had wanted quick results and Nizam had been confident of delivering them. However, Baidu insisted on adapting every idea to suit his latest caprice. His enormous personal conceit jeopardised their goals. His insistence that the attempt on the Italian's life should appear an accident had led to its failure.

As for the fiasco in the boy's apartment, on the eve of Kartir's arrival in the capital, had that been Mongol efficiency at its very best? It was as well no harm had come to the boy. He could not have relied on Kartir's silence if Hassan had died.

Now he wondered how much the child had overheard. Probably no more than the mother would already have guessed, certainly not enough to halt the next phase of Baidu's plan. Nizam now regretted making so clear his distaste for Tabriz. It was true he was about to escape from the city again, but he would be under the watchful eye of Timur or another of the prince's spies. There would be no opportunity to back out, to go running back to Ashraf with his commission - to sabotage the Christian treaty - unfulfilled.

The Sultan was unforgiving of failure. Nizam knew that if Arghun's plans of conquest were not halted he could not go back. He shuddered at the thought of finding himself again in a damp, stinking dungeon. Twice during his fifty-five years he had experienced captivity. There had been the six months in the old fortress of Baghdad, condemned to near starvation with others of the Caliph's kin, living in a cell with his own excrement when his only crime had been loyal service to his lord. He had escaped to Kerman by bribing his gaolers with all that remained of the Caliph's treasure - three gold coins he had swallowed on his arrest.

The Emir of Kerman had welcomed him. After all, he had skill at managing accounts as well as his talent for espionage. But it had all ended when Hulegu invaded the south, and when a man who had presided over his degradation was appointed as a governor. Though, until then, Nizam had never met Kartir, he blamed him for his misfortune, for the humiliation of the Caliph, the laughter of the Shiites and the blossoming prosperity of the Christians and Jews.

After his abortive attempt at revenge, Nizam had again found himself in prison. Fearing Kartir's wrath, he had fled to the Syrian border only to be arrested as a Mongol spy and thrown into a Mamluk dungeon. He had spent almost a year among the dregs of humanity - blasphemers, thieves, cut-throats and sodomites - until Sultan Ashraf, recognising in him a man who might be more useful alive than dead, had personally ordered his release.

Nizam forced himself to return to the present. He must not contemplate failure. The plan was a good one and if it succeeded he would be rewarded with riches beyond his dreams. First Arghun, then Ghazan; perhaps the Italian was incidental. And he would find another opportunity to pursue his personal revenge against the Viceroy of Kerman.

The horrors of his prison experience had taught Nizam a great deal about men and their depravity but he had also learned something about himself. He knew with certainty that he would betray, thieve, murder and even commit acts of the vilest bestiality rather than lose his freedom again.

The autumn sun had not yet broken through the morning haze. The olive plantation was deserted save for a few rodents scuttling among the debris of twigs and fallen leaves. Giovanni swung the scimitar from side to side, flexing the muscles of his wrist. The weapon was heavier than he expected but it could at least be wielded from the saddle. He prayed he would not be forced to use it. The poison and loss of blood had weakened his shoulders and arms. He had already decided the longer rapier was useless and had given it to Nadia to stow in the wagon.

The pony Hassan had brought him was more suited to his size than the ones he had recently ridden. Giovanni manoeuvred it with his knees, testing his grip and the animal's responses. His leg throbbed but it was less uncomfortable than when he walked. He regarded the thick bandages ruefully. Although there was no visible leakage from the wound, he wondered how it would respond to several days on horseback.

He swung the scimitar again and urged his mount at a steady pace through the olive grove. When he reached the far side he tucked the weapon into his belt beside his own short sword, turned, and began a slow canter round the perimeter. He felt a twinge of pain in his thigh with every stride, but it was bearable. Anyway, he no longer had a choice but to accompany Nadia to Baghcha and conclude his mission there.

Hassan's adventure and the merchant Umid's disturbing intelligence had brought home to him the reality of his position. Baidu was negotiating an alliance with the Sultan of Egypt; he would embrace Islam and give up Baghdad in exchange for Mamluk support to defeat Arghun. A treaty between the Il-khan and the Western monarchs would spoil their plans. Ashraf could not leave Syria undefended if the Crusaders were planning to take Jerusalem, and he would not be foolish enough to invade with half an army.

But, Giovanni had reasoned, with himself dead and the threat of the treaty removed, the Sultan could consolidate his position in Palestine then mobilise in the direction of Baghdad. The Crusaders' fragile hold on Asia Minor would be broken. Baidu, probably with his cousin Gaikatu's support, would make his move against the Il-khan.

All this made perfect sense to Giovanni, but he was unable to judge the role played by Nizam in the conspiracy. Clearly, the man's path had crossed with Kartir's at some date in the past and he was now suspected by the viceroy of having a hand in the attempted kidnapping. However, neither Nadia nor her father showed willingness to confide to a stranger any detail of what seemed to be a closely-guarded family secret.

Giovanni completed two painful circuits of the plantation, slowed his mount to a walk and glanced back towards the priest's villa. Hassan was harnessing a pony to the wagon. The two Persian merchants whom Kartir had left as escorts the previous evening were attentively saddling and bridling their own animals.

The choice had been made for him. He was not well enough to return to Venice, and he could not remain in Tabriz to be a target for

Timur's assassins. Moreover, both Nadia and Hassan were in danger as long as they remained with him outside Arghun's protection.

Kartir had wanted to accompany them to Baghcha, but Nadia was adamant.

'If Timur were to send a squadron after us, you would die too, Father,' she said resolutely. 'But I wager he will not. This is not open revolt we have uncovered but lurking treason.'

'But Nizam may strike again.' As he pronounce the name, the viceroy's jaw tightened.

'I think we are safe for the moment,' Nadia replied. 'When Umid has explained all to Taghachar, the riots will be put down and the conspirators will go underground. Their plans are sabotaged, Father. They will not act alone.'

'You may not overtake Arghun and it's a long way to Baghcha.'

'It's not a hazardous road,' said Nadia reassuringly, 'and I shall be spoiled for protection with my son, Signor Giovanni, and the two men of Kerman you promised us. Besides, Father, you must go to Ghazan. This unholy alliance between Baidu and al-Ashraf will bring chaos, and you know it. Encouraged by a Muslim sultan in Baghdad, the zealots will declare a bloody Jihad. It will be Persian against Persian, while the Chagatai and the Golden Horde ravage the North.'

'Then be careful, Nadia.'

'You too, Father.'

She had kissed him on the cheek and Giovanni had seen uncertainty as well as tears in her eyes.

Nadia was waiting for him in the tiny front garden of the villa. She had exchanged her silks for a plain brown caftan and had discarded her fashionable sandals in favour of leather riding boots.

'The wound should not inconvenience me too much, My Lady,' Giovanni said in response to her questioning look. 'In any case, you can afford to delay no longer.'

'Then we shall go now, ' said she tersely. She signalled to Hassan and the Persians that they should mount. 'If God wills, we shall intercept him before he reaches the River Arax.'

'I'm in your hands, madam.'

'You are indeed, sir,' said she, affecting a lighter mood which could not disguise her uneasiness. She took the reins of the remaining pony and climbed neatly into the saddle. 'But you shall drive the wagon for the rest of today. It will give your wound a better chance to knit.'

Her tone did not invite argument. Hiding his discomfort as best he could, but grateful for the respite, Giovanni eased himself from his horse's back, hitched it to the wagon and climbed on board.

*

XVII

The fire in the hearth was low and Gobras was dreaming. So often now, in the solitary silence of early evening, he withdrew into his world of dreams and visions, where spectres of the past and realities of the present mingled, sometimes indistinguishably, with phantoms of the future.

Sometimes he was in the grand temple of Istakhr, or in the palace at Ctesiphon, where ghosts of priests and kings, pale shades, still offered their prayers and made their sacrifices . On other days, he was at the altar in Kerman, suffering again with the unavenged souls of the innocents condemned by a lie and slaughtered there.

Tonight, the images were clear. He was in a room dimly lit by candles. Their flickering light illuminated paintings of animals and birds that decorated the walls. The air was filled with the scent of burning herbs and resins. In the shadows, two figures moved. Their robes were the colour of congealed blood, their faces hidden by dark hoods.

Near the centre of the room was a bed, on it the body of a man. His linen and the pillows on which he lay were stained red. His eyes were wide and staring. From behind his clenched teeth came the sound of gurgling. One of the shadowy figures approached, in his hand an object that glistened in the candlelight. The man on the bed reached towards it, seized it. Then, overcome by violent spasms of his chest and arms, he released it and fell back on the pillows. His teeth parted, the gurgling grew louder and from his open mouth erupted a torrent of blood.

In his dream, Gobras froze in horror. The bright object had fallen on the floor, a gold cross with the span of a man's hand, one whose hooked arms were turned to the left and at whose centre was the engraving of a crescent moon.

And as the Patriarch watched, the arms blackened and shrivelled until nothing remained of it but a bundle of smouldering ash.

*

PART TWO
The Treaty

I
Bagcha, Two Months Later

Giovanni stood at a window. The rain fell in the courtyard, turning the earth to mud and forming brown rivulets that ran like miniature torrents towards the palace gate and onwards through the fields to the river. The distant hills were enveloped in banks of dark grey cloud. Somewhere, over the sea to the east, thunder rumbled.

But for a few anxious days at the beginning, his first month at Baghcha had passed pleasantly. The stiffness in his leg had gradually worn off and he was able to remain in the saddle for longer periods without feeling any discomfort. He had mastered the art of riding without stirrups and this enhanced his enjoyment of excursions through the cool, damp forests. On fine days he fished on the lake, using a small boat that Arghun put at his disposal, and which he shared with Hassan and Oljeitu.

Nadia had been proved correct. They had not been pursued from Tabriz and had met the Il-khan's party on the banks of the River Arax after two days riding. Arghun's journey from Urmia had been without incident. He had reacted with cold anger to their news, sending his seal to Taghachar with orders to bring him the heads of Timur and Qutlugh; Nizam was to be taken alive. Any further riots in Tabriz were to be put down ruthlessly, the instigators condemned to death by strangling.

'These knaves will pay dearly for plotting your death, Ambassador,' Arghun said. 'There will be no trials. I'll hang this Nizam by the hair till he screams my cousin's name. Then I'll castrate him and cut out his tongue!'

His anger was short lived. Apparently satisfied that the threatened revolt was thwarted, he became affability itself. The air around Baghcha seemed to agree with him. Giovanni found himself the centre of attention, as his host strove to make amends for his recent pain and discomfort.

Arghun's winter residence was a palatial villa, built round a central courtyard, and grander though less spacious than the castle of Tabriz. The doors to the apartments opened onto two covered verandas, one at ground level, the other supported on it, so that all parts of the complex could be reached without going outside. The floors and the stairs leading to the upper storey were tiled, the pillars and inner walls decorated with mosaic.

Opposite the main gate was an imposing flight of steps leading to a marbled hall where Arghun received visiting dignitaries in style, and which doubled as a banqueting room. The Il-khan's own apartments were on the right, next to them the garrison and a Turkish bathhouse. To the left were quartered the royal women, eight in all including Nadia, Tolaghan and Arghun's daughters Oljei and Doquz. Others were widows of previous rulers, whom custom had demanded the Il-khan marry.

Giovanni's apartments, to the left of the gate, comprised an atrium and two chambers, one reserved for eating, the other for sleeping and bathing. Both were laid with carpets. There were no rooms on the upper floor, but an inner staircase led to the roof, which was sunken and planted with roses and flowering shrubs, all dull and lifeless in the present season. This garden, whilst affording some privacy from its neighbour by a wall, commanded a full view of the complex, and of river, lake and woods beyond.

On the same wing were accommodated the Il-khan's military and civil advisers, while on the other side of the gate were the quarters of artisans who maintained the property and stoked the fires in the bathhouse. Across the courtyard, adjacent to the royal family, were housed women employed in domestic duties.

The palace's strangest residents were two Buddhist monks who had joined Arghun's entourage on the road from Urmia. They were to be seen rarely, shuffling along the veranda, muffled in their orange-brown robes, their faces hidden by flapping cowls. They were an incongruous pair, the one short and fat, the other angular and wraith-like. Many of Giovanni's prejudices against other faiths had softened, but he could not look at these false clerics without a certain amount of disgust.

Between palace and river Arghun had erected a splendid tent that he seemed to prefer to the luxury of the palace rooms. Its walls were painted white, and round the inside were colour drawings of hunting scenes. The entrance flaps were decorated with pictures of exotic creatures that Giovanni had never seen. There was a central hearth and smoke hole, and the boards forming the floor were strewn with animal pelts, fine Persian rugs and cushions. Similar, smaller tents, but without the paintings, were set up nearby for Hassan and Oljeitu who, Giovanni observed, revelled in their experience of the old Mongol way of life.

Hunting was the chief diversion but, as the parties were small, it did not have the savagery of the Tabriz hunts. Giovanni lost his aversion to it. He discovered to his delight that Arghun was acquainted with hawking, and had made good his promise to acquire a pair of birds for his guest's pleasure.

As an adopted member of the Il-khan's circle of friends, it would have been impossible for him to avoid Nadia's company. The women ate and drank with the men. Some hunted. Local emirs and functionaries were entertained with their wives and children.

He saw her frequently. She would seek his opinion on features of the landscape, on the progress of Hassan's skills as a hunter and fisherman, or on the quality of the meat, but their dialogue was invariably of short duration.

Even Tolaghan and other womenfolk occasionally addressed him in a familiar manner. However, to initiate a conversation would have breached the rules of hospitality by which Arghun set great store. An exception was made in the case of Oljei and Doquz, who were pert and precocious with everyone and were treated freely in return. The former, the full sister of Ghazan and daughter of Arghun's first, but now dead wife, was a small, chubby maiden just growing into womanhood who flirted inexhaustibly with men, young and old; the latter, Tolaghan's own child, was a gangling girl of nine or ten.

Though much of the cold formality of Tabriz was swept away, it was replaced by rigid rules that even family members ignored at their peril. Crimes against property carried the death penalty and consequently there were none. Drunkenness, gluttony, intolerance and quarrelling among men and women alike were punishable by a sound beating. That Giovanni's understanding of this moral code grew was largely due to

Arghun's military commander, Mohammed Sabbah. A native Persian, Sabbah occupied a privileged position in the household, and his knowledge of the laws of Genghis Khan was profound.

A bond of friendship grew between them. The commander was an educated man and from him Giovanni also gained an understanding of the religion of Islam whilst imparting in return some appreciation of his own faith.

The belief in a risen Saviour, at the core of Christianity, was absent from the Muslims' creed, but they acknowledged His goodness with humility and reverence. The two faiths shared with the Jews the commandments of Moses. Muslims believed too in the oneness of God, and in being charitable to those less fortunate than themselves.

It was true that Islam had added much that was still alien and disagreeable to his mind, but Giovanni saw nothing in the two faiths that justified, from the perspective of either, the centuries of hatred and bitterness. It would, he decided, be just a short step for a devout Muslim to take from the acceptance of Christ's prophecy to full salvation.

Despite the agreeable manner in which he was entertained, Giovanni had occasionally detected an air of uneasy expectancy in those around him. The first hint of inclement weather had only added to the presageful mood.

At the start of winter, he had been summoned regularly to the Il-khan's tent for discussion of the alliance. He would repeat his arguments and would be questioned at length about the motives and commitment of the western monarchs. Maps would be produced and Arghun would draw on them to illustrate his preferences for assault on the Sultan's strongholds.

Giovanni foresaw at last the fulfilment of his mission. However, in the fortnight leading up to the solstice, the meetings became less frequent. Arghun was seen less in public. For whole days he would closet himself with the Buddhist priests. During these periods of fasting and prayer no one else was permitted to approach him. Moreover, the rituals seemed to depress him and it would take the excitement of a hunt to restore his good humour.

Giovanni found his host's behaviour irksome. His feelings were confused. Arghun was affable, likeable even, except on the now rare occasions when he over- indulged in liquor. However, he had promised an agreement and there was none. Not only that but he was Nadia's husband, and that made him a rival.

During their frantic ride north, Giovanni had almost convinced himself that she returned his feelings. In Gobras's house she had been warm and alluring. Now she was cool and remote. He tried to dismiss all thought of her from his mind. However, the effort only tormented him and, instead of abating, his passion and frustrations grew.

The weather had broken a week after the solstice and was now at its worst. All outdoor activities had been suspended. There was no communal feasting and the fires in the bathhouse were unlit. Giovanni had hardly stirred out of doors for three days. The hunting, fishing and riding had provided the distraction he needed but, with those gone, he was alone with his thoughts.

The silence of his villa was disturbed only by the drumming of rain on the veranda roof. The dampness crept through his bones. His mission unaccomplished, he had nevertheless had his fill of Tabriz, Baghcha and Persia. He wanted only to be away from this godless country and its unrelenting climate. He needed the sun-kissed vineyards and the comforts of his father's estate. He might never truly love again, but he needed the soothing attentions of a sweetheart.

He glanced round as the door of atrium creaked open. While there was no banqueting, he was served in his quarters by two veiled women who, in early evening, brought him a basket of bread, smoked meats and fish, a flask of wine and a pitcher of water.

The two attendants entered dressed in their plain caftans. As usual, their faces were covered. The taller carried the pitcher, which she laid on the floor at the entrance to his bedroom; the shorter placed her basket on a table beside the stairs. Giovanni thanked them and resumed his idle contemplation of the deserted, rain-soaked yard. He heard the outer door close.

'My lord ....'

The sound of the voice startled him and he turned again. The woman with the pitcher had not withdrawn and was lingering expectantly in the inner doorway. Though the veil hid most of her features, he realised she was not one of his usual attendants. She was more erect than either and had an agreeable figure the caftan could not hide. He detected the faint odour of perfume.

'You wish to speak to me?' he enquired kindly.

'I only want to serve you, my lord,' she replied, advancing into the room, dropping onto one knee and bowing her veiled head. It was a young voice.

'You have done so already,' said Giovanni, taken aback but feeling a thrill at her proximity. The scent of perfume was stronger now. 'And I'm neither god nor king that you should feel obliged to kneel to me.'

'I have a gentle hand as well as a strong arm, my lord, and would be greatly honoured if you would allow me to wash you.'

'To wash me,' repeated Giovanni. 'There is no need. I can manage well enough ....'

'Will you only look at me?' the woman begged. She unwound her veil, loosened her hair, and raised her eyes to his face.

Giovanni's senses stirred. She was a maiden of seventeen or eighteen years. Unlike any of the Tabriz women, either Mongol or Persian, she was fair of complexion, with green eyes. Her light brown hair fell in ringlets over her slim shoulders.

'You do not think me ugly?'

Giovanni recognised her now, one of the girls who had attended him in the massage room of the Turkish bathhouse, but who was forbidden by custom or law from speaking there.

He touched her lightly on the shoulder. 'Ugly? No, you are beautiful. What is your name?'

'Pidorka, my lord.' said the maiden, 'and I am glad and honoured that you find me appealing. These short, dark days and long nights must be lonely for a strong man when he has no woman to share his bed.'

'Loneliness is a misfortune of my profession,' said Giovanni lamely.

' 'Tis a misfortune you need bear no longer, my lord,' said she, blushing. 'I have seen these weeks how sad you are. Perhaps because you are far away from your homeland. I ask only that you let me love you; that you let me soothe away your loneliness and relieve your sadness in the recesses of my body.'

Before he could reply, she clasped his leg and slid her hands over his calf and along his thigh. Giovanni winced as she reached the spot where, two months earlier, the arrowhead had penetrated his flesh, but he did not interfere with her caress. Her hands were soft and their touch aroused pleasure. It had been almost two years since he had lain with a woman.

He knelt beside her, unfastened the sash of her caftan and drew it open at the front. She had firm, well-rounded breasts and shapely hips. Her skin was pale, her nipples pink and proud. Her lips were parted, tempting him to a kiss.

The sight of her and the continuing caress of her hand drove Giovanni to a wild passion. The emotions he had denied himself for so long swept over him. He pulled her to him and pressed his mouth against hers, savouring the perfume of her hair, feeling the warmth of her body and the beating of her heart against his chest. One of her hands was beneath his tunic, the fingers clasping his lower back. The other was between his legs, stroking him gently and urgently.

Giovanni edged them both towards the thick rug beside his divan, aware that her hands were now fumbling, seeking an opening in the unfamiliar breeches, struggling with their fastenings until she had found the means to pull them from his buttocks.

Then he was free and she was pushing against him, trembling as she enfolded him between her warm thighs. As soon as he was fully inside her, she threw her arms about his neck and clung to him fiercely until their ardour was cooled.

The foul weather continued. The lake spilled over into the nearby meadows, increasing its surface area by almost half. The rivers overflowed their banks and flooded the valley roads, making travel hazardous. The tents, though secure, were abandoned.

In the daytime, Giovanni found other diversions to clear his mind of fantasies. Hassan had brought his magnificent chess pieces in his luggage and demanded that they resume their contests. When it rained they played. When the rain stopped he watched the boys engage in their earnest swordplay, in which victories and defeats were shared almost equally. The officers of the militia too sometimes found pleasure in this activity, only their weapons were of blunted steel and the game frequently ended with some blood being spilt, though never fatally.

Pidorka came to him in the evenings. She shared his meal and remained with him until morning. As they ate, they talked. Her family was Russian. Her parents had been brought to Armenia as slaves by the Mongols of the Golden Horde, but had been released by Arghun. Though free to return to their homeland, they had decided to remain and were now willing servants of the royal family.

After they had made love, they would lie together silently on the divan, her head nestling against his chest and her breasts on his belly while he stroked her hair and neck. Sometimes, the gentle coaxing of her knee and the warm dampness on her thighs aroused him a second or third time and they shared their bodies again until, fulfilled and exhausted, they fell asleep in one another's arms.

Unlike many women he had known, she made no demands, but was always eager to please. She gave companionship without pretence, and pleasure without thought of reward. It became clear to Giovanni that she loved him.

However, his emotions were mixed. Though he had grown fond of her, he felt twinges of guilt. Their intimacy was a deception when the lips he longed for and the body he desired were those of another. Another he could never possess.

One evening, Pidorka arrived fresh and sweetly perfumed, her eyes bright with desire and anticipation. Giovanni removed her veil, unfastened her robe and stood admiring the shapeliness of her form. He wore only a toga and already he could feel his hardness grow beneath it. Pidorka raised her face towards him and he took it between his hands. It had a soft, sensuous beauty.

'Do you want me now, my lord?' she asked, tempting him. She grasped his arms and manoeuvred him onto the bed. 'My heart is so full of love tonight. I can think of nothing but you.'

'You know I want you, Pidorka, only ....'

She threw herself on top of him, pressing her mouth against his in a passionate kiss, exploring with her tongue and stifling his words.

Giovanni fought against the embrace. He knew that in a few seconds he would succumb, but he could not continue to pretend. He pulled his mouth away. 'Pidorka ....'

'Giovanni?' There was surprise and hurt in her eyes. 'Have I displeased you, my lord?'

'You could never displease me, Pidorka. But what if this love were a pretence?'

Pidorka released him and sat back on her haunches. 'A pretence, my lord? How can it be so when what I give is given freely; when your pleasure becomes my pleasure? Is that not all there is between a man and a woman, save for the making of new life?'

'But if I love another?'

'Are Venetian men from another world, Giovanni, that they cannot love two or three equally,' said Pidorka with a strained smile. 'If you were to give your love to me alone, I would accept it gladly. But I do not demand it.'

Giovanni struggled with his desire. She was still close to him on the divan and beautiful in her nakedness. 'If I could truly love you, I would, Pidorka,' he said. 'But my world *is* different from yours. You should have a husband who can protect you and give you many fine children. I cannot offer you these things. And our intimacy is a violation when there is always another in my thoughts. I ask your pardon for having used you.'

'I do not care that there is another,' cried Pidorka. 'And even if you are thinking of her, there is enough love in me for both of us. Only let me show you.'

She lifted the hem of his toga, slipped her arm round his waist and put her head in his lap. Her mouth travelled downwards to encircle him in its moist embrace.

'No!'

His resistance had almost melted but he held on to his determination and tried to ease her away. Pidorka looked up at him, her expression fearful.

'Do not send me away, Giovanni,' she pleaded. 'Do not forbid me coming to you, or His Majesty will be angered!'

Giovanni's passion was suddenly cooled. Suspicion took root in his mind and he thrust her from him.. He felt his cheeks flush with annoyance.

'His Majesty!' he exclaimed. 'Was it the Il-khan who sent you to me?'

'Do not be angry, My Lord,' stammered Pidorka.

'But it was Arghun who sent you?' Giovanni insisted hotly.

'I am no harlot, My Lord, and he did not force me. My father overheard the Il-khan say you were in need of a companion. In the bathhouse you had looked at me with favour, and I found your person pleasing, so I offered. His Majesty wished only to honour you. I did not think ...' She broke down in tears. 'Please, Giovanni, I'm not ashamed of what my heart feels, but I will not speak of it again, if that is what you wish.'

Though she had lowered her eyes, she had made no attempt to cover her nakedness. Giovanni fought the impulse to take her again in his arms but instead reached for her robe and placed it around her shoulders. Whatever had been Arghun's intention, the tenderness and love she had shown him were not expressions of duty but of true affection. To the guilt he already felt was added shame at having doubted her sincerity.

But he knew all efforts to return her love would be in vain. Whenever he looked at her, he saw only Nadia. When she spoke meaningless endearments in his ear, it was Nadia's voice he heard, and when he lay at the climax of arousal on her breast, it was thoughts of Nadia that filled his heart and imagination.

'That is my wish,' he said softly. 'You are truly beautiful but, in my country, love between man and woman is not something that is easily shared with another. I should have spoken sooner. Forgive me if I have hurt you.'

Pidorka rose from the divan and silently refastened her dress. When she had done so, she touched his arm briefly without again raising her eyes. 'If it is not to be, I forgive you, My Lord,' she said. 'I shall bear the hurt with the memory of our pleasure.

II

At last the weather improved. The ponies sniffed the cold, dry air as if spring was just round the corner and pranced with delight in the damp meadows in anticipation of a chase. The heavy, flat-bottomed boats had lain on the lake shore throughout the worst of the storms and were now wedged firmly in the mud and filled to the brim with water. They were tipped over, drained, cleaned and made ready for use. The hunting, riding and fishing were resumed.

Giovanni's mood lightened. After the vigour of a day's sport he slept soundly and the hours of darkness did not seem so long. Pidorka had not come again to his villa, but he saw her still in the massage room where she would smile brightly as he entered and left. He felt pleasure as she worked the muscles of his shoulders with her skilled fingers and was tempted several times to beg her to renew their trysts, but he resisted. Sabbah, who regularly accompanied him, often remarked that the girl lavished more attention on him than on the other men, and he had to endure in silence the commander's amused glances as they lay relaxing on the tables.

Another month passed. Negotiations with Arghun became more serious and a provisional plan of campaign was agreed. The Il-khan confided the disposition of his armies along the River Tigris at Mosul and his intention of launching an attack on Damascus from the north. If the Christians were to assemble a force to relieve Acre and capture Jerusalem at the same time, the objectives of the allies would be achieved all the sooner.

Giovanni was worried that the project might be hindered by the talked of alliance between Baidu and the Sultan, but Arghun laughed at his concerns.

'Just wait and see, Ambassador,' he said mysteriously. 'That has been taken care of.'

Towards the middle of the month, General Taghachar arrived in Baghcha with a squadron of picked men.

'Tabriz is calm, Your Majesty,' he reported. 'There have been minor protests by both Muslims and Jews, but my forces are vigilant.

Commander Berke will act at the first sign of escalation.'

'And Timur?' scowled Arghun.

'He retreated to the Zagros with two hundred men, Your Majesty. We overtook them in As-Suleimanya. I promise you none reached Baghdad.'

'Then you've brought me what I demanded?' Arghun enquired grimly.

'Timur's head you may have, Sire,' said the general. 'The other, Qutlugh, is long since food for the crows. The very day I learned of his attack on the boy, I found him at the gates of Tabriz Castle with his throat cut.'

'So, what of the Persian of whose company my cousin Baidu once seemed so fond - Nizam?'

'Disappeared, Your Majesty. Vanished without trace.'

'He's gone crawling back to Baidu, I'll warrant,' said Arghun. 'Let him stay there. His time will come, as will my cousin's. I have plans for Baghdad.'

'I'll vouch for it that if he's in Baghdad he'll not leave it, Sire, unless it be to run to the Egyptian. Your forces are blocking all roads to the north and east of the province.'

'By Genghis's tomb, you see how my enemies treat their friends, Giovanni,' said Arghun scornfully, when the general had been dismissed. 'Let us waste no more time in settling our affairs!'

During the following week, messengers arrived from Isfahan and from the Lake of Van. Arghun's mood was buoyant.

'It all comes together, Giovanni,' he announced. 'The regiments in Yazd and Isfahan are on the alert, al-Ashraf has pulled back from the Euphrates, and my agents in Rum are watching every move Gaikatu makes. My only regret is that I have not heard from Ghazan. Still, as soon as his armies are mobilised, we'll be ready.'

The treaty was concluded within days. If ratified by the kings of Europe, the joint offensive would take place the following spring. A year would be sufficient time to complete the preparations.

Despatches were written and the agreement celebrated with a

flagon of wine. Giovanni was persuaded to remain for a further ten days, by which time the road through Armenia would be passable and the danger of further flooding would have receded. He would travel to Italy by way of Constantinople, and return with the Christian answer. Arghun promised an escort as far as the Persian border, or until they encountered a merchant caravan bound for the Black Sea ports.

Arghun now began to take an interest in the outings on the lake, as well as in the hunting, insisting that the whole of his extended family participate in them. Whereas he had previously been alone with Hassan and Oljeitu, Giovanni now found they were often accompanied by a second boat, and occasionally a third.

On some days, Arghun himself would arrive, accompanied by Nadia, Tolaghan or another of his mistresses. On others, one or more of the women came, alone but for a personal servant. Sabbah frequently joined them, along with Oljei and Doquz, who giggled and shrieked as their boat's prow rose and dipped, splashing them with icy water. The girls, so different in appearance, seemed so alike in character.

'They have their father's temperament,' Sabbah observed wryly, 'but if you had met Prince Ghazan you would not wonder at Oljei's looks.'

A full week elapsed pleasurably. One afternoon, while Arghun was closeted with the Buddhists, Giovanni found himself in the small boat in the company of Nadia, Hassan and Oljeitu, while a second craft was shared by Sabbah, Tolaghan and the girls. They were all well wrapped in furs against the cold. The fish were plentiful. Giovanni hauled in an excellent catch, ably assisted by the Mongol boy. Hassan however seemed unable to concentrate on the sport. He sat moodily in the bottom of the boat, rarely participating and avoiding Giovanni's eyes. Neither his mother's coaxing nor his stepbrother's excited cries when another fish was netted had any effect.

'I do believe he would accompany you to Venice, Giovanni,' said Nadia, when they had beached the boat and were walking slowly back to where they had left the ponies. The coolness he had fancied in her was not apparent. 'Hassan cares nothing for politics and alliances, only that he is about to lose a friend.'

'Not to lose, madam,' rejoined Giovanni. 'I may be gone several months, but I will return.'

'If my son keeps that same dismal countenance until then, he will drive me to madness, ' said she, attempting a laugh.

'Then I have more than one reason for hastening back,' said Giovanni, looking meaningfully at her, ' - to fulfil my duty, to rescue Hassan from his depression and to save you from madness.'

'But which is the stronger motive,' she asked, avoiding his gaze, ' - duty or friendship?'

'One does not choose the first, madam, yet it is no less powerful as a shaper of one's destiny.'

They were quite close together and Giovanni became aware she had rested a fur clad hand on his sleeve.

'And the second?'

'Friendship, like love, is sublime, or so the Holy Scriptures of my faith would have us believe. However, it imposes duties of its own. I would not wish to separate the two.'

'Tell me, Giovanni,' said she. 'What does this holy book of yours say about love?'

'That it suffers; that it is unselfish, hopeful, truthful; that it demands sacrifice, even the sacrifice of one's life, in its name.'

'Truly, that is a love worth tasting,' said Nadia.

She had not withdrawn her hand and even through the thickness of two animal skins Giovanni sensed that she had increased the pressure of it.

'One that might be yours, Nadia .....'

He had forgotten himself and would have thrown discretion to the winds if she had not silenced him. The hand that had touched his sleeve was raised to his mouth to prevent him continuing.

'Say no more, I beg you,' she warned. 'Whatever we may desire, I fear that in our contests between love and duty it will always be duty that is the winner.'

The following day Arghun dismissed the priests and led a hunting party in the forest. The day after that he retired to his tent and took to his bed. Giovanni supposed he had either drunk too much or had caught a chill from the damp air, and began preparations for his departure. He had few belongings and checking that everything was in order was a simple matter.

Hassan had come out of his black mood and for a few days was a constant visitor. Even when they were not playing chess or discussing the finer points of swordplay, the boy would loiter in the vicinity of his quarters on any pretext, his young face grave, his dark eyes near to tears.

'Must you go, Giovanni?' he asked when the eve of the Venetian's planned departure approached.

'I fear so, Hassan,' said Giovanni, 'but if God wills it, I shall be back well within the year.'

'May I accompany you part of the way?'

'With His Majesty's permission - and if your mother does not object, you may travel half a day with me.'

'She does not object,' said Hassan firmly. 'I have already asked her, and I shall ask my father's permission straightway.'

It was settled within the hour. Hassan would be provided with an additional escort as far as Van. Giovanni was glad of the prospect of company. He had grown fond of the boy, and parting from him would be one of his few regrets on quitting Persia. He had hoped to see Nadia one last time, but the final day wore on and he saw no sign of her. Arghun remained indisposed and did not appear either.

He was debating with himself whether to risk an enquiry of Hassan, and even to dare requesting an interview with his mother, when the door of the atrium opened silently and Hassan himself entered looking flushed and embarrassed.

'My mother is outside, and asks if she may speak with you.'

Through the open doorway Giovanni could see a cloaked and veiled figure and his heart leapt in his chest.

'May I enter, sir?' said Nadia's voice from beneath the veil. 'Hassan, remain in the courtyard and knock if anyone comes.'

'Madam, you honour me,' said Giovanni. He remained in the shadows so that she would not see his limbs tremble.

'You know the risk I take in coming here,' said Nadia, 'but I cannot allow you to go without speaking.'

She raised the upper portion of the veil so that her eyes were visible. Giovanni waited, afraid to reply lest his voice betray his feelings.

'You once swore friendship to me,' continued Nadia, 'and I'm here to call upon that friendship now. Delay your departure. Do not leave Baghcha.'

'I shall always be your most devoted friend, madam,' said Giovanni, regaining some of his self control, 'and saying goodbye to friends is always a wrench. However, you told me not long ago that duty will always be the winner over friendship. I have my duty, just as you have yours. I cannot remain here.'

Nadia gave a sob. She removed her veil entirely, grasped Giovanni's hand and knelt before him. He saw that her face was pale and her eyes tearful.

'This is not meant to be, Giovanni,' she cried. 'Our parting. This alliance. Neither is meant to be!'

'The treaty is concluded, madam, and my mission is over,' said Giovanni, hearing in her words only contradiction. 'Would you have me break my word?'

'No, not that,' said she, confused. 'I cannot properly explain. Since I was a child, I have been frightened by dreams of a future that has sometimes come to pass. There are dark days ahead for you, My Lord. Dark days for us both. If you go now I fear you will never return to Persia.'

'What is this talk of dreams and visions?' stammered Giovanni, his heart beating ever more rapidly. 'Only God knows the future and He does not reveal it to mankind.'

'I do not pretend to this faith of yours, Giovanni,' she said, 'but neither do I scorn it. There is a God, that I know - one God only, and he has a purpose for all of us. I do not wish to be cursed by half-formed visions of what tomorrow holds. I'm a woman with woman's needs and longings - a secure home, a strong man to lie with and love, children to suckle and nourish. Was I wrong to think you wished to be that man?'

Giovanni clasped both her hands and raised her so that she stood trembling, her upturned face level with his shoulder. 'Not wrong, Nadia,' he said quite overcome with emotion. 'I wished nothing more than to love you, to lie with you and have you bear children for me. I have loved you since the very first day you walked past my apartment in the castle at Tabriz. I loved you even more when you sat at my side and treated my wound at the priest's house, and when I spoke your name in my sleep. In another place, another life, you and I might have been more than friends, but as things are, it is as friends that we must part. Even if it were not for my word to bring the Il-khan's letters to Rome, do you think I could remain here to be tortured by thoughts of you in his embrace when my own arms long to hold you ....'

'Do not torture *me* with the might-have-been,' cried she passionately. 'It is the *now* that concerns me. Arghun is ill. He will die, and your treaty will die with him!'

Giovanni released her suddenly and stepped back. 'Die!' he exclaimed. 'How can you know this, madam? Is his indisposition so serious or is there some new dire plot to destroy him and the work we have accomplished together?'

She gazed up at him, her face a picture of misery, and shook her head. ' 'Tis enough that I know it,' she answered. 'My husband will die, not by the hand of an enemy, but by a wasting of his inside. It may not happen this week, nor this month, but it will not be long. I have long tried to slow the disease's progress, but I cannot do so for ever. In the name of our friendship, at least delay your departure until the equinox, or until Ghazan arrives. It can do no harm, and Arghun will not challenge it. After that, you may keep your word.'

'I cannot believe in your visions, My Lady,' said Giovanni. He took her hands again and kissed them. 'However, if by delaying I please you, I will delay. You have my promise to stay until the equinox. Now go before we are discovered together.'

*

III

Arghun remained in his splendid tent for a week during which time Nadia nursed him dutifully. Between her visits, he would see only the Buddhists, and reacted angrily if anyone else sought an audience. His brow was fevered. The cramps in his insides were more severe than they had ever been and had come upon him suddenly.

The respite from his illness was over. He had his treaty, but he might not live to see Ashraf humiliated. Moreover, Ghazan had not come, and it was now apparent their reunion might not take place for some time. Even if his son had succeeded in putting down the Khorasan rebellion and had set out for Baghcha, he would have to travel westwards by a more indirect route. The passes of the Alburz Mountains lay under snow.

At least Nadia would be free if he died, Arghun reflected. He knew that Kartir had reached Rayy. The documents he had entrusted to Nadia's care, and which she had judged best to give to her father - his will and the Great Khan's letter, would now be in Ghazan's hands. Ghazan would respect his wishes and console himself with the Chinese princess Kublai was sending to Persia as a royal gift. It would be ironic, thought Arghun, if the ageing despot, the great-uncle with whom he felt no true ties of kinship and who was surely the last of the great Mongol emperors, outlived the bridegroom for whom the gift was intended.

On the eighth day of his sickness, the Il-khan awoke from a disturbed sleep with the taste of blood on his tongue. He attempted to rise from his divan but his arms would not support him and he fell back on the pillow with a groan. A water jug lay at his bedside. He reached for it weakly and brought it to his lips, spilling part of the contents on the divan.

He swallowed half a mouthful of the liquid and felt its coolness trickle down his gullet. A moment later, a stab of pain, more agonising than any sword thrust, racked his abdomen, causing him to double up and retch violently. The jug fell from his grasp and broke into a dozen pieces on the hard wood of the floor.

Arghun wiped his lips with his sleeve and saw to his horror that the night-shirt was stained red. A cold sweat formed on his forehead. His heart was pounding and his lungs were gasping for breath. In mortal fear he called out for help. He became dimly aware of voices at the door of the tent and again tried to rise. With determination, he turned onto his belly and, clinging to the bed for support, slid his legs over the edge. His feet touched the floor and he felt the soft pile of a rug between his toes. He tried to stand, but his knees buckled and his senses swam.

He recovered consciousness to see Nadia bending over him. With great effort, he hauled himself back onto the divan, and lay there drained while she washed the blood from his mouth and gave him more water from the fresh supply she had brought. As he had done so often in the past, he watched silently while she prepared a herbal tincture then allowed her to feed it to him on a spoon.

The medicine soothed him and, after a few moments, he raised himself wearily from the pillow. His breathing was returning to normal.

'Am I dying, Nadia?'

'The illness should not have progressed so far, My Lord,' she answered, 'but it may still be checked.'

'I had not thought the end would come so quickly,' said Arghun weakly. He had noticed uncertainty in her voice. 'These last months I've felt quite my old self, and began to believe I was cured. Is there any news of Ghazan?'

'No, My Lord.'

'He will come. But my illness must be kept a secret as long as possible, or my brother and cousin will take full advantage.' He paused, breathless. 'At least the alliance with the West has been secured. Has the Venetian gone?'

'No, My Lord,' said Nadia. 'There is flooding up-river as well as snow on the mountains. By the spring equinox the weather will have improved and his journey will be less arduous. But there is sport here and often, of an afternoon, he plays Hassan at chess.'

Arghun tried to force a smile. 'So they play chess while I die,' he said. 'Tell him no more than you must. Oljeitu and Hassan too should be spared details. Tolaghan avoids my sick bed. Even Oljei does not wish to see me.' He lay back again and half-closed his eyes. 'Now you should leave, Nadia. Send the Buddhists to me, and bid them bring candles and incense.'

By afternoon the cramps had lessened and he felt well enough to rise and take a walk in the fresh air. Nadia visited him at dusk, the first occasion in many months she had done so at this time of day, and again fed him the tincture of herbs.

Over the next few days his condition improved. There was no more bleeding and he became more relaxed again. He was able to take a little food. He quit the tent and returned to the palace.

The respite was short-lived. After another week the cramps returned with a renewed intensity. Arghun could feel his life ebbing away. He summoned his priests, but their rituals tired him. He dismissed them and fell into a fevered sleep. When he awoke, he tried to drink a goblet of wine, but had no sooner swallowed a mouthful than he vomited on the bed.

Nadia had endured days of anguish. She had felt sure a crisis was approaching without being able to divine its nature or outcome. The disease she had laboured hard to control was progressing so quickly that she began to suspect more sinister causes of the deterioration in Arghun's health. Her suspicions were strengthened by a new wave of disturbing visions but, though she saw death everywhere, the phantoms were indistinct.

However, there seemed to be no opportunity for an enemy to take advantage of Arghun's indisposition. After finding him with blood on his clothing, she had visited him twice daily with her medicines. He had eaten and drunk scarcely at all, and then only those things whose preparation she herself supervised. Then, when his condition became no worse and, indeed, as a result of her prescriptions, he began to recover some of his strength, she was relieved, and her suspicions abated.

After his return to the palace, she found the Buddhists frequently in his chamber. Nadia had paid scant attention to them before, but she now began to notice details of their appearance. The taller of the two was so emaciated that his shrunken head, withered shoulders and spindly arms were almost lost in the folds of his tawny robe. By contrast, the second had an ample figure that testified to liberal diet and sedentary occupation. Though she never saw his full face, there seemed to be an unhealthy greyness to his whole person.

Nadia's tolerance in religious matters allowed her to view their esoteric rituals with indifference. Nevertheless, she noticed that the monks seemed hostile to her presence and would retire to an anteroom while she remained at her husband's side.

Her visions came back. She was on the banks of a swollen river, running for her life, panting, her bare feet slithering over slime-covered rocks. Chasms opened in front of her and closed again. Some were filled with wild beasts, roaring, hissing, their hideous jaws gaping and their teeth bared horribly to tear her flesh. She fell, screaming silently as her body was swallowed up in a vast river of blood. She was borne along on its current to a place she recognised, a valley between two mountains, only its grass had withered and its trees were twisted and bare of leaves or fruit.

These fantasies interwove with more rational thoughts and fears. If Arghun died, what would she do? Nadia derived no comfort from his promise that she would be set free. Ghazan, who, by his father's will would release her, had not come. Though she tolerated the company of the other women and was tolerated in return, she felt surrounded by unfriendly eyes. With Arghun's other wives and children, she had no ties of love or duty. Mongol law alone bound them together as possessions of their husband and ruler.

She no longer denied her feelings for Giovanni. Since the day in the boats, she could not dismiss him from her thoughts. She wanted to confide in him; she wanted more, - to feel the touch of his lips on her mouth, neck and breasts, to experience the thrill of intimacy and the warmth of his life force as he thrust himself inside her. If only she could say to him what was in her heart; if only he could confess what she believed was in his, she might more easily bear his absence.

At length she had dared to cross the courtyard to his villa. He loved her and had consented to stay. It was an impossible, despairing love, without hope of fulfilment, but the knowledge of it strengthened her for what she was sure lay ahead.

The Il-khan was sound asleep and snoring loudly. Near his bed, on a low chest, the casket carved with the gammadion symbol lay open, its contents half consumed.

An orange-robed priest stood motionless at the door of the room. His hood was thrown back. On his shaven head, grey bristles were beginning to show. His round, flabby face wore a frown. After a few moments of watching and listening, he pulled the cowl over his brow and moved stealthily across the room. He skirted the table on which two candles and some incense still burned, and stopped at the edge of the bed.

Suddenly, Arghun's body heaved and his throat let out an agonising groan. The priest held his breath. Drops of sweat formed on his forehead and ran down his cheeks.

The Il-khan's snoring resumed. Relieved, the priest mopped away the sweat with his wide sleeves. He threw one final glance at the man on the bed then, very cautiously, extended a hand towards the wooden casket.

Shortly after dawn on the fifteenth day of the Il-khan's illness, Nadia awoke with a deepening sense of foreboding. The courtyard was empty. She donned a cloak, gathered up her medicines and made her way to Arghun's chamber. He lay on his bed, his body bathed in sweat, his clothing soaked in blood and vomit. He was barely conscious. Evidence of the Buddhist rituals lay on a table. Though the candles had been snuffed, the wax was scarcely dry. Beside them lay an incense burner containing a dark residue. A wine goblet had been upset, spilling its contents on the floor.

Nadia cleaned her husband's face and gave him water to drink. The cool liquid seemed to bring him to his senses.

'I wish you had not come,' he breathed, dragging himself painfully onto one elbow. 'I'd rather spare you a sight of me in this foul state. Send someone to clear away the dirt and stench, and bring me some fresh linen.'

'My Lord, I can still be of comfort to you. Allow me to remain.'

'Obey me, wench,' he cried wildly. Her refusal irked him. He writhed on the bed in an effort to get up and in the process dislodged an object that had been secreted beneath the coverlet. Nadia saw it was a wooden casket. She stooped and picked it up. On seeing the decoration on the lid, she felt the blood rush to her head and almost went into a faint.

'What is this, My Lord?' she enquired, opening the box and holding it to her nose.

Arghun had fallen backwards helplessly. 'It's nothing.'

Nadia tasted some of the paste and grimaced. 'Have you been taking this mixture, My Lord?' she asked in horror.

'It's merely an elixir to restore good health,' gasped Arghun. 'But it's a fraud! I hope the sage who gave it to me roasts in hell.'

With a cry of despair, Nadia summoned all her strength and threw the casket with such violence into a far corner of the room that it broke in two, dispersing the contents over the carpet. 'What have you done?' she groaned. 'This substance contains mercury in high proportion. It is a slow poison. Instead of restoring you to health, your elixir is sapping all your vital energy. Instead of curing it is killing.'

Arghun managed only a slight movement of his head. His eyes stared in terror and his ashen face ran with sweat. 'Send for the holy monks,' he croaked.

Nadia went obediently to the door of the room, called to one of the ever-present guards and relayed the commands. 'Shall I remain, My Lord?'

'No,' hissed Arghun. 'I'm more composed now. Fetch a woman to tidy this bed as I asked and, when that's done, command my other wives and my children to attend me.'

'As you wish, My Lord,' said Nadia. She spoke again to the guard then made to go herself.

Arghun called her back. 'Forgive me, Nadia,' he begged. 'I spoke hastily. It's too late. Don't leave me!'

She returned to the bedside and bathed his face in water. His breathing was uneven and he began retching again.

'I wish ... I wish you could have loved me ... instead of hating me for what my father did,' he said.

'Lie still, My Lord,' whispered Nadia tenderly. 'Be assured I do not hate you. I have often told you so. Throughout our marriage you have treated me with nothing but honour. I have been Queen in everything but name and served you willingly.'

'But without love,' said Arghun. 'It was your love I wanted most.'

'I tried, Arghun, but I could not give it. Even after Kerman, I could not give it.'

'Kerman?' His voice was weak and his breathing even more laboured.

She tried to summon up the memory of him as he was, to blot out the picture of wretchedness he had become. 'You remember My Lord? It was only ten years ago. You were a fine general then.'

Arghun sighed. 'And you a pretty child .... with hair like the mane of a wild stallion ... only ten times more beautiful. I remember, Nadia. I would have married you then if my father had allowed it ... but instead he sent you to Teguder.'

'Yes, My Lord.'

'A pretty child with a new bridegroom. One that we took forcibly from you and sent to his death.'

'I was sixteen, My Lord ... and a virgin.'

Arghun opened his eyes wide and stared up at her. Nadia focused on them through the mist that was forming over her own. She bent forward over the bed and with tears running from her cheeks, whispered in his ear the secret she had shared with only one other living soul.

The Il-khan's eyes closed again. A faint smile crossed his lips and the last words he spoke were in a whisper that was scarcely audible.

'He handles the bow like a Mongol!'

*

IV

Giovanni had completed his preparations for departure. By his reckoning, it was already the month of March and the equinox was only a fortnight away.

His days were spent at leisure, fishing with the boys, riding alone or with Hassan in the forest, playing chess or conversing with Sabbah. At times, he would loiter on the roof garden, watching Nadia go to and from Arghun's quarters and counting the minutes she spent there. He noticed too that the Buddhists were regular visitors. Despite Nadia's ominous words, he had supposed the Il-khan's indisposition was no more than a chill, and that he would soon recover from it. However, the ever more frequent sight of the priests' tawny robes made him uneasy. He felt a new tension in the air. Sabbah had increased security around the royal apartments and the commander himself seemed on edge.

On the ninth day of the month by his calculation, Giovanni rode out early with Hassan, returning to his villa only as daylight was fading. On the morning of the tenth, he was aroused by the clamour of voices and the beating of gongs. It was well past dawn. After long days in the fresh air, he had come to rely on the boys to wake him, but neither had done so.

Rubbing the sleep from his eyes, he climbed to the roof garden. The entrance to the palace apartments was surrounded by a troop of soldiers, among them Sabbah and Taghachar. At the head of the steps were the royal women, beside them the two Buddhists, and in the doorway Doquz and Oljei, clutching one another tightly and weeping. He could see neither Oljeitu nor Hassan.

As he watched, the priests came down the steps carrying their gongs and hammers. They quit the palace complex by the gate and climbed the knoll overlooking the river, beating a solemn clang as they went. Giovanni descended to his bedroom, dressed, and went out into the courtyard. By then it was empty and ominously silent.

Suddenly, the gongs began to sound again, their ever more rapid beat echoing plaintively in the damp air. Giovanni ran to the gate with their grim message ringing in his ears. A single voice raised above the din proclaimed what his heart already knew but wished to deny.

'The Il-khan is dead. Arghun is dead!'

Arghun's body was laid out in the marbled hall of the royal apartments, dressed in a general's costume with cloak and plumed helmet. His once full face had shrunk. His cheeks were hollow and across his ashen forehead was written the pain that had never been evident in life. On the stretcher beside him were a sabre and lance. Across his breast lay a Mongol bow fitted loosely with two arrows, one long and slender with a fine barb, the other short and thick. His bloodless left hand had been placed over the haft and the fingers of his right round the strings.

Twenty men of the garrison stood to attention on both sides of the hall. Round the bier wives and children mingled in silence with friends and adherents, town dignitaries and servants. Faces were solemn. By contrast, the courtyard was noisy. The gates were shut, but some curious Baghcha citizens had gathered outside, eager to learn if the rumours were true. Soldiers of Taghachar's squadron stood around indifferently in groups, drinking from communal flagons. Their loud, slurred conversation carried through the open door of the palace. There was even some laughter.

Giovanni took a last look at the corpse and turned away from the bier. Nadia was standing behind him, all in black and veiled. He bowed stiffly.

Surely he should feel something, he thought - pity, grief, anger; joy, hope - but no emotion came. His mind was numb and he had not even begun to consider what he would do next. He knew only that his treaty was in tatters. It had depended on Arghun, and Arghun was dead.

My husband will die.

Nadia's so recent prediction echoed in his head.

It may not happen this week, or this month, but it will not be long.

A suspicion formed in his brain and with it a chilling fear. The wasting disease of which she had spoken was a lingering one. Even if she were truly cursed with visions of the future, this sudden end was not what she had foreseen. Were secret enemies still at work, and had they taken advantage of Arghun's weakness to ensure his illness was of short duration? Had daggers and arrows been put aside in favour of poison and, if so, was he to become a target again?

On his way out of the hall, he met Sabbah who took him by the arm. The commander was clearly agitated.

'I must speak with you, Giovanni,' he whispered when they reached the head of the steps. He gestured towards the groups of militia in the courtyard. 'But not in front of this rabble!'

They crossed to Giovanni's villa. Once inside, Sabbah relaxed, but his jaw was set grimly.

'This may be our last chance to talk in private. You should leave Baghcha, my friend. Taghachar may declare for Gaikatu.'

'For Gaikatu? But surely Ghazan will succeed?'

'Take nothing for granted,' said Sabbah. 'Ghazan has not been publicly named so the succession will be decided by the Mongol Council. Both Baidu and Gaikatu will contest Ghazan's claim and neither is sympathetic to your alliance. Even my position here is precarious.'

'But your commission ...'

'You don't understand, Giovanni. Arghun called me friend. He returned my father's property to me after Teguder seized it illegally. I am commander only by his will.'

'Then what will you do?'

'I don't know. The Council could be months away. But you can be sure the struggle for power has already begun.'

From the courtyard came more laughter and swearing. A voice barked an order. That was followed by a chorus of Mongol battle cries, the clank of weapons and the shuffling of feet. Gradually the sounds died away.

'You hear them?' growled Sabbah. 'They are horsemen and do not march well, but they are ruthless killers. If Taghachar *does* pledge his support to Gaikatu ....' He shrugged helplessly. 'Take my advice, Giovanni. Leave Persia - while you're still free to do so!'

Giovanni studied the hardened soldier's face. He knew he should take Sabbah's advice. No more could be expected of him. He could be surrounded by enemies, both secret and overt. And, though he had accepted Pope Nicholas's commission in true expectation that he could succeed, he did not have the zeal of the Templar Knights, to accept death as the price of failure.

Yet in him burned a different zeal. He had travelled to Persia driven as much by a desire for adventure as by the prompting of his Christian conscience, and the adventure was not done. The woman he loved was free and might still be his. Moreover, he still had Arghun's letters. Ghazan might yet be Il-khan and would respect his father's wishes.

Giovanni's spirits rose. Not only could he win Nadia, but he might also have his treaty. As soon as the funeral was over, he would court her and, if all else failed, snatch her from under Taghachar's nose.

'I'm grateful for your warning, Mohammed,' he said firmly, 'but I cannot leave so long as there is hope of success ... so long as there is hope of Ghazan succeeding.'

'Then Allah grant you patience and courage, my friend. You may have a long wait.'

'Then wait I shall,' said Giovanni. 'When the mourning is over I will decide my course of action!'

Arghun's lying in state was followed by a general fast which lasted for three days. His interment was a very private affair, attended only by his surviving wives and children, together with his closest friends. No mausoleum was to be built to house his remains.

The rituals were hardly over when the members of the royal party began their preparations for the return to Tabriz. Taghachar and his Mongols had withdrawn to their billet near the river and the palace complex was quiet.

After the funeral, Giovanni retired early to make his plans. He had no intention of returning to the capital or of observing the lengthy mourning. The following night he would go to Nadia and ask her to be his wife. If she consented, they would leave immediately for Khorasan and take refuge under Ghazan's protection; if not, he would abandon his mission and take the road north west, to Constantinople.

He was only too aware of the law that forbade a man from setting foot in the female quarters, but it was a risk worth taking. Over the winter, he had discovered that illicit assignations between Arghun's advisers and the free women were not uncommon. He knew for certain that the awkward but pubescent Oljei had lately seduced more than one youth from the militia. Moreover, since the Il-khan's death, the guard had become lax again and he did not expect to be hindered.

Resolved on his course of action, Giovanni slept soundly to be awakened late by a loud banging on the door of the atrium and the sound of his name being pronounced shrilly and urgently. It was Hassan. From somewhere outside the palace came a babble of noise, the clanking of weapons, raised voices, women screaming and men bellowing orders.

Thinking the palace was under attack, Giovanni grabbed his sword and staggered to the door. When he had opened it barely a fraction, Hassan squeezed through. His face was flushed and his breathing punctuated with sobs.

'Giovanni, Giovanni, come quickly. They're taking her away.'

'Taking whom?' Giovanni was still only half awake.

'My mother! They're taking my mother. They say she caused the Il-khan's death by witchcraft.'

'Witchcraft!' Giovanni was suddenly alert. He seized the boy frantically by the shoulders. 'What do you mean? Tell me!'

'Because my stepfather's illness worsened suddenly... It was my mother who found him ... spitting blood .... There was blood on her clothes. And they found a casket with poison. Now they are accusing her.'

'What casket? Who is accusing her?'

'I don't know. I know only they're taking her away!'

Giovanni pulled on his breeches, took up his sword and rushed into the courtyard. The royal apartments were unguarded and the gates were wide open. On the knoll above the river, Arghun's tent was surrounded by a Mongol detachment wearing Taghachar's colours. Facing them were a dozen officers of Sabbah's guard. Bands of townspeople had arrived and were straining their necks for a view.

Giovanni raced towards the mound with Hassan close on his heels. He pushed past a few bystanders. Behind the soldiers, voices were raised angrily. At the tent entrance stood Taghachar himself, brandishing a scimitar. On his left, his men were holding two struggling women. A third was on her knees at the general's feet, pleading with him.

Even at a distance, Giovanni would have known Nadia anywhere.

He broke through the crowd. Cries of *poison* and *witchcraft* reached his ears.

'What's going on?' he demanded of one of Sabbah's swordsmen.

'The Il-khan was poisoned,' the man shouted above the din. 'His wife and two accomplices are accused of poisoning him by magic!'

Giovanni forced his way past to confront the ring of Taghachar's Mongols. They moved menacingly to block his path. But he could now see more clearly. The two Buddhist monks had just emerged from the tent. One was clutching a bundle of bloodstained garments while the other held aloft what seemed to be a plain wooden box. Nadia's head was sunk helplessly on her breast. Hassan had crawled between a soldier's legs was beating Taghachar with his fists.

'This is impossible ... a mistake!' cried Giovanni to no one in particular. He tried to push past the Mongols but immediately found two sabres at his throat and one at his ribs.

'We do not wish you harm, Man of the West,' grunted one of the men, 'but you cannot pass. The Il-khan's wife has been arrested. Evidence against her was found in his tent.'

'Evidence,' demanded Giovanni hotly, ' - what evidence? If there was a crime, it was not committed by Nadia.'

'Who else? Arghun's blood was on her clothes.'

'That is no proof!' cried Giovanni, seized with a sudden madness. Though threatened by the Mongol weapons, he had not been forced to release his own. He feinted backwards. A sharp blade cut into his side but, ignoring the pain, he brought his sword upwards in a desperate motion and swept aside the two aimed at his neck. With all the power of his shoulder he elbowed one of the guards aside and strode into the gap.

He caught another glimpse of Nadia, held by the waist and one arm and struggling to her feet. Hassan was clinging to the hem of her soiled gown.

The soldiers closed round him. Before he could take another step, Giovanni was struck forcibly between the shoulder blades. The blow drove all the breath from his body and propelled him forward. He fell and, in so doing, hit his head on a stone and lost consciousness.

*

V

Nadia knew her husband had been murdered.

Though the mercury substance in the casket she had so angrily cast aside would have killed in sufficient quantity, the little science she knew told her it would have been a slow, creeping death. Arghun's violent retching in his last moments, and the eruption of blood she had witnessed could only be the result of deliberate poisoning. Yet she was slow to suspect who the poisoner was, or how the deed had been managed.

Then she remembered the upset goblet and, earlier, the broken jug. The poison could have been in the wine or the water. But when had it been added, and by whom?

Two days of fasting had passed before the truth struck her with awful certainty. The first evening, she developed a headache and pain in her abdomen. Initially, she supposed it to be due to the lack of food and a reaction to the horror she had recently witnessed. However, on the second night, in the silence and loneliness of her apartment, the pain became so acute that she was gripped by the fear that she too had been poisoned and was about to die the same agonising death as Arghun. She fought down her fear and nausea. She must think clearly. Others could be in danger, Hassan or Giovanni.

Nadia rose from her divan and prepared a drink of herbs which she swallowed hurriedly. To her relief, the pain subsided. She lay down again, but her sleep was restless. Since hearing the story of Arnawaz, she had been continually haunted by the inverse gammadion symbol and, as she tossed on her bed, she could not rid herself of its image. The carved casket? Had the legs of the gammadion bent to right or left? She could not recall.

However, she had sampled the paste. What if the mixture had contained not only quicksilver, but another more deadly substance? Had poison been added to it in the sure knowledge that Arghun, believing in the paste's healing properties, would ingest it?

She joined the funeral procession, though scarcely well enough. Afterwards, feeling better, she questioned the two women who had washed and anointed Arghun's body. His chamber had been quickly cleaned and stripped of all artefacts. They did not remember the casket but had, on orders from the monks, packed the bloodstained clothing and some other items in a chest, and had taken it to the Il-khan's tent.

At dawn the next morning, she left the palace and climbed the knoll. The two matrons accompanied her. The air inside the tent was cold and damp. The flooring had been cleared of rugs, tables had been removed, and the divan lay bare of cushions or covering. In the central hearth, the stump of a candle and pieces of a broken flagon lay in the ashen remains of the last fire, now more than a week old.

The chest had been pushed into the darkest corner of the tent. Its lid had not been replaced properly, and pieces of crumpled silk and flannel hung out over the rim. Coldness descended on Nadia's heart, as if hidden eyes were watching her. The tent smelled of betrayal and death.

At her signal, the women pushed the lid aside and allowed it to fall with a thud on the bare boards. The sound echoed. The paintings of hunters and quarry seemed to spring to life. Nadia watched as her servants removed the topmost garments and explored gingerly down the sides of the chest. At length one withdrew a shirt with full sleeves of the finest Persian linen that Arghun had worn on his death bed. The collar and one sleeve were stained red.

The casket fell from its folds. Nadia picked it up, opened it and again smelled the contents. Behind her, there was a gasp and then a child's cry. She turned. Hassan ran into her arms. Oljeitu, standing at the entrance to the tent with a look of abject horror on his face, began to scream. Before she could calm him, one of Taghachar's Mongols appeared at the door of the tent, then others. They would not let her leave.

Then the Buddhists came. The short, stout one pointed to the casket accusingly. The other picked up the bloody linen. More soldiers came with Taghachar at their head. They formed a ring around the tent.

The two matrons were seized, the two boys bundled away. She saw Taghachar and Sabbah arguing and heard the shouts of *poison* and *witchcraft*. With her brain whirling, she remembered Gobras's warning. Her tolerance of all faiths had blinded her, had shrouded her enemies in robes of red. Only the Buddhists could be guilty, and they had planned her death as surely as they had taken Arghun's.

Despite her protests of innocence, she too was seized by one of

Taghachar's lieutenants. She knew only too well the penalty for witchcraft. Would they dare? She could no longer resist. Her belly was hurting again - like the pains of childbirth, only more severe. Her mouth was dry and sweat broke out on her forehead.

Her legs grew weak. The world was red behind her closed eyelids. She would never see her son again. She was dying.

Hassan .... Giovanni ....

*

VI

Giovanni regained consciousness. He was lying on his stomach, his arms outstretched. His throat was parched, his head ached and with every breath he took pain racked his lungs.

At first, he thought his back must be broken because a numbness spread across his body from waist to neck. He moved his hands and cautiously felt his neck. With effort, he raised the upper portion of his body from the ground and turned on his side. He felt his legs and slowly flexed the muscles of his calves. They were stiff but otherwise functioned normally.

He sat up and realised to his surprise that he was in the atrium of the villa.

Nadia! The thought of her immediately brought him to his senses and memory flooded back. Panic seized him and he struggled to his feet. He had to find her, to save her.

He tried taking shallow breaths. This helped relieve the pain in his lungs but the ache in the centre of his back would not go away. He pressed his hand against his spine. His shirt was wet and sticky and when he looked at the hand he saw it was covered in blood. There were also bloodstains on the front of his shirt where the Mongol sabre had pierced it.

He touched his temple and felt the outline of the contusion there. Sharp pains shot through his head. He staggered across the atrium and through the rooms he had occupied. All his possessions, credits and Arghun's letters were still there. Only his sword was missing.

Still confused, he rushed to the outer door and tried to throw it open, but it had been locked or barred from the outside. In anger and frustration, he beat his fists against it with all his strength. The force of his blows bruised his knuckles and the rough wood tore the skin from his fingers.

He went to a window and looked out. There was no one in the courtyard. At the foot of the steps leading to the banqueting hall a pair of scavenging birds pecked at the remains of a dead rat.

He thought of the roof garden. Perhaps he could lower himself to the upper veranda from there and swing down onto the lower. However, as he turned towards the inner staircase he was arrested by the sound of whimpering coming from a dim corner of the atrium. Behind one of the mosaic pillars he discovered Hassan curled up on the floor, his head between his knees and his whole body quivering convulsively. His hair was damp and his face smeared with dirt.

Giovanni put out a hand and touched him on the shoulder. The boy cringed from him.

'It's me, Hassan. Giovanni,' croaked the Venetian. He tried salivating to relieve the dryness in his mouth.

'Giovanni - you're alive!'

'Yes, I'm alive.'

'But you're wounded,' cried Hassan, staring as if unsure whether or not he saw an apparition. 'There's blood all over your face and on your tunic.'

'It can't be too serious,' replied Giovanni hoarsely. He tried to sound unconcerned, though his head, back and both shoulders still pained him. 'But, tell me quickly, where is Nadia? Where is your mother?'

'They took them. Taghachar's men took them away. My mother and two others.' He broke down in sobs. Giovanni stroked his the damp curls.

'Took them where?'

'To the river. She is dead, Giovanni. My mother is dead. They called her a witch and have drowned her, I know it.'

Giovanni fought down the despair in his heart. 'That cannot be so,' he said. 'They would not kill the Il-khan's wife. We shall go after her together.'

'It's useless, Giovanni. She's dead. I heard Taghachar say they must pay the price. And all the others have gone too. Oljeitu and the women. Back to Tabriz. They wanted to take me too but I ran away and hid.'

'How did I get back here, Hassan? How long have I been unconscious?'

'I don't know, Giovanni.' Hassan wiped his tears away but they only began to flow anew. 'I know only that my mother is dead, and the others have gone.'

'Let us go and look anyway,' said Giovanni, trying to sound

hopeful. He patted the boy's head and helped him to his feet. 'But first we have to get out of here. The door has been barricaded or locked from outside and we are prisoners.'

Hassan's spirits perked up. 'I climbed through that window, Giovanni,' he said, pointing to an opening in the atrium wall scarcely bigger than a grown man's head. 'There was a key in the lock but I was trembling and couldn't turn it. I can easily go back the way I came and try again. There's no one outside. I have heard no voices.'

The boy hoisted himself onto a ledge and started to squeeze through the gap. His head and shoulders disappeared, and finally his legs. There was silence, then the sound of feet on the veranda, much panting and the grate of metal against metal.

'It is too stiff, Giovanni. I can't turn it all the way.'

'Find something to use as a lever: a dagger; a stick; anything.'

'My bow. I can use that,' cried the boy excitedly. 'It's in my tent. Wait while I fetch it.'

Again there was the patter of youthful feet on the veranda, followed by silence.

Giovanni went to the room where he usually washed. The pitcher from the previous evening had not been taken away, and a little water remained. He emptied half into the basin and used it to clean the blood from his face and hands. He then raised the pitcher to his lips and poured the residue over his parched tongue and throat.

He climbed the stairs to the roof garden and looked out over the escarp to the fields. From the position of the sun he could tell it was late afternoon. The Mongol camp was gone.

The tent previously occupied by the boys was not visible from the villa, nor could he see any sign of Hassan, but Arghun's tent was still there on the mound, deserted save for two Persian soldiers who loitered in front of its entrance. Giovanni was considering whether to call out when one nudged his companion and pointed towards him. They engaged for a moment in conversation then disappeared into the tent only to re-emerge a moment later accompanied by two other men, one of whom Giovanni, with mixed emotions, recognised as Sabbah.

The key in the lock turned and the door opened.

'You can come out now, my friend,' Sabbah said gruffly.

Giovanni remained in the shadows, uncertain how to greet the commander. Over the long winter months, their intercourse had been nothing but friendly. Sabbah had been an intimate of Arghun's family and had enjoyed the Il-khan's high esteem; Giovanni liked him. But he had allowed Nadia to be unjustly accused of murder. He had sanctioned her arrest and possibly condemned her to die. If he had not been directly responsible for Giovanni's detention, he had at least connived at it. However, neither Sabbah nor his men had drawn their weapons.

Giovanni came out into the light. 'You call me friend, yet you lock me up in my quarters and leave me for dead,' he said savagely.

'If you had been dead, there would have been no cause to lock you up,' retorted Sabbah. There was censure in his voice, but the tone was far from hostile.

'And is it friendship that leads you to betray your sovereign's mistress and give her up to a mob?'

Sabbah came into the atrium and leaned against a pillar. The light fell on his face. It was stern and unsmiling. His eyes were tired and red-rimmed. 'Do you think so little of me? If you've any idea of what has occurred here, you must surely know that none of it has given me any pleasure.'

'I know only that a king has been murdered, and an innocent woman betrayed,' Giovanni went on in bitter reproach.

'You understand so little of our people and our ways, Giovanni,' Sabbah replied sadly. 'Of the Mongol princes who rule us even less. Taghachar would have cut your throat for your interference. Many more innocents might have died, and still you would not have saved her, nor the others who were taken.'

'So it's true? Nadia charged and sentenced? Drowned in the river?'

'As Allah is my witness, Giovanni, I do not know.' Sabbah came farther into the room. 'I know only that she was arrested with some servants and has disappeared. What would you have had me do? I honour womanhood and cannot bring myself to believe in witchcraft, but I pled with Taghachar to no avail. I have twenty men at my disposal, and cannot fight an army. Taghachar's picked troops would have killed us all if I had continued to defy him, and he would have taken reprisals against the townspeople.'

'Yet I might have prevented them from harming her if I had not been struck from behind,' said Giovanni in anguish.

'Your foolish chivalry would have achieved nothing. Another step and you would have been cut to pieces.'

'Cut to pieces perhaps, but I might have taken two of her murderers with me,' said Giovanni angrily. He paused. 'Yet I was not cut down, but struck from behind.'

'If it'll make you feel any better, you may strike your attacker in return.' said Sabbah. 'Eye for eye, tooth for tooth, hand for hand, as Moses said.'

Giovanni stared at him. 'You?' he muttered.

'Yes, it was I who hit you, though it gave me no satisfaction,' confessed Sabbah. 'You'll be bruised for a week, but the blow saved your life.'

Giovanni sat down miserably at the foot of the pillar and buried his face in his hands. 'What purpose would it serve us to fight?'

'None, other than to relieve your anger,' said Sabbah after a moment's silence. He joined Giovanni on the floor. 'So what do we do now?'

'It has all been too quick,' said Giovanni, 'as if it had been planned. Tell me what happened after you locked me in here.'

'I can tell you little more than you already know,' Sabbah replied. 'Just after dawn, the two boys followed Nadia and two woman servants to Arghun's tent. They found them rummaging in a chest containing bloodstained clothing. Oljeitu saw the blood and cried out.'

'Did Nadia not give an explanation?'

'She was given little chance. The child wakened half the town with his yelling. You must sleep like the dead, my friend, that you did not hear him. First a guard or two came, then the monks, then the rest of Taghachar's men. Soon there was a crowd. No doubt some passing townspeople spread the word round Baghcha. Nadia was arrested, and the two who were with her.'

'Who accused her?'

'The Buddhists. It was they who found the box. They denounced Nadia as a witch and ....'

'Box - what box?' Giovanni leapt to his feet.

'A wooden casket with an emblem on its lid, - a cross like the necklace the lady always wears. The monks claimed it contained a poison, and that Nadia, knowing it to be evidence of her guilt, was about to remove it.'

'What has happened to it?'

'It's still there in the tent with the clothing for all I know. If you think it has significance, you have my permission to look for it, though what you hope to prove I can't imagine. I have ordered the chest containing the clothing to be burnt, so you'll have to hurry.'

Hassan scampered across the fields. He avoided the mound, where the two guards kept half-hearted watch over Arghun's tent, and reached his own within minutes of leaving the palace. He was panting from exertion, and sat on the ground to recover his breath.

The discovery that Giovanni was alive had cheered his spirits and kept burning the slender hope that at any moment he would hear his mother's voice and see her run towards him with arms outstretched. However, as he contemplated the plain grey walls, all his wretchedness returned, and his lack of comprehension of everything that had occurred only made his grief more profound.

His first emotion had been anger. He had been snatched from Nadia's side, kicking and screaming every obscenity he had ever learned without knowing the meaning of the words. He had watched her dragged away, and had seen Giovanni, who might have protected her, fall. In the previous half year, Hassan had been the instrument of the deaths of two men. He had seen two more die. Now, he wanted only to kill some more - to strike at the enemies who had once pretended friendship, to plunge a sword through their hearts, to watch their life blood spill on the sand and see their lives slowly ebb away.

After the anger had come fear. He was alone. His hands and feet had been bound with cord to prevent him struggling and he had been carried, still screaming, into Arghun's tent.

The minutes had passed. The clamour had died down. The sound of voices receded. In the silence that followed he managed to free himself and slip unseen from the tent. Driven by the desire to discover where his mother and the others had been taken, he descended towards the River Kura, slithering in the mud as he approached the swirling spring currents. There were tracks in all directions but so many and confusing that he could not tell whether they had been made recently or days previously.

Trial by river water, he had heard the soldiers say. Hassan had not at first known what they meant, but their cold sarcasm had frozen his blood. Only later, as he wandered by the rocks and muddy pools, did the grim significance of the words dawn on him and fill his young soul with terror. He fled from the river bank, skirted the mound and ran towards the palace. The gates were open. Outside the women's quarters were two wagons, loaded in preparation for a journey.

He had heard horses approaching, then voices cursing loudly. He dodged behind a pillar, then slipped into Nadia's apartment just as the first of the Mongol soldiers came through the gates. Shortly afterwards he heard Oljei and Doquz calling his name. He had not wanted to face them and cowered in a dark corner until they gave up the search. When all was quiet again, his tears burst forth. He felt cold all over and was shivering. Without quite knowing why, he crossed the courtyard to Giovanni's villa, tried to turn the key in the lock and, finally, unable to shift it more than a fraction, climbed through the little window.

Giovanni pushed aside the heavy flap that served as a door to the royal tent and entered. It was much as he remembered only most of the furnishings had been removed. Only the divan remained, along with a plain chest.

He knelt by the chest, opened it, and looked inside. In addition to garments, there were a pillow and some blankets, all stained red. 'But you said he bled from inside, Mohammed. Surely this much blood could only be the result of a sword cut?'

Sabbah shook his head. 'There were no wounds on the body.'

'Then poison it must have been!' said Giovanni. 'What else but a virulent substance could have caused so much bleeding?'

Doubts began to nag at his brain. There had been Nadia's dire predictions and her confession that they might have been more than friends. Her knowledge of herbs and medicines was profound. What if, after all, she had been responsible?

He shook his head to rid himself of the suspicion. 'Never,' he said to himself. 'I'll never believe it.'

He threw the clothes and bedding aside. Near the bottom of the chest was the casket, lying open and damaged beyond repair. Most of its contents had been spilled.

Giovanni picked it up and ran his fingers over the emblem on its lid. *The cross of Arnawaz.* He shuddered involuntarily.

Sabbah was staring at him quizzically.

'Just an evil omen, if you believe in such things,' said Giovanni, trying to dispel the unnatural chill that pervaded him. 'A legend, Nadia told me, - two crosses, one bent to the right like the one she wore, the other to the left like this carving. A sinister plot has been hatched here, Mohammed. Someone wanted the Il-khan dead and Nadia accused.'

'It may be as you say, my friend,' said Sabbah, 'but how, and to what end, will you pursue the truth? Arghun is dead. Nadia too in all likelihood.'

'Are you so sure?'

'Only Allah knows. The penalty for witchcraft is drowning, and she has disappeared. She was not with Taghachar when he took the others back to Tabriz. And if the women were drowned, their bodies will have been washed into the sea. There will be no trace.'

Thoughtfully, Giovanni studied the casket and smelt what remained of its contents. The chill had lifted and he now felt only anger. 'I'm no alchemist and this residue is a mystery to me,' he said. 'But I swear whoever plotted these foul deeds will pay dearly for them.'

Hassan was so immersed in his grief that he almost forgot his mission. He snatched up his miniature bow and quiver of arrows then, remembering something else, went to the box where he kept his toys and games. Among them he found Giovanni's icon of the Madonna and child. He had always meant to return it, but found special meaning in it. He kissed it now, returned it to the box and quit the tent. Sabbah and Giovanni had just emerged from the palace gate together. There was no evidence of coercion. The commander's sword was sheathed and the three Persian guards sauntering several paces behind seemed in no way threatening.

Yet Hassan was confused. He no longer trusted anyone. It was soldiers who had seized his mother. He crouched in a depression until the men had reached Arghun's tent and Sabbah and Giovanni had gone inside. He waited. One of the guards settled himself on a boulder while the other two wandered off deep in conversation. Hassan grew calmer. It was time for boldness, he told himself. He had been raised the son of a prince, and princes did not run from their enemies. Whatever was afoot, he would discover it. If, despite appearances, Giovanni was in danger, he would rescue him. After all, Sabbah had not prevented his mother's arrest, and who but he could have locked Giovanni in the villa.

Hassan strung his bow. He fitted an arrow to it and began creeping slowly up the little hill. There was no cover on the knoll for a fully grown man, but the scattered boulders and tree stumps were just large enough to conceal him from the casual glance of the nearest guard. He had proceeded most of the way and was congratulating himself that he could easily reach the tent without attracting attention, when his foot caught on an exposed and rotting root. It snapped with a loud crack. Startled and off balance, Hassan released his arrow. It flew at an angle and imbedded itself in the soft earth. The nearest Persian was already on his feet with his sword drawn. He shouted a warning to the others and started down the slope.

Thus discovered and with his boldness gone, Hassan's only option was to flee. He took to his heels and ran back across the field, with the guards in pursuit. He headed again for the Kura. His feet sank in the mud of the track and he lost his sandals, but he plodded on regardless with the shouts of the men ringing in his ears. Once among the trees and rocks that lined the river bank, he could evade them, find somewhere to hide until they gave up the search.

To his left, the field fell towards the river in an escarp. The bad weather had eroded the soil, making the slope even steeper in places and more treacherous overall. Little caring where it led, Hassan gripped his bow tightly and leapt over the edge. He landed on his rump and slid between saplings and over rotting vegetation all the way to the bottom. Here the ground was stonier. He picked himself up and began to run again without looking back. He reached some woods. The trees had only just begun to bud, but he dodged among them, searching for a hollowed trunk where he might conceal himself.

He heard his name pronounced, faintly but distinctly. He slowed his pace and turned to check behind him. He could not see his pursuers, but surely that was Giovanni's voice he had heard. He stopped running and climbed a tree to obtain a better view. The three Persians were no longer chasing him and had turned back. He heard his name called again, saw two figures emerge at the top of the escarp, a long way behind, and recognised Giovanni from the style of his clothing.

Hassan asked himself why he was running. If the Venetian was searching for him, there could be nothing to fear. Anyway, he was cold and hungry, his feet hurt where the stones of the path had cut him, and there was ultimately nowhere to run to. He gripped a branch and looked down for the nearest foothold. As he did so, his eye caught an unexpected movement close to the river and some distance from where he perched, a shapeless bundle of pale blue and white that lay in the hollow of a rock, half-immersed in the lapping spring current. Hassan froze against the trunk then, plucking up his courage, looked again. The object was still there, but it no longer moved. He climbed down from the tree and, picking his steps carefully, walked along the treacherous ridge, looking for somewhere to descend.

He found a place where the bank was less steep. Using outcrops of rock as a natural ladder, he clambered down. The mysterious bundle was about thirty paces away and, as he drew closer, Hassan saw with mounting horror that it was the body of a woman, spread stiffly and unnaturally, face down on a bed of mud and stones. Her legs trailed in the water. The hem of her stained and bloody garment had caught on the rock and it rose and fell flaccidly with each ebb and flow of the Kura's current. The exposed flesh of her arms was a ghastly white, and in the curve of her shoulder, where the gown had been torn away, something glinted in the weak afternoon sun.

Hassan uttered a howl of despair. He rushed forward, fell on his knees by the side of the corpse and threw himself, groaning, on the ice-cold and lifeless neck.

*

VII

Giovanni and Sabbah were alerted by the cry of the guard.

The commander laid his hand on his sword, but Giovanni restrained him.

'It will be Hassan returning,' he said. 'I had almost forgotten him.'

'Nadia's boy? Then he did not go back to Tabriz with the others?'

'He climbed through a tiny window into my apartments and hid there. I sent him to find something to turn the key.'

They ran outside. Two guards were already half way across the field in pursuit of Hassan. The third had stopped to pick up something from the ground outside the tent.

'Come back, you fellows,' yelled Sabbah. 'It's only a child. Nadia's son!'

'A child perhaps, but one with a deadly sting,' cried the third Persian. He waved a miniature arrow in the air.

'After what he's witnessed today, he can't distinguish enemy from friend,' said Sabbah. 'You frightened him, most probably. I've seen the boy shoot. If he had meant to fire at you, you would be dead. Call the others back. The Venetian and I will follow him and reassure him.'

They found Hassan kneeling in the mud of the river bank, with Nadia's gammadion round his neck. His eyes were staring, his teeth chattering and his shoulders shaking violently. Giovanni put an arm round him and lifted him gently to his feet.

Sabbah knelt by the body and reverently turned it over. He gave a gasp of surprise. 'This isn't the Il-khan's wife,' he exclaimed.

Hassan clung to Giovanni's belt. He was still shaking. 'She was wearing the necklace so I took it,' he sobbed. 'I couldn't look at her face, but I knew it wasn't she. I knew it wasn't my mother!'

'Then do not look now, Hassan,' said Giovanni.

He bent over the corpse and drew his breath sharply. Death had sucked all beauty from her pallid features. There was a bloodless gash on her cheek and her forehead was a mass of contusions. On the left side of her head was a gaping wound where a rock had torn hair and flesh from her skull. Her eyes were still open, frozen with a look of extreme terror.

'Do you know this girl, Giovanni?' Sabbah enquired.

'We both know her, Mohammed,' said Giovanni faintly. His stomach heaved and he vomited into the lapping current.

He recovered quickly from the spasm. His grief and anger were bubbling over. He knelt by the body, closed the staring eyes, then clasped the limp, wet form to his breast, remembering how she had once been.

'It's Pidorka,' he exclaimed. 'An innocent child. May all the demons of Hell pursue the perpetrators of this deed, and feed on their flesh and bones for all eternity!'

Giovanni carried the girl's body back reverently to the palace while Sabbah sent an officer to find her parents and break the news to them. Later, they searched the riverbank until dusk but saw no trace of other victims.

Food was plentiful in the kitchen, and Sabbah procured sufficient rations to provide them with a cold supper. Hassan would not leave Giovanni's side until, overcome with exhaustion, he lay down on the floor of the atrium and fell soundly asleep.

Giovanni lit a lamp and he and Sabbah faced one another in its flickering light.

'What was Pidorka doing on the river bank?' the commander asked. 'She was not one of those arrested.'

'And how did she come to be wearing the gammadion? Nadia would not have parted with it willingly.'

Sabbah shrugged. 'I only wish I had answers, my friend. What will you do now?'

'In truth, I do not know, Mohammed. I no longer have the patience you urged upon me so recently. In my heart burns a rage I've never felt before. The Il-khan was coldly murdered. I can think only of discovering the truth and of avenging the innocents blamed for his death.'

'You're so sure it was poison?'

'I'm sure.'

'Suppose you are right,' said Sabbah. 'What can you do? What dare you do?' He laid a friendly hand on Giovanni's shoulder, where he had formerly struck him and Giovanni winced.

'I'm a soldier, my friend,' Sabbah went on, 'and death is a soldier's constant companion. For all that, I'm not made of stone, and the sight of that poor broken body moved me more than I can say. Such an act cries out for vengeance!

'I also know how Nadia saved you at Tabriz and, as a man of passionate desires myself, I have several times wondered ....' He paused. 'No, that is the past, and I will ask no questions. Whatever she was to you, God alone grants life and death. Allah al-Muntaqim, al-Hakam - the Avenger and Judge will decide the murderers' fate, if murderers there be. Is that not also what your faith teaches?'

'That is what I used to believe,' replied Giovanni. 'But I'm not the man I was when I came to Persia, perhaps not even the man I was this morning.'

'Get what rest you can,' Sabbah advised. 'Tomorrow you may feel differently.'

As most of Il-khan's servants had returned to Tabriz with his family, Giovanni drew his own water. He bathed and changed his clothing. The pain in his back had eased and the injury proved to be no more than a bad bruising. The sword cut in his side was superficial. Sleep was far from his mind and he sat down by lamplight to consider the future.

Hassan belonged with his grandfather. Kartir was the boy's nearest true kin. But, if the viceroy had returned to Kerman as he supposed, how was the boy to get there?

As for finding Arghun's murderers and avenging Nadia and Pidorka, Giovanni told himself that Sabbah was right. Even if he knew how the poisoning had been managed and who had administered the fatal dose, what could or dare he do? If either Gaikatu or Baidu were the instigators, both were much too powerful to be challenged.

Was Nadia a victim because she had discovered the means - the casket bearing the sign of Arnawaz, - and had perhaps also identified the killer? Had she been arrested and condemned only to prevent her revealing the truth, or was the plot more subtle? And why was Pidorka wearing the hooked cross?

Without finding any answers to his questions, Giovanni drifted into sleep punctuated by meaningless nightmares. He awoke before dawn, stiff and sore, and with a pounding head. The lamps had died and he rekindled them. The flames flickered, casting silent shadows against the walls and across the floor of the apartment. His eye caught sight of the chess table, the pieces toppled as Hassan had left them after their last game together. Absent-mindedly, he picked them up and began resetting them on the playing surface. In his real life drama too, all the pieces were there - kings and queens, castles, mounted archers and leering footsoldiers, all playing their parts. Only the moves were unknown.

He was distracted by the sound of movement behind him. Hassan had already risen and was rubbing the sleep from his eyes.

'What are you doing, Giovanni?'

'I'm not of a mind to play,' said Giovanni, continuing with his rearrangement of the chess men. 'It's merely that I hoped to find answers in these symbols, to discover the truth behind these plots and counterplots that threatened first your life and mine, then succeeded in taking that of your mother.'

'But you are mistaken, Giovanni,' cried Hassan with just a trace of enthusiasm. 'You've set all the pieces wrongly. The table should be rotated through a right angle. And, look, the white priests occupy the knights' positions.'

Giovanni stirred from his reverie and looked at what he had been doing. He had indeed arranged two priests wrongly. In addition, the board lay at ninety degrees to its correct position, and he had set all the pieces along the sides adjacent to the ones they should have occupied.

He leapt to his feet in sudden inspiration.

The priests? Why had he not considered it before? What better way for a murderer to cover his tracks than to pronounce witchcraft was involved.

Hassan was gazing at him in astonishment. 'What is it, Giovanni? What's the matter?'

Giovanni did not answer. He was staring again at the chess board. Another memory stirred, Nadia's words to him as they parted that first day in Tabriz Castle.

All doors look alike to anyone unfamiliar with the corridors.

As the absurd simplicity of the idea struck him, he laughed aloud.
'What is it?' cried Hassan in alarm. 'Are you no longer unhappy?'
'Believe me, Hassan,' said Giovanni, 'I'm the most unhappy of men, but I may at least have found the solution to a puzzle!'

As morning wore on, the theory gradually took shape in Giovanni's mind. His negotiations with Arghun had posed a threat and he had been the target of an assassin once. Why not twice? Supposing everyone was wrong about the attempted kidnapping, and that he, not Hassan, had been the intended victim. The assassins had bungled. In the darkness and confusion of the corridors, they had mistaken the apartment, just as he had done in broad daylight. All the tutor's talk was superstitious nonsense.

Now Arghun had been struck down, and Nadia too, - perhaps because she knew the murderers, or because they feared her influence. Though he had no evidence to connect the princes to the crime, he was sure that either Gaikatu or Baidu was to blame. Taghachar had appeared to be loyal, but there could be no doubt now he was implicated.

By early afternoon he had made his decision. Some of Sabbah's men had gone with Taghachar and others had gone back to their wives. The commander was leaving the next day for Khorasan, to join Ghazan's army.

'I am coming with you,' Giovanni announced as they shared a midday meal.

'It's not an easy journey. I pray Allah, the road through the Alburz is clear of snow.'

'Clear or not, we will come. Hassan needs a guardian, and the princes of the West an ally.'

'So be it then.' Sabbah held out his hand. 'I'll be glad of your company.'

'And I of yours,' said Giovanni. He gripped the commander's hand. 'But now answer me this if you will, Mohammed. What became of the two Buddhists? Did they return with Taghachar's troops to Tabriz?'

'I neither know nor care what became of them.' Sabbah looked puzzled. 'What interest can a Christian have in two heathen monks?' he asked indifferently.

'As much as a Muslim, if one was Arghun's poisoner, or both, as I suspect.' said Giovanni.

A frown of anger crossed Sabbah's brow. 'A priest?'

'Why not, if he were not one? Who other than a supposed cleric would have a better opportunity? And, as Ghazan too favours the Buddhist religion, I ask myself if they plan his death in a similar manner. Even if I'm wrong, Mohammed, we should at least warn him!'

*

VIII

It was raining again, a heavy downpour from clouds that seemed to hover over the trees. In the six months at Tabriz, Giovanni had seen hardly any rain at all, perhaps two or three light showers that did no more than damp the earth. The climate at Baghcha resembled that of Venice and he had relished the change, but now the weather depressed him. Every moment reminded him of Nadia, of their ride north on Arghun's trail, of the day in the boats, and of their last conversation the day before the Il-khan's death.

They had left Baghcha at first light. Giovanni armed himself in the Mongol fashion with bow, arrows and reinforced leather shield. He had found a short sword among the weapons in the palace armoury and this hung from his belt. Hassan carried his own weapons, the miniature bow and quiver. Sabbah and twelve loyal followers made up their party of fifteen.

They rode in silence. Occasionally, Sabbah would try to engage Giovanni in conversation but neither could sustain it. For five days they travelled along the wet coastal plain, often within sight of the sea. Their tents were loaded already erected on carts, and camps were made and struck with ease. On the morning of the sixth day they changed horses at Rasht and turned inland towards the mountains, following the Sefid River along their westernmost edge. It became much colder, although most of the snow had melted from the lower slopes.

'Where now?' asked Giovanni.

'We'll make for the town of Qazvin. There we'll change the ponies again and enquire for news of Ghazan.'

Their road led through a gorge between two mountain peaks which, though not as high as Sahand, seemed dark and menacing because of their proximity to them. Giovanni was reminded of Italy and the mountains of the High Tirol that lay no more than a few days ride north of Venice. He had never been there in winter but could imagine the wind howling down from the crags of the *Gran Venezia* or San Giacomo Heights and chilling his bones just as the icy blasts from these alien peaks chilled him now.

They climbed higher. Although the path was clear, flakes of

freezing snow gusted at intervals through the valley, stinging their faces and obscuring the way ahead. Giovanni was overcome by a longing for his homeland. His adventure had palled. Perhaps the mission had been doomed from the outset. Nadia had said the alliance was never meant to be. Was her certainty due to an understanding of his heart, or an inspiration from heaven?

Several times he considered abandoning the journey. He would head for the Silk Road, return to Tabriz and find a merchant caravan bound for Venice. Only a glance at the boy, muffled in a thick goatskin coat, riding uncomplaining at his side, made him despise his own lack of resolution. At nights, they would curl up together under the skins in the warmth of the Mongol tent, and Giovanni was glad of the comfort this proximity gave him.

Nadia! How many times he had repeated her name in his dreams, unsure if he spoke it in the silence of his thoughts or aloud. How many times he had returned to the cellar beneath the old priest's villa to receive the caresses of the woman of his desires. They were dreams without the wakening to reality, where his fantasies could be explored without hindrance.

He had not had the dream since leaving Baghcha but on the ninth night of the journey he was restless. Once again he felt the warm excitation in his belly and the hardness in his loins. He spoke Nadia's name and reached out to cast aside the talisman that lay between him and his gratification. Before, he had always encountered a pillow or bedpost. This time, his hands touched living flesh. The warmth of the other body woke him. Hassan had crept even closer than usual. His body nestled against Giovanni's chest, and he had thrown one arm round his neck.

Giovanni recoiled from its touch and threw aside the skins. The arm was removed and in the darkness of the tent he heard Hassan's quickened breathing.

The boy sat up. 'What's wrong, Giovanni?'

'It's nothing, Hassan. I was dreaming. Go back to sleep.'

'Do you think often of my mother, Giovanni?'

'Why do you ask me that?' Giovanni asked guiltily.

'It's just that you spoke her name three times, and I've heard you pronounce it before, on other nights when I couldn't sleep.'

'Yes, I admit I sometimes think of her,' said Giovanni.

'I knew it,' said Hassan. 'I do too, all the time. Sometimes I feel she is there inside me.'

'She will always be inside you, Hassan. The people we love and who love us, never truly die, but stay with us forever, in our thoughts and in our dreams.'

'Did you love my mother, Giovanni? She often spoke to me about you, and after we had been together hunting, or playing chess she would ask me questions. What had occurred that day, what had we talked about, how you behaved towards me, and had you mentioned her? I think ... I'm sure she thought pleasurably of you and would have gladly lain in your bed.'

Giovanni's heart beat faster in the darkness. 'What do you know of such things?' he demanded.

'There's very little mystery,' said Hassan sleepily. 'I watched my father and Tolaghan once. Doquz, Oljeitu and I crept into their bedchamber. Afterwards, I tried to do it with Oljei because she is older and likes kissing, but that bit of me was too limp. Later, my mother told me how men and women join their bodies, and have pleasure together, and how the seed goes from the man to the woman to make the child. Then she sighed and said she wished she could know that pleasure again.'

Giovanni could think of nothing to say. The boy was a man in so many ways, but he surely could not understand a man's longing. He was warrior and philosopher, but in matters of love he was still a child. Yet Giovanni knew there was no one else to whom he could ever confess his secret desire or his pain.

Hassan lay back on the floor of the tent. 'She sighed and looked so sad,' he yawned. 'And it was the same sigh she gave when she spoke of you.'

Giovanni stroked the boy's curls and replaced the skins over them both. 'Yes I loved her, Hassan,' he whispered, and the bond between them was complete. Whatever hardships and dangers faced them in Khorasan he could not now turn back.

'And she will always be there inside me too,' he added, but Hassan was already asleep.

In the morning they began the descent towards Qazvin and reached it within another two days. To the east, the towering, snow-clad peaks of the Alburz were hidden in cloud, dull and unwelcoming. However, in the valley, the weather was warmer and the trees showed the first signs of spring.

The town's garrison was loyal to Ghazan, but they had no recent word of their prince. Fighting in the plains of Semnan had been reported prior to the onset of winter. Ghazan's disagreement with his deputy governor, Nauruz, had spilled over into open hostilities between their forces.

'If Nauruz joins the Chagatai, that will be as great a threat to our country as the accession of Gaikatu might pose,' Sabbah growled. 'Ghazan's hopes of gaining support will wither if he cannot put down this rebellion.'

'Chagatai?'

'A fierce Mongol tribe. The descendants of Genghis who rule Transoxiana. They would dearly love to extend their territory and influence.'

'Then I'm taking Hassan into a war region.'

'It's not too late to turn back. You could take the boy to Kerman.'

Giovanni had already considered this possibility and rejected it. He had no map of the region and doubted he could find his way to Kerman, even if Hassan were willing to try it.

'No, we shall go on with you,' he said.

The ponies were changed and they set off eastwards towards Rayy, following the foothills of the mountain range. The way became easier. The clouds had lifted. All but the highest peaks were now visible. For fourteen days they had met few travellers and encountered no armed patrols but now that they had returned to the traders' routes merchant caravans passed them regularly in both directions. The signs of military activity were becoming more frequent. Armed horsemen, with bow and hooked lance, many with a second animal in tow, met and challenged them at approaches to villages along the route. Surly footsoldiers squatting on rocks or on the low roofs of houses watched them suspiciously.

Giovanni was apprehensive lest they encounter a squadron loyal to Ghazan's enemies and be detained or robbed, but at each outpost Sabbah showed the Il-khan's seal and they were waved through without question.

On the morning of the sixteenth day they reached the outskirts of Ghazan's capital and by noon were inside its walls. News of Arghun's death had reached Rayy a week previously but it was garbled. There had been no hint that the Il-khan's death was other than a natural one. The prince had posted troops to guard the city but had already departed with his main army for Semnan. Nauruz was rumoured to have twenty thousand men there, mostly his own Persian followers, but also a reinforcement of Chagatai Mongols.

The party moved on. They passed another outpost unhindered and descended into a narrow valley. Giovanni had ridden ahead of the small column when, suddenly, Sabbah called him back and pointed at the northern horizon. On the crest of the nearest ridge, lined against the grey of the sky, appeared a band of horsemen, fifty or more strong. Giovanni instinctively reached for his sword.

'Wait,' cautioned Sabbah.

The riders came down the hill at a trot, moving into an arc reminiscent of the Tabriz hunt. Some carried flags. Bows were drawn.

The arc gradually tightened.

'I'm not afraid of a fight,' said Giovanni, 'but we are outnumbered three to one and if we are to run, we should do so now.'

'Run?' echoed Sabbah with a forced laugh. 'And where would we run to, I wonder?'

He wheeled his mount and gestured to the rear. Another troop of cavalry was approaching out of the sun, the foremost riders forming a column three abreast, the rearmost a line that was already fanning out, forming a second arc and barring their retreat.

Giovanni's hand tightened on his sword hilt.

'Don't move hastily, my friend,' said Sabbah. 'If they had seen us as an enemy, they would have already shot their arrows. But I don't recognise these colours, and I don't think they recognise mine.'

One of the leading riders of the second troop came towards them, a powerfully built Mongol wearing a general's helmet and carrying a sabre. 'Identify yourselves!'

Sabbah dismounted. 'Mohammed Sabbah, commander of the Il-khan's forces at Baghcha,' he said.

'Arghun's dead, we've heard,' rejoined the other indifferently. 'What's your business in Rayy?'

'We've ridden with the news from Baghcha, but clearly it has gone ahead of us,' said Sabbah, motioning Hassan forward from his position at Giovanni's side. 'I have a boy with me, who wishes to join his brother, Prince Ghazan.'

The officer looked Hassan over, not missing his short sword and the tiny bow fastened to his saddle, then laughed heartily. 'What's your name, boy?'

'Mahmoud Hassan.'

'So the prince is your kin? That's just as well - and just as well too for your escort,' said the Mongol. 'There are rebellious traitors everywhere, and we've been sent out to hunt them down. I'm General Musa of Yazd, and pleased to meet you.' He caught sight of Giovanni. 'And you? You've a foreign look about you. Are you also the prince's friend?'

'I do not have that honour,' said Giovanni. 'However, I have brought him letters written by his father. My name is Giovanni di Montecervino from the city of Venice.'

'Very well,' said Musa. He signalled to his ring of warriors to lower their bows. 'You may ride with us, Commander Sabbah and Master Giovanni of Venice. You too, Master Hassan. We're on our way to rejoin Prince Ghazan and his allies. His camp is only an hour or two's ride from here.'

The prince's regiments were camped on the plain between two river beds. In all directions, as far as Giovanni could see, were row upon row and line upon line of tents, tents of all sizes, descriptions and colours. On his left, they reached almost to the foothills of the mountains that lined the horizon from west to east. Hovering above them and dominating the northern sky was a gigantic snow-capped peak that poked its way through a retreating bank of rain cloud.

On his right, the tents fanned out towards the desert like a shapeless mosaic of white and grey tiles on a background of pale green and gold. Some were round in the Mongol style, one large central pole and shorter ones framing the whitewashed walls, resembling the one that had been his bedroom for fifteen nights. Many were square or rectangular. Others were little more than awnings - sheets of canvas supported on inverted lances to provide shelter from the midday sun. A few fierce-looking women in battle dress, moved among the men or squatted inelegantly at their posts.

Sabbah halted his men at the perimeter of the camp and ordered them to unload the tents and equipment from the carts. Musa's regiment marked out an area of ground as near to water as they could manage and proceeded to set up its own camp.

The tent of the commander-in-chief was easily distinguishable. It was larger than the others and stood in a clearing surrounded by a troop of mounted warriors. A second troop lined the only approach to it. Pennons of red and white fluttered lazily from its roof and hung from lances impaled in the soft ground.

Giovanni and Hassan dismounted, leaving their ponies and pack animals in the charge of two turbaned servants. Sabbah did likewise. They followed Musa along the human avenue towards the central pavilion. A servant stationed near the entrance struck a gong.

The flap of the tent opened and three men emerged, one behind the other. The first wore armour. He was about nineteen or twenty years of age, and small and stocky with unmistakable Mongol features. Giovanni noticed that one of his eyes was set higher than the other, giving his face and ogreish look. The second was perhaps ten years older and in civilian dress. He was no Mongol, rather his profile and the cut of his beard were what Giovanni characterised as belonging to the Jewish people. The third to emerge from the tent was Nadia's father, Ahmed Kartir.

*

IX

The viceroy had aged. His bearing was less erect, his eyes had lost their vitality, his cheeks were sunken and his hair and beard contained more grey than before.

While Giovanni was recovering from his surprise at the change, Hassan rushed forward and threw his arms about Kartir's waist. The emotions he had controlled with such manly determination since leaving Baghcha boiled over. His tears flowed freely and his breathing was choked with sobs.

'Grandfather!'

The young Mongol watched this reunion for a moment without interrupting, then turned to his other companion. 'So this is the stepbrother I've heard so much about, Rashid,' he said.

'It would seem so, Your Highness,' replied the man of Jewish appearance.

'Hassan, then. That is his name,' said the Mongol to no one in particular. 'And General Musa ... and two strangers.'

'One the Venetian ambassador, perhaps,' suggested the man called Rashid.

'But which, Rashid, which?' enquired the Mongol. 'Neither looks like a diplomat to me. Perhaps Musa can enlighten us.'

Giovanni struggled to hide his amazement. Surely this small, ugly youth could not be Arghun's son.

The general performed curt introductions, saluted and left.

'So, you're the Christian, eh?' said Ghazan. He was a full head shorter than Giovanni and squinted up at him grotesquely.

Giovanni could for the moment think of no suitable reply. He acknowledged the prince's question with a formal bow.

'And I suppose you'll want to convert me too, eh?' said Ghazan. 'As if I didn't have enough advisers. This one here, Rashid, was born a Jew but now staunchly proclaims his devotion to Mahommet. The viceroy of Kerman, descended from a long line of Gabars, does the same. They both would have me cast off the mantle of Buddhism and become an adherent of Islam. What are you, Master Italian - a converted Hindu?'

'I've always been a Christian, Your Highness,' said Giovanni, recovering his tongue, 'and I have no intention of becoming anything else. However, I have to say that since arriving in your country, I've learned something. So long as we love God and respect our fellow men, we are best left to worship and serve in our own way.'

'By Genghis's beard, that was well said, Master Italian,' cried Ghazan with enthusiasm. 'What do you say now, Rashid?'

'Only what I have said many times already, Your Highness. This is a Muslim country. It has been so for nearly seven hundred years. Most of the people are Muslim, and they need a Muslim as ruler.'

'And Kartir agrees with you, I know,' said Ghazan with a touch of impatience. 'But both of you forget I've a war on my hands. When that traitorous fellow Nauruz is at my feet in chains and begging my forgiveness for the trouble he's caused, I will think more about your suggestion.'

Rashid inclined his head resignedly.

Kartir, having released Hassan from his embrace, regarded Giovanni gravely as if there was something on his mind he wished to communicate. It was Ghazan however who took the initiative.

'I hope you bring some better news to us, Master Giovanni,' he said. 'There has been nothing but gloom about the camp since the rider from Baghcha brought news of my father's death. I'm sorry he's dead, and of course I feel deeply for the governor of Kerman that his daughter should have been judged the cause.'

Giovanni glanced at the viceroy. The very mention of Nadia, even if not by name, opened the door of his memory and allowed all his feelings of despair, anger and guilt to spill into his consciousness. He imagined Kartir was looking at him accusingly.

'We had thought to be bearers of the news, Your Highness,' he said flatly. 'I confess to being surprised it arrived before us.'

'We Mongols don't waste time,' said Ghazan. 'Genghis's generals crossed the country from north to south in less than a week. There have been two messages. The first merely told me my father was dead. Then, my own man from Tabriz to acquaint me of events - Arghun dead, his wife arrested. Witchcraft, by all the infernal powers! What do you say, Master

Venetian, eh?'

'Tales for the gullible, Your Highness!' said Giovanni. He glanced at Kartir and fancied he saw expectation in the other's eyes. The viceroy was paler than ever and was leaning against the stiff tent wall for support. 'The truth is more sordid. Your father was certainly poisoned, but no one who knew the lady could believe her capable ....'

He broke off the sentence as Kartir staggered and slumped silently to the ground clutching one of the impaled lances. Hassan went to his aid. Kartir tried to get up, but seemed incapable of further movement.

'Help him, Rashid,' said Ghazan shortly. 'And take the boy too!'

Rashid and Sabbah lifted the viceroy to his feet and, supporting him on their shoulders, carried him back to the tent. Hassan followed them.

'So, Master Giovanni,' went on the prince when they had gone, 'what's all this about poison, eh?'

'His Majesty's death was planned, I am convinced,' Giovanni said. 'Indeed, I may hold proof of it in my possession.'

'Then let me see it, and any last messages from my father,' demanded Ghazan impatiently. 'By the gods, this could change everything. Perhaps Kartir was right in his predictions ....'

He was interrupted by sudden shouts from somewhere on the perimeter of the encampment. Dust rose on the horizon. Pennons were raised in the air.

'Enemy horses!' yelled the prince, springing into action. He seized a lance and waved it. 'No time for letters now.'

There was great commotion. Like a disturbed colony of ants, the army began to move. Weapons serving utility purposes were seized, ponies mounted and within a few seconds whole sections of the plain were devoid of their primitive tents. Sabbah reappeared, then the viceroy supported by Rashid, with Hassan at their heels. The man with the gong banged it furiously. The line of guards broke as each man ran towards his horse. Giovanni found himself hustled towards where his own mount was tethered.

'Pull back into the foothills,' Ghazan ordered his officers. 'Divide your forces in three. When the enemy pursues, we use the pincers to entrap them. I'll ride with the left flank.'

Kartir had taken the reins of a pony and was trying to haul himself up laboriously.

'Help him with the stirrup, Rashid,' shouted the prince urgently. 'And get to the wagons. Hassan, Giovanni, stay with me!'

Giovanni grasped Hassan by the waist and almost threw him into the saddle. He loosed the animals, slapped both on the rump and, as they broke into a trot, leapt agilely onto his horse's back.

With incredible speed the camp was struck. Tents were either collapsed or loaded still erected onto wagons. Loose animals carrying other equipment and provisions were herded together by the women. What had been an army in repose became in the space of a few moments one mounted and ready for action.

They moved out of the river bed in close formation. The army split, the centre heading straight towards the mountains, the two wings fanning out over the plain. They gathered pace, spurring the ponies into a brisk trot, then into a fierce gallop, with Ghazan at the head waving a red and white pennon as encouragement.

When they reached the undulating country that marked the beginning of the mountain range, the left wing halted. Giovanni, on the prince's tail, was perspiring heavily. Beside him, Hassan panted with excitement.

'I've never been in a battle before!'

'Guard your life with that small shield, and pray you live through it, Little Brother,' Ghazan admonished.

They waited and watched, concealed just below the summit of a ridge. From the river valley, in the distance, emerged a horde of riders, their colours green and gold. The sun was now up and, as they drove forward, bows drawn, it glinted on the polished metal of the leaders' helmets and on the tips of the lances that hung from the saddles.

The central regiments of Ghazan's army, having reached the edge of the plain, turned and began to advance along the direction they had come. They were still at least three hundred paces from the enemy when they drew their bows and released a merciless hail of long arrows in the direction of their foes. Shields were raised but that did not prevent a score or more of the leading horsemen from falling, either struck fatally by the sharp barbs or propelled to the earth as their mounts died under them.

The enemy returned fire. Ghazan's regiments wheeled full circle and retreated towards the foothills, leaving their dead and wounded to be trampled by the beasts of their pursuers.

'Now!' yelled Ghazan above the thud of the horses' hooves and the chilling battle-cry of the advancing Mongols. 'May the spirits of our ancestors defend us. They're Chagatai. If you escape their arrows, beware the hooks on their lances.'

He raised his pennon. The left flank mounted the ridge and descended it at a furious pace. At the same time, the right wing, similarly concealed on the other side of the plain broke cover and went into the attack. Like the pincers of a gigantic crab, they closed on the belly of the enemy.

The bowmen rode with their knees, both hands free, and shot at the gallop. The van of the Chagatai, caught off guard and separated from the middle and rear by the two-pronged attack, was cut down. The two forces met and engaged. The bows were of little use now, and in the melee that ensued the weapons were sword and lance, the latter being used to good effect in unhorsing the riders or in bringing down their mounts.

Giovanni watched from the ridge. He was conscious of the non-combatants and women camp followers waiting apprehensively behind him with their loaded wagons, among them Rashid, motionless but alert, and Kartir, pale and haggard. He felt not only conspicuous but guilty with the Mongol bow hung on his pommel and the sword at his side. He knew all their lives would be threatened if Nauruz's forces broke through, yet he hesitated. It was not his war.

He had forgotten Hassan and, when he turned, the boy was no longer beside him. Then he saw him, bent low in the saddle, his tiny bow at the ready, riding madly in the wake of Ghazan's troops, in his excitement totally oblivious to the danger from a group of outriders in a second wave of enemy attack.

Giovanni no longer hesitated. He crossed himself and kicked his pony into a gallop. He had no skill with the Mongol bow, but he fixed the leather shield firmly on his left arm and drew the sword from his belt. He had overtaken the tail of Ghazan's troop and was half way down the slope when a shower of arrows descended on them from the sky. A dozen of the men fell. A deadly barb embedded itself in his shield. A second shaft glanced from it and fell harmlessly to the earth.

Hassan fared less well. His small shield protected his person from injury, but an arrow penetrated his pony's ribs. The animal whinnied pitiably, reared, and threw its rider to the ground where he lay stunned and motionless. A single Chagatai moved in, his lance raised for the kill. Giovanni acted instinctively. He rode straight into the Mongol's path. In the act of throwing, the Mongol swerved and turned to face the new enemy. Their mounts collided. The lance met Giovanni's shield at an acute angle and tore it from his arm. The Mongol reached for his scimitar, but Giovanni's short sword struck his clavicle and almost severed his arm from his body.

Hassan stirred. All around him lay the bodies of the dead and dying, both men and animals. Nearby, his unfortunate pony lay mortally wounded, its forelegs jerking in a vain effort to rise, its foam- and sweat-covered breast heaving as it drew its last painful breaths. Giovanni, already half unseated by the force of the impact with the Chagatai warrior, slid from the saddle and, still gripping his own horse's bridle, took the boy by the collar of his tunic and heaved him onto the animal's withers.

A second Chagatai bore down on them. Giovanni seized the fallen lance and swung it in a circle with all his strength. The hooked end connected with the Mongol's temple, ripping flesh and hair from bone and splitting his skull. The man fell without uttering a sound. Giovanni leapt on his horse's back and retreated to the relative safety of the ridge.

In a few more moments the battle was over. Caught by surprise, Nauruz's force disengaged and fled. Ghazan, blood-spattered, breathless, and without his pennon rejoined the observers.

'It's not over yet, by the gods,' he growled. 'Today we had the better of them, but there have been three such skirmishes in the month, and this is the first where I have not come off worst.'

'But you taught Nauruz a lesson, Your Highness,' proclaimed Rashid. 'I confess too, I find Venetians more manly than I had thought them. As for this stepbrother of yours, he looks like a Persian child, but I'll swear by the Prophet's beard there's more of your noble father in him than we were led to believe. He brought down two hairy fellows with his toy bow before the enemy arrow felled his animal.'

'We're all in your debt, Master Giovanni,' said the prince. 'My little brother most of all, eh? I saw the way you took that vicious Chagatai's face. That was a sight I'll not forget in a hurry. Well, Rashid, what is our strategy to be now?'

Rashid glanced at the carnage with seeming indifference. 'You are right, Prince,' he replied dryly. 'It's far from over. I recommend you withdraw to Rayy and enlist some reinforcements. The Chagatai have scattered and the rest of Nauruz's army is to the south, so we have several days to consider our next move.'

'I'll return to Rayy then,' Ghazan declared soberly. 'In fact, I begin to be sorry I ever left it. Have Viceroy Kartir taken to my villa and the walking wounded to the citadel. The bulk of the army can camp here, but we'll post the sentinels along the River Golu and on the Semnan road to give us more warning of an attack.'

*

X

The ancient city that Ghazan had made his headquarters lay between the Alburz and the Great Plateau. Standing in the path of Genghis's advance, it had suffered more than most Persian cities from the destruction wrought by his armies, and much of its once fine architecture lay in ruins. The blue earthenware that had decorated its walls and towers was, where they still stood, cracked and blackened by the heat and smoke of countless fires. The splendour of its palaces and villas, which had outshone even that of Baghdad itself, was dimmed.

The population of Rayy was small. Most who had survived the wars of seventy years earlier had migrated northwards, taking with them their skills in pottery, painting and silk weaving, if little else. Few of their descendants had returned and now carried on their artistry and trade from the nearby town of Teheran, which by a quirk of Fate had begun to prosper under Ghazan's satrapy.

Some proud families had determined to return their city to its former glory. Parts of the damaged outer walls had been rebuilt, a tower and mosque or two had been restored, and some usable land had been ploughed and its drains relaid. But their efforts were largely in vain. Ghazan, threatened continually by the Chagatai, and now faced with a rebellion from within his own ranks, had little time for architecture or husbandry. Rayy now served a mainly military purpose.

Giovanni followed the prince and Rashid along an avenue of elm and linden towards the citadel. The branches of the trees were broken and the trunks split. On either side, what had once been gardens was, after fifty years of neglect, a jumble of wild grasses, decaying wood and fallen rose-arches. Ruins of plinths, small columns and miniature temples lay scattered amidst the tangled vegetation.

The citadel itself was a cheerless edifice of crumbling brickwork. The steps leading up to it were hollowed and the door was defaced by lewd drawings. Over the doorway, the remains of a decorative arch hung so loosely that the slightest vibration would have brought it crashing down. The topmost step was dislodged entirely, exposing a cavity as wide as a man's foot.

At the entrance waited a wild-looking man, half Mongol, half Persian, whom Ghazan immediately engaged in excited conversation. Giovanni could tell that the fellow had been riding hard as his boots were dusty and his face and clothes caked with filth. Two leather flagons fastened together with a thong hung round his neck.

Giovanni paused on the threshold to survey in horror the scene that met his gaze. Hassan, bringing up the rear, clutched his sleeve. The boy's mouth was agape and his eyes were wide and disbelieving.

Inside the building was more decay. The floors were worn, the tiling had lost its glaze and pieces of plaster littered the ground below the cupola. On the lower part of the walls were more drawings and scrawled obscenities.

The sights and sounds of war were everywhere. Men with gashed arms and torn skulls, or with broken arrows embedded in their sides, sprawled against pillars and writhed in agony on horse blankets, moaning, retching and gasping for breath. In the centre of the atrium, water spurted from a damaged fountain and trickled along the flagstones, mixing with the blood that oozed from their open wounds. Abandoned shields and bows, dark red-encrusted swords and lances lay all around.

The most seriously wounded had been left to die on the battlefield, but Giovanni could see that many of those who had been brought back to the city in the carts would not survive the day. A harassed physician moved among them, ignoring the screams of the more hopeless cases and muttering profanities as he passed on to the treatable.

Avoiding the prostrate torsos and limbs, Ghazan and his visitor crossed the atrium, entered a court at the far end and disappeared into an ante-room. Rashid stopped at the fountain. He filled a discarded kettle with water, bathed the faces of some of the dying and held their heads while they drank. Despairing eyes followed him. Parched tongues lolled on cracked lips. Hands reached out feebly to touch his jubbah.

Giovanni had seen such sights before but never had he been struck so forcibly by the senselessness of warfare. And it would get worse. In every small town of the plain there had been evidence of fighting. The garrisons there were no defence against guerrilla attacks by marauding

Chagatai. Farms had been burnt and their owners put to the sword. It would be only a matter of time before Ghazan, having marshalled his reinforcements, would march out again to engage with the rebels. There would be more blood and wasted flesh, more widows and orphans.

What reason did he have for remaining in Persia now, Giovanni wondered. His part in the recent battle had sickened him. He had done what needed to be done, but this was neither his country nor his fight. He had been away from Venice too long. His ageing father might well be dead; his mother and her brother, the Duke, might well have given him up as surely the Holy Father must have done. He was an only child. Who would inherit the Montecervino estates if he did not return? He thought with longing of the lush green Po valley and the ordered rows of vines that would now just be budding in the spring sun.

The pressure of a young hand on his arm brought him back to the reality of the present and, with a sigh, he led Hassan across the bloody flagstones to the court where Rashid, having done what he could for the wounded, joined them.

Ghazan was in a black mood and pacing the floor of his room. He beckoned to them impatiently. He had been drinking. Giovanni could smell the sickly mares' milk liquor on his breath. The wild-looking man sat at a table. He had untied the flagons and was quenching his thirst from one of them. His disagreeable odour and that of the fermented drink mingled with the smell of horse sweat.

'The tidings are bad on all fronts, Master Venetian,' frowned Ghazan, gesturing towards a charred bench and indicating to Giovanni that he should sit. 'My agent has just come from Tabriz. The Wazir ad-Daulah has been killed. Baidu is making overtures to the leaders of the Muslims. And Gaikatu's lording it in the capital, pretending surprise at my father's death. Does that make him the more guilty, eh?'

'Possibly, Your Highness.'

'Gaikatu has never been one for religion, nor Taghachar by all accounts,' mused the prince. He stopped pacing and stood in the middle of the room with his arms folded, tapping one foot restlessly. 'If they sent assassins to Baghcha it wouldn't surprise me. Poisoners. That was what you hinted, Giovanni, eh?'

'That is my belief, Your Highness.'

Ghazan began pacing again. Then he stopped suddenly and brought his fist down hard on the table. His agent released the flagon and, sobered, jumped to his feet and stood to attention.

'Tell the Venetian what you told me, Sadr,' Ghazan enjoined.

The envoy wiped some surplus liquor from his mouth. 'Prince Gaikatu plotted to bring down ad-Daulah,' he said. 'Many'll testify to that now. And Baidu and Timur were in it with him. Irregularities were to be found in the treasury accounts, and the Jew pronounced an embezzler. The Muslims would be enraged and Gaikatu would lead a revolt with the promise of fiscal reforms. Arghun would be deposed.'

'Deposed,' the prince repeated. 'Deposed, but not murdered, eh Sadr?'

'No, Sir. Murder was not intended. Gaikatu cautioned against it.'

'Go on,' snapped Ghazan. He nodded towards the flagon. 'Wet your throat again and tell the Christian the rest of your feeble tale.'

Sadr took a long drink of the liquor. His eyes flitted from Giovanni to the prince and back again. 'Prince Baidu was impatient, Your Excellency,' he went on volubly. 'He thought he could gain the crown with the support of the Mamluk Sultan, if he promised to convert to Islam. But his plan was threatened by Your Excellency's friendship with Arghun. Your Excellency was to be killed!'

'But the scheme failed, Giovanni, eh?' remarked Ghazan. He gave an ogreish wink. 'You're not an easy man to kill, even with poisoned arrows.'

'No, Your Highness,' Giovanni acknowledged with a muted smile, 'but I fancy there was more than one attempt on my life. In the first, Hassan was nearly killed instead.'

'Yes, Your Excellency,' Sadr agreed. 'Two attempts *were* made at Tabriz. Baidu laughed when the first went wrong. Everyone thought it was a bungled kidnapping.'

'And what about the Venetian's theory that my father was poisoned?' asked Ghazan.

'My source knew nothing of that, Your Excellency.'

'Your source?'

'A Persian girl, Sire. One who knew more of the Mongol tongue than either Gaikatu or Baidu realised.' Seeing he was not been forbidden from drinking, Sadr took another swig of liquor, emptying the flagon. 'Of course, there are rumours.'

'There are always rumours,' said Ghazan. 'But are they true, eh?'

Sadr shrugged. 'There's talk among the militia, Your Highness. They say Baidu sent two assassins to Baghcha to poison the Il-khan's food. The Italian was to die too. Their deaths were to look natural.'

'If they had poisoned the food, half the Baghcha population would be dead,' said Ghazan, turning to Giovanni and winking again. 'I don't see how it could be managed with Arghun on the alert.'

'If you'll permit, Your Highness, I will outline my theory,' said Giovanni. 'The assassins were disguised as priests.'

'Priests?' Rashid looked sceptical. He had not sat down but was listening keenly from the doorway.

'Buddhist monks,' Giovanni corrected. 'Their poison was added to the contents of a decorated box - a medicine, or a delicacy His Majesty enjoyed. I have it here, or what is left of it. But I think something went wrong, Your Highness. Perhaps they used too much poison. Your father was sick already and vomited blood. The killers panicked and needed someone to blame ....'

'By Temuchin, it's plausible, Giovanni.' The prince folded his arms and began tapping his foot once more. 'Buddhist monks, eh? What do you say, Sadr? Surely my uncle Gaikatu was implicated.'

'He's denying it, Your Highness.'

'Denying it, eh. So what's he up to? Gaikatu's no Muslim.'

'He's publicly promising amnesties to all. They say he has plans to reform the tax system. To bring in a new currency.'

'New coins with his effigy, no doubt,' scowled Ghazan.

'No, Your Highness. A scheme from China. Paper money.'

Ghazan's face lightened in one of his more grotesque grins. 'Paper? What do you think of that, Rashid?'

'Does my opinion count for anything?' asked Rashid sulkily.

'Come, Rashid, you're still my chief adviser,' said the prince. 'You can't go in the huff just because we argued on the way here. I'm not about to treat with Nauruz - nor to adopt Islam, though it's tempting if the Buddhists are such rogues. But you're right about this mares' liquor. It leaves a foul taste. Oblige me by fetching some water.' He turned back to the envoy. 'Now, Sadr, what else is there?'

Sadr looked uncomfortable. He licked his lips and stole another glance at the second flagon of fermented mares milk. Ghazan pushed it across the table to him.

'There are the women, Your Highness.'

'Women? What women?'

'Arghun's wives and relatives, Sire. Prince Gaikatu shows his contempt for Your Highness's claims by marrying two of them. Two others that were unwilling have been restrained in a private villa.'

Ghazan flushed with anger.

'That's an outrage,' he fumed. 'What of my little sister - Oljei? By the Great Khan's beard, if Gaikatu has touched her, I'll cut off his privates.'

'The princess has not been harmed, Sire. She's safe in the castle.'

'But there are two prisoners?'

'Yes, Your Highness. One is Keremun ....'

'She's a child, by all the infernal gods,' roared Ghazan, his face now contorted with helpless rage. His squint was more prominent than ever. 'Keremun was never Arghun's wife, and she's no relation. She was promised to me as a virgin bride on my accession. And the other?'

'The other is the Persian lady, Sire - that Taghachar arrested in Baghcha. Nadia, the mother of that boy there!'

Giovanni felt the blood drain from his face and the saliva from his tongue. His heart missed a beat. He rose unsteadily, but could only stand speechless. Hassan however leapt on Sadr like a wild beast, tearing at his clothing and beating him about the chest and neck.

'It cannot be my mother,' he screamed. 'She's dead. Tell him it cannot be she.'

'Dead?' growled Ghazan. 'What nonsense is this? Who said she was dead?'

'That is what we believed,' said Giovanni. His voice shook. 'Commander Sabbah and Hassan saw her dragged away. We thought she had been drowned with the others. We found her necklace ....'

'Taghachar had to pacify the mob, but he wouldn't dare execute her,' snorted Ghazan, still enraged. 'Gaikatu would have ripped out his intestines. My uncle's enamoured of the woman, by the gods, and the general knows it. Nadia was taken to Tabriz. How can you have thought otherwise, eh? Taghachar's men threw two serving crones in the Kura to keep the mob happy.'

'Not crones, Prince!' cried Giovanni. He remembered Pidorka's appealing eyes, soft breasts and gentle hands and his suppressed anger bubbled over. 'We found one body - a maid of seventeen. Wearing Nadia's gold necklace.'

Ghazan glared. 'Impossible!' he said incredulously. 'Taghachar would not kill a maid who could pleasure him.'

'Even so, it is true.'

Ghazan squinted at him, then at his chief adviser, who had returned with a jug full of water. 'We've touched on a mystery here, Rashid,' he grunted, 'and on something else if I'm not mistaken. Our Venetian is less the diplomat and more the cavalier than we had thought. What do you know of this, Sadr?'

'One maid did die, I heard, Your Highness,' replied the envoy, 'but it was none of Taghachar's doing. Some wenches were abducted. As they left Baghcha, one leapt out of a cart and ran back along the river bank. They say she slipped on the wet rocks, fell over the edge and disappeared.'

Giovanni groaned. Nadia was alive, a prisoner, and Pidorka's death had been an accident. Yet the story did not explain why she had been wearing the gammadion. And something else niggled. If, indeed, the Buddhists panicked when Arghun bled, why had they not made good their escape? Four days had elapsed between Arghun's death and Nadia's arrest. Why had they waited?

Ghazan had begun to pace again. His anger had eased and he seemed less the prince, more the helpless youth.

'What am I to do, Rashid?'

'You know my opinion,' said Rashid. 'This changes nothing. Your Highness's only hope of the crown is to make peace.'

'But my mother is alive,' pleaded Hassan. He grasped Ghazan by the knees. 'You have to go to Tabriz. We must save her.'

'I would like to take your mother from Gaikatu's clutches, believe me, Little Brother,' Ghazan rejoined. 'But what can I do, eh? I can't desert my army in the middle of a war, nor can I concede to Nauruz, whatever my advisers think.'

The tears welled up in Hassan's eyes and he ran from the room. Ghazan seemed quite moved.

'Go after him, Rashid,' he said. 'You have children. Explain my predicament.'

'I'll do my best, Your Highness,' said Rashid. He turned in the doorway and frowned at the prince like a stern father. 'But forgive me for saying so again. The war could be over tomorrow if both you and Nauruz swallowed your pride. The day after tomorrow, you could be on your way to Tabriz. It was a stupid quarrel and I forget even how it started.'

'Don't forget yourself, Rashid, by the gods,' cried Ghazan petulantly to the retreating figure of his adviser. He took a drink from the water jug then emptied it over his head and face. He ran his hands through his wet hair. 'It *was* a stupid quarrel, Giovanni, but how can I end it when Nauruz is burning Khorasan? How can I send even one platoon to Tabriz to free the woman?'

Giovanni's heart was beating furiously. He knew what he must do. 'If you'll permit it, Your Highness, I will go with Hassan and attempt it.'

'You, Master Venetian?'

'A platoon, if you could spare one, would be seen as a threat. In this situation, one man can accomplish as much as an army. I ask only that Commander Sabbah share the adventure with me, if he is willing. Someone familiar with the roads from here to Tabriz will be invaluable.'

'I confess I'll never understand Christians,' said Ghazan. 'Gaikatu'll make short work of you. You would risk your life. Throw it away for a ....' He broke off in mid sentence as his eyes met Giovanni's. 'By my ancestor's tomb, I see!' he exclaimed. 'You and the boy .... Why else? You want Nadia for yourself!'

'Does it matter if I go for my own sake or for Hassan's, Your Highness?' asked Giovanni. He held the prince's stare.

'By the pox, you're a daring fellow,' said Ghazan admiringly. 'You can take Sabbah with you and, if you succeed, you may have the woman. Arghun's will freed her. I swear no ancient Mongol custom will stand in your way. And if her father recovers from his illness, he'll not deny you. I'll see to it.'

'Thank you, Your Highness,' said Giovanni. 'And perhaps I may live to surprise you again. It is no part of my plan to engage Gaikatu in a contest of swords, nor to appear in Tabriz as myself. I fancy a Muslim merchant with a full purse can do the job whereas a foreign diplomat might not.'

The young Mongol gave him a puzzled squint, then laughed jovially.

'A disguise!' he exclaimed. 'I begin to see sense, and some hope, behind your bravado. You have a very Persian look, Giovanni. I've always thought so. And with those beady eyes of yours, and that black beard, you would make a very fine imam. The costume is easily obtained, and you may use the post horses. However, do me one favour. Rescue the princess Keremun as well as Nadia and I shall be forever in your debt. And if by some distant chance, Gaikatu or Baidu should die at your hands, I'll give you half of Persia as a reward.'

*

XI

Nadia's recollection of her denunciation and arrest was hazy. It had all happened so suddenly.

When she came to her senses, she was lying in a moving wagon. A crude awning had been erected over it. The atmosphere was damp. She could not imagine how she had come to be there. Though the pain in her insides had gone, she felt sick and empty. Her clothing stank of vomit.

Someone was kneeling beside her and wiping her forehead with muslin soaked in water. Nadia focused her eyes. She recognised Pidorka, who had been her personal attendant at Baghcha two years earlier.

'Where are we?' she demanded weakly. 'Where is Hassan?'

'We are on the way to Tabriz, My Lady.'

Nadia tried to sit up. A pain shot through her temple and she cried out.

'Lie still a moment, My Lady,' said Pidorka. She supported Nadia's head and, having shifted her position on the boards, allowed it to sink back slowly onto her lap.

Nadia felt the soothing touch of hands on her neck, massaging gently and easing away the ache. She remembered how this girl had an extraordinary talent for manipulating the spine and muscles of the shoulder. Then Arghun had learned of it and had sent Pidorka to the bathhouse to work as a masseuse.

After a few moments more recent memories flooded back. She sat up.

'Where are the two women who were with me?'

A look of terror came over Pidorka's face.

'I do not know, My Lady, but I fear they are dead. The Mongol soldiers called them hell-hags. Poisoners. They seized them and carried them off. I was afraid they would kill me too, though I have done nothing. And you, My Lady. But the general said you were too valuable a prize. They were taking you to Tabriz and I was to be your companion. I have brought a box with clothing ....'

'My son!' cried Nadia. 'I must go back.'

'You are still unwell, My Lady. Besides, we are guarded.'

Nadia felt the sickness passing. She struggled to her feet, pushed the awning aside and looked out. A Mongol warrior drove the wagon, his woman at his side. Two more of Taghachar's men rode escort on their left. On their right was the river. Two spare ponies were tethered to the rear.

'You say there's a box with clothing, Pidorka,' she said desperately. 'Help me find something other than this gown and cape to wear. I must go to my son. He must know I am alive.'

'You cannot, My Lady. Tagachar has left ten of his men on the road behind in case you run.'

'Help me dress while we consider a plan,' said Nadia. She pulled off her soiled gown and shivered in the dampness. Pidorka threw the gown into the furthest corner, selected another from the box and gave it to her. Nadia dressed in it and combed her disarranged hair with her fingers. 'There are woods nearby,' she went on. 'Perhaps if we take the two ponies we can outpace them and hide there.'

Pidorka looked doubtful. 'I can ride, My Lady. Baghcha is my home and I don't want to leave it. If I take one of the ponies, they may not pursue me. Then I can take a message to your son.'

Nadia considered, then she unfastened her necklace and placed it round Pidorka's neck.

'Very well. Take the fylfot as a token. And find the Venetian ambassador. Beg him to take care of my son until we can be reunited.'

'Yes, My Lady.'

Nadia saw the blush on the girl's cheek and for a second felt the pangs of jealousy. She knew Pidorka had served Giovanni, that she had been sent to him by Arghun as a companion and that, in all likelihood, he had succumbed to her charms. Why would he not? The girl had true northern beauty. Her features were finely sculptured and she had a lithe, youthful body.

She shook her head to rid it of unwanted images. It no longer mattered that they had found comfort together, only that Pidorka should escape. She helped her onto the tail of the cart and watched her climb agilely onto the back of one of the ponies, slip its tether and kick the animal into a gallop. Clods of earth and muddy water flew from its hooves.

The escorts had seen her. They wheeled their mounts and one

turned in pursuit. Nadia grasped the rope that held the remaining riderless animal to the wagon, but the pony shied out of reach and she almost lost her balance.

The second Mongol came menacingly towards her. Nadia made another grab for the rope, but he seized her by the waist and hauled her onto the saddle in front of him. She swung her fist and struck him in the face.

'You're asking for it, witch,' the man leered. 'I always fancied tumbling a khan's woman.'

The cart had halted on the brow of a hill.

'Leave her,' snarled the driver. 'Taghachar'll have you castrated if there's a mark on her.' He cursed savagely. 'And help that fool bring the maiden back!'

Nadia's captor deposited her reluctantly but effortlessly in the back of the wagon and took off after his fellow. The first Mongol had circled in an effort to head Pidorka off, but she was making good ground and evaded him.

Nadia gripped the edge of the awning. The other pony was now directly behind her. Again she took hold of the rope, trying to pull the animal closer. She thought of leaping for its back, but her dress hindered her movement.

She looked up. Pidorka's pursuers had slowed and seemed to be giving up the chase. The plan was working.

However, no sooner had hope filled her heart when the girl's pony missed its footing in the mud and stumbled. Pidorka was thrown head first over its neck, landed on the treacherous Kura embankment and lay still. The two Mongols spurred forward. They had almost reached her when Pidorka rose shakily to her feet and began to run.

The bank gave way. Pidorka screamed. Even the escort seemed transfixed in horror, and when they moved to assist her it was too late. The girl vanished over the edge amidst fragments of rock and clay.

Nadia gave a moan of despair, turned her head away from the awful scene and sank to the floor of the cart, drained of all resistance.

XII
Tabriz

She remembered little of the rest of the journey. There was a supply of food in the cart, and her captors stopped twice to replenish it and to collect fresh water. However, though Nadia's sickness had begun to leave her, she was so crushed and grieved by Pidorka's fate that she could scarcely eat.

They had almost reached Tabriz when Taghachar, riding hard with a single troop of his men, overtook the wagon. The general had always pretended loyalty to Arghun and Nadia had never once suspected him of treachery. Even when his men had seized her in the tent, she had told herself they had done it to protect her from the consequences of the accusations hurled at her. However, when he refused her freedom, kept her under close guard and would not answer any questions about where she was being taken or why, she knew his true allegiance now lay with one of the princes. She surmised that her implication in Arghun's murder and seizure were part of a cleverly engineered plan.

Her life was in no immediate danger. However, she knew only too well the intemperate natures of Gaikatu and Baidu and their weakness for fleshly pleasures, and she looked forward with increasing dread to the day when either would return to Tabriz as Il-khan. Moreover, she was afraid for Hassan, left at the mercy of a clever enemy. Even Giovanni, who she was sure would have protected him, might be dead. They had tried once to kill him and might have succeeded at the second attempt.

The villa where they took her was comfortable if not sumptuous in its decoration and furniture. She was housed in one of two wings, built on either side of the courtyard and of the two gates. The apartments were entered from a covered veranda decorated with brightly-coloured tile. The structure was well maintained. Although the gates were unlocked, there were bars on the outside and, even without them, the permanent presence of two sentries at each exit prevented her leaving.

For the first few days of her captivity, Nadia saw only the guards and an elderly matron who prepared and brought her food, and none was inclined to conversation. She was perfectly free to move about within the villa itself, but the weather was cold, and for most of the time she remained indoors, except to draw water from the well, risking only a daily walk in the courtyard and round its small central garden to maintain the suppleness of her limbs. Although she had been allowed a supply of her herbs and medicines, she had no opportunity to practice her skills. Her routine became tedious and she began to long for a companion with whom she could converse.

The guards met her requests for information with stony silence. However, the old woman eventually gave her to understand that the second wing of the villa, though presently empty apart from a room in which she herself lodged, was being prepared for a new occupant.

Nadia considered escape. If she could only pass the guards, she had many friends in Tabriz who would shelter her. However, though she might have dealt with one guard - drugged his wine when he came into the villa for refreshment or perhaps, given sufficient time, dulled his wits - there was always another outside and two more at the opposite end. Moreover, she would be risking her friends' lives by involving them. Given the obstacles, she decided to wait and study the habits of her keepers at greater length.

Towards the second week of her captivity, she was aroused in early morning as usual by the call of the muezzin from the nearest mosque. On going to her window, she saw that one gate lay wide open and a group of three persons, followed by one of the sentries, was proceeding along the veranda towards a door on the opposite wing. One of the new arrivals was clearly there reluctantly. She was a small, underdeveloped Mongol girl of thirteen or fourteen years of age, escorted by the woman who brought the food. Behind them was Gaikatu, smiling toothily as always. Nadia's heart skipped a beat and she stepped back behind the window pillar. The small party entered the apartments, the guard returned to his post and the courtyard was once again deserted.

Several minutes passed. Gaikatu and the matron reappeared, conversed briefly under the veranda, then parted, she to the gate which closed behind her, he in the direction of Nadia's wing. Nadia waited apprehensively. To her surprise, the prince knocked and called out politely to enquire whether she would permit him to enter.

'Since it appears I'm quartered here at your pleasure, I can scarcely object,' said Nadia acidly.

Gaikatu showed no annoyance at her reply but came in, smiling broadly.

'I trust you are in good health and find my humble residence to your liking, My Lady Nadia,' he began, with a casual glance round at the room's furnishings.

'I'm as well as can be expected for one who is shut up against her will,' she replied boldly. 'What do you mean by detaining me here, away from my son and servants? How dare you treat me as a criminal!'

'I suppose you'd rather I'd let them drown you in the Kura with the others,' Gaikatu responded with a sly grin. 'As to me detaining you, it's a temporary measure only. Once I'm proclaimed Il-khan and we are married, you'll be free as any of my wives. Or you can save yourself the wait and marry me now!'

'You should have drowned me,' said Nadia, 'because I shall not be the wife of a man whose crimes include treason and fratricide.'

'You'll do as you're told,' growled Gaikatu. 'And let's be clear about one other thing. Of aspiring to the throne I plead guilty, but as far as my brother's death is concerned, I'm as innocent as you are yourself.'

'You may continue to deny it, but I know you had a hand in his poisoning, even if you did not administer the fatal dose. I know too that both you and Baidu were behind the plot to murder Giovanni di Montecervino.'

'The Christian's wounding was none of my doing, I swear,' said Gaikatu. He appeared amused rather than offended by the accusation. 'And Arghun's death was my cousin's work alone. Though I don't pretend sadness at it, poison would not have been my way. That was how our father died.' He smiled grotesquely. 'It was a subtle scheme for all that. Baidu's men disguised as priests, by Genghis!'

'Then it was as I suspected,' said Nadia. 'The Buddhists were the assassins and I their scapegoat. And the Italian ambassador was to be next.'

Her assertion seemed to annoy Gaikatu.

'By then, the Christian's life was a matter of indifference,' he frowned. 'And you were never meant to be harmed. The villains were supposed to disappear as soon as Arghun breathed his last. Instead of that, they leave clues lying around for you to discover. They exceeded their authority, by the gods, and if I find out who they were, they'll rot in a dungeon. My cousin too, if he's been lying to me. As it is, thank the gods for Taghachar's vigilance.' The frown vanished and he shrugged. 'But why are we discussing the past, My Lady? I came here to talk about our future together. You must know that our laws and customs give me the right to take you as a wife. Life for both of us will be much more pleasant if you submit to me willingly.'

'You have no right. You are not Il-khan yet.'

'I soon will be.' Again the prince smiled broadly. He grabbed her suddenly by her hair, which had not yet been bound, pulled her roughly towards him and, before she had time to resist, kissed her on the mouth. His touch was moist and his breath stank of liquor.

Nadia broke free, pushed him away and rubbed the saliva from her lips.

'You have my answer,' she cried vehemently. 'Kill me if you like, but I shall not be your wife nor submit to you.'

Gaikatu again grasped her long hair, drew his scimitar and, with a stroke which passed within a blade's width of her cheek, removed a handful of her dark tresses.

'It would indeed be a pity to cut such a beautiful throat,' he said calmly. He allowed the flat of the sword to rest briefly against her neck, then, very slowly and deliberately, he brought it across her shoulder, between her breasts and down over her abdomen and thighs.

Though Nadia continued to defy him with her eyes, she inwardly trembled. She felt only horror and revulsion as if, instead of the blade, the prince's hands were touching her and performing this violation of her person. Helpless, she allowed the blade to caress her body, and watched Gaikatu's features twist lustfully as he pursued his perverted game.

All at once, he seemed to tire of it.

'Before the next month is over, I'll be proclaimed the new ruler of Persia,' he said, replacing the scimitar in his belt and turning abruptly towards the exit. 'I vow then you'll think more favourably of me.'

Nadia sat on her divan trying to calm her quivering emotions and control the shaking in her limbs. Not since Kerman had she felt so alone and afraid, and then she had been little more than a child. If Gaikatu was to be believed, Arghun's killers had wanted her dead, not because Baidu had ordered it, but for some sinister reason of their own. But who were these enemies of whom Gobras had warned her, and why had they ignored Baidu's order that she be not harmed?

Strangely, she no longer feared for Hassan but only for herself. She knew now he was alive and safe. The strange, uncontrollable power that gave her brief glimpses of the future, had twice during her time at the villa shown him to her fully grown, on one occasion at the head of an army, on the other aboard a fine sailing ship. These visions did not occur in dreams but came to her as reflections in her mirror or in the rippling surface of the water as she bathed, and she silently thanked Allah, or whichever other god had chosen to send them to her.

More than once over the past weeks, she had thought of Giovanni and now, as her mind became calmer, she thought of him again and of what might have been. She pictured his solemn yet handsome face and tall, muscular figure with great longing. He had loved her, but surely, believing her dead, he would have returned to his homeland, his love forgotten.

She was so preoccupied in her thoughts that she did not hear the soft footsteps on her veranda. Her door open and a hand touched her on the shoulder. Nadia looked up with rekindling terror, but instead of the hated face of her captor, she beheld the pale and frightened face of the Mongol girl. Her jet black hair was uncombed and her pallid complexion was stained and dirty from much crying. Her breasts were scarcely grown and her hips were straight like a youth's.

'Are you a prisoner too?' The voice was shrill with the inquisitive intonation of a small boy.

Nadia nodded.

'I guessed,' the girl went on. 'I saw *him* enter and leave, and I guessed. What is your name, beautiful lady?'

Nadia had recovered her composure and smiled at this odd and flattering address.

'I am Nadia, widow of Arghun,' she replied. 'And you?'

'Keremun,' said the girl. 'Keremun, daughter of Anbarji and Borka. My parents are cousins of the Il-khan. When they heard he was dead, they tried to send me away, but *he* prevented them.'

'Gaikatu?'

'He wants to marry me though I'm only fourteen and am already promised as a bride to Arghun's son.' Keremun burst into tears. 'I don't want to marry Gaikatu, and I'm afraid. He has threatened to execute my father if I refuse.'

Even younger than I was, thought Nadia. She drew the girl onto the divan beside her, put a friendly arm around her shoulders and wiped her tears away with a finger.

'Has he forced you to bed with him?' she asked.

Keremun shook her head violently. 'No, but he has said he'll do so when he returns.'

'I only wish I could reassure you, Keremun,' sighed Nadia. 'However, I fear we are in the hands of Fate. But cry no more. If you know when Gaikatu plans to return, tell me, and anything else you know about happenings in the city. It may be a forlorn hope, but at least let us consider together how we might escape from this place.'

Much of what Keremun was able to relate was hearsay. She had seen fighting in the streets but did not know what it was about. She had heard the Wazir had been convicted of treason but did not grasp the nature of the crime he was supposed to have committed. However, Nadia was able to piece together an account of the previous month's events from her companion's sketchy information and her own understanding of the politics.

News had reached Tabriz that Arghun was ill and might not survive the winter. The occasional disturbances in the city streets, especially those directed at Jews and supporters of the Wazir's policies, had escalated, fanned by propaganda from the followers of Baidu and Gaikatu. Though officially in Baghdad, the former was rumoured to be in the city and, according to reports, had gathered his forces for an assault on the castle. When it was reported that Arghun's condition was worsening, the rebellion became more open. Ad-Daulah was charged with corrupting the currency and embezzling state funds. He was arrested and imprisoned along with members of his family and a dozen Mongol aides. The forces of several emirs had stormed the castle and put to the sword loyal followers of Arghun who remained in the city and who had taken refuge there. The city guard and its new commander, Berke, had changed sides. The names of Baidu and Gaikatu were being shouted everywhere.

Keremun's parents discussed the situation continually and when, at length, Daulah and his family were put to death, they became very nervous. Anbarji and Borka were adherents of the Christian religion and feared the suspicion and violence against Jews would spill over into the Christian quarter. They had almost completed preparations for a journey to Fars when the messenger bearing news of Arghun's death arrived from Baghcha.

'It was then my father tried to send me with an escort to the provinces, but we were stopped by Gaikatu not a day's ride from the city,' concluded Keremun. 'His soldiers killed the escort and took me prisoner. I heard them say there's to be a gathering of all the Mongol nobles to elect the new Il-khan. Like my father, I hope it'll be Ghazan, but I fear support for Gaikatu will be too strong.'

'Where this gathering to be?' asked Nadia. 'Do you know that?'

'I have heard it will be at the Lake of Van, though I don't know for sure,' said Keremun. 'That is where *he* has gone. I heard him tell the old woman to look after me until he returned.'

'That is several days journey there and back, even on a fast pony, and if there's to be a council, it will take at least a week,' said Nadia. She tried to sound confident though he heart was filled with despair. 'That gives us time. And the old woman comes and goes freely for supplies. I have watched her. An opportunity for our flight may present itself.'

They took their evening meal together. When it was over, Keremun seemed reluctant to leave her company and wept copiously until, in pity, Nadia agreed she could remain until morning and share her divan.

As she undressed and bathed, Nadia saw the girl was staring at her with tearful but admiring eyes. She combed her hair, still watched closely, and fastened it.

At length, Keremun dried her tears and hesitantly reached out her hand. 'May I touch it?'

'My hair? You may if it pleases you, but it is very ordinary hair.'

'It is beautiful, and so smooth,' said the girl. 'I have never seen such beautiful hair. Mine is so coarse and dry, and my body is so pale and thin. Yours is so rounded and your skin is such a golden colour. Why would a man want me when he had you to look at and caress?'

'Men can be undiscerning in their desires,' said Nadia. 'Most think of nothing but that which hangs between their legs. They are easily and quickly satisfied, whereas we women long for a kind word and the touch of a gentle hand. They give out, we endure. But do not undervalue yourself, Keremun. Your body will grow and change, and some simple oils and balms can beautify your hair and skin. If you like, I will teach you what I know so that when, pray God, you have a husband you wish to please, he will see in you more than a mere possession for his gratification.'

Keremun's face brightened and then darkened almost immediately to the point of further tears.

'I don't want to please Gaikatu, Nadia,' she said. 'Will it hurt when he beds me forcibly?'

'It will hurt, Keremun, though 'tis more a pain of the soul. Do not think of it but of whoever you would have love you, be he flesh and blood or the Alexander or Rustum of your dreams. When a woman is willing and the man kind, the joining is less of a hurt and more a wondrous pleasure.'

'You are very wise, Nadia, and I only wish I could believe that to be true,' sighed Keremun.

'Believe it, and believe also you will not have to endure him,' said Nadia. 'We shall escape from this place together.'

She put her arm round Keremun's shoulder, kissed her on the brow and stroked her hair and cheek. The girl responded by clasping her tightly round the waist and pressing her head against Nadia's breast. Her touch was that of a child, free of any desire other than to be comforted by a sister or friend.

They remained in this innocent embrace until Nadia, anxious to complete her toilet, released herself from it.

O, Hassan... Hassan, she thought, if only I knew where you are at this very moment.

Giovanni ... Giovanni, will I ever see you again?

*

PART THREE
The Patriarch

I
Tabriz

Giovanni found the streets of Tabriz much the same as he remembered. A tense calm had descended on the city. After the disruption of recent weeks, life and trade had resumed their normal course, but Giovanni noticed the tattle and argument in the markets and at street corners was less robust than formerly. He saw too a new wariness in the eyes of the merchants as they haggled over their prices. There was an army post in every quarter and he wondered if the commanders had yet decided to which of the princes they would offer their allegiance.

He had remained three more days at Rayy, rehearsing with Hassan in the city bazaars their roles as merchant father and son. Satisfied that their disguises were as complete as they could make them, they had departed in the company of Sabbah and two of his warriors. Kartir's health had improved in the care of Ghazan's women and, though his cheeks were still pale and he was coughing badly, he had insisted on accompanying them to his villa in Qazvin.

Giovanni and Hassan had travelled into Tabriz alone. Once the Silk Road lay before him, Giovanni had no need of a guide. Sabbah was persuaded to wait at an outpost a day or two's ride from the city, where Ghazan's seal was still respected. There he would arrange a change of horses.

If the rescue bid succeeded, they would all return together to Qazvin where the viceroy would meet them. Sabbah would escort Keremun back to Rayy.

Giovanni had not given much thought to his own plans. He loved Nadia and wanted her, and he had the prince's permission for the match, but he could see that Kartir looked on the prospect of a Christian son-in-law with less favour. And it was yet probable that Nadia would prefer to return south with her father, rather than be his wife or mistress.

The costume he had adopted was comfortable and he regretted he had not discovered its merits sooner. The folds of the robe protected him from the cool of the night as well as from the midday heat. He had quite lost track of the weeks since leaving Baghcha, but he guessed by the position of the sun and by the signs of spring on the lower mountain slopes that it was already late April.

Hassan had exchanged his usual jerkin and breeches for more traditional Persian attire and with their turbans pulled well down to disguise any dissimilarity of feature and colouring, they might be taken for any Muslim father and son. Giovanni had little fear they would be recognised. He knew that, unless he came face to face with Baidu or Gaikatu, or with one of Arghun's former ministers, his disguise was unlikely to be penetrated.

They stabled the horses and by dispensing a few extra coins learned the princes were not in the city. By the same means, he discovered that Gaikatu owned three properties in the environs, and learning their location proved a simple and inexpensive matter.

To discover in which of these Nadia was held presented greater difficulty. Giovanni did not risk open enquiry for fear his curiosity would betray him. A much stronger fear and one which caused his heart to beat increasingly faster was that Ghazan had been misinformed - that Nadia was dead as he had believed and that Gaikatu held some other Persian mistress for his carnal gratification. However, he suppressed these feelings and, with Hassan at his side to show the way, began an innocent reconnaissance of the prince's villas.

He reasoned that the building being used as a prison was likely to be more heavily guarded than the others. On the other hand, he had no evidence that Nadia and Keremun were imprisoned together, or that they were the only women detained by the prince. However, he was quickly able to eliminate one house from the search. It was deserted and, from its state of disrepair, Giovanni guessed it had not been occupied for a considerable time. The second was surrounded on four sides by a high, whitewashed wall. Close to one corner was a double-sided gate.

They halted in the shade of a tall elm that grew fifty paces from this entrance. A group of travellers approached and passed by with a polite greeting.

'There are no patrols,' said Hassan, when they were out of earshot.

'There may be soldiers guarding the house from inside the walls,' rejoined Giovanni. 'Wait here and I will find out.'

He felt for the hilt of his short sword hidden in the folds of his jubbah and, reassured, strolled over to the gate. The two halves were fastened together by a heavy bar on both sides, but without any locking mechanism. He peered through the grating. Beyond was a courtyard and a garden of trees, with the house itself just visible behind the thick spring blossom and greenery. There was no sign of life. Cautiously, Giovanni raised the bars, pushed the gate open and took a few steps inside.

A loud snarl greeted him. He turned his head in the direction of the sound. Resting in the fork of a large tree was a huge creature with the face of a cat and a sleek, flame-coloured body, covered all over with black markings like hoofprints. Its jaws were wide open and displayed a set of savage, flesh-tearing teeth. At the foot of the tree and over the courtyard were littered the carcasses and entrails of smaller animals, the remains of previous meals.

Giovanni reached for his sword, but it had scarcely cleared his belt when the creature leapt from the tree and straight at him, roaring like a fiend from hell. Instinctively, he dropped on one knee with his sword arm outstretched and his other raised to protect his face. He felt sure his last moment had come and began reciting an Ave Maria. However, the creature's leap ended a pace or two in front of him and there it remained, snarling furiously at the end of the heavy chain by which it was tethered to the tree trunk.

Trying not to make any sudden movement that would enrage the animal more and perhaps allow it to escape from its collar, Giovanni retreated backwards to the gate, slipped through the gap and replaced the bar. He was still shaking when he rejoined Hassan under the elm tree.

'What's the matter, Giovanni?' exclaimed the boy. 'Have you found her?'

'She is not there,' replied the Venetian, offering no explanation for his disquiet and rapid breathing. 'That leaves one more residence to try. But first, we should make some purchases to assist our escape.'

'Purchases?'

'Two extra horses, provisions and, I think, some clothing such as a youth might wear.'

'What use do you have for boy's clothing, Giovanni?' Hassan asked.

'You will see in good time,' Giovanni said solemnly.

Nadia's prison was built on rising ground overlooking the city walls. There were trees on three sides. The road leading to it was long and straight with only one converging lane on the left.

'It's a fortress,' breathed Hassan unhappily. 'There are two sentries. We can't approach without being seen.'

'At least two,' said Giovanni. 'There may be others out of sight.'

'What are we to do?'

'Reaching the villa may not be difficult. Getting inside and escaping from it are another matter. You will have noticed there are other residences at this end of the road, and only plantations at the other. Here we are at the crossing of several ways, one leading to the west gate and the market, another encircling the walls. It's a busy junction. People are passing constantly in all directions. If we could only reach the trees, it would be an easy matter to merge with the crowds. But first we need a pretext for approaching the villa and a scheme to fool the guards. We'll loiter here for an hour or two and see what traffic turns into the road.'

They squatted on the dry earth at the cross-roads and waited. Several traders, some with wagons, others with heavily-loaded donkeys crossed the street and entered a large plain building at the corner of the road leading to Gaikatu's villa. Giovanni decided it must be a storage depot. A group of veiled women passed going towards the city wall and made it clear by signs that they would welcome his attentions. A youthful imam in sparkling white robes coming from the other direction caught the eye of one, and they hastened on, chattering incessantly.

No one went near the villa. Any citizens who took the road went only as far as the plantations and turned into the lane. A few emerged from it and came towards the cross-roads. Giovanni decided to investigate and beckoned Hassan to follow him. The mouth of the lane, he discovered, was only just visible from the gate of the villa. It skirted the trees for a dozen paces, then turned downhill towards a densely populated part of the city.

'Even better,' murmured Giovanni. 'It will mean a long walk but it can be done.'

They returned to their observation post and patiently resumed their watch on the villa. A caravan of merchants passed and a few artisans. A coarse fellow with a portable grindstone stopped and eyed Giovanni with interest.

'I see you're a man of quality, good sir,' said he obsequiously, 'and your son is a handsome lad. No doubt you have a fine dagger in your belt. Allow me to sharpen it. Two dirhams only is my price.'

Giovanni saw no harm in the fellow's request and was about to offer him his weapon when the germ of an idea crossed his mind.

'Tell me,' he said, 'how much would it cost to purchase a grindstone such as yours?'

The other looked at him keenly and Giovanni wondered if he had just made an error of accent or idiom, but after a few seconds the knife-sharpener lowered his eyes and bowed politely.

'A grindstone such as this may be bought for a silver dinar, sir,' he said. 'Why do you ask?'

'That is good trade,' said Giovanni lightly. 'A dinar for the stone and two dirhams for each sharpening gives you profit after four swords have been serviced.'

'I can see you're a man of business,' replied the artisan. 'For you, I offer a special price. If the young man also has a knife, I'll sharpen both at one dirham each.'

'I have a better idea,' countered the Italian. 'Your stone appears to be fairly new. I'll give you one silver dinar for it and another for your trouble. You can easily purchase a replacement.'

'And thereby find myself in competition,' added the other shrewdly.

'I have no desire to join your profession,' said Giovanni with a laugh. 'I have quite another use for the stone. Will you sell it to me or not?'

'I'll sell it to you, sir, and may Allah the Seer go with you,' said the artisan. He laid the grindstone on the ground at Giovanni's feet and stood expectantly. Giovanni rose from his squatting position, dusted himself and took two silver coins from his purse. He was aware that Hassan was tugging gently at the hem of his robe but he ignored it. The artisan took the money eagerly and hastened off in the direction from which he had come.

'You've been swindled, Giovanni!' cried Hassan, leaping up and regarding him with horror. 'A whole armoury may be sharpened for two dirhams, and five such stones may be purchased for a silver coin. How can this trade possibly help my mother?'

'Believe me, Hassan, I'm not such a fool,' said Giovanni calmly. 'I had my reasons for the exchange. Do you trust me?'

'Do you need to ask? We are friends, are we not?'

'Then, if you trust me, my friend, it's time for us to part company. Is there anywhere in the city where you can hide safely for a full day? Do you have any other friends ...?'

'There's the house of the priest,' said Hassan, 'the patriarch of the Gabars. He will shelter us. But I don't want us to be parted, Giovanni.'

'It is necessary, Hassan. If I succeed in rescuing your mother from Gaikatu's clutches, there must be somewhere I can bring her safely until the hue and cry dies down. There will be no time for us to fetch our horses if we remain together. The prince's followers will search once they know she's gone, and I cannot kill them all.

'I'll give you half my purse. Reclaim our horses and purchases, and pay for the extra stabling. I pray you do not have an adventure equal to when you last performed such a task. Go to the priest's house and wait for me. If I do not join you by first light the day after tomorrow I will have failed. Wait no longer but ride as fast as you can back to Sabbah and your grandfather at Qazvin.'

*

II

Nadia too had lost count of the days. The tedium of her captivity vexed her less since the arrival of Keremun and they spent many hours talking and eating together. The matron who fetched supplies and prepared the meals became more communicative as time went on. Her name was Zobeida. She had a Persian father and Mongol mother and had once served Abaqa. She had been present at Gaikatu's birth and apparently had an obligation to him, although unwilling to say what it was. Nadia quickly realised that her gaoler, though free to come and go through the villa gates, was as much a prisoner as she.

Though constantly on the lookout for a means of escape, Nadia, after more than a month's confinement had been unable to discover one. The sentries performed their duties in shifts, coming inside the gates only at the end of their period for a meal and leaving their replacements already on watch outside. At no time did they enter any part of the house. Once fed and wined, they always departed promptly to their billet in another quarter of the city. During the hours of darkness they patrolled with the assistance of oil lamps.

Nadia had several times tried to engage them in conversation but they remained as taciturn as ever. She had twice approached the gate during the changeover period and tried to step outside, but the sentries made it clear by gestures that this was not allowed.

Since Gaikatu's departure, there had been only three other visitors, a tradesman bringing supplies, a mason to repair some broken tiles on the veranda and a merchant selling carpets and embroidery, this latter at the request of Keremun who had found her quarters less than comfortable. It was clear that the prince took particular pride in maintaining the fabric of this particular residence and had instructed Zobeida to indulge his unwilling guests' every whim short of freedom. Nadia had requested she be allowed some new clothes, and spices and perfumes for her toilet, and Zobeida had brought them without argument.

Her intercourse with Keremun raised Nadia's spirits, but the Mongol girl was prone to attacks of extreme depression. Some days she would weep continuously and shut herself up in her quarters, refusing to come out. Twice, Nadia allowed her to share her bed.

The weather had become warmer and Nadia spent a great deal of time in the garden. The trees were in full bloom and the subtle scents of the blossom wafted over the courtyard reminding her of other gardens and of happier years. She continued to think of Giovanni, not only on her walks but in the silence of her bedroom. Once, he entered her strange visions. She was at the head of the staircase in a grand palace. At its foot was a lake and just disembarking from a trim barque was Hassan. As she watched, the Italian too leapt ashore and, smiling, put his arm on her son's shoulder. Together, they began to climb the steps towards her only to vanish before they reached half way. These occasional visions now comforted her as much as they had once disturbed her, and she began to hope again.

One afternoon, Keremun had departed tearfully to her apartment and Nadia was alone in the courtyard when the south gate opened to admit one sentry in the company of an artisan with a whetstone. As, on the advice of Zobeida, she was not expected to be abroad when the sentries or any male visitor was inside the walls, Nadia immediately retired to her quarters, but continued to watch through her window with interest to see what transpired. The sentry spoke a few words with Zobeida, then withdrew. The grinder bowed repeatedly and with his stone under his arm, followed the gaoleress into her small cell next to the kitchen.

Several minutes passed and the man re-emerged alone. He no longer carried the stone and, though his appearance had not essentially changed, it seemed to Nadia that he had grown taller. To her infinite surprise and consternation, instead of proceeding to the gate, he crossed the courtyard and entered the covered passage leading to her door.

*

III

Giovanni had not slept. Having with great difficulty persuaded Hassan to embark on the tasks vital to their flight from Tabriz, he had vacated the rooms they had hired at an inn and had spent the night in silent watch of Gaikatu's villa. He had noted the previous night that, though there was a crescent moon, it had clouded over, and he prayed that during his vigil it would be no different. As the sun went down, he watched the guard at the south gate of the villa change, and saw the new sentries light their lamps.

Darkness fell. With nothing but infrequent lamps to guide him and a faint glow from the sky to illuminate any obstacles at his feet, Giovanni crept along the road towards the villa. He kept as close to the intervening buildings as he could and, on reaching the plantations, slipped noiselessly among the trees. The sentries' lamps lit the ground in front of the villa for no more than twenty paces. Giovanni dropped to the ground and began to crawl on his belly along the line of shadow, keeping well within the region of darkness.

Circling the walls of the residence proved a slow and painful process. The ground was dry and the dust irritated his lungs so that breathing silently became difficult. He dared not clear his throat for fear that the guards would hear him. His hands became rough and his knees chafed through the material of his jubbah. Small animals scuttled in and out of the vegetation and night insects buzzed round his head, biting the unprotected flesh of his face and neck.

It was almost dawn when he returned to his starting point. He had discovered the second gate and noted that it was guarded like the first. Plantations encircled the villa to north, east and west and might provide cover for an escape but, though he had devised a scheme for gaining access to the villa, he had as yet formed no idea of how he might leave it with Nadia, if indeed it proved she was being held there. However, he was in no doubt that the villa did house a prisoner, because he had noted how vigilantly the guards patrolled the walls. He concluded that to protect the property alone, Gaikatu would have resorted to a creature like the one he had already encountered. That animal, he had learned from Hassan, was a leopard, and the only necessity to maintain this form of guard was an adequate supply of goats and small deer for its nourishment.

As the sun showed above the horizon, he returned to his former position at the cross-roads and, worn with fatigue, squatted beside his wheel and the roadside. Four soldiers passed, heading for the villa and Giovanni guessed he was about to witness the changing of the guard. The four exchanged brief greeting with the two on duty who immediately raised the bar of the gate and went inside. Two of the newcomers disappeared behind the trees of the plantation to take up their positions at the north entrance. Shortly afterwards, the gate opened again and the four night guards, now relieved of duty, walked none too steadily down the road, past Giovanni and along the street towards the market.

Giovanni waited only a moment then, picking up the grindstone, ambled along the road towards the villa. He hunched his shoulders to disguise his height and forced himself to adopt a limp which was none too difficult as both legs ached from his exertions of the night. His pulse was racing. He tried to time his arrival at the gate to coincide with a moment when the sentries were some distance apart. There was no guarantee his stratagem would work, and he had determined if it failed to quickly cut one soldier's throat and take his chance with the other before help could arrive from the north side.

He reached the gate just as one sentry came to the west corner of the wall.

'What do you want, fellow?' demanded the other. He was a pure Mongol youth of about seventeen years, and strongly built. 'We've no money to waste on knife- sharpening.'

Giovanni suppressed his inclination to drop the stone and run. He bowed and turned his dirty face and matted beard in the direction of the guard and, trying to adopt the mien and accent of the grinder, addressed him as humbly as he could.

'This is, I'm told, a residence of his most worthy Highness, Prince Gaikatu,' he said.

'And if it is, what of it?' growled the sentry. Giovanni noticed that his companion, curiosity aroused, had turned and was making his way back towards the gate.

'Only that I cannot aspire to whet the sword of the most worthy prince, future ruler of our kingdom, but it'll be an honour to be of service to one of his trusted generals. Allow me to sharpen your weapons free of charge.'

The man looked pleased at the compliment to his rank, but hesitated to draw his sword or dagger. His companion had now arrived on the scene. He was older, and a Persian.

'And you, sir?' persisted Giovanni, beginning to sweat profusely under his turban. 'Let me put a keen edge on your scimitar.'

The Persian shrugged and handed over his scimitar while keeping firm grip of his dagger. Giovanni squatted, wedged the grinding wheel between his knees and began slowly to whet the already sharp blade.

'There's no harm in it,' he heard the older man say, 'especially as we do not have to pay.'

'May Allah strike down your enemies,' Giovanni said. A year previously, he would not have risked damnation by uttering the name of an alien god, but he had become used to Muslim ways and expressions, and since it was necessary for him to remain in character he now spoke the phrase with hardly a prick of conscience.

He finished working on the sword, returned it to its owner, and held out his hand for another, praying that the guards would not have noticed his lack of expertise with the wheel. However, they seemed content with his work. Giovanni, emboldened by his success at the first phase of his plan, was ready to move on to the second. If they refused his request, he was back where he started but no worse off than before.

'In such a grand house, there must be other knives in need of attention - perhaps in the kitchens. In years to come, I may tell my grandchildren that I once put my humble craft at the disposal of the illustrious Il-khan, His Majesty Gaikatu.' He wondered if he had gone too far. If the guards had been retained only by payment of gold, they might be unimpressed by such grand compliments to their employer.

The Persian sentry however grinned.

'I fancy Mistress Zobeida can make use of him in her kitchen,' he said. 'The fellow can do no harm, and she can have service without paying a single dirham.'

The Mongol nodded and raised the bar of the gate, allowing Giovanni to pass through. He pointed toward a low door at the end of one wing of the house where an elderly woman stood suspiciously. In one hand she held a little bell, which she rang as if as a signal. Giovanni glanced quickly round the courtyard. It was empty save for a second woman in a yashmak who strolled among the trees of the central garden. His heart leapt in his chest and his throat, already dry with thirst and from the dust he had swallowed, almost closed in terror. It was Nadia beyond doubt. What if she should recognise him and cry out? However, at the sound of the bell, she turned away and headed towards the veranda on the other side.

The younger sentry beckoned to the woman and spoke briefly to her. Giovanni saw she was reassured. The sentry withdrew. The gate was shut again and barred from outside.

Giovanni allowed the woman to lead him into the house. Once inside, he shook off all pretence. He slammed the door shut, seized her bell and clapped his hand over her mouth.

'I do not wish to murder you in cold blood, mistress, but I will do so if you call out. And if I die at the hands of those fellows at the gate, God knows I shall have the satisfaction of taking you to Purgatory with me.'

The woman did not struggle but shook her head as furiously as Giovanni's firm grip of her mouth would allow. Her eyes bulged with terror. Giovanni, who had now drawn his short sword, released her and she fell back against a table. As she did so, he caught sight of a small trinket swept to the floor by the sleeve of her dress. It was a crude wooden cross.

'You are a Christian, mistress?' he stammered, now unsure of his next move.

The woman nodded.

'As God is my witness, madam, I mean you no harm. I too am a follower of Christ. I only beg that you allow me to speak with the Lady Nadia. After that, I will be gone and the guards will learn nothing of my purpose in being here.'

The matron had got over her terror.

'Do you have some proof of what you say?' she breathed.

'None, mistress, but I swear to you by the blood of Our Lord that it is the truth. I am a Christian from the kingdom of Italy.'

She peered at him wisely through the grime and sweat of his face.

'Your eyes speak truly, master,' she replied. She poured a goblet of wine from a flask on the table and held it out to him. 'I will not betray you. My name is Zobeida, and I have been a Christian since childhood, though few know it.'

'God be with you for your small kindness, madam,' said Giovanni gratefully, relaxing his grip on his sword's hilt and taking the wine. He drank it thirstily. 'My one desire at the moment is to speak with the Lady Nadia and to reassure her of her son's safety.'

'And to rescue her from this place, I'll vow,' said Zobeida. 'Otherwise, you would have come as yourself instead of in disguise. I have lived sixty years and know when someone wishes to deceive me. That you are a Christian, I have no doubt, but your purpose is rescue, not mere reassurance.'

'And if it is?' asked Giovanni. 'Would I have been admitted as myself?'

Zobeida smiled. 'What do you care for these Muslims, if you are a true follower of Christ?'

'Perhaps you are a mother yourself, and will know how a mother aches for the sight of her child,' Giovanni replied with passion. 'Nadia's son is eleven years old and has no woman to take care of him.'

'I only ask for the truth,' said Zobeida, and again she peered at him wisely. 'If you love her and wish to convert her to the one true God, I will not hinder you, but you must know you can never leave here except alone and in the same guise as you entered.'

'And suppose there were to be a way,' said Giovanni. 'Would you still not hinder me? And would you be safe from Gaikatu's revenge?'

'The prince will not hurt me for his mother's sake,' Zobeida replied. 'Like me, she was a Christian and when she was dying, still a young woman, begged me to watch over him. I was his nurse and loved him once. If his prisoners escape, he will rage and perhaps execute a guard or two, but he will let me be.'

She gathered up her cross. 'Go quickly,' she added. 'Speak to your lady. She is quartered in the wing opposite. The sentries will not trouble you unless I call them, and I swear on this emblem that I will not do so.'

Giovanni saw no alternative but to trust her. Whether he stayed or attempted to leave as the knife grinder he had claimed to be, he was in her hands. In anger and frustration he might have struck her down but he could not kill in cold blood. He opened the door of the cell, glanced at the gateway to assure himself that the sentries had truly withdrawn, and strode across the courtyard towards Nadia's apartments.

The door was barred from inside. Despite the wine he had drunk, Giovanni's throat was still raw and he knew his voice had changed as much as his appearance. Nadia would be unlikely to recognise it.

'My Lady,' he called hoarsely through the closed door, 'I bring you news of Prince Hassan ....'

There was a rustle of silk and the door opened a crack.

'Who are you, sir,' demanded Nadia, 'and what do you know of Hassan?'

'Only that he is well, and waits for you at the house of the priest of Zoroaster.'

The door was opened a little more and Nadia appeared on the threshold, still veiled. She stared unrecognising at his dirty robes, stained turban, rough artisan's face and matted beard.

Through the opening in the yashmak, Giovanni saw that her eyes still held their sparkle. Though she seemed to have grown thinner since he had seen her last, her figure had not lost its shapeliness and, despite the danger of his adventure and the risk he knew he was taking every moment he remained within the villa walls, his old love and desire for her was awakened. He swallowed.

'I see you do not know me, Nadia,' he said, trying to recollect how his voice had once sounded, at the same time removing the turban and stepping back into the morning sunlight so that she should have a better view of his face. 'Have I altered so much since we last conversed?'

Nadia stared hard at him and a sudden change came over her. Her eyes opened wide with astonishment. In a movement that took Giovanni completely by surprise, she tore the yashmak from her head and, rushing towards him, threw her arms about his neck and pressed her face against his chest.

'Giovanni. Oh Giovanni,' she cried. She released his neck and pulled him by the sleeve through the door. The Venetian saw her eyes were wet with tears.

'Nadia!'

'Giovanni! I dreamed ... I hoped ... I did not think it possible you would come. But you should not have ....'

'My Lady ....'

'And Zobeida,' continued Nadia, with a glance through the open door and across at the gaoleress's cell. 'Have you killed her?'

'How could you think it, My Lady? Zobeida is a Christian like me, and has given her oath not to hinder us.'

'But you should not have come, Giovanni,' repeated Nadia, now sobbing quietly. She barred the door and fell again on his neck, her hands stroking his untidy hair and her mouth covering his coarse chin with kisses.

Giovanni was choked with emotion and could not speak. He raised her lovely head and taking her face gently between his roughened hands, kissed first her eyes, then her cheek and finally her mouth. Instead of resisting this liberty as he had feared, Nadia responded eagerly to the kiss. Her lips parted, and in a moment her moist tongue was in his mouth, relieving its dryness and pressing urgently against his teeth.

He ran his fingers through her hair, over her throat and down towards her breasts, which he cupped lovingly within his palms. He could feel her quiver through her clothing, but still she did not resist, but pressed herself ever more closely to him.

'Nadia.' His voice shook. 'I have wanted you for so long, Nadia, but did not dare dream of a reunion like this.'

'I know it,' she replied. 'I have always known it - even before I tended your wound. And it has been so long for me too, Giovanni - an aching eternity. And now, to have your strong arms around me, to have your throbbing loins so near to mine, I have no other wish in life than to feel you inside me and to see my son again.'

Without releasing her, Giovanni reached inside his robe, drew his sword and laid it on a nearby chest. He kissed her again on the lips, then

with his free right hand lifted the hem of her gown and pulled her gently
onto the divan.

*

IV

Giovanni had closed his eyes for what seemed a moment. When he opened them, Nadia was pouring water from a jug into her palm and washing his face and upper body. The coolness of the freshly drawn water revived him and he sat up, gripped by sudden fear.

'Did I fall asleep?'

'For an instant only, my love,' said Nadia, stroking his forehead, 'but you must go now.'

She took the water jug, poured some of the reviving liquid into a goblet and held it out to him.

'My one purpose was to rescue you from this place, and I shall not go without you,' said Giovanni stubbornly.

'But how?' she said anxiously. 'There are two guards at each gate and even if they allow you past, I cannot come with you.'

'There must be a way,' he said, taking her again in his arms and kissing her brow. 'Having found you again, I will not lose you. If I engage the men at one entrance there may be a chance.'

'I cannot allow it. The clamour would attract the others and you would be killed.'

Giovanni glanced round the room.

'There is a window,' he observed hopefully.

Nadia shook her head sadly.

'A child could not squeeze through there.'

He rose and went into the adjoining apartment.

'This has two,' he said, 'and they are larger.'

'And with two bars on each,' she objected. There was despair in her voice.

'Yet from either of those windows, one could easily drop to the ground. Is it possible to reach the roof without being seen?'

She considered.

'I believe so,' she said. Giovanni saw her eyes brighten with hope. 'There's a tree that climbs the wall. It might bear your weight and mine. However the wall is the height of three tall men. We would break our legs in the fall, if not our necks.'

'It can be done,' he insisted. 'Come, show me the tree.'

She hesitated.

'There is Keremun to think of. We cannot leave her alone.'

'Keremun? Then she *is* here? I saw none other than Zobeida and yourself.'

'You know the name?'

'She is promised to Ghazan. I swore to him I would free her if I could.'

'Her quarters are on the other side of the courtyard.'

'Bring her here while I resume the character of the knife-grinder,' Giovanni ordered, 'and here is something else which may reassure you of our success.'

He opened his purse and took out her hooked cross.

'My fylfot,' cried Nadia with delight, taking the talisman and fastening it about her neck. 'God be praised. Now I may hope even more that we shall escape from here.' Her eyes saddened again and she looked at him almost accusingly. 'Yet it's return is bitter-sweet. Pidorka did not deserve to die so!'

She hastened off before he could reply and returned a few moments later with the Mongol girl. Giovanni had meantime dressed again in the costume of the artisan and, satisfied with the disguise, he slipped out cautiously into the open.

He easily identified the tree, an ancient beech that grew at the south end of Nadia's veranda in the shade of the wall and out of sight of either gate. It had been cut down so that its highest point was just below the pinnacle of the wall. A climbing shrub had attached powerful suckers to its trunk and wound strong, leafy tendrils round its branches. The upper parts of the tree, the wall, and the roof of the veranda were covered in fragrant, white blossom. The way to freedom was open, he told himself, if he had not underestimated the height of the roof.

He took firm hold of one of the tendrils and began to climb. An insect stung his wrist but he ignored it and continued hand over hand until he had reached the top and hauled himself onto the tiles. He beckoned to the women to come after him.

First Keremun, then Nadia followed his example. They joined him breathlessly on the roof. The guards were out of sight.

'If I take your hands and lower you one at a time, can you reach that opening and take hold of the bars?' he asked, pointing at the barred window directly below them.

Nadia looked down. 'It's a long way, but I can do it,' she said.

Keremun on the other hand shook her head violently. She clung to Nadia's dress.

'You can,' the latter whispered. 'You must!'

'Come, Keremun,' said Giovanni. He reached for her hands and she reluctantly allowed him to take them. 'Trust in me. I will not let you fall. When your feet are secure on the window ledge, let go of my left hand and grasp hold of the bar with your right. Then release me altogether. Lower yourself down the wall. It's not so far. When your arms are fully extended, jump. Bend your knees and relax your body. When you reach the ground, run quickly to the trees.'

Slowly, he lowered her over the edge. She was no great weight. Twice, her sandals slipped on the dry whitewash but she reached the ledge without mishap. Giovanni watched her feel for a foothold and then felt the strain on his arms relax.

'Now, your right hand, Keremun. Reach down and grasp the bar.'

Keremun looked up at him appealingly and again shook her head.

'Keremun!' Now Nadia spoke, her voice insistent but with the same soothing magic he had once heard in the house of the Patriarch. 'Trust him, Keremun. Loose his hand and grasp the bar. See how close it is. You will be safe.'

The Mongol girl bit her lip. She leant down uncertainly, felt for one of the window bars and gripped it tightly. Then, encouraged by her success, she let go of Giovanni altogether, missed her footing and fell against the wall, still clutching the single bar grimly with her right hand, her feet suspended more than her own height from the hard earth.

Nadia gave a gasp of terror and Giovanni felt her body stiffen beside him.

'Jump, Keremun, jump,' he hissed.

Keremun jumped and landed in a heap. Giovanni crossed himself and leant as far forward on the tiles as he dared to ascertain the extent of her injury. However, in a moment, the girl regained her feet and apparently none the worse for her fall, took to her heels and disappeared into the plantation.

One of the guards reached the south east corner of the wall, gave the empty road a cursory glance and turned on his heel . Giovanni waited until the sentry at the north side had done the same.

'Now you, My Lady.'

'But what about you, Giovanni? You cannot reach the ground without assistance.'

'I shall do what I always planned, and leave by the gate.' He smiled wanly. 'Trust in God, Nadia, and think only of our love.'

He clasped her hands, kissed them, and gently lowered her to the window. Nadia released his hands one at a time as he had instructed, took firm hold of both bars, allowed her sandals to slide a few paces down the wall. and leapt clumsily but safely to the ground.

Giovanni hastily climbed down the tree, checked that both gates were still closed, and crossed to Zobeida's cell. The gaoleress made the sign of the cross.

'I watched you on the roof, master. Is it done? Have they truly gone?'

'Thanks to you and God's mercy, good Mother,' said Giovanni, taking up his grindstone and quickly polishing the edge of two kitchen knives. 'Now, if it will truly bring you no harm, do me one last favour. Ring your bell and, if you can, distract the sentries until I reach the gate. Perform your usual routines for one more day if you can before you give the alarm. If Gaikatu believes their escape was accomplished by magic, so much the better.'

Zobeida nodded agreement. There was no betrayal in her eyes.

Giovanni watched the gate swing slowly open and the younger sentry come through it in answer to the bell. Zobeida beckoned to the lad and he came towards them. Giovanni hunched his back, picked up the grindstone and limped towards the exit. It seemed to recede from him, but he dared not run. Every step seemed like ten. Perspiration ran from his pores. He could feel the Mongol sentry's eyes burn into his back.

He reached the gate. Outside, the Persian guard was urinating against the wall and paid him no attention. Giovanni measured the distance to the lane. It was not far, if only his nerve would hold. He gripped the stone tightly in the crook of his left arm, felt the comfort of the hidden sword hilt with his right and began hobbling down the hill.

'Hey, fellow!'

Giovanni froze in his tracks. He turned. The Persian had finished relieving himself and was gesturing to him. Giovanni heard the chink of money as two dirham coins landed at his feet.

'Prince Gaikatu's debts are his own,' grunted the guard. His face broke into a friendly grin. 'I always settle mine. Take that for your impertinence.'

With affected gratitude, Giovanni fumbled for the money, scooped it up and put it in his purse. Through the half-open gate, he could see Zobeida still in conversation with the younger sentry.

'Allah reward you for your generosity, General,' said he, concealing only with difficulty his amusement at the irony. 'And may He bless you with many fine sons!'

*

V

Nadia and Keremun were asleep. The Patriarch's housekeeper, Djamila, had put her own apartment on the ground level and some items of her clothing at their disposal and had retired to an anteroom. Hassan lay on the floor of the temple, his body supported by two cushions and his head resting on the belly of the old priest's hound. Both child and dog slept peacefully.

Gobras himself did not seem to need rest and kept unseeing and silent vigil over them. He sat upright with his legs crossed. His eyes were closed, his head was sunk in his beard, and his slow, almost inaudible breathing was punctuated by the occasional involuntary sigh. In the near darkness, he found comfort in the animal's fur and from time to time would stroke it with his bony fingers.

Giovanni squatted beside the hearth opposite him and watched the dying fire. Occasionally, its orange embers would throw out a bright blue and yellow flame. Their reflection flickered among the figures of the triptych panel. Giovanni stared at the images, fascinated.

'Tell me about the visions,' he said.

The dog raised its head, sniffed at him inquisitively and, apparently satisfied, resumed its repose.

The old priest chuckled softly. In the ghostly light, his teeth seemed more broken and yellowed, his hollow cheeks more cadaverous than before.

'You do not believe, yet you ask me that?'

'I doubt, but my mind is open. Even I have dreams.'

Gobras chuckled again, showing his broken teeth.

'Ormazd sprinkles the earth with his essence, and the sons and daughters of mortals prophesy,' he sang quietly. 'The young are sent visions; it is for the old to dream.'

'My visions are fantasies of the mind,' said Giovanni. 'They have no meaning. But perhaps your dreams say more: what dangers we face in the days to come; how we might avoid them?'

'The fire is dark tonight,' said the Patriarch solemnly, 'but I do not need the fire to tell me you are in great danger as long as you remain here.

Once, in a dream, I saw a man die ....'

'Arghun?'

'Believe it, Giovanni of Venice. I saw the deed done, saw his blood on the hands of his killers, saw the cross of Ahriman stamped on their brows. It was a warning that came too late.'

'Then you knew the truth?' said Giovanni. One corner of the hearth flared up again brightly. He watched the light play on the metal panel. 'You knew the assassins were in the guise of monks, perhaps that, having poisoned Arghun, they would deliver Nadia to a mob. Perhaps you even know the identity of these false priests.'

'It was a dream only, Christian,' Gobras answered, 'and dreams fade into the morning. Though the fire has given up its secrets, it is with our reason too that we must solve puzzles. I listened to your talk, to Nadia's, and the boy's, and that told me much.'

'And what does the fire and your reason tell you, Gobras?'

For a while, in silence, the Patriarch stroked his hound's ears. At length he broke the silence with a question.

'You remember when you came before, - and what we said to one another?'

'I remember.'

'Who was it desired your life, and why? Then Ahmed Kartir and the boy Hassan came, and they spoke of conspiracies.'

'Yes.'

'Arghun must die if Baidu is to gain the throne. And there must be no alliance that will bring the kings of Europe and their Crusader knights to Syria. The murder of Master Giovanni of Venice is arranged, only the murderers mistake the apartment. We know now it was not the boy they wanted.'

'Yes.'

'There is a second attempt, and it is Nadia, Arghun's wife, who foils it. But now there is a new mind at work. Who is this Nizam who plots with the Mongol generals - who serves Baidu and treats with the Egyptian Sultan? A fearful man, but also a man full of hate. Once he served the Caliph of Baghdad, once the Emir of Kerman. Once he deceived Ahmed Kartir; once he betrayed my people to Abaqa!'

'Nizam?'

'Do not forget him, Christian, for he will have forgotten neither you nor the woman you love.- a little fat man whose turban falls over his eyes - a stout Buddhist monk whose face is always hidden by an orange cowl. Foiled once ....'

'Nizam - the assassin?' breathed Giovanni incredulously.

'Who else? Who but Nizam himself, his turban removed, his head and face shaved like a monk, could be better trusted to perform the deed if Baidu promised him gold. And who else, faced with discovery, would defy a Mongol prince to denounce the daughter of his bitterest enemy?'

'If this is true ....'

'Believe it, Christian!'

'And the other priest?'

'Once a real monk perhaps, or a renegade of my faith - a man familiar with Buddhist ritual, who knows the legend of Jemshid and the two crosses.'

Giovanni stared thoughtfully at the glowing hearth. Could it really be, he wondered, that past, present and future were to be seen in the patterns of orange and yellow, in the blue flickering flame, in the intricate designs of the triptych. Though he still doubted, he felt a disturbing assurance that the Patriarch's theory, part mysticism, part deduction, held the truth, - that it was indeed Nizam who had added poison to the carved casket.

'What should I do, Gobras?' he asked, half to himself.

'I think you know that already, Giovanni of Venice,' Gobras answered, 'and only Ormazd can change what is written. For now, sleep if you can. Tonight there is no danger in the dark.'

It was a warm night. The moon had risen and its diffuse light just caught the eastern slope of Sahand, showing up the forbidding outline in relief against the star-studded heavens. The lower ridges of the mountain were lost in impenetrable darkness, and the villas and their surrounding plantations were in shadow.

Giovanni had become accustomed to nights spent in the open. It was stuffy in the temple and he had left the Patriarch motionless and spectre-like by the hearth while he wandered into the small villa garden. He had brought with him a cushion which he laid in the corner of a wall beside a fragrant bush. But he could not sleep, and the time passed slowly. He watched the moon rise towards its meridian and the shadow of Sahand's first peak creep across the buildings and plantations. At length, when the trees were bathed in light and the road to Tabriz clearly illuminated, he left the villa, crossed to the olive grove and sat on the ground at its edge.

Still the adventure was not over. He had to make good his promise to escort Keremun as far as Qazvin but, after that, despite Gobras's confidence that his future was fixed, he was not sure what to do. Could he remain in Persia? Ghazan, though protesting his allegiance to the Buddhist faith like his father, had indicated his sympathy for a western alliance. However, without his presence at the Mongol Council the succession would be decided in Gaikatu's or Baidu's favour.

Giovanni had made an enemy of both. Gaikatu, whatever his political or religious leanings, was not likely to look with favour on a man who had robbed him of a mistress, and Baidu's agents had twice already tried to take his life.

He watched a shooting star flash across the night sky and fall behind the mountain's second peak. Above the aroma of the olive trees, he noted another scent like jasmine. There was a footfall on the path and a gentle hand touched his shoulder. Nadia stood beside him. She had found a plain cloak in her new wardrobe, and had wrapped it round her shoulders and body. Her feet were bare and her calves visible. In the moonlight, she seemed to Giovanni more desirable than ever.

'I heard you and the Patriarch talk,' she said. 'It woke me.'

Giovanni rose, took her hands in his and pressed them to his lips.

'Then you are a light sleeper, My Lady, and I'm glad of it.'

She sighed and laid her head against his chest.

'I am too,' she murmured. ' 'Twas on nights such as this that the Empress Shahrazade gave her husband a cup of wine and charmed him with her tales of love, magic and strange lands. Under that brilliant sky it's easy to forget the danger we are in. Will you share your thoughts with me, Giovanni?'

'Only that I love you,' he whispered. 'How can I think of anything else, when we are together?'

'And I love you.'

'Then will you honour me by coming with me to Venice as my wife?'

'I will come gladly, My Lord,' said she, 'but let us go now, before morning.'

'There is my promise to Ghazan. You know I cannot leave yet'

'I know it,' sighed Nadia. 'You and I are cursed, it seems, by duty and promises.'

'Cursed or blessed, there is only one road we can take, and that is the one to Qazvin.'

'And after that, how are we to find our way to Venice if Gaikatu's troops block the road?' said Nadia bitterly. 'He will never give up searching for me. Better that you send me back to him. I shall spend the rest of my life in misery, but at least I'll know you are alive.'

'I would rather die than send you back to Gaikatu. If Taghachar comes after us, I will kill him.'

'And if he kills you, I will die too.'

'So be it then,' said Giovanni. 'We shall live or die together. However, neither Taghachar nor Gaikatu himself will kill me. And Baidu's assassins will not stop us. I lived too long in the desperate hope of winning your love, and for an eternity in the darkness of hell when I believed you were lost to me, to give up my life now. Tomorrow we'll ride for Qazvin. You and Keremun will wear men's clothes so that you can sit astride the ponies. That way we shall travel faster. When I have fulfilled my promise, we shall devise another plan to bring us to safety.'

'Then I will put my trust in your bravery just as you once put yours in my skill,' said Nadia. 'If this is to be my last night as a woman, let me spend the rest of it with you under those bright stars.'

She released her hands from his grasp and loosened the cloak. Underneath it she was naked.

Giovanni gazed at her in wonder. It seemed to him that never had he seen such beauty. Her body glistened with fresh oils in the moonlight. Her breasts were full, the curves of her hips and thighs perfectly formed.

The perfume of her skin and hair wafted into his nostrils and invaded his senses.

'If this were to be my last night as a man, I would wish to spend it nowhere else but in your arms,' he breathed.

He took the cloak from her shoulders and spread it at the foot of an olive tree. His arm encircled her waist and coaxed her down and towards him in an embrace. As their lips met and their bodies entwined, he reached for the edge of the cloak, pulled it over and wrapped it round them both.

Then, careless of their danger, they lay together on the earth of the plantation until the first rays of sun touched the mountain.

Nadia and Keremun dressed in the youths' clothes that Giovanni had insisted on purchasing. The disguise fitted the Mongol girl perfectly and she looked every inch a boy of twelve.

'Now I see your stratagem, Giovanni,' exclaimed Hassan excitedly. 'Keremun can be my brother.'

'She will easily be taken for a boy, I'm pleased to say,' agreed Giovanni. 'However, I fear your mother will never pass as a man.'

He regarded Nadia with a worried frown. The breeches and boots would serve, but the tunic was too small and even a jubbah did not hide her full figure. All attempts to bind her hair inside the turban had failed.

Though unable to see the results of the women's efforts, Gobras had followed the proceedings with great interest.

'If only I still had my eyes,' he sighed, then gave a quiet chuckle. 'I have not seen a woman in almost five years, and I would give another of my senses to see one again, even one dressed in man's clothing.'

'Yet you understand the problem, Gobras,' said Giovanni, his tension returning. 'Lady Nadia is too much a woman to be hidden in a child's costume.'

'I remember Nadia's looks, Christian,' said the priest, 'and it will be a near profanity to cut her hair. However, I judge it necessary if you are to escape detection. You are a tall man, well proportioned, and your sex will never be questioned. Let the lady have your over-garment. I will provide you with another robe which, though it may be a poor fit, will keep the sun from your shoulders.'

At Gobras's order, Djamila fetched a white toga similar to the one the priest himself wore. Giovanni took off his jubbah and gave it to Nadia who then retired with Keremun to the upper apartment. He donned the toga watched by Hassan, who laughed when he saw the result. The garment was tight in his armpits and left his lower arm exposed. In length it barely reached his knees.

'It will serve its purpose,' said the Venetian with a smile which hid his misgivings. He clapped Hassan playfully on the back. 'Now, let us go and saddle the horses while we wait on your new brother and our other travelling companion.'

*

VI

'Gone? How can they have gone?' screamed Gaikatu. He stood at the south gate of his villa surveying the empty courtyard. Taghachar was at his side and behind lingered four of the troop who had recently served as sentries.

'They disappeared in the night, Prince,' said the general nervously. 'I told you the woman Nadia was a witch!'

'Magic! Witches!' fumed Gaikatu. 'You're a fool, Taghachar. She's no more a witch than you're the ghost of my dead brother. The guards were asleep, and the women slipped past.'

'The guards swear that no one passed,' said Taghachar. 'And you know the gates were always barred from the outside.'

'The guards have tongues, I suppose, and can speak for themselves,' said Gaikatu, turning and pointing to one of the men at the gate. 'You! Were you on duty when the escape was discovered?'

'Yes, Your Highness.' The sentry came forward reluctantly. 'All four of us were here and we will swear no one passed through the gates during our shift.'

'And were you here all night?' demanded Gaikatu angrily.

'No, Your Highness. We were here on the forenoon, and returned to our duty at dawn the following day.'

'I have questioned the night sentries as well as the four they replaced at dusk,' said Taghachar. 'All swear that no one came out.'

Gaikatu glared at him. 'By the pox, they did not fly, you can be sure. They must have gone over the walls.'

'Impossible, Your Highness, unless they had help. No woman could leap from that height and live. Even a tall man ....'

'And who helped them,' sneered the prince, ' - Zobeida, I suppose. What does the old woman have to say?'

'Nothing, Highness. She prepared the women's breakfast as usual but when she took it their rooms she found them empty. I will punish her if she assisted them in their escape.'

'Then you will get nothing from her,' said Gaikatu, baring his teeth. 'Zobeida is a simple soul, Taghachar. I will question her myself. Zobeida!'

he called. 'Come out, old nurse! '

He strode towards the gaoleress's cell and threw open the door. Zobeida was seated at her table with her simple wooden cross between her hands. She rose and timidly approached him, clutching the symbol of her faith.

'Well, old nurse,' cried the prince. 'So my prisoners have disappeared by magic, have they?'

'I don't know if 'twas magic,' replied Zobeida. She did not look up at Gaikatu, but held the cross more tightly. 'I know only that they're gone, and that they did not pass through either gateway.'

'Magic is for fools,' said Gaikatu, baring his teeth in a mirthless grin. 'We both know it. Tell me how it was done. Did they overpower you, Zobeida? Did Nadia drug the sentries' liquor?'

'I told you, Highness,' interrupted Taghachar, who had followed the prince across the courtyard, 'the sentries were at their posts and both gates barred ....'

'Shut your cock-sucking mouth, Taghachar,' snarled Gaikatu. He seized Zobeida by the chin and forcibly raised her head so that she could no longer avoid his eye. 'They did not fly, and they did not come through the gates, so they could only have climbed the wall. Did you help them, old nurse - mmm?'

He squeezed Zobeida's cheeks between his thumb and forefinger and she squealed in pain.

'Do not hurt me, My Lord, I beg. I will tell you what I know.'

Gaikatu released her.

'So there is more to this affair,' he said triumphantly. 'Speak up, Zobeida. I will not punish you. When did you last see them?'

'I cannot say exactly. 'Twas of a morning certainly,' said Zobeida vaguely. 'After that I didn't see either of them. But I didn't aid them, My Lord - and they didn't leave by the gate. After the knife-grinder went ....'

'Knife-grinder!' exclaimed the prince. 'You said nothing about a knife-grinder, Taghachar.'

'You gave no instructions regarding tradesmen, Highness, only that Nadia and Keremun should not leave. Supplies had to be brought in, and there were some tiles to be mended.'

'Why did no one mention tradesmen?' cried Gaikatu. 'You fellows? Did you see anyone?'

'We saw the mason, My Lord,' said one of the guards, 'and, a morning or two before the escape, someone did come wanting to sharpen our blades. But both left alone.'

'Before the escape? Not the same day?'

'No, My Lord.'

'Mmm. We'll see,' mused Gaikatu. 'I am interested in this knife-grinder, Zobeida. Did he see the prisoners?'

Zobeida hung her head and said nothing. Again the prince seized her and compressed her face between his fingers.

'Well?'

'Yes, My Lord. He saw the Lady Nadia and spoke to her.'

'So you permitted a ruffian to address the lady?'

'No, My Lord,' said Zobeida. She held the wooden cross to her lips. 'At least, he addressed her, but he wasn't a ruffian. I didn't learn his name, but he was noble, an' a Christian like me. I couldn't betray him. So I allowed it.'

'By the jaws of the underworld - the Venetian!' cried Gaikatu in a passion of rage. 'Why didn't I think of that. My cousin Baidu was right after all, and I was wrong. You should have killed the Christian at Baghcha, Taghachar.'

'He has four days start, Highness,' said Taghachar, 'but he cannot have travelled far with the women.'

'But in which direction, and who are his accomplices?' said Gaikatu. 'And where is the boy? Those are the questions we need answers to.'

'To Kerman,' suggested Taghachar. 'The boy's grandfather is there. Or perhaps they have gone to join Ghazan.'

'I want them found, Taghachar!' cried the prince. 'The woman is mine, - and the child. Send a platoon in each direction, and another on the Baghdad road. Have your men search Tabriz. And find my murdering cousin or his deviate Muslim cronies. They can help. Nadia has friends in the city and may have gone into hiding.'

He bared his teeth again, and for once there was a trace of real amusement in his smile. 'By the gods, Taghachar, this Christian is a worthy adversary. When you find them do not kill him. I'll enjoy slitting his throat myself.'

*

VII

Nadia's first taste of freedom was bittersweet. She had made her decision without hesitation. Often, in the loneliness of the villa, she had dreamed of being Giovanni's wife and of bearing his children, scarce daring to hope that her dreams could become reality. And when, in answer to her prayers but against all expectation, he had come, she knew that nothing mattered but her love for him.

Yet, as she sped east from Tabriz with Giovanni and Hassan at her side, her joy, her anticipation of a new life, her elation at having escaped Gaikatu's clutches, were dampened by the prospect of causing her father more pain. She had hurt him by revealing Nizam's deception and now she would hurt him again by revealing her own.

Giovanni's thoughtful preparations repaid themselves and they reached Qazvin in less than five days. Kartir awaited their arrival expectantly at his villa. It was the moment Nadia had dreaded. She knew he had been ill, but the change in him shocked her. His beard had become very grey and the flesh had fallen from his face, but it was not only his appearance that was different. He seemed distant, subdued. He did not recognise her and was only persuaded it was she when she unwound the turban to reveal her shorn locks.

'Your beauty is half gone,' was all he would say as he embraced her.

Nadia took his hands in hers and raised them to her cheek. For a while they looked at one another in silence. She gathered her courage.

'You know I cannot come with you to Kerman, Father.'

Kartir nodded gravely and led her away from the others.

'So it is *goodbye*, Daughter, when we've only just been reunited?' he asked her.

'Gaikatu will not give up, Father. As long as I remain in Persia, I'll be a fugitive, and your life too will be endangered. By Arghun's will, I am free, and I have chosen to spend my freedom in Venice. Giovanni has asked me to be his wife.'

'His wife!' the viceroy exclaimed, but with less passion than she had expected.

'I love you dearly, Father, but we are like strangers. There is both

good and evil among those who follow Islam, just as there is both
wickedness and nobility among those who worship the gods of our
ancestors, or the Prophet Jesus. Yes, Giovanni is a Christian, but what does
religion matter if we truly love one another? Allah sees into our hearts and
will bless us.'

'I know it, Nadia,' acknowledged Kartir. He smiled wanly. 'But
whether He does or not, I have no power to prevent this union, any more
than I could prevent your last.'

She looked at him apprehensively.

'But you would forbid it if you could?'

'Forbid it? No. But consider, Nadia. You *are* free. You could again
be the daughter of a viceroy. I am in Ghazan's favour and have no doubt
he will eventually claim the throne of Persia. In Venice, what will you be?
What will you have?'

'I will have a husband, Father,' she cried, 'and he will be king to me,
whatever his rank or profession. What is your wealth if I cannot have
love?'

'Think of your son. He has the blood of the Magians, even if not of
the Shahs. Perhaps what I once planned may still come to pass. If Allah is
willing, he might one day be Persia's ruler.'

'Not even you believes in magic crosses, Father, or in prophecies of
long dead priests of Zoroaster!' Nadia cried. She lowered her eyes and
held her breath for a moment, hesitating, but her secret no longer
mattered. 'And it is for Hassan's sake as much as my own that I must go.
I have to protect him from his heritage, at least until he is grown.'

'His heritage?'

'To the title of Il-khan only two have a better claim,' she blurted out.
'Even if Roxanne were to have been Jalal's heir, Hassan would not have
his blood. Mahmoud never touched me. We were too much brother and
sister ever to be lovers.'

Kartir drew away from her and she watched his hollowed face
become ashen grey.

'I don't understand, Nadia.'

'Don't you see, Father? Hassan is Arghun's son. I lay with him
before we were ever husband and wife. That is reason enough why I can

never return to Kerman.'

'That cannot be so,' cried Kartir, disbelieving. 'It cannot be .....'

'We cannot erase the past, Father. Do you remember when Abaqa's forces rode into Kerman? I was alone. The soldiers were wild, drunk, looking for their pleasure wherever they could find it. Three of them seized me. They threw me to the ground, bruised me, tore my clothes.' She closed her eyes, recalling her terror. 'They would have violated me too if Arghun had not come. He gave me his cloak, took me to his tent and attended to my injuries. I had never known a man, but my feelings were awakened and I was curious. We lay together in the tent and when I knew I was with child, I pretended his father was the man I had married. I even pretended to Arghun. Until he lay dying, he did not learn the truth.'

'And Teguder?'

'To Teguder, I was a mere possession. I learned to cool his passion with a look, and with the help of garlic odour and some herbs added to his wine. Perhaps if I had married Arghun straightway, my life would have been different. As it was, I never let him make another child with me, though he was a good husband and father.'

'And will this Venetian be a good husband and father?'

'The best in the world. And we shall have sons and daughters together, so long as God wills it. I will do nothing to prevent it.' She paused and touched him on the cheek. Now that she had told him, she felt relief. He might never condone her sin but surely he, of all people, would understand it. 'What could I be in your house, Father? I am no housekeeper, and I am no virgin to be married off to a rich Muslim merchant. Or would you have me stoned as an adulteress?'

'You know I'm no zealot, Nadia, and I could forgive even that if you came back to me.'

'And if not?'

'I have lived too long by the laws of Islam to pretend I am not hurt by your confession,' replied Kartir bowing his head but not quickly enough to prevent her seeing the tear that had formed in the corner of one eye. 'I shall need time to adjust. Yet I wish only for your happiness. Giovanni has proved his right to your hand. He has twice saved the life of your child, and he has given you back to me, even if only for a day. Go to

Venice with my blessing, but hurry before you break my heart even more by staying.'

She kissed him solemnly.

'Why not come with us, Father? If Ghazan is deprived of his birthright, Persia will be a sad country. And you are in danger too from this Nizam. You can make a new life with us in the West.'

Kartir shook his head.

'My life is here,' he said. 'Persia may be a sad country, but she is *my* country. Maybe in the years that remain to me, I can make some slight difference.'

'But if Gaikatu or Baidu becomes Il-khan ....,' protested Nadia. 'Neither will forgive you for being Arghun's friend. You will be deprived of your post, perhaps even of your life.'

'Allah's will be done, Daughter,' Kartir answered, 'though I do not think I have anything to fear. Nizam is an obsequious fool, but he was right in one respect. Those princes are weak men. Whoever wins the throne will need a strong hand in the South. Perhaps I can give them the peace and stability they need and crave.'

Giovanni was eager for them to be on their way. He had said goodbye to Keremun and to Sabbah, who embraced him silently like a brother before departing for Rayy with his young charge. Fresh horses were purchased, three for Nadia, Hassan and himself, and a fourth to carry provisions and a few belongings.

Hassan pranced around, paying little attention to his mother's efforts to calm him or Giovanni's to impress on him the perils of the journey they were about to commence.

'We're going to Venice,' he shouted excitedly. 'We're all going to Venice!'

Kartir watched their preparations serenely, but Giovanni saw the shadow on his brow and lingered, hoping for a word. He sensed that, at their previous parting two weeks before, the viceroy had been aware of his intentions, even if he had not been fully aware of them himself. Then, they had spoken of nothing but the plans for rescue. Now, he guessed what was in the viceroy's mind, that he was not to be easily reconciled to his daughter's decision, that he might even have tried to dissuade her from it.

When he had finished saddling and loading their ponies, Giovanni led them across the villa courtyard towards its gate. Hassan had already mounted. Nadia was with her father in the shade of the building. Giovanni felt a surge of apprehension. What if she had changed her mind and would not come with him? Perhaps her love for him was not strong enough to sustain the parting from her native land or the uncertainty of months of travel across hostile terrain. The dangers of their journey could be scarcely preferable to the dangers of remaining. Even if they reached the Persian border and crossed to the Turkish coast, they faced the additional hazard of a long sea voyage.

However, as he took the bridle in his hand and prepared to mount, both she and Kartir came towards him. Nadia was smiling through her tears. The viceroy had recovered some of his lost colour and he too smiled faintly, the first time Giovanni had ever seen him do so.

'Take care of my family!'

'We shall put our trust in God,' said Giovanni. 'He will bring us to Venice safely.'

'In God, and in your sword, Ambassador? You'll forgive me for continuing to call you that.'

'I have become used to the title, Excellency,' replied Giovanni, 'though I fear I may have undertaken my first and last mission.'

'I suspected at Rayy you had not always been a diplomat.'

'I'm no more than soldier of fortune, much to my father's chagrin.'

'Soldier and diplomat; it is a contradiction. Which is my daughter to marry?'

'Both, - and neither, Excellency,' answered Giovanni. 'But whatever I am, you have my promise to guard Nadia with my life.'

'You are a brave man, Giovanni di Montecervino,' said the viceroy. 'If Muslims and Christians are ever to put aside their differences, it is through men like you that it will be done. Stay! Put your diplomacy and your sword to good use in Persia's service.'

'You know I cannot,' said Giovanni. 'Besides, I have had my fill of war. As for diplomacy, I fancy that, after the excitement of this adventure,

I would find it tedious.'

'What will you do?'

'Who knows? I may seek a place on the Council of Venice, or find my destiny in husbandry. Our family owns rich land and wants only a son to manage it. Will you give me your blessing?'

Instead of replying immediately, Kartir drew a paper from beneath the folds of his robe and held it out. Giovanni took it in his hand. On the front were written the words - *My House is Your House*. He opened it but could make nothing of the neat Persian script.

'You have my blessing a thousandfold,' said the viceroy, 'but you shall have a dowry too. In Maragha, I have a fine property, the reward of many years service to this country's rulers. Travel there; it is on your way. Give this letter to Master Shirazi at the observatory. He has the house's title and will give it to you. Perhaps you will return to Persia in happier times.'

'Thank you, Excellency,' Giovanni replied. 'You are most generous. As to the future - again, who knows?'

'Our futures are in the hands of God, Giovanni,' said Kartir gravely, 'and only He knows whether we shall meet again.'

By chance, a group of traders returning to Tabriz from Herat happened to be in the town, and the three travellers joined them. The merchants had their womenfolk with them and, as Nadia's former disguise would have come under close scrutiny and would have made explanations difficult, she exchanged it for a caftan and yashmak.

They travelled more slowly now. The merchants stopped frequently to exchange gossip, and more than a week elapsed before they glimpsed the peaks of Mount Sahand in the hazy distance.

Giovanni remained tense throughout the journey. Although he had become accustomed to the Persian guise he had assumed and had long lost his Italian accent, he dared not relax his guard lest a minor slip betray him as a foreigner. Nadia seemed happy and cheerful, but he knew her outward demeanour hid a deep sadness at the parting from her father, and from the only country she had known. He suspected too that, like himself, she had not discounted the possibility that Gaikatu was searching for her, and that he would anticipate their journey and prepare a trap for them.

As they emerged into the plain of Tabriz on the tenth morning after leaving Qazvin, the weather was sultry and oppressive. The sky was grey to the south and west. The air was still as if presaging a storm. The horses seemed less willing and responded only to strong pressure from the knees.

'Surely it is not the season for rains,' said Giovanni. As if in answer, a faint, distant rumble reached his ears. His mount snorted.

'It is odd,' admitted Nadia with a glance at the ominous sky. 'My ancestors would have said it is the cloak of the dark god, and that the sound is the wheels of his chariot.'

'We have seen no sign of Gaikatu's troops, nor any armed Mongols that might be part of a search party.'

'The difficulties will come when we are again alone. The Patriarch will give us hospitality, but I do not wish to endanger him by remaining long under his protection.'

They parted from the caravan at the east gate, skirted the walls and took the mountain path. The sun was approaching its zenith when they reached the olive plantations, and it was hot. The low southern and western skies, however, retained the ominous greyness they had observed earlier on leaving the Uzan valley. The groves were silent as if the birds that normally twittered languidly in the midday heat had taken shelter from a coming deluge. Even the insects had desisted from their excited chattering, and a few feeble cheeps were all that greeted them from the grass. The rocks, usually alive with lizards, were bare.

A group of militia sprawling lazily in the shade of an apple orchard were the only other human beings in sight. They drank from their water bottles, laughed boisterously, but scarcely looked up as the three travellers passed.

'I have never known a day like this,' said Nadia. 'There are omens to be seen in the heavens, and I fear more than ever that our danger is not over.'

At the Patriarch's villa, Djamila welcomed them courteously, and led them indoors, but she was clearly agitated.

'You must not stay here, My Lady,' she said. 'Prince Gaikatu has returned to the city. He learned of your escape, and how it was accomplished. Many in the Christian quarter were arrested and questioned.'

'He has guessed then at my involvement,' said Giovanni, 'and is taking reprisals.'

'And it is I who have brought his anger down on them,' said Nadia, greatly distressed. 'It was never my wish to endanger the lives of the poor people of the city.'

'There have been no deaths. They say Gaikatu has an aversion to bloodletting. It has been nearly three weeks, and his anger has cooled. The prisoners were released, though I cannot swear he has given up the search for you, My Lady. Nor for you, sir.'

'Then he must have believed we were still in Tabriz,' said Giovanni.

'As soon as your escape was discovered, Taghachar sealed all the main routes out of the city, and it seems he persuaded the prince you could not have left it.' Djamila's countenance lightened and she smiled slyly. 'The hue and cry was not raised until two days after you rode for Qazvin!'

'Two days,' echoed Giovanni. 'God bless Zobeida! I asked for a day, and she gave us two. Yet we saw no patrols that would trouble us, only some lazy fellows in an orchard.'

Djamila's smile faded and she became very grim.

'It is nearly midday, and the sun is at its hottest. At other times they hail and question caravans leaving the city. And six men are stationed past the ridge, on the way to Maragha. The Patriarch thinks it only a matter of time before the Mongols come here - though it is not Gaikatu he fears seemingly, but the other.'

'Taghachar?'

'Baidu, sir.'

'Baidu is in Tabriz?'

'There is a pact and the succession is to be determined by a vote. But it is not that. The Patriarch mutters incessantly to himself about death, the Dark One and the shaking earth. I fear he may be losing his wits.'

The sound of Gobras's bell interrupted their conversation. They descended to the lower apartment. The Patriarch sat close to the fire, his sightless eyes turned towards it as if staring into the embers. The black and white hound padded silently up and down the long room. At intervals, it paused expectantly, as if listening to a sound beyond human hearing, sniffed the air and growled softly. As the visitors approached the altar, it returned obediently to it master's side and lay down with its nose nuzzling his bony hand. Gobras stroked it.

'It is almost noon, and you must be gone from here by then,' he chanted. His agitation was only too obvious.

Nadia went to him, knelt at his side and gently laid her hand on his shoulder. 'Patriarch ....'

The ancient turned his face toward the sound of her voice.

'I have seen death .... and murder, Daughter of Kartir. Murder ..... betrayal.'

Nadia drew in her breath.

'Ours?'

Gobras shook his head. 'I have not seen that, child, but the husband you once knew ...... His assassin in close by.'

'Nizam? What have you seen? We shall not go until you tell me that.'

'I see only a servant of the Dark Lord.' The Patriarch became very agitated. 'I know him now - one who betrays his people for gold and dreams of power. You must go before it is too late. Ride like the wind for Maragha. Ormazd will protect you.'

'More visions!' Giovanni cried impatiently. 'Tell us what you have seen.'

The old priest's frame shook as if it would break, then he grew calmer.

'Mine has been a long life, Christian, and I will die soon,' he said. 'That I have seen in the fire. Ahura Mazda has spoken to me. He is the same whatever men call him. Whether his prophets be Zoroaster, Mahommet, or Christ. And He will protect you, but you must go now.'

'You are frightening me, Patriarch,' said Nadia. 'What harm can we come to here? Gaikatu knows nothing of this temple.'

Gobras showed his cracked, yellow teeth in a sad smile.

'Once you came to me with a secret, Nadia, Daughter of Kartir. You trusted me to preserve it, and I have done so. Trust me again now. Take your child, and your man, and ride for Maragha.'

'But the patrol?' insisted Giovanni. He appealed to Djamila. 'I cannot fight six.'

'The patrol will not harm you,' said Gobras. 'Trust me.'

Nadia kissed the wrinkled forehead.

'I do not understand these visions, and I am in terror when they come to me, but I trust you, Patriarch. We shall do what you say.'

'Then let's be on our way,' said Giovanni. He took Nadia's arm and tried to lead her away from the hearth, but the old priest gripped her hand tightly.

'Wait but a second, child,' he cried. 'Let me touch the talisman one more time - the gammadion you wear at your throat.'

Giovanni watched, not comprehending. Nadia stared at the glowing hearth, then at the triptych. She freed herself from Gobras's grasp, reached for her gammadion and held it out to him. His withered hand found it. The exploring fingers stroked briefly the bent arms, lingered, then allowed the ornament to fall back against her breast. He turned away and resumed his motionless vigil over the embers.

Nadia rose. She was trembling.

'Let us go, Giovanni,' she said. 'Let us go now, before the earth shakes!'

*

VIII

Nizam was sweating like a pig. The rim of his turban was damp against his forehead. Drops of perspiration fell from his eyebrows. He wiped them away with his sleeve. He had never known such a morning, grey and oppressive like winter, but with the heat of midsummer.

'It is tragic enough to be amusing, Master Nizam.' Prince Baidu was at his most sardonic. 'Only my cousin isn't laughing!'

'No, Your Highness.'

'*No, Your Highness,*' squeaked Baidu in a falsetto. 'Is that all you have to say to me? It's lucky for you Gaikatu doesn't know who you are, or you'd be a eunuch by now.'

Nizam's head and chin began to itch. Although his hair was growing back and his beard was stubble once more, few days passed without him imagining the touch of the blade against his scalp, without him feeling the coarse fabric of the discarded monk's hood against his raw skin. At times he even fancied his nostrils could still detect the aroma of candle wax, the pungency of burning incense or worse, the smell of Arghun's blood.

'Yes, Your Highness,' he said nervously. 'What more can I say? I have apologised. It was a moment of panic.'

'Forget Baghcha,' said the prince. He raised the flagon of liquor at his side and took a long drink from it. 'We have a more diverting task for you. Find the woman!'

Nizam rubbed his head through his turban and scratched his chin. It was not easy to forget Baghcha. The simple poison, ingested slowly, should have first caused narcolepsy, then death, leaving no trace, raising no suspicion that it had been anything but natural. Instead, Arghun had taken more than a week to die, and had done so in a violent and bloody manner. Nizam had indeed panicked, but he had recovered his nerve quickly. When the Indian told him the significance of the gammadion on the casket lid, he had seen the chance of not only averting suspicion, if there was any, but of securing a personal triumph.

That the casket's maker, as Nizam supposed, had mistakenly carved on it the left-handed cross, not the right, would be the ultimate irony. The Il-khan's wife would follow her husband to the grave and he, Nizam, would be avenged on his hated enemy . Ahmed Kartir, who had colluded with the Mongol conquerors in the overthrow of the Emir of Kerman, who had been their ally against the Caliph and who, with the treacherous Juvaini, had presided over the destruction of all that was sacred to Sunni tradition.

His second moment of panic had come when, searching hastily in the damp, crimson-stained bedlinen and beside the still warm body, he had failed to find the casket. Nadia had found it and drawn the only possible conclusion.

The Indian had urged that they make their escape, but Nizam turned a deaf ear. He calmed down. There had been no cries of murder, no accusations. All he had to do was to watch Nadia and wait for the right opportunity to turn his plan into action. And the opportunity had come.

But it had all been for nothing. Nadia had escaped his justice. Taghachar, his loyalty already transferred to Gaikatu, had recognised her value and taken her as a prisoner to Tabriz. Faced with his cousin's wrath, Baidu had confessed to being author of the murder plot. There was talk of a truce. Sultan al-Ashraf, preferring the certainty of a quick victory over the Crusader remnants to the uncertainty of a prolonged struggle between the cousins for the Persian succession, had withdrawn his army to Palestine.

And now the woman had escaped for a second time, had gone to ground somewhere in Tabriz with her son and the Christian.

The prince was watching him through narrowed, liquor-drugged eyes.

'Well? Do you have any idea where she might be?'

'They may have already left the city, Your Highness.'

'I don't see how,' scowled Baidu. 'The gates are patrolled day and night. The Italian's a cunning fellow by all accounts, but even those fools of guards couldn't mistake Nadia for a knife-grinder.'

'Perhaps they left before the alarm was raised.'

'Mmm.' Baidu took another mouthful from his flagon, gargled and then swallowed. 'That gives me a notion. I wonder if my cousin has looked outside the city walls. There was some talk of Nadia going to a villa on the mountain road, but the fellow got himself killed in the skirmishes before he could find out any more. Olive and pumpkin farms, that was it. Do you know the place?'

'No, Your Highness, but I should be able to find it,' said Nizam, grateful for the chance to make up for his disobedience.

'Then do so,' snapped the prince. 'And when you do, have a few of my useless conscripts guard the road. Gaikatu has men at the mountain pass, but two or three more won't do any harm. Amuse me and I'll give you fifty dinars. Fail and I'll have your balls for dinner!'

*

IX

Djamila accompanied them to the villa entrance. She waited until they replenished their water supplies and mounted their ponies before disappearing again indoors.

They crossed the plantation. Giovanni led the way, with Nadia in the centre and Hassan bringing up the rear with the fourth pony in tow. He could feel the air heavier than ever. He turned his eyes towards the grey southern sky. Another distant rumble reached his ears. The animals snorted nervously.

'It's very close now,' he observed. 'Are we to escape Tabriz in a storm? Will the dark skies, the thunder and the lightning hide us from our enemies?'

'Not a storm, Giovanni,' said Nadia. 'I used to be told that every hundred years the mountain breathed out fire and smoke, and that the plains opened and swallowed the unbelievers. Such tales!'

She shook her head, but Giovanni noticed she was trembling again.

'What then?' he asked.

'It is the quaking earth, My Lord. All the stories hide a truth, this one no less than the others.'

'What is it, Mother?' breathed Hassan. 'What's the quaking earth?'

As if in answer, there was yet another rumbling sound, much closer this time, and the ground beneath their feet seemed to move. The ponies quivered and strained at the bridle.

'It has begun,' Nadia exclaimed. 'Keep a tight rein and stay firmly in the saddle. I had forgotten. One night, the year of Arghun's accession, the castle of Tabriz shook, and some loose stones fell from the walls. And it happened once, when I was a child. I ran to my mother's bed in terror. The next day, the roof of the residency had to be repaired and the veranda rebuilt.'

Again the ground shook. The men in the apple orchard were on their feet, staring fearfully at the heavens. Two of their horses had bolted, carrying their bows and scimitars. The others had strayed a distance away.

'If they are Gaikatu's men, they will not trouble us,' cried Giovanni. 'Stick close together!'

He shortened the rein and dug his knees hard into his pony's side. It responded by lunging forward into a wild canter. Nadia's and Hassan's mounts followed suit. The animal carrying their boxes bucked violently and tore the tether from the boy's hand.

'Mother!'

'Leave it!' panted Nadia. 'We have no need of it.'

There was a deafening crack. A chasm, as wide as the path itself, opened not twenty paces behind them. The unfortunate pony, cast adrift and riderless, but following valiantly in the wake of its companions, stumbled, and was swallowed up by the hungry earth, which closed up after it. The orchard heaved. A complete row of trees toppled, throwing branches, twigs and newly-formed fruit in all directions. The three terrified soldiers vanished into the pits left by the roots.

The hillside erupted. Rocks appeared where there had been none previously, and rivers of stones and debris cascaded down along the newly-formed crevices.

'Ride for your lives,' yelled Giovanni, and he pressed his pony even harder. However, none of the animals needed any encouragement. They snorted in panic and, with flared nostrils, gathered speed in the only direction the tightened reins would allow them to go.

They were on rising ground, but still the ponies did not slacken. Giovanni had never ridden at such a pace. His face burnt and his eyes stung with pain. Hassan had overtaken him. He rode forward on his pony's neck, grasping the bridle, with his face buried in the creature's long mane. His saddle had loosened but he clung to it skilfully with his knees and thighs, striving to hold it in position.

Giovanni glanced back anxiously. Nadia was on his tail and a little to the left. She too rode forward, clutching her horse's neck. She had lost her yashmak and her caftan streamed out behind her like the jib of a single-master. There was another crack and they were showered with fragments of rock and small stones. A boulder struck the path and rolled into the valley, narrowly missing them.

Still they rode at a gallop, ponies and riders panting from exertion, the animals sweating and bathed in foam. The fierce sun beat relentlessly on their heads. Time seemed to have stopped.

The ground was levelling off but small, new eruptions appeared, throwing the terrified horses into even greater confusion. They zigzagged hither and thither, heads down, necks straining, muzzles frothy white, hooves thudding on the hard earth. Hassan had drawn further ahead and Giovanni saw he was now balanced precariously on his pony's withers. The saddle had slipped askew and the fully loaded bags were trailing below the animal's belly, hampering its free movement.

Giovanni slackened his pace and called out, but his voice was lost to the mountain. Again he looked back. Nadia was now some distance away. Behind her, the city of Tabriz was spread out in the haze of the plain. Above, grey rocks cast twisted shadows across the road.

They were climbing again, and the ponies were tiring. Suddenly, Giovanni was aware that he could hear only the clatter of iron against rock and the whistling of the air past his ears. The rumbling and the tremors seemed to have stopped. He spurred forward, overtook Hassan and signalled him to draw rein. The boy did so and slid awkwardly from his horse's neck.

Nadia too halted. Her brow and cheek had been cut by the flying stones. She wiped the blood away with her hand.

'Are you hurt, My Lady?' Giovanni asked breathlessly.

'It is nothing,' she replied. 'At least, it's no worse than what you suffered.'

Giovanni realised that his face too was bleeding.

'Is it over, Mother?' asked Hassan. Only he seemed to have escaped the stones.

'I do not know,' Nadia answered. 'Be silent a moment, and perhaps we shall learn.'

They listened, but could hear nothing.

'More tremors may come later,' she said, 'but I think we are safe for the present.'

Giovanni refastened Hassan's saddle and they continued on foot. The hillside above began to be peppered with cave openings. Ahead of them was a rocky ridge. To the west, the ground fell away in a smooth escarpment.

'What of Gaikatu's patrol?' Nadia asked.

'Perhaps they took refuge up there,' suggested Hassan, indicating the caves.

'I think not,' said Giovanni. He signalled them to pull into the shadow of the hillside. Less than fifty paces away, near the top of the ridge, with his back towards them, squatted a Mongol bowman.

Nadia gasped.

'Can we pass him without being seen?'

'We have no choice but to try, My Lady,' said Giovanni. 'We cannot go back, and this is the only road.'

'And the others? Djamila said there would be six.'

Giovanni drew his short sword and edged forward, straining his eyes to detect signs of movement. If there were six men, they could be stationed at intervals on the other side of the ridge. His only chance was to take one at a time.

He dropped to his knees and began crawling towards his quarry. The bowman seemed unaware of their presence and there was something eery and unnatural about his posture. He sat quite motionless, his head tilted to one side and his right arm resting on a boulder. His left hand gripped his bow but there was no sign of a quiver or arrows.

Giovanni crept closer and prepared to attack. He saw the man clearly now, but he saw too the reason for his lack of awareness. The Mongol was dead, his neck broken, his temple crushed by a flying rock. His legs were buried to the thighs in rubble and his trunk remained upright thanks only to the boulder against which he had been thrown. Nearby, on the escarpment, lay a second Mongol bow and further down, half embedded in the seemingly solid ground, was a human forearm and hand still holding a scimitar in its death grip. As Giovanni became accustomed to the tricks played by the sunlight on the rocks and among the shadows, he spotted other horrors: the corpse of a man, ripped in two by the terrifying power of the quake; a soldier's boot containing the remains of a leg, and the head and neck of a grey pony, protruding grotesquely between two boulders.

He rose to his feet, aghast. Beyond the ridge, lying sprawled on their faces were two more bodies, bloody and torn by wounds. As he turned away from this dreadful spectacle and made his way back slowly to where he had left his companions, they came to join him. Hassan turned pale. Nadia averted her eyes.

'Was this what you saw in the fire, My Lady?' asked Giovanni. 'Are these the visions of the future that so frightened you?'

'Never that, Giovanni. Never that,' said she, clinging to his neck and weeping silently. 'They would have stopped us, I know, perhaps killed us even. But these were once living, breathing creatures like us. Once, they may have been Arghun's friends and mine. I could not wish my most bitter enemy such an end.'

'Yet it could so nearly have been us, Nadia, crushed or entombed inside this angry mountain. I begin to believe in these predictions, and that God does indeed have some other plan in mind for us.'

'Let us not tempt Him more by remaining here. The tremors have done their work and the road has much altered since my last journey, but I think our way lies over there, beyond the caves. We are not far from the summit of the mountain. There is said to be a lake near the top into which the snows melt. From it, several streams run, so we shall not want for water.'

They continued their journey, sometimes walking, sometimes trotting. In places, the path was so uneven they had to dismount and pick their way through the fallen rocks. They stopped on the banks of a narrow river to quench their thirst, refill their water bottles and wipe some of the blood and dirt from their faces. The day wore on. From time to time Sahand rumbled and they halted again as mild tremors loosened more debris from the hillside.

At last their route turned downhill. The air lost its sultriness. The terrain changed. The earth became darker and more fertile again. Another stream, dammed and diverted by the eruptions of the ground, crossed their path and fell, splashing, over the stones and boulders. It flowed into a gully where spring grass grew, sparsely at first, then in profusion as the vista opened out into the broad panorama of the Maragha valley. Ahead and below spread a patchwork of rich greens and browns, with splashes of pink, orange and white: avenues of cultivated trees, neatly-planted vineyards and fields of tender corn lit warmly by the early evening sun; isolated farms, clusters of low brick villas and, rising beyond them, Nasr's splendid observatory and the imposing Turkish towers. To the west, in the distance, the sunlight glinted on water.

They halted on a rock terrace overlooking the view. Giovanni drew in his breath.

'It is an earthly paradise,' he said simply.

'Truly,' Nadia replied. 'My father often said it was here that Adam first bedded Eve, but no doubt that is a myth like the others. I have seen the view often and have become used to it, yet never before was there so welcoming a sight.'

They rode wearily into the valley, through the lush pastures and blossoming orchards. The approaches to the town were quiet. The setting sun had turned the slopes of the mountain red. The scents of jasmine, citrus, and almond-blossom wafted across the gardens and along the narrow, empty streets. Here and there was evidence of the tremors - a few broken tiles, a cracked wall, some uprooted vines, but otherwise Maragha seemed to have suffered no damage.

It was the time of prayer. From somewhere beyond the dome of the observatory and the Turkish towers, across the roofs of villas, came the wailing summons of the muezzin:

God is greater! God is greater!
I bear witness!
There is no God but God. Mahommet is the prophet of God.
I bear witness!
Come to prayer! Come to prayer!

Giovanni listened. He was drawn to the sound as never before. The words no longer jarred; they were no longer the abhorrence to him they had been a year ago. He had long neglected the spiritual duties of his own faith. Weeks of travel and danger had allowed no time for them, and in his guise as Muslim merchant he had been obliged often to pretend devotion to his companions' rituals.

He knew their dangers were not over. Yet, for the moment at least, he felt that he and Nadia had reached a sanctuary, a place to safely lay their heads, recover their resolve and, above all, thank God for His mercy.

What had the Patriarch said? *One God, whatever men call Him. One God, whether his prophets be Zoroaster, Mahommet or Christ.*

Giovanni dismounted from his exhausted pony, knelt at the roadside and bowed his head reverently towards the earth. He crossed himself, began to recite the Pater Noster, then stopped, unable to recall the Latin words.

How long he remained there, drained of strength and empty of thoughts, he did not know. At length he was aware of movement at his side. Nadia touched his shoulder. She too was kneeling. Her eyes were soft, and her dust-covered cheeks were wet with tears.

'Forgive me for disturbing your prayer, My Lord,' she whispered. 'It is almost dark. Let us hurry to my uncle Shirazi so that, for tonight at least, he remembers he has a niece.'

*

X
Maragha

Jafar greeted his former pupil with pleasure.

'You have grown in the six months since I saw you, Hassan,' he said. 'I do believe you will be able to reach the topmost shelves of the library without toppling the stool!'

Shirazi offered them a share of his supper, but Giovanni could see he was worried.

'The sooner you put a few days' journey between yourselves and Lake Urmia the better,' he frowned, when they had washed and refreshed themselves with a goblet of wine. 'I cannot protect you here, Nadia. Gaikatu's men have twice passed through the town looking for you. He knows that both you and Hassan were frequent visitors in former times, and have many friends here.'

'We ask for one night only, Uncle,' said Nadia. 'After that, we'll be on our way to Urmia. From there, there is a road to Van and thence to Constantinople.'

'I cannot deny you refuge, and will not, Nadia,' said Shirazi hastily. 'I mean only to warn you against lingering. Though I'm certain none in the observatory will betray you, there are always soldiers in Maragha who would betray their whole families for a silver dinar. As for this ....' He tapped the letter Giovanni had given him. 'Of course, you may have the title, but I fear possession of the house must wait. It is some distance from the observatory.'

'Be assured we shall be on our way as soon as the sun is up, Master Shirazi,' said Giovanni. 'We fully entrust you with His Excellency's marriage gift until another time. We do not wish to endanger you. However, if some new clothes can be found for us without attracting attention, we will be grateful. I still have a few gold coins and some bills of exchange, and can afford to pay well for this small service.'

'Keep your bills and money,' smiled Shirazi. 'You shall have what you need. And if you can read a map, which I suppose you can, I will make you a gift of one that I prepared for the Il-khan. It will assist your journey to Van and beyond. Pray Allah you encounter a caravan, for it is a dangerous route for a man, woman and child travelling without escort.'

The sun had just touched the top of Mount Sahand when Giovanni awoke. Nadia was already on her feet, dressed in a plain white caftan and yashmak that Shirazi had procured for her.

'We should be on our way while the morning is still cool, My Lord,' she said. 'And we had better leave Maragha before the population stirs.'

Giovanni examined the clothing the Master had left for him. He pulled on the coarse vest and breeches, wound the turban round his head, and eyed the scholarly jubbah with amusement. He had slept soundly and his weariness had gone.

'Like the one I wore previously, it'll barely reach my knees,' he observed dryly, 'but at least it will not hinder my movements.'

They loaded the animals, fresh again after their early morning grazing. Giovanni slung a heavy scimitar, rescued from the mountain, over his saddle-horn and concealed his short sword in unscholarly fashion beneath the ill-fitting outer garment.

'Hassan!' Nadia called when these preparations were complete. 'Are you ready?'

There was no response.

'He spent the night in Jafar's quarters,' said Giovanni forcing himself to laugh. 'Perhaps he has gone to the library to test the tutor's theory about his height.'

They looked, but the library was empty.

'He must have risen before the sun and gone to breathe the morning air,' Giovanni suggested.

'Wayward as ever,' Nadia breathed. 'Even after all that has occurred, danger and risk have no meaning for him. But if he has left the observatory grounds, he cannot have gone far in the grey dawn. Hassan!'

She made for the outer gate but halted suddenly and gave a cry of alarm. Before she reached it, the gate swung open to reveal a Mongol soldier. He carried a bow into which a shaft was already fitted. At his side, wielding a naked scimitar and smiling toothily with self-satisfaction was Prince Gaikatu.

Giovanni reached for his short sword and half drew it, but stopped as the archer brought up his bow and aimed the weapon steadily at him.

'Back, fellow!' ordered the prince. He swaggered to the fore, a look of triumph on his face. 'And the sword! Throw it to the ground.'

Giovanni obeyed. He dropped the short sword and backed slowly towards where the horses were tethered. Out of the corner of his eye he saw Jafar in the doorway. His first thought was that the tutor had betrayed him, but he immediately dismissed it as unworthy. His second was that there were only two men, his next that the prince had not recognised him in his Persian costume. That gave him a moment's comfort. If only Nadia did not speak his name, if he could distract the bowman, force him to loose his arrow early, perhaps he could reach the scimitar.

Nadia stood frozen to the spot in terror. She was staring at Gaikatu in disbelief.

'You are surprised, My Lady,' said the prince sardonically. 'Do you take me for a fool? I have spies who sell me information, and I store it for my own purposes. You were recognised a fortnight since in Qazvin and news was brought to me that you had left it, travelling west with the traders. I gambled that sooner or later you would come over the mountain, and I have waited here long days for you. I too have friends in Maragha. Where else in the world would you go for aid than to your mother's brother?'

Very cautiously Giovanni shifted the position of his feet. The bowman's arrow was still pointing at his heart, but Gaikatu had not once looked directly at him. Behind him, in the doorway, stood the tutor, unarmed and helpless to intervene. The prince continued to taunt Nadia.

'As you have survived the shaking earth, we can now go back to Tabriz. I promised to marry you, and this time you'll not deny me that pleasure.'

'I'll deny it you as long as I breathe,' cried Nadia bravely. 'Kill me if you wish. I will not be your wife.'

Gaikatu laughed.

'Perhaps I can make you change your mind, My Lady. You so readily choose death for yourself. Are you equally ready to choose for your son?' He swung the scimitar at a nearby plant and neatly severed flower and leaves from stem. 'Mangke!'

From behind the gate pillar appeared a second Mongol soldier, his scimitar wedged firmly in his belt. With his right arm he held the squirming form of Hassan, while his left hand was placed over the boy's mouth to prevent him uttering a cry.

'To find the boy walking alone was a happy chance,' Gaikatu continued, savouring his triumph. 'Now, madam, I ask you to choose.'

'You would not kill a child!' cried Nadia in horror.

'Kill?' mocked Gaikatu. 'Why would I kill him when his tender flesh can grant me the pleasure you deny me? Now choose quickly while my patience lasts!'

Nadia half turned towards Giovanni with a look of hopeless despair and the Venetian's heart sank. He was trapped. Gaikatu had followed her gaze.

'Giov .....'

'By the gods, it's the Christian,' screamed the prince. 'Kill him!'

The bowman drew back the string just as Nadia threw herself in front of Giovanni and clung to his robe. The bowman hesitated.

There was a cry of anguish from the doorway behind and Jafar rushed forward like a raging madman.

'No!'

Giovanni moved. He thrust Nadia from him and leapt desperately towards his tethered pony. At almost the same moment, Hassan sank his teeth into the hand that covered his mouth.

The Mongol bowman shifted his position to meet the new threat. His arrow, formerly aimed at Giovanni's heart, pierced the charging tutor in the upper chest, just below the neck. Jafar slowed but did not stop. He grappled with the bowman and both fell. The tutor seemed to have the strength of two men. His left hand closed round his opponent's throat, pinning him to the ground. With his right, he tore the arrow from his chest and plunged it beneath the Mongol's breast bone. The man shuddered, coughed blood, and lay still. Jafar, mortally wounded, collapsed across the body.

The distraction lasted only seconds, but it was enough. Giovanni reached his scimitar, grasped its hilt and turned. Mangke had meantime released Hassan and had drawn his own weapon. Gaikatu, no longer the swaggering youth, but cool and deadly, advanced slowly.

'Leave the Venetian to me, Mangke,' he hissed, 'and see the boy does not get away.'

It was his one mistake. Faced with two powerful antagonists, Giovanni would have been overwhelmed. Mangke made a grab for Hassan who scrambled away and reached the spot where Giovanni's short sword lay in the dust. Hassan gripped the weapon in two hands and, just as the Mongol made a second lunge for him, thrust it with all his strength into the man's groin. A river of blood sprang from his severed artery and he fell, beating the ground and screaming in agony.

Giovanni moved warily, watching the prince's eyes. He now faced only one opponent, but one who was his equal in height and weight and little more than half his age. Gaikatu swung his scimitar twice, almost casually, slicing the air, then in a sudden change of tactic that almost caught the Venetian unawares, lunged forward.

Their blades connected. Giovanni, gripping his weapon in both hands, forced his opponent's blade away. Gaikatu stepped agilely aside and swung the scimitar right to left. Giovanni saw confidence in his expression, sensed ability in his easy movements. If he did not use his years wisely to end this contest early, they would tell against him. If he tired, he could expect no mercy from this arrogant youth who had gambled for a kingdom and would continue to gamble alone for the woman he coveted.

The prince too held his scimitar with both hands. Another lunge, another swing right to left. Giovanni met the blade each time, forcing it away, and went on the offensive himself. He aimed a blow at the prince's exposed left shoulder but Gaikatu was too quick. He ducked aside and, crouching low, swung his scimitar yet again, this time at the level of Giovanni's knees. Giovanni leapt back just in time. His days of anxiety had taken their toll and he was already conscious of the perspiration beneath his turban and of his own heavy breathing. He had slept soundly one night in twenty whereas the prince was fresh.

They circled one another. Gaikatu lunged using his right hand alone, now to the breast, then to the thigh. Twice more their blades met. Twice more Giovanni parried. Twice more he himself swung and scythed the air. Still he watched his opponent's eyes. To the left, always right to left. It was a game, if only he could anticipate all the moves. His breath was coming faster now, and he could feel the sword grow heavier. The prince too was perspiring, but showed no sign of tiring.

Another lunge. Another parry. Scimitars locked. Another swing right to left. Giovanni gripped the scimitar hilt tightly and swung furiously, attacking Gaikatu's sword arm, and retreated as the prince absorbed the blow and went on the offensive.

Then Giovanni saw his opponent's eyes flicker. He too would have to gamble. *When your enemy is in the open crying victory ......*

He retreated another pace, stumbled clumsily, and brought the scimitar across his body to defend against a right to left swing. Behind him, Nadia screamed but he shut out the sound. Gaikatu's weapon was in his left hand, swinging the other way, from left to right.

Had Giovanni's stumble been other than a ruse, the force of the blow would have separated his head from his trunk. However, he had correctly anticipated the change of tactic. At the last possible moment, with both feet firmly planted, he leant backwards from the waist and dropped onto one knee. The prince, following through, momentarily lost his balance and cleaved a deep furrow in the earth. Giovanni's blade struck him from behind, cutting through his heavy leather corslet and opening a deep gash near the shoulder-blade. In an instant, Giovanni was over him, with one foot planted on his left forearm.

Gaikatu reached for his scimitar with his right hand but Giovanni kicked it away.

'Finish it then, Christian,' breathed the prince. He raised himself to a sitting position and looked up, defiant and fearless.

Giovanni took a step back and raised his sword to strike. Then he caught sight of Nadia standing close to where the tutor had fallen. The shadows had gone from the courtyard, and she was in full sun. She had removed the yashmak and the morning light touched her face and the ebony and gold of her hair, not unlike when he had first set eyes on her that summer evening in the castle of Tabriz. Hassan was by her side, his arm encircling her waist, his head buried in the folds of her caftan. So nearly a man in words and action, yet still a boy in need of a mother's comfort and love. He thought of his portrait of Madonna and child, now buried forever in the bosom of the mountain.

He saw too that the contest had attracted spectators. Shirazi himself was in the doorway of the observatory with the other scholars, impassioned, curious. Several members of the town garrison had arrived at the gate and stood there, bemused and uncertain, with hands on weapons.

Giovanni lowered his scimitar and held it steadily with its broad point just below Gaikatu's ear. His eyes met the prince's. Was it only resignation that he saw there, or was there something else - hurt pride, even admiration?

'I could kill you, Prince,' he said. 'I could kill you, and be hacked to pieces by those fellows at the gate. However, I have seen too much blood in the last weeks to see any more while I live. And it is the people of this land, not I, who should decide their rulers.

'You gambled when you might have brought half an army to meet us here. It is now my turn to gamble that, if I spare your life, you will neither pursue us nor take reprisals against those who have given us their friendship.'

He stepped back slowly but with sword still at the ready. Gaikatu rose rather unsteadily clutching his shoulder to staunch the flow of blood from his wound. The men at the gate shuffled uneasily. One or two made to draw their weapons.

'Leave him!' growled Gaikatu. He showed his teeth in a grim smile. 'Do not expect me to thank you for my life, Christian. I would kill you without hesitation if our positions were reversed. But you are right. Too much blood has been spilled. And the Master of Maragha is too valuable a servant to be the object of my revenge. Take the woman. She is yours. Leave Persia, but do not return while I'm ruler here, or by my ancestor's tomb, you will certainly never leave it again.'

Giovanni glanced again at Nadia. She was kneeling by Jafar's body. The disfigured side of the tutor's face lay uppermost, a mask more grotesque in death than it had ever been in life. Nadia's eyes were moist. She bent forward and kissed the scarred cheek.

'His debt to my father is paid,' she said solemnly.

Gaikatu was on his feet. His arm was crimson with blood, his face pale and his teeth were hidden behind his firmly-set mouth.

'I shall not return. Of that you can be sure,' said Giovanni, regarding his former adversary coldly. 'But, meantime, I recommend to Your Highness that you allow Master Shirazi to attend that wound, otherwise nature may prove less merciful than I have been.'

*

XI

Gobras squatted motionless by the dying embers of his hearth. His sightless eyes were closed and he breathed scarcely at all, listening intently as the faint rumbling gradually died away. The second quake had come to nothing. The spirits of the earth were asleep again.

The Patriarch rose from his cushion, leaning on the dog for support, and made his way towards the triptych panel which he lovingly caressed with his bony fingers, feeling the outlines.

Suddenly the dog growled softly.

Gobras felt its neck stiffen and calmly stroked the bristle. He was grateful for the animal's loyalty but the warning was needless. Years of living in the dark, sightless world had sharpened his other senses. The spirits of the earth slept, but there were new vibrations. Horses were approaching along the road from the city, four, perhaps five, at a gallop. Gobras felt his way back to the cushion and rang his bell to summon the housekeeper.

'They will be here soon, Djamila,' he said urgently. 'Go quickly, before it is too late.'

He was conscious of her hesitation.

'I will not leave you, Patriarch,' said Djamila wretchedly. 'Perhaps they will pass by.'

'If only that were so,' said Gobras with resignation. 'You must go, Djamila. One sacrifice will be enough. May Ahura Mazda watch over you.'

'And over you, Patriarch.'

Gobras felt her lips press briefly against his hand and heard her steps retreat across the altar. He rose from his cushion again, followed her to the panel and waited until the second rasp of metal against stone told him she was hidden in the underground room. There would just be time for her to reach the secret exit at the rear of the villa. He sighed. The boy and his mother were long gone, and now Djamila would be safe too.

He listened as the thud of hooves grew in volume, and waited for the timbre to change as the riders forsook the well-trodden ground for the softer earth of the plantation where in years gone by the young soldiers had played their noisy military games.

The sound of hoofbeats grew even louder, then stopped. A thunderous banging on the rotting outer door of the villa was followed by a drunken bellow.

'Open up, old man!'

'Break the door down!' cried another voice impatiently. It too was slurred by liquor.

Gobras felt the chill of fear. This was no visit by anonymous off-duty palace guards. Baidu, prince of Mongol blood, cousin to the murdered Il-khan, did not waste his time on games. He had plotted with a single purpose - to clear his own path to the throne of Persia. Gaikatu might defeat him, but he would not be diverted by a weak and sightless priest. Throughout his long life, Gobras had seen many things clearly in the fire and his last vision had been the clearest of all.

The dog barked. Gobras clutched at its coat and held it, comforted by the feel of the coarse fur. The sound of splintering wood was followed by the clatter of iron on tile. The intruders and their mounts were in the corridor, smashing the decaying mosaics and yelling their drunken, blood-curdling war-cries.

They had reached the door of the temple. Gobras heard the snorts of the ponies and the echoing obscenities of the men as they urged the frightened animals down the broken tessellated steps. There were four of them, Gobras decided - Baidu and three others, just enough to silence a frail old man. Their voices betrayed their number.

The intruders had dismounted. Gobras heard hasty footsteps, the shuffle of leather against marble. They were closer now. Strong body odours reached his nostrils. Their breath reeked of fermented mares' milk.

The dog growled angrily and leapt from Gobras's grip. There were more obscenities, the thud of leather connecting with soft flesh, a yelp of pain and then silence. One of the Mongols laughed.

'Give the priest a taste of his own fire! Let him tell the future with his nose in the hearth.'

'By Genghis's tomb, we'll have no more prophecy,' cried another, Baidu himself from the tone of authority. 'We'll take his tongue as well as his eyes and have an end to it.'

Gobras felt a gloved hand grasp his beard and another hand with strong naked fingers take hold of his shoulder. The foul smell of the Mongol liquor nauseated him. He struggled but was pushed to the ground. His bony cheek struck the cold marble of the altar and he lay there, tasting dust and blood, feeling only pain.

Again there was the clatter of hoof on tile and the sound of footsteps in the upper passageway. A door slammed. The youths on the temple floor uttered further obscenities.

'They're not here, Your Highness,' called a voice from the stairs, an older voice not slurred by alcohol. 'The house is empty!'

Gobras raised his head painfully and listened. It had been long ago, more than ten years, but the accent and intonation were the same.

'Would you condemn me a second time, Nizam?'

The man on the stairs took a few steps and halted. His tread was heavy, his breathing laboured.

'Gobras!' The voice held surprise and fear.

'Do you forget so easily those you condemn?' demanded the Patriarch.

'You should have died at Kerman, old man, along with the others of your tribe.'

Gobras struggled to his knees. His exploring hands touched the fur of the hound. The animal stirred and a low murmur came from its throat. At least his people would have their revenge, he thought, and Nadia her justice.

'The fires have taken twenty years to give up all their secrets,' he said. 'Did you fear us so much?'

Nizam did not reply.

'If it had been I alone, I could have understood perhaps,' the Patriarch went on. 'Only I and Khalafi knew that both Jalal's children died without issue. Kartir did not believe in prophecies, or in Jemshid's cross, but he wanted to believe an heir to the Shah existed. So you deceived him.'

'It was no more than he deserved,' said Nizam. 'My family served the old order for generations. Kartir and his kind betrayed us, and his faith.'

'Was it necessary to denounce the followers of Zoroaster as Abaqa's enemies, and send twenty to their deaths?' challenged Gobras, summoning all his remaining strength. He was aware of the Mongols blundering around the room, overturning the meagre furniture and tearing the astrakhans from the walls in their search for concealed openings. There was a clang of metal on metal as one struck the triptych panel with his sword hilt.

'What's this nonsense, Nizam?' demanded the youth Gobras had identified as Baidu. 'You told us they would be here. Did we coax a few tongues to no purpose?'

'There are other houses, Your Highness,' said Nizam. There was uncertainty in his voice. 'Perhaps it was not they who came from Qazvin ......'

'Who else?' cried Baidu. 'A woman - a boy - a tall man in Muslim dress. Is my cousin to be denied his concubine? Search the upper apartments again, and bring the priest to me!'

Gobras was hauled roughly to his feet. His senses reeled and every bone in his body ached. Twice before, he had stared death in the face and had cheated it but this time he knew his fate was sealed.

'Where are Nadia and the boy?' demanded Baidu. 'I know you helped her in the past - that you hid the Venetian here when he was wounded.'

Gobras did not answer. Instead, he again addressed Nizam.

'Was it to become the servant of these inebriates that you sacrificed my people, Nizam?' he said defiantly. 'Was it for this that you poisoned the woman Roxanne too, lest she speak your secret? Yet it was all in vain. No one man can alter what is written in the flames. Temuchin's children were destined to rule, and will rule until Fate decrees otherwise. Arghun was destined to die, and would have died within a year without your interference.'

There was more commotion on the floor above as one of Baidu's henchmen repeated the search. Another sword struck the metal close by.

'Over here, Prince!'

Gobras was released. They had found the opening, but it was too late. Nadia and her lover had gone, the boy too. He saw her as he remembered her, before his sight had failed. Nadia, daughter of the Magians, in all her youthful beauty. The Il-khan's wife, wearing the

Gammadion of the Sun.

Nizam had drawn in his breath sharply. 'Roxanne's death was natural!'

'You poisoned her!'

'What do you know, old man?' muttered Nizam. 'Your fires could not have told you that.'

'I know,' said Gobras weakly. He was dimly conscious that the dog was awake and on its feet. 'In my sightless world, I see many things - how, with an accomplice, you attached yourself to Arghun's court in the guise of a monk. Perhaps nature lent a hand, but poisoning was always your plan. And when he was dead, you denounced an innocent wife. Would you have killed the child too if Ormazd himself had not covered him in darkness.?'

'Enough of this, devil priest!' cried Nizam. He took hold of Gobras by the two strands of his beard.

The dog growled savagely and leapt. Gobras felt the swirl of air. He heard Nizam's scream of terror as the beast sunk its teeth in his throat, a dull thud and a crack as animal and man toppled on the marble. Another sound as the blade of a sword split fur and flesh, and spattered him with canine blood.

He was seized again by the beard and gasped.

'I asked you a question, old man.' Baidu again.

Gobras was silent. Despite his great age and the roaring in his head, he would stubbornly cling to life and the truth. A shudder of agony shot through his fragile body as the prince struck him forcibly on the jaw. Involuntarily, he spat a mouthful of blood and broken yellow teeth over his persecutor's tunic.

'Where are they?'

They are not here; they are safe, thought Gobras. The fire that had given him warning had also told him that much. He was barely conscious of being again pushed to the ground. His arms and legs were bound with thongs. Something was thrown over his head and he could not breathe freely. He recognised the texture of Astrakhan.

Gobras had long known that Hassan was Arghun's son, but that did not matter. The blood of the Magians, of the kings, of Kartir the Great and

Ardashir flowed in his veins. There was the prophecy, and there was the Cross of Jemshid. The child would grow, and he would return to fulfil his destiny, perhaps even to avenge the death of an old man. He had been raised in an alien faith, but Ahura Mazda would guide his hand for all that.

Another rug was laid on him, one of those that had adorned the walls of the upper apartments. Execution by carpet - reserved by the Mongols for their royal enemies. Gobras knew their customs.

They were beating the rugs with their swords and treading them with their boots, screaming obscenities. Suffocating, driving the life from his body. He could not feel pain, could not hear them, but it was what he had seen in the sacred flame. Darkness no longer. Nadia!

Gobras saw the gammadion clearly now. The engraving at its centre glowed, drawing him ever more closely into its light.

*

Epilogue
Venice, April 1292 CE

Umid Malikshah stood at the prow of a merchantman watching the Venice Arsenal loom out of the spring mist. A cool, early evening wind blew over the lagoon. Umid was glad of it. A week of squally weather had confined him below deck, where the air was stale and the animal stench of the sailors almost unbearable. By the end of the long voyage from the Black Sea, despite frequent landfalls to take on new supplies, provisions were always low and much of the food that remained was bad or turning.

The vessel was Byzantine, its captain a half-Greek with whom Umid had sailed more than once and who was honest in his dealings if careless in his personal habits. The merchant had made the journey four times in the past but this one was by far the worst. He had escaped the fever that claimed two lives before they reached the Dalmatian coast but since embarking again had suffered stomach and bowel pains and regular bouts of vomiting.

The fresh air made Umid feel almost human again and, as they glided at half sail through the sand banks and past the outer islands towards their moorings, he watched with pleasure the slim, colourful harbour craft bobbing lightly on the swell. Though the pains had eased and he felt hungry, he politely declined the Greek's invitation to sup with him at a tavern on the grounds that his business would not wait. With most of his affairs completed at Ragusa, he was left with only one important commission, and he had ten days to discharge it while the ship was refitted and its crew refreshed in the taverns and bordellos of Venice.

Umid knew the city well. He had many acquaintances among its residents, Christians and Jews as well as merchants of his own faith who had made their home among the infidel. These men formed a close knit brotherhood and, as in Persia, traded information along with the goods they bought and sold. A silver coin purchased for him the services of a boatman and, within an hour of dropping anchor, Umid arrived at his destination, a Gothic-style *palazzo* fronting the *Gran Canale*.

The *palazzo's* owner, an elderly Italian dealer in jewels, first stared hard at his visitor, then allowed his bronzed face to crease in an expression of happy astonishment.

'*Benvenuto a Venezia, Signor Malikshah,*' he cried warmly. 'And you are no less welcome because your visit is unexpected. You are often in my prayers.'

'As you are in mine, Maffeo,' replied the Persian. He embraced the Christian like a favourite brother. 'Did you suffer much when the Mamluks took Acre?'

'I was sorry to lose the Syrian trade,' confessed the Italian, 'though it will come back in time. Indeed, the Sultan's intervention may have been a blessing in disguise. After Acre, I and many of my fellow Venetians turned our attention again to Constantinople. I have to admit that by last autumn I had gained as much as I had lost.' He paused and scrutinised Umid's haggard face. 'However, let us eat first,' he suggested. 'You have been ill, I think. A seaman's rations do not suit you. While we fill our bellies with fine Venetian cooking, and enjoy my wife's company, you can give me the latest news from the Levant. Afterwards, we can talk business.'

Umid accepted gratefully the invitation to dine. However, he ate sparingly, preferring to sample only a little from the dishes presented to him, rather then aggravate his digestive disorder. While they ate, he talked of al-Ashraf's sudden withdrawal from the Persian border and of the new Il-khan's debauchery and fiscal extravagance.

Baidu's overtures to the Sultan had come to nothing. Realising, on Arghun's death, that prospects of an alliance between the Il-khanate and the Christian West were receding, al-Ashraf had first redeployed his army in a siege of the Crusader stronghold at Acre, which had fallen the previous summer. Then, flushed with success, and with no thoughts of a Persian alliance, the Sultan pursued the war against the remaining Frankish fortresses in his territory. Before the onset of winter, these enclaves had either been destroyed or had surrendered.

Gaikatu had been proclaimed Il-khan within a month of al-Ashraf's victory at Acre. Contrary to the predictions of many, no bloodbath had followed his coronation. Umid had expected a purge of the emirs who had supported Baidu, but Gaikatu had dealt leniently with those who opposed him, appointing many of them to positions of authority. The new ruler's excesses were personal rather than political.

Baidu was confirmed in his governorship of Baghdad and Taghachar given a new commission to dislodge all remaining Syrian forces from their entrenched positions along the Euphrates. Kartir was allowed to resume his duties in Kerman, his favouring of Ghazan's cause either ignored or forgotten. Ghazan himself continued to be preoccupied with the civil war in Khorasan.

When the meal was over and he was again alone with the Italian, Umid turned immediately to the matter that had brought him to Venice.

'The Montecervino family?' Maffeo exclaimed. 'Theirs is one of the largest estates in the Po valley. And one of the wealthiest. The Signora di Montecervino is a sister of the Duke.'

'The *Signora*?' Umid raised his eyebrows.

'Yes, my friend. It is unusual even among our people. The lady is a widow. Her husband sat on the Council. Since his death a year ago, she has managed the estate.'

'But there are children ...?' began Umid hopefully.

'There was a son,' said Maffeo. 'Giovanni. Wild and rebellious as a youth. A renowned swordsman. He distinguished himself in the Sicilian Revolt, but ...' He stopped in mid sentence and waved his arms in a gesture of inspired understanding. 'Aha - perhaps I see where your enquiries are headed. This son of the Montecervinos disappeared. Two years ago. Some said he had taken service in Rome, but there were other stories that he had followed the steps of another young man, and had gone to China!'

Umid's heart sank. He had hoped to take better news back to Kerman. Nadia had not reached Venice. She, her son and her Christian lover had not survived their flight across Turkey.

'Then who will inherit, should the young Montecervino not return?'

'There are nephews on the Duke's side,' said Maffeo. 'But such talk may be premature. Young Giovanni may still come home. It's less than a month since I myself returned from Anatolia and I have not yet caught up with the gossip. If you wish to meet the lady, his mother, it can easily be arranged!'

Grazia di Montecervino was younger than Umid had expected. She was much too pale, he thought, even by Venetian standards, and too tall and angular to be beautiful, but she carried herself well. She was elegantly dressed in a brocade gown and her hair was bound beneath a silk cap.

'Signor Umid Malikshah,' said she, acknowledging his polite bow with a slight inclination of her head. Umid noticed she had her son's eyes. 'From Kerman. A trader in fine fabrics, and a Muslim?'

'I confess it, madam.'

'Indeed, signor.' A flicker of a smile crossed her countenance. 'Christians believe that confession is good for the soul. Is that also what the priests of Islam preach?'

'Our faith has no priests, madam, only imams. Teachers. But to be able to open one's heart to a friend is worth a thousand elixirs.'

'I feel sure you exaggerate, Signor Malikshah,' said Grazia, impassive again, 'but I concur with your sentiment. You have brought me some samples perhaps?'

Throughout his two day wait for his invitation and during his ride through the verdant countryside of vineyards, lemon plantations and olive groves, Umid had rehearsed this meeting, how he would explain what had occurred in Persia and break the news to a recent widow that her only son might never be coming home. In truth, he did not know for certain whether Giovanni was alive or dead, but almost a year had elapsed since the Master of Maragha had witnessed his battle with Gaikatu and had bade him farewell on the road to Urmia. Surely, if he and Nadia had survived the journey, they would have reached Venice long before now.

The unexpectedness of the Signora's question drove the prepared speech from his mind. Clearly, his errand had not been explained.

'Your pardon, madam, I am not here to trade,' he said. 'I came hoping for some news, or at worst to impart some.'

'News?' Grazia frowned.

'Of your son.'

'*My son!*' she echoed, moving elegantly across the room towards a small table on which stood a gong. Umid followed her with his eyes, trying to comprehend the emotion behind her impassive mask. There had been neither surprise nor anxiety in her reaction to his enquiry. 'While we talk, will you have a cup of wine?'

Without waiting for his reply, she struck the gong firmly, and turned to face him. It occurred to Umid that she could be a formidable woman if she chose. Again she frowned.

'My son,' she repeated, and there was sharp censure in her tone. 'Now there's a fine topic of conversation! My son is in Rome, Signor Malikshah. First, he vanishes with not a word. I do not see him for more than a year. Then, with his father scarce cold, he returns, fills my house with his new family and, with hardly a breath, goes off again. Is that how Persian sons treat their mothers?'

As Umid stood in silent embarrassment, she suddenly laughed.

'Forgive me, sir,' she begged him, 'but I have rarely seen a merchant lost for words. Your name was unknown to me, but I guessed the reason for your visit. I am well content with my new daughter, and of course you may see her. And bring her news of Persia.'

She struck the gong a second time. Almost immediately an inner door opened and a maidservant appeared with a tray bearing refreshments. Behind her was Nadia. Her face was as lovely as Umid remembered but held none of the strain he had seen eighteen months earlier in Tabriz. Her loose robe could not disguise the swelling of her figure. The Signora withdrew gracefully from the apartment and left them alone.

Nadia held out her hand and Umid kissed it fervently. They appraised one another silently.

'Master Umid. You have not changed.'

'Nor have you, My Lady.'

Nadia patted her abdomen.

'You can see I have truly changed much,' she said lightly. 'I had quite forgotten what it is to be fat with child.'

'Allah has blessed you, My Lady,' said Umid. 'I pray you have found what you were seeking.'

'I have found happiness, Umid,' said she more seriously. 'My one regret is that my father is not here to share it with me. Is he well?'

'His Excellency is well enough and will thank Allah you are safe. Perhaps one day .....'

'I shall never return to Kerman, Umid,' said Nadia wistfully. 'We both know that. But you may tell my father that I love him, and when my son or daughter is born, I shall find a way to send word to him.'

'I will tell him, My Lady,' said Umid. 'And what of young Master Hassan? What shall I say to His Excellency of him?'

'Hassan has gone with my husband to Rome. I would have gone too but Giovanni feared the journey would tire me. My time is only a week or two away. But you should know, Umid, that I no longer speak for my son.'

'Still, a mother knows what's in her son's heart, even if she does not know what the future holds for him.'

Nadia sighed. 'Persia is in his heart, Umid, and in his blood too. That will never change. One day he will return to his homeland and fulfil his destiny, whatever that might be.'

'Fate will decide, My Lady.'

'Fate draws an incomplete map of our lives,' said Nadia pensively. 'Its moving finger writes on the parchment of time, as the poet Omar so wisely wrote, but it cannot mark out all the ways we may travel. God has given us free will. Tell my father that too, Umid. He will understand. Hassan will choose his own path, just as I have chosen mine.'

The End

Other Books by the Same Author:

Novels -
The Dark Side of the Fylfot
The Tiger and the Cauldron

And writing as Drew Greenfield -
Sweeter Than Wine
Sweet Entanglement
The Sweetest Lie (in preparation)

Family History -
Tapestry: the story of a family
Patterns: a family journey

Miscellaneous -
The Lion, the Sun and the Eternal Blue Sky (non-fiction)
It's a Fantasy World (reviews)
Classic Reviews
In My Own Write (short stories and essays)

Printed by Amazon Italia Logistica S.r.l.
Torrazza Piemonte (TO), Italy

40748487R00188